Packed Up In Vegas

Lexie Quinn

ISBN: 978-1-988931-35-7 (Ebook Edition)

ISBN: 978-1-988931-36-4 (Paperback Edition)

Content Notes

Welcome to Lexie's omegaverse!

Heats happen every ~3 months and last ~3 days.

Ruts typically happen during the context of a heat when an alpha gets overwhelmed.

Bonding happens in the context of a heat and requires a bite from both parties to complete.

Spicy stuff: exhibitionism (live spicy shows), group scenes, four peens in one omega (and various other ratios), knotting, breeding.

Possibly upsetting stuff: injections (to induce heat, for birth control, and to neutralize scent blockers), financial abuse, abusive cheating ex, verbal abuse (outside the pack), harassment (outside the pack), abandoned FMC, panic attack/delirium episode, reference to past drug use, bank fraud, use of slut (predominantly in the context of dirty talk, but a couple times in verbal abuse by the ex).

Content Notes

Welcome to Lexie's omegaverse!

Heats happen every ~3 months and last ~3 days.

Ruts typically happen during the context of a heat when an alpha gets overwhelmed.

Bonding happens in the context of a heat and requires a bite from both parties to complete.

Spicy stuff: exhibitionism (live spicy shows), group scenes, four peens in one omega (and various other ratios), knotting, breeding.

Possibly upsetting stuff: injections (to induce heat, for birth control, and to neutralize scent blockers), financial abuse, abusive cheating ex, verbal abuse (outside the pack), harassment (outside the pack), abandoned FMC, panic attack/delirium episode, reference to past drug use, bank fraud, use of slut (predominantly in the context of dirty talk, but a couple times in verbal abuse by the ex).

Chapter 1
Callie

I was startled awake by the slam of the hotel door, sitting bolt upright to see my fiancé standing there, looking like he'd rolled through a gutter. "Hey, babe. Are you just getting back?"

Jerry stomped past me and into the bathroom, turning on the shower. His usually clean, mild beta scent was tainted with sweat, alcohol, and a herby lemon fragrance that made my nose wrinkle. Scent blockers drowned out my omega scent—Jerry's preference, he said it was overwhelming—and usually muted my response to others', but some were unpleasant enough to override the blockers.

I tiptoed out of bed to peek in on him. "Were you out all night? Are you okay?"

"Jesus, I'm fucking *fine*." He shoved a hand through his sandy blond hair, making it stick up in every direction. "I was at the casino. I don't need you grilling me over nothing."

I chewed my lip. "Okay, sorry. Why don't we have a rest day today? Chill by the pool instead of going to see the Hoover Dam."

"*Callie*. For god's sake. Stop bothering me and let me shower and sleep."

"Fine. I'll be down at the pool after you've rested." I certainly didn't want to stay up here if he was going to be an asshole. I changed into my swimsuit; wrapped a sarong around my hips; put on my flip-flops; grabbed my tote with my sunscreen, hat, and book; and abandoned the hotel room.

It was hot as balls outside. We'd come in July at Jerry's insistence that it was off-season and cheaper. I didn't bother arguing that it was off-season because it was miserable that time of year. I didn't win many arguments in our household and I'd honestly stopped trying at this point. I ordered myself an iced coffee and some breakfast after taking up a spot on a lounge chair in the shade. The good thing about being chased out of the room this early was that almost no one else was at the pool yet, which meant I had my pick of spots. I braided my dark hair to keep it off my skin and tucked it under my hat before liber-ally applying sunscreen so I didn't burst into flames from the sun reflecting off the water.

I was halfway through my book by the time I finished the last of my drink and had consumed every bite. Jerry still hadn't made his way down, but I reasoned if he had been out all night I probably wouldn't see him for a few more hours. He was going to be pissy after fucking up his sleep schedule like this, but I'd rather deal with him rested than hungover.

The day got progressively hotter and I ordered myself a

slushy drink a little after noon, sitting on the edge of the pool under a shade with my feet in the water.

"Ma'am." One of the servers approached me with a frown.

I lifted my sunglasses to see him better. "Yeah?"

"I'm afraid we weren't able to put the drink on your room tab."

"Oh, that's weird. It was working fine earlier." I pulled out my phone to call Jerry to ask if he could look into the issue, but it went straight to voicemail. With a sigh, I focused on the server. "I left my purse up in my room and I don't have cash or card down here with me. Can I go up, get it, and come right back?"

"Do you have anything you can leave to ensure you'll return?"

I passed over my phone. "Does this work?"

"Yes, ma'am. I'll watch for you to come back." His tone was unnecessarily judgy, but it probably wasn't the first time he'd encountered a non-paying customer, though it was definitely my first time being one.

Annoyed, I made my way back into the hotel and upstairs. I didn't want to see Jerry when he was in a mood, and I'd been intending to stay out of his way until he was ready to see me, but that couldn't be avoided now. When I stepped off the elevator and turned down the hall toward our room, I saw all my things in the hallway.

What the fuck?

The cleaning staff were coming up the hall from the opposite direction, looking at me curiously. I swiped my keycard and the light blinked red. "Come on."

I swiped it again, and it remained resolutely red.

One of the staff approached me. "Miss, do you need help?"

"Please. My card won't work. I don't know why my

luggage is out here when we're not supposed to check out for a couple more days."

Jerry was probably having a hissy fit, which I didn't want to broadcast to them. It wasn't the first time he'd tossed something of mine out a door or window when he couldn't handle his emotions.

They opened up the room for me, but Jerry wasn't inside, nor were any of his things. I stood in the entryway, trying to figure out what had happened. I couldn't call him again with my phone back with the pool staff, but surely he hadn't gone far. Maybe he was down at one of the restaurants? But then why were all of his things gone?

Okay, Callie, just breathe. What was I supposed to do now?

First, I needed my purse. I opened up my suitcase, the contents spilling out. My purse was among the chaos, and I took a few moments to repack everything properly and change into regular clothes before I thanked the staff and went to reclaim my phone and pay for my drink with some cash in my wallet.

I tried phoning Jerry again and it went to voicemail once more.

Fuck.

Where the hell was he?

I wheeled my suitcase down to the front desk and waited in line until the check-in staff could see me.

The woman at the desk beamed at me. "Hi there! Ready to check in?"

"Actually, I'm already staying here, but my keycard isn't working, and I wasn't able to charge my last purchase to the room even though it was fine earlier in the day."

"Oh dear, let me look into it. What's your room number?"

I gave her the info and she tapped away. "Hmm, it looks

like Mr. McIntosh checked out a couple of hours ago and canceled the remainder of your stay with us."

The world dropped out from under me. "Excuse me? What do you mean he *checked out*?"

"I'm so sorry, ma'am. That's what the computer says."

Okay. Don't panic. I just needed to go over the facts. 1) My fiancé wasn't answering calls. 2) He'd left my luggage in the hall. 3) He'd apparently checked out even though we had two more days booked.

"Is my car still in the hotel lot?"

"I'm not sure. Let me call the valet."

I gave her the info on it, and, sure enough, it was gone too. Jerry had done a lot of stupid things in the eight years we'd been together, but stealing my car and abandoning me in Vegas was a new low.

I sank onto one of the many chairs in the lobby, trying to sort out what my next step should be. I could report my car stolen, but that would lead to a massive fight, and by the time anyone looked into anything, it would probably be back at the apartment. Plenty of buses went between LA and Vegas, so it wouldn't be too difficult to get home, at the very least. I checked ticket prices and then went to the banking app on my phone to see if I could afford it. Student loans had been up my ass and we had budgeted so carefully for this vacation.

Zero dollars remaining.

I stared at the number incomprehensibly and refreshed the app, but the amount of money in my account remained a big fat goose egg. How was that possible? All our rent, all the money we had put aside for the vacation. Gone.

I dialed Jerry again, half-surprised when he actually answered. "Hey, Cal."

"Hey yourself. Where the fuck are you?"

5

"Um, coming up on Barstow?"

"What the sweet fuck are you doing in California? Did you seriously leave me in Nevada? What the hell is wrong with you?"

"Listen...I've been rethinking some things in my life."

"Oh, have you now?"

"Yeah, so, I'm married."

"What the fuck do you mean you're *married*? We're *engaged*."

"Yeah, I know. But Katrina ate my ass in a back alley and you're not that fun, babe."

I stared off into the middle distance, tinnitus blaring in my ears, my skin hotter and pricklier than even the weather demanded. "You abandoned your fiancée in another state because some woman ate your ass?"

"I mean, I did also blow all of our money gambling, and those casino people are not nice about it when you can't pay."

"You lost all our money *and* got married? Who the hell even is this woman?"

"I met her at the blackjack tables when you refused to come down and wanted to sleep. Katrina and I got *super* drunk last night, we ended up at the chapel, and then I kind of panicked this morning. Sorry about all this, but you'll figure it out."

"You're *sorry*?! Jerry!"

"Later, Cal."

He hung up on me and I dropped my face into my hands, letting out a scream that turned my throat raw and drew every eye in the lobby.

Over.

My life was over.

How the hell was anyone supposed to come back from something like this?

We'd already been living paycheck to paycheck since Jerry had lost his job, and I was barely keeping us afloat between the exorbitant rent in LA, my student loans, and debt repayment from before he'd *told me* he'd lost his job. How could he have gambled everything away when we were barely surviving as it was?

Maybe his *wife*—ugh, the word nauseated me—had money and it was all some elaborate ploy to get her money and then come back to me... No, that was stupid. Fuck! How was I supposed to get home? My only credit card was back at home in the freezer to keep me from spending over our means. That didn't do me a lick of good when I was over four hours away with a cleaned-out account.

I didn't want to call my family in Seattle. They already hated Jerry and I would have a full-on breakdown if I had to hear an "I told you so" right now. I didn't have many friends in LA after moving there for Jerry, and the contacts I did have were my video editing clients. There was no way in hell I was going to ask any of them to bail me out. I could figure this out. Somehow...

Everyone was looking at me, staring really. The hotel graciously agreed to watch my suitcase for me and I wandered to a nearby coffee shop, away from all the eyes who had watched me freak out on the phone.

I stood in line, dissociating to cope, and wanting an iced chai to push back the impending doom, but of course when I tried to pay, *declined* flashed across the terminal. I'd half forgotten everything was gone, even though it loomed over me like a specter of the end. I tried with my card for my personal account, hoping I'd somehow left at least a few dollars behind when I'd transferred over the money for our vacation.

Declined.

"Let me see if I've got enough change." I dug through my purse, finding only a few coins. My eyes burned, tears sneaking up on me as the line behind me grew, and my fingers found nothing else. I hiccuped, a little sob breaking free. I was so fucked.

Chapter 2
Miles

The sweetest omega whimper I had ever heard drove me out of my own head as I stood in line at the coffee shop. I glanced down at the dark hair of the woman in front of me, standing before an unimpressed barista.

"Ma'am, your card declined."

"Let me see if I've got enough change." She rifled through her purse, managing to fish out a few quarters and dimes. Definitely not enough to pay for her drink. I could smell her tears from here, and when she hiccuped before a tiny sob escaped, I couldn't stop myself from sliding my credit card across the counter from behind her.

"It's on me."

The omega turned to me, chocolate-brown eyes luminous

with tears, her bottom lip wobbling. Her pale skin was flushed pink and blotchy from crying, but she still had a soft sort of beauty and triggered all of my protective instincts.

"Thank you," she said quietly.

"It's no problem. Let's add a couple cake pops to the order, and I'll get a medium flat white."

The barista updated the order, and I tapped my card. Then I ushered the omega over to the side, where we could wait for our drinks, reaching out my hand to shake hers. "My name's Miles."

She stared at my hand for a moment before her brain caught up to the social niceties, and she took my hand. "Oh, I'm Callie."

It was only her petite size and her sounds that had given her omega status away. In all likelihood she was on scent blockers, a courtesy to the rest of the world, especially when she was distressed, but it made me wonder what she smelled like without those drugs in her system. The only scent she carried was a faint whisper of sugar that every omega smelled like beneath their unique fragrance.

"Having a rough day?" I asked.

Her lip wobbled dangerously again. "You could say that."

Our orders arrived, and she sipped at her iced chai latte, clutching the paper bag of cake pops to her chest like a lifeline.

"Do you want to talk about it? You look like you could use a friend."

She nodded after a moment of hesitation, and we snagged a tiny table near the door that got blasted with the Vegas July heat every time someone stepped inside.

"Money is tight. Too tight, to be honest. I just wanted a little boost to cheer myself up today. I don't even know what to do. So much is fucked up right now."

up. She needed the money, and I needed to not have a hundred pissed-off patrons.

Another whimper escaped Callie.

"I take it that amount sounds enticing?"

She bought herself a few moments of silence by sipping on her iced chai. "What would I have to do?"

"Why don't we walk and talk?"

Her hesitation was easy to see, but the money was too tempting for her to resist. "Sure."

She whined again the second we stepped out of the air conditioning. "Why is it so ungodly hot? I didn't even want to come here this time of year, but Jerry insisted because everything was on sale. Well, no fucking wonder it's on sale when it feels like you're stepping into Satan's asshole when you're outside."

I couldn't help but laugh, swinging my arm over her shoulder as we meandered toward the Strip. "I feel the same way. But there's only so many places where a business like the one I work for can thrive, so I have to suffer."

"So, spill," she demanded. "Money like that is going to involve something super shady. Is it sex, murder, or drugs?"

I laughed again. This little cutie had spunk. "Sex. The club I recruit for does live shows. Young, innocent omegas getting defiled by alphas in front of an audience."

Callie squeezed her drink so hard the lid popped off and she cursed as it sloshed over the sides and onto her hands. I offered her a napkin I had stuffed in my pocket, and she took her time tidying herself up as we continued to walk and I held her drink.

"I'm *sorry*. A *live sex* club? Are you being serious right now?"

"Very serious, sweetheart. I know it's a lot to take in, but it's very safe, everyone is a professional, and we take really good care of the omegas involved."

Eventually Callie said, "But don't you want models for something like that? I'm not polished *at all*. I've got squishy bits and body hair, and you don't see that in porn."

"You do if you know where to look, but in any case, porn isn't reality. The patrons want a more realistic experience."

"I barely have real experience, though. Besides my fiancé, there was one drunken night for my twenty-first birthday—we were on a break—where I thought it would be a good idea to sleep with my lab partner and ring in full adulthood with a fling. It was...not great. And while I love Jerry, scratch that, *loved* with a *D* at the end 'cause I can't say I actually love him anymore... Anyway, we didn't do anything especially creative. I don't even know why I'm telling you all this. But I really don't think I could do a live sex show. It's not me."

"You mean, you don't *know* if it's you. You can't say for certain if you've never had an experience like this. All the alphas are professional and regularly tested. They know how to take care of omegas and it sounds like you could use some extra care right now. All you would have to do is show up and go through with it. No worrying about outfits, body maintenance, after-care. We cover all of that, plus your hotel room while you're here and all your meals. We can charge extra for clients to watch a virgin get taken so you can boost your pay by another ten grand. Plus you'll get tips."

"But I'm not a virgin."

I shrugged. "Close enough. I'm pretty sure you'll give enough genuine reactions to things being experienced for the first time, and that's the important part. Have you been with an alpha before?"

Callie shook her head.

"That'll definitely work in your favor for the show, then. It's a whole different ballgame moving from betas to alphas as an omega. The audience would eat it up."

Some of the tension was slowly leaking out of her, and I couldn't tell if the flush in her cheeks was due to the heat or to the idea of what I was proposing.

"Even though it's a terrible idea, could you give me a little bit more info?"

"Absolutely." Hopefully this meant she was coming around to the concept. "You'll have a penthouse suite, and prior to your heat starting, you'll get to know the alphas there while eating to your heart's content to prepare for the marathon."

Callie's brows pinched. "But my heat isn't due for another two months."

"That's not a problem. There've been some...developments. Not exactly approved or legal quite yet, but we've had no issues and it works really well."

Callie swallowed hard. "What kind of developments?"

"Just a simple injection. It'll trigger your heat within a couple of hours. We'd also give you something to neutralize the scent blockers you're on."

"I don't like needles," Callie said, staring at her feet.

"I promise you'll barely feel it. Our on-site medical staff are amazing, and I can be there with you the whole time if you want."

When she finally looked up at me again, her lip was wobbling once more.

"Hey, it's all going to be okay." I pulled her into my arms, and she didn't hesitate, melting against me in a way that had my instincts screaming at me to protect her. "By the end of the week, you'll have a fresh new life one way or the other. If you want to start it with a nest egg, I'll help you through every step of the way to getting that. If you want to get on a bus and go back to wherever you came from, I'll give you all the cash in my wallet to get you there."

"Why do you want to help me?"

"Well, for one thing, I have a bit of a soft spot for women I find crying in coffee shops, and for another you would actually be doing *me* a favor if you went through with this."

Callie extracted herself and I restrained myself from pulling her back in.

"It's too fucking hot for hugs right now," she said. "How would I be doing you a favor?"

"That call I took earlier was my omega for tonight telling me she has food poisoning. So I have dozens of well-paying patrons expecting a show, and no star to give them one."

"Do you get in trouble because she backed out?"

"Not in trouble exactly, but none of the alphas who signed up will get paid if the show doesn't happen. Now, sweetheart, I don't want you to feel pressured one way or the other. This is an opportunity, not an obligation, and if you don't want to, there are other omegas I can call to fill in."

Callie didn't seem repulsed by the idea, so I wanted to give her the chance to accept or reject before I looked elsewhere. "What happens after the heat is over?"

"You'll stay in the penthouse for a few more nights until you feel well enough to head on your way, at least one of the alphas will stay with you for as long as you choose, and you'll have full access to the spa and room service."

"And during?"

I truly hadn't expected to get this far with her, but I was happy to answer as many questions as she might have if it would put her at ease. "Three alphas are scheduled for tonight's show, and through the heat you'll be with all of them in basically every combination you can imagine."

Callie sucked in a shaky breath. "Are they nice?"

"The ones tonight are actually my packmates, and I can promise they'll take incredible care of you. They're some of the best men I know. Do you want to tell me what's going through your head?"

"Too many things." She laughed. "My brain feels like a box of bouncy balls I chucked down the stairs. I can't tell if I should be fascinated, disgusted, or into it. Definitely feeling awkward, though. How the fuck would I even begin to prepare for sex with *three* alphas when I've never even had sex with *one* before?"

I sent a silent prayer of thanks to the universe for gifting me the most perfect omega to turn this into our best show yet. "That's the beauty of being an omega. Your body knows how to handle a pack even if your brain doesn't. And I promise you'll get an exquisite amount of tips if I can pitch to our patrons that you've never had an alpha before."

Her nose wrinkled adorably. "Do they actually care about that?"

"They absolutely fucking do. You're going to make yourself a fortune."

"The club too, I'm sure," she said with a roll of her eyes.

"Of course, sweetheart. The club makes its money one way or the other, but they pay well."

"Can I have some time to think about it?"

"I can give you an hour before I have to get someone else. I would give you more time if I could, but the show's tonight. In the meantime, though..." I pulled out what cash I had in my wallet—roughly four hundred dollars—and passed it to her along with a business card. "I want you to get home safe regardless of whether you end up doing this. Text me when you've decided. I've got to get everything set up for tonight."

I slipped into a sleek black rideshare and tried not to look back at the sweet omega. She would agree or she wouldn't, but at least I wouldn't have any guilt over abandoning her in her time of need.

I arrived at the hotel where the shows took place, and by the time I made my way upstairs to the penthouse where my pack was waiting, my phone buzzed.

UNSAVED NUMBER:

Fuck it. I'll do it.

Chapter 3
Callie

W *hat the fuck have I gotten myself into?*
I didn't even like when Jerry left the lights on. How was I supposed to have sex in front of a room full of people? The universe was unfair.

I hovered outside the hotel, my luggage at my side, when a black SUV rolled up with a painfully beautiful alpha in the driver's seat. His hair was longer than I'd expected, falling past his shoulders like a sheet of black silk, and his eyes were a gorgeous golden brown. He hopped out with a smile and beelined straight for me. "Callie?"

"Yep," I squeaked out.

"Nice to meet you. I'm Kai, one of the alphas who'll be taking care of you for your heat."

Even his name was pretty. Miles had sent me a photo of him so I wouldn't get scooped up by the wrong person.

"Ready to go?"

I barely finished a nod before he was taking my luggage to put it in the back, and then he opened the front passenger door for me, those warm golden eyes watching me expectantly. I hopped into the front seat, trying to buckle so quickly I accidentally locked the belt.

Kai chuckled and took it out of my hands, resetting the mechanism and buckling me in properly. "Excited or nervous?"

"Both? I feel like I might pass out."

"We'll get you relaxed in no time." He kissed my cheek and I bit down on a whimper as he rounded the vehicle and climbed into his seat before zipping out into the traffic.

Sweet mother. He was so fucking pretty. It was like someone had ripped him off the pages of a magazine, and he was going to *touch me*. Why didn't I have a pillow to scream into right now?

I had a white-knuckle grip on the door handle, my other hand fidgeting with my hair.

"Deep breaths." Kai laced our fingers together. I stared down at where we touched, the fizz of electricity traveling up my arm. "I promise we're going to take very good care of you. I know I can tell you not to be nervous, but it won't make a difference, so instead I'll tell you to keep breathing."

He had no alpha scent. He was probably on scent blockers like me, but it would've been easier to chill out if he could have just shut off my brain with a burst of whatever he smelled like.

The drive was short and I spent most of it internally screaming and trying not to sweat all over Kai's palm.

"Here we are," Kai said as he pulled to a stop.

It wasn't a hotel I recognized, but then I didn't know any

that weren't on the Strip, and it looked snazzy with teal glass that shone in the sun. The valet took the vehicle, and Kai took my hand again, wheeling my suitcase behind him to lead me inside. The brief stretch of heat between the air-conditioned vehicle and the hotel already had me sweating.

Kai chuckled. "Not used to the desert?"

"No. I'm *suffering*."

"Well, I promise you don't have to leave the AC for a while now."

Thank goodness for small miracles.

On the way up, Kai dropped his arm around my shoulder and it took every ounce of fortitude not to simply melt against him. I wanted to know what he smelled like. Miles too. Scent blockers might be the courteous thing, but they did absolutely nothing to assuage my omega curiosity.

It wasn't really polite to speculate, but considering what was going to be happening between me and Kai tonight, I felt a little entitled to know. How awkward would it be if his scent repulsed me? How the fuck would I get through a heat in that case?

"Are you on scent blockers too?" I asked.

"Yep. The other alphas are as well. We all get everything neutralized at the same time."

"But what if someone doesn't like someone's scent? Then isn't it too late to back out?"

He gave me a cheeky look. "Should I be offended you think my scent is going to be gross, little dove?"

Heat flared in my cheeks. "That's not what I meant. You could think *mine* is gross."

"Basically impossible with how cute I think you are."

All the blood rushing into my cheeks was making me lightheaded.

"Diego and Amir are the other two who will be taking care of you," Kai told me as we slipped into an immaculate open-concept penthouse suite.

"Holy shit, this is pretty." A view of the city filled one wall through an enormous window, and the bedroom double doors were wide open to show off the biggest bed I had ever seen in real life. The bathroom was all white marble and sparkling glass, and the living room was set up with plush couches, a fire-place, and an enormous TV.

Two alphas emerged from the kitchenette area, looking oddly twin-like with their dark hair and eyes, beautifully bronze skin, and athletic forms. The easiest differentiation I could make with a two-second glance was that one had floppy curls and the other's hair was cut short on the sides with just enough length on top to grab. I flushed at that thought being the first to enter my mind. Floppy Curls also had a sun tattoo on his hip.

"Guys, this is Callie," Kai said, and then gestured to each of them in turn. "Callie, this is Diego and Amir."

Diego was the one with the tattoo.

"Hi," I squeaked.

Kai left me there with them to deposit my luggage in the bedroom and I stood frozen under their scrutiny. What did they see when they looked at me? I wasn't entirely certain if my coloring had shifted enough so I didn't betray my recent crying.

All the little hairs on the back of my neck stood straight up when Amir approached me, hooking his fingers beneath my chin. "Questions?"

Fuck me, his touch was full of sparks that had my stomach clenching.

"Only a million," I said, trying at levity.

"Miles gave her the rundown," said Kai as he returned. "We can cover anything else."

"Where *is* Miles?" I asked. "He said he would be here."

"He will be. He's just making sure everything else is running smoothly for tonight," replied Diego. "You should go shower. Hair and makeup will be here in about an hour, and Miles will have paperwork for you. Also, if you want to eat, I would order room service now so you have time to digest."

I swallowed hard. Everything felt like it was careening toward me now that I was here.

"I'll order for you," Kai offered. "What would you like?"

"Spaghetti and meatballs? I usually carb load before a heat."

Kai gave me a soft smile. "I'll put in the order now."

I disappeared into the bathroom, grateful to have a reprieve. They were all certainly attractive enough to put on a show; I just had to reconcile myself to the fact that I was going to be a part of that. This was my last chance to be clean for a few days, so I might as well take the opportunity to indulge. I stood face-first under the spray until I felt a little steadier, and then set about scrubbing myself head to toe. Was I supposed to shave everything? Miles had said the audience wanted an authentic experience, but how far did that apply?

"Um, is anyone nearby to answer a question?" I called out. I cringed, letting my forehead rest against the glass while I tried not to let my embarrassment swallow me whole.

The door cracked open and Diego stepped inside. "What's up?"

I crossed my arms over my chest.

He laughed quietly. "I'm going to see a lot more of you soon, and so is everyone else. No need to be shy. What's your question?"

"Is this like an everything shower where I shave head to toe? I don't know what to do."

Diego's eyes gleamed. "Only take off what you actually want to. I'm going to wreck you regardless."

Oh god.

Heat rolled through me and I didn't miss his appreciative look when I braced one hand on the glass, my fingers curling.

"If you don't want to shave a single hair, then don't. Probably better not to, quite honestly. Don't want you to nick yourself and have to deal with any extra discomfort."

Extra discomfort. How much would there actually be?

Diego parked himself on top of the marble vanity. "Hurry up with your shower. Your food will be here in a few minutes."

"You're just going to watch?"

"You need to get used to eyes on you."

A tiny whimper escaped.

"Amir, Kai, the little omega needs to practice having some attention."

Oh sweet baby Jesus. Then the three of them were in the bathroom with me, all watching me through the steamed-up glass.

"Don't be shy, little dove. If you can't handle this, you won't be able to handle tonight."

I bit my lip and tried not to focus on the fact that they could all see me naked as a spring day while I took the hair off my underarms and lower legs. By the time I was rinsing out my conditioner, feeling their gazes wasn't quite so intrusive. But then I had to step out from the protective barrier of the fogged glass.

Kai held out a towel, dangling it from his fingers far enough away that I wouldn't be able to reach. "Come on out, sweetness."

With a deep, shaky breath, I stepped out of the shower and closer to them so Kai could wrap the towel around me. Diego dropped another over my head and squeezed the water from my hair.

"See," Diego said. "Not so bad."

Was I red as a beet? Yes. Had I fainted putting myself in front of these unfairly beautiful alphas while butt naked? No. I counted that as a win.

A knock on the door signaled the arrival of my food and Amir scooped me up to carry me over to the couch while Kai brought the cart in. I wrapped my arms around his neck, wishing that the scent blockers were already gone so I could tell what he smelled like. I craved the knowledge like a tangible thing, my omega instincts demanding to know.

In addition to the spaghetti and meatballs I had requested, they'd also ordered cheesy bread, two carafes of juices, and one of water.

Kai and Diego each took a spot at my sides and worked lotion into my skin until goosebumps covered every bit of me and I was dizzy from breathing so hard.

"Open," Amir commanded, gesturing to my mouth with a forkful of pasta twisted around half a meatball.

I accepted the bite, still shivering when Kai scooped one of my feet onto his lap and dug out the tension with his thumbs.

"There's a lot of things happening at once right now," I commented once I had swallowed.

"That'll be the next three days," Amir reminded me. "You need to get used to it. We don't want you to have a panic attack out there."

"Right." I swallowed another bite of pasta Amir offered and almost died of bliss when Kai shifted me, leaning my back to his chest and Diego lifted my legs onto his lap. So comfy.

With a quiet hum, I let myself melt, leaning into his warmth that was actually enjoyable now that I was in air conditioning.

The suite door opened and Miles swept inside. "I see you're all getting acquainted. Callie, sweetheart, I have a contract for you to sign and I'll need your banking information so we can deposit the first chunk of your money as soon as I submit the paperwork."

Miles grinned at me, his blue eyes bright beneath his tousled brown waves. He passed over the clipboard with the paperwork and I read all of the intricate details, feeling like I was signing my soul away when I laid down my name.

"Perfect," Miles crooned. "One step closer to your new life and the best sex you'll ever have."

Chapter 4
Callie

"D on't look at it, little dove."

I dragged my gaze away from the needle the nurse was bringing closer.

"Hey." Kai took my face in both of his hands. "Look at me. I've got you."

I'd much rather look at him than a needle, so I let myself focus on the warmth of his golden brown eyes, the sweep of straight lashes, the fullness of his lips that I had decided were kissable the moment I saw them. It seemed rude to drop my gaze further, even though he wasn't wearing a shirt and the lean, muscled planes of his body practically begged to be admired.

They'd already administered the medication to reverse the scent blockers—which would take a little while to take full effect—and I'd immediately burst into tears. I'd always been like that with needles. I whimpered as the heat serum was injected under my skin, the burning tingle slowly spreading up my arm, followed immediately by a dose of birth control. They'd put me through one of the rapid-test clinics dotted around the city to make sure I didn't have anything that required extra precautions, and luckily Jerry hadn't brought anything to our bed.

"Well done," the nurse praised. "You'll have about an hour before it kicks in fully, but you'll start feeling the effects in a few minutes. I'm sorry to say that it can make you a bit emotional, so don't worry about that too much when it happens. You'll settle quickly once you're out on stage."

"Deep breaths." Kai stroked my cheeks with his thumbs, before sweeping one over my wobbling bottom lip. He pulled me onto his lap. The hyperventilation started almost immediately, panic galloping through my system, setting my heart to racing, and making my head feel like it was going to float away into the stratosphere. I clung to him, desperate for an anchor. His grip tightened until it bordered on pain and I felt like his arms were the only thing keeping me together.

This wasn't fucking fair. Not twenty-four hours ago I'd been engaged and now...

Fuck.

I wiped the tears streaking down my face.

"She can't cry on stage," Diego murmured, sitting next to us with his shirt off too.

"Sure she can," Amir said. "Tons of those rich bitches have a crying kink."

"Don't be dicks," Kai snapped.

"Rude," Amir said with a laugh. "That's literally all we're here for. It's just the serum wigging her out, not a big deal."

Maybe it wasn't a big deal for him, but he wasn't experiencing it. I buried my face against Kai's chest with a soft whine, that omega sound of distress ratcheting tension through him. "Where's Miles?"

"Right here, sweetheart." Miles stroked a hand over my hair. "I know it's a lot. The drugs will settle soon."

I sniffled miserably. "I hate it."

Kai nuzzled the top of my head. "You're doing great."

"Mhmm," Miles agreed. "And your first twenty-thousand was just deposited in your account."

I popped my head up. "Really?"

Fuck. That already made me feel better, knowing those dollars were sitting there waiting for me on the other side of this.

"When do I get more?"

"Another twenty on each day of the heat, and the rest once it's all over."

I settled against Kai, still sniffling, but holding on to the knowledge that everything would be okay when this was over. But then my mind wandered to why I wasn't okay in the first place and the sobs came in soul-crushing waves.

God, I couldn't do this. But I would be even *more* fucked than before if I backed out now. Right back to square one, abandoned and broke, but with a heat on the way.

Fucking Jerry.

My life before today hadn't been *great*, but it had been mine. It had been...comfortable, predictable, if nothing else. I just wanted to go back. If only there were something to go back to.

Kai continued to hold me, purring away until I got my sobs

down to a manageable level. He nudged me to lean back far enough to see my face, his eyes flickering over the hair and makeup they had done for me before I had gotten the injection. I thought I looked ridiculous. I never wore this much makeup, but the artist had said something about the audience liking to be able to see the tear tracks from the mascara and I'd almost thrown up on the spot.

"I think we have to run you through makeup again real quick," Kai said.

"I'll probably just cry it off again."

"Probably," he agreed, "but try to keep that to when we're on stage."

I squirmed in his lap, the faintest hint of *something* tweaking the back of my brain. It crept in molecule by molecule, the scent blockers dissolving by the second.

Cinnamon.

Warm, like cinnamon rolls fresh out of the oven, and spicy like those candy hearts I ate every Valentine's until my tongue went numb.

I bucked and shuddered like I'd stuck a fork into an electric socket, shoving my face against Kai's throat. Sweet fuckity fuck. My tongue swept over his skin, soaking up that flavor, and suddenly I was in the air.

"Whoa there, sweetheart. It's not time to start yet."

I whined as Miles hauled me away and onto his lap.

"Miles... I—I think we might have a problem," Kai said slowly, staring at me like he had no idea what to make of me. All I wanted was to climb back into his lap and breathe him in.

"Miles, please, I *need*." I fought against his grip, trying to get back to Kai and suddenly Diego and Amir were there too.

"Calm down." Amir's voice was firm, but did absolutely nothing to temper my desire to get to Kai, or at least it didn't until I caught a whiff of *him*. Rich, sunbaked cedar, all sticky and sweet in the height of summer. Fuck me sideways. I grabbed onto him and dragged him closer, whining as I got my face up to his throat.

Yes.

Perfect.

"This feels like more than a heat, Miles." Diego did his best to extract me from Amir, but then he was close enough to scent too. Warm clove and nutmeg, like my favorite chai and the most delicious cookies.

A whine rocked through my chest, a whispered chorus of *oh, fuck* moving through the men around me. Heat sat like embers in my belly. I needed all of them all over *me*. Immediately.

"Okay, sweetness, don't worry." Miles opened a drawer and forced a respirator over my face so I could get a breath that wasn't laden with alpha deliciousness. The others very quickly donned their own, followed by scent-blocking patches. I didn't want those scents to go away, but with every clear breath it was easier to think and keep some semblance of control over myself.

My whine rang in my ears.

"Deep breaths," Miles crooned, pulling me away from Amir and into his arms. "You're okay."

I clutched the front of his suit, letting him comfort me, his hands smoothing down my back as I clawed my way back to sanity. When my shoulders finally relaxed, I looked up at Miles, my mind full of questions. "I don't understand."

"It's going to be okay, sweetness. Rest for a minute. We just need to figure out a few things." His voice soothed me, sliding over me like velvet and untangling some of the knots of panic in my chest.

"Miles, we can't take her out there," said Diego. "We can't let people see her."

"If you don't do the show, none of you are getting paid. All four of you are under contract. If Callie backs out now, she has to give back everything she's been paid so far and still go through a heat, just not on stage. We can't turn off the heat now that she's been given the serum."

"I don't want that. I don't..."

Miles stroked a soft hand over my hair. "She's already agreed to the show and it kills two birds with one stone. We owe her. Where else is she supposed to find heat partners this close to the start? You have to. You know she doesn't get paid if you back out."

"What?!" It came out as a muffled shriek through the respirator. "I don't get paid if *they* back out? That's not fair. Why is anyone backing out? What's going on?"

Fucking hell. Could my day get any worse? I was broker than broke, stranded in Sin City, and about to go into heat.

"Please."

The simple word had all four of them softening. I had played by all of their rules and they could ruin it for me anyway. Men were not very high on my list today. They always got so damn creative finding new and exciting ways to ruin my life. I supposed that blocking a payday wasn't as bad as what my fiancé had done, but still.

Without their scents to distract me, I had only my own nerves and the serum coursing through my blood turning me into a basket case. I didn't know what was going on, but the tension in the group was setting off an instinctual panic. The alphas were mad about something. Maybe they didn't want me now that my scent had come in? Maybe they couldn't bear to go through a heat with me?

"If you don't want me…" I began.

"Don't," said Kai. "That's not what this is about."

"But no one's telling me what it *is* about. What else am I supposed to think?"

Kai gathered me up and even though I couldn't smell him anymore, the contact smoothed off the rough edge of my worries.

"Miles, this is fucked up," said Amir. "What are we supposed to do?"

"I already told you. We have to do the show."

"I am *not* letting those people see her," Amir hissed.

"Why do you get to decide who sees me?" I snapped. "You're not the one with an empty bank account. You're not the one who got abandoned by your fucking fiancé in Las Vegas after he drunk-married someone else, or the one who has to face their goddamn family who told you not to date that asshole to begin with. You don't get to make this choice for me. You can't trigger my heat and then deny me everything I need to get my fucking life back on track."

Amir's growl sent a ripple of fear and desire through me, like my brain couldn't make up its mind if he was growling *at* me, or at the injustices done *to* me.

"Let's get through the show," Miles said softly. "We can figure out everything afterward. Everyone will get paid and we won't book anything new. Callie's right that this is her choice and not yours."

Amir looked so pissed that I shrank against Kai.

"If you give me a good reason, I'll consider it," I said. "But so far you're all just being cryptic weirdos."

Amir growled again. "We can't go out there and fuck our mate in front of a goddamn audience."

I stared at him, trying to process the words through the

rapidly rising stew of heat hormones in my brain. Then it clicked. "Your *what*?!"

Mates. The alphas I was about to fuck for three days in front of a room full of people were my *mates*.

Chapter 5
Callie

They were all looking at me. This was absolutely ridiculous. How was I supposed to cope with the fact that these guys were my mates and I had just been dumped by my fiancé? Now I was heading into a heat I couldn't stop, and on contract to have sex in a room full of wealthy people with a bunch of alphas who seemed to want to back out at the last minute.

Too much.

My brain was not equipped to handle this level of fuckery.

Kai smoothed a hand down my back. "You don't have to go out there."

"I do if I want to get paid."

Amir sat down hard next to Kai and me, draping himself

lazily over the back of the couch. "Fine. Your choice, princess. I have no interest in showing off my mate to the world. Frankly I'm not even interested in *having* a mate, and while I don't want to give up a payday, I won't be dragging you out there if you don't want to go."

It wasn't fair that Amir saying he didn't want a mate was like a knife to the heart. I didn't want a mate either so it made no sense that it would hurt if it was reciprocal.

I sucked in a deep breath, half-grateful their scents weren't there to muddle things, and half-annoyed that I couldn't drown in those fragrances. I didn't have a choice but to go out there. The pay was so good and it was the only way I was ever going to recover from how hard Jerry had fucked me over. I had to.

"The show starts in twenty minutes," Miles said quietly.

"I have to do it," I told them. "I need the money and I don't want to get anyone in trouble."

"What do you need that much money for?" Diego asked.

I turned to him, watching his hands flex like he was trying to keep himself from reaching for me. I didn't have the mental fortitude to tell the whole story. Maybe after the heat when I wasn't so raw. I didn't want them to know how badly I had fucked up trusting Jerry. I had already spilled that he had betrayed me, but they didn't know everything.

"It doesn't matter," I said. "I'll do it. Please don't ruin this opportunity for me."

Miles looked relieved, and Amir looked the opposite, quietly stewing with his brows pinched.

"If we need to get other alphas to help me—"

"No!" they chorused.

"Okay, okay," said Amir. "This is complete insanity, but I'd rather let them see her than let anyone else touch her."

Diego sat down on the other side of Kai and hauled me onto his lap. My conscious mind managed a half second of protest before my body went feral and I locked every limb around him. "I've got you," Diego said quietly.

"What the hell are we even supposed to do with a mate?" Amir asked. "We can't keep doing this job if we have an omega at home."

Diego adjusted my weight and put his hands over my ears as if I were a toddler they were afraid of cursing around. "We'll talk about it later."

"Let me take care of her," said Miles. "I haven't taken any neutralizers for my scent blockers so she's not going to react to me the same way as you guys. I'll watch her until it's time to get her on stage. You can all go out there and wait."

Not a single one of them looked like they wanted to do that, but they all complied, Diego passing me over to Miles.

When they had left the room, Miles let me take the respirator off. The air was still thick with their scents, sending goosebumps rippling over my skin, and slick pooling between my thighs, but it wasn't as strong as if they were in front of me.

"I'm sorry," said Miles as he did his best to tidy my makeup while I was stuck to him.

"For?" I snuggled up against his chest, needing the security of his arms.

"I never would have offered you this job if I had known you were our mate."

I pressed my fingers to his lips to silence him. I didn't want to think about that part right now. The encroaching heat was making it too difficult to think and I didn't dare consider the future, or what having mates actually meant. Only the next few days mattered.

"Nest?" I mumbled. All I wanted in this second was to

crawl into a mountain of blankets and drag the alphas in after me.

"I'm sorry, sweetness. There's no nest on stage, but I promise there will be something here for you whenever you need a break. It won't be as good as a nest you make yourself, but I'll get something put together once the show starts."

"You're still sure I'm going to be good at this?"

"Absolutely."

"You don't mind them seeing me?"

"I look at all of this a bit differently than the others. I don't want anyone in that audience to touch you, but I do love the idea of them squirming with jealousy and desire for someone they can never have."

That declaration had lust curling in my belly, my brain summoning up the images of all those people salivating over me, and my body lit up at the concept.

Miles only grinned at me. "I take it the idea isn't unsavory to you?"

"It should be," I admitted. "I've never been watched or thought I would like it, and maybe it's the heat hormones, but fuuuck me. The other people out there can't touch me, right?"

"That will be your choice," said Miles. "It depends on how many tips you want and whether the others are going to be willing to allow anyone to touch you."

"I don't know how to do this, Miles. It was already a lot before the whole mates thing."

"The only thing you have to do is let them take care of you. They might break you a little, but I promise they're very good putting their playmates back together."

Desire was like a heartbeat pounding through my body and I squirmed, curling my fingers against Miles's shirt.

"They'll make sure you like it. We've never had any complaints from an omega who performed with them."

My brain screamed, two thoughts ping-ponging around in my head. One—I despised the mention of them doing things with other omegas with a fiery fucking passion. Two—my pussy was taking on a life of its own at the thought of what they would do to me.

"I know they're going to take extra care with you being who you are," Miles added. "Your only job is to take everything they give you. Allow them to get you through this heat."

"Are you always on scent blockers?"

"Usually. At least one of our pack needs to be clearheaded, so I'm not going to neutralize mine until your heat is over."

I pouted. I really wanted to know what his scent was. I knew Miles wasn't going to perform with me, but if I was a mate to his pack, I was probably a mate to him as well. How would I react to him? I was already embarrassed as fuck over how I'd reacted over the others. I'd always been familiar with the phrase "wanting to climb someone like a tree," but I had never experienced it before.

"What do I do when I go out there?"

"Just walk through the door. They'll be out there already. Go straight to Kai. There's usually a slower work-up to the show, but honestly I have no idea if they're going to be able to hold themselves back once they get close to you."

I gasped at the rush of slick, my panties turning damp and heat rolling up my spine. Miles's grip on me tensed.

"Fuck me, you smell so good, sweetheart."

I didn't even care that I couldn't smell Miles right now, I wanted him to flatten me out on the couch and have his way with me. "Miles..."

"Easy does it. As much as I would love to take care of you

39

myself, I can't do that. I'm not on contract with you, and you can't fully consent to anything new once the serum has been administered. Kai, Diego, and Amir are the only ones who can touch you."

I whined. My skin was so hot and my pussy was throbbing. "Please."

"I'm sorry. The show starts in a few minutes. Everyone is getting seated and then you can go out and you'll forget all about me."

I clung to coherency, but I could feel it slipping away with every moment that passed.

"You're going to have so much fun," Miles promised. "They are *very* good at what they do and you deserve nothing less than to be ruined while feeling like the most exquisite, desired omega in the world. Every single eye out there is paying a fucking fortune to be here; they're paying to see *you*. So let's give them a proper show, yes?"

Part of me wanted to tell all those people to go fuck themselves, another part wanted me to drag Miles to the floor and take what I needed, but the quieter third part very much wanted to know what the other alphas would be like.

I wasn't an actress; I was just desperate, and in three days I could save myself from everything that had been taken from me.

I swallowed hard, glancing toward the door that would take me to the stage. Miles looped an arm around my waist and led me down the hall to the elevator that would take us directly to the theater.

Miles kept his arms around me while we waited for the countdown clock atop the doors to run out. Someone from the crew attached a mic to me.

"It won't be on long," Miles explained. "It helps set the tone for the start. Ready?"

"I think so."

He nuzzled my cheek and whispered in my ear. "Have fun out there for me. I'll be watching."

Then he pushed me toward the door, his palms warm against my shoulder blades.

"And three, two, one..."

He nudged me through the door and out under the spotlight that swiveled to illuminate me.

Their combined scents almost took me out at the knees.

Sunbaked cedar.

Clove and nutmeg.

All wrapped up in Kai's cinnamon.

Fucking hell. I'd be lucky if I remembered my own name during this, let alone the fact that a room full of people were already staring at me, waiting for me to get railed.

Reality fell away like grains of sand in an hourglass. All I was able to focus on was the three alphas in front of me.

Showtime.

Chapter 6
Kai

Nerves rocked me down to my toes. I was *never* nervous. But this was my *mate*. The first time I was going to kiss her and fuck her would be here in front of all these people. I fought against every instinct that demanded I drag her right back through that door and bend her over the couch.

Her sweet candied apple scent hung like a thick cloud around her, as tempting a lure as I had ever experienced. Callie's dark brown hair gleamed in the lights, teasing out hints of copper and gold. Her little white sundress was rendered basically see-through under the intensity of the spotlights. She stood there, shaking like a leaf, her arms crossed over her chest, and she stared at us with wide eyes.

I walked toward her, trying to keep the stiffness from my

movements, to appear calm and confident so she could draw that same energy from me. I cupped her cheeks like I had done before and she offered me a wobbly smile.

Callie let me take her hand and I drew her over to the center of the stage, where Diego and Amir were waiting. Her breathing picked up the closer we got to them, the sound sharp in the speakers. The audience loved sounds like that, the little hints of panic and emotion slipping through. That was the authenticity they craved and Callie was certainly giving it to them.

I positioned her at center stage, her back to my chest and leaned down, nipping her earlobe to draw out a gasp that had my cock rising against her ass. "You're doing so well, little dove. Let us take care of you."

I slipped one hand around her waist, gliding up her stomach and the curve of her breasts to hold her throat, encouraging her to tip her head back and surrender. She melted in my grip, tensing only when Amir and Diego each took one of her wrists and tugged down the spaghetti straps of her dress.

Callie's perfect whine echoed through the space, and I didn't miss the wave of shifting through the audience as they reacted to the sound. Her body bowed and flexed when I got my mouth on her throat, teasing her scent gland with my teeth and indulging myself in the flavor of her candied apple scent on my tongue. Bright, tart, and sweet as hell.

All I wanted to do was drown in her, and once this was all over, I was going to keep her. I couldn't let her go now that I'd tasted her. I had to keep my head in the game for the show, but fuck me if Callie's soft sounds and delicious scent weren't making that really difficult.

Amir and Diego had tugged her dress down to her waist,

leaving only the lacy strapless bra that barely contained the spill of her breasts.

Callie let out the most glorious inhuman sound and I glanced down to see Diego's mouth on her breast. If she was going to sound like that when we got a mouth on her tits, I could only imagine what she would sound like when I got my face between her thighs. I growled against her skin and rocked my hips against her ass.

Her squirming got unruly when Amir joined Diego, unhooking the bra entirely and tossing it over his head. Her hands locked around their heads and she was arched like a bow, breathless and panting as they got their first tastes of her. The heat radiating from her skin would've told me how fast she was falling under the sway of the serum if all of her delicious sounds hadn't done that for me.

I closed my eyes, ignoring the people watching us, dipping into the fantasy that it was just Callie and us, our mate letting us take her apart for our own pleasure. I pulled away long enough to flick off her mic, and undo the zipper at the back of her dress, Diego dragging it to her feet and Amir guiding her to lift each foot so the dress could be tossed aside. I couldn't hide her from the audience, but I took the opportunity to cup her breasts, cradling the heavy softness and teasing her nipples while the others waited patiently.

My hands felt like they were aflame, knowing how many eyes were watching their descent down Callie's stomach and under the waistband of her pink panties. She twitched hard when I dipped my fingers between her folds, finding the fountain of slick that let me glide through easily and burrow into her cunt. She made another one of those perfect inhuman sounds and bucked hard against my hand.

Amir tugged down her panties and then they were each

hoisting one of her soft thighs onto their shoulders, spreading Callie's dripping core. I took my time thrusting my fingers into her while she writhed between all three of us, giving her a few moments to adjust to being touched like this, for her body to welcome everything we were about to give her.

Diego pulled my hand away and replaced it with his own, Callie's breathing shifting at the new angle and the rough grind of his thumb against her clit. I watched it all with rapt fascination and carefully raised my slick-drenched fingers to her mouth. Tracing her lips was all it took for that mouth to pop open and her tongue to lap her flavor off of my skin.

Fuck me sideways.

She was perfect. If we could keep her distracted, she wouldn't even notice the audience. She was definitely loud enough, but hopefully they wouldn't mind obscured views if any of us fell too hard into the instinct to guard her.

Callie's whimpers and the rhythmic tensing of her body told all of us how close she was. Diego was watching her face like she had hung the moon, waiting for the moment she broke for him.

Callie cried out, her muscles shaking.

"There we go. Good girl, taking your pleasure."

Diego's gaze flipped to me. "She liked that. Praise her again."

"You sound so fucking good, little dove. I can't wait to make you sing for me."

"Dibs" was all Diego said before he stood, snatched up our omega and spread her out on the bed.

Asshole. He couldn't call fucking *dibs* on our mate.

I couldn't fight him for her on stage, so I let it be and moved to the head of the bed. Callie's eyes were wide and desperate as she reached for me the second she realized I was close, dragging me down until she devoured me, her lips meeting mine in a needy clash. My hair swept down, a curtain blocking us from the audience, but I couldn't bring myself to care. My mate was kissing me. I couldn't even begin to drink my fill of her. She tasted like summer and nostalgia, sweet and sharp.

Diego, the absolute fucker, was the first to get his mouth on her cunt and Callie arched like a cat beneath the attention. Amir was back on her tit, and our sweet little mate could barely contain herself. She had a white-knuckle grip on Amir's and Diego's hair, and I had to pull back for her to catch her breath, her panting growing as frantic as the roll of her hips.

I wanted to get my cock into her so fucking badly.

Realistically, I could. It was a bit out of order, but Callie could decline if she didn't want to. I shucked my pants and climbed properly onto the bed, lifting her head to rest on my thighs. I waited until Diego shattered her, letting her ride that wave before pressing my cock close enough for her to reach. Her tongue laved along the underside and I nearly came out of my skin. I had to check every instinct to lace my fingers into her hair and turn her head so I could fuck straight into those perfect lips.

Maybe later.

Callie sucked at the skin and wiggled around, whining at me until I lifted her head enough that she could get her mouth on the tip of my cock.

Plenty of omegas had done this for me—hell, plenty of *people* in general—but none of them compared to every eager, muffled sound my omega made as she used my hand to support her bobbing on my cock. Diego might've gotten his mouth on her first, but I had the honor of being the first of us she took of her own volition.

"That's my good girl. Hungry for cock, are you?"

Her eyes popped open, a half second of clarity in them before Amir wrapped his hand over her throat and obliterated whatever self-consciousness had managed to slip through her heat.

That was the goal, after all. Make her so deliciously, desperately needy that she wouldn't have a spare bit of space in her brain to feel anything but desire.

"So perfect, and all ours."

Whether it was Miles or fate that had dropped her in our laps, I didn't even fucking care at this moment. All that mattered was that Callie was ours.

Chapter 7
Callie

I couldn't think. All I could do was feel every mouth and hand on me. Who gave Kai the right to taste so fucking good? Whoever had designed alphas and omegas so that cum and slick tasted like our scents was a fucking genius.

I had never liked sucking Jerry's dick, though it was certainly one of *his* favorite activities. With Kai I couldn't get enough. That cinnamon flavor bathed my tongue and I savored every shuddering breath I drew out of him. With my eyes squeezed shut, I couldn't tell who else was where, only that fingers were buried in my pussy, a tongue was on my clit, and an insistent mouth was teasing my nipple.

Pleasure ratcheted tight and deep and I broke apart again, heat making my head swim and my hips writhe.

"Ready, princess?"

I blinked blurry eyes, seeing Amir looking at me. "Ready for what?"

A ripple of laughter in the distance snapped me to attention and I whipped my gaze toward the theater seating. They were all fuzzy blobs thanks to the spotlight, but I'd almost forgotten they were there.

Amir grabbed my chin and turned me back to him. "Don't look at them. Be a good girl and get on your hands and knees for me."

When I didn't immediately move, he smacked my thigh. I squeaked, though it hadn't been hard enough to hurt, just to get my attention. As loath as I was to pull away from who I now knew was Diego between my thighs, I complied with Amir's instruction. I groaned as I shifted, Diego's fingers sliding free. Kai helped me balance as I unsteadily got onto my knees. Amir adjusted my position so that I was parallel to the crowd.

I looked at Kai for reassurance.

"I'm right here, little dove. Are you going to be a good girl and let Amir fuck you? I'll be so proud of you taking him."

I nodded like a bobblehead and leaned into his soft hand stroking over my hair.

I held stock-still when Amir grabbed my hips and I felt the first bit of pressure from the tip of his cock notching in my pussy.

Anticipation filled the air and I glanced over at the crowd. Amir's hand cracked against my ass and I yelped, squeezing against the little bit of him he had gotten inside me. "What did I say, princess?"

I turned back to Kai.

49

"Why don't you give Diego some attention after he took such good care of you?"

"Okay." I shivered.

Kai moved over and Diego took his place, his cock standing proudly, his clove and nutmeg scent instantly filling my senses. I let my forehead rest against Diego's stomach, my breath hitching at the slow invasion of Amir. My pussy stretched, the slight burn making me lightheaded as I carefully rocked to take him in. Amir wasn't patient for long and dragged me back until my ass cheeks were pressed to his stomach.

"Fuck." I panted against Diego, who had a comforting hand on my hair. That comfort only gave me another moment of reprieve before his fingers curled in my hair and lifted my head.

Just like with Kai, my mouth popped open on reflex so I could get the flavor of him on my tongue. Amir's first proper thrust had my eyes rolling back and I moaned around Diego's cock. Then he moved too, the two of them trapping me between them, and I couldn't do a damn thing except hold still and take it.

Kai reached for me, his fingers going to town on my clit until I was squirming and squeaking, helpless to move.

So much.

Too much.

I was going to burst. I'd never been so fucking turned on in my whole life. It felt like a disservice to everyone to think about how Jerry paled in comparison to this, to think about him at all when I had three alphas taking me apart, but the thought was there all the same. I hadn't been good enough for him, but maybe...

Amir fucked in with hard strokes, cutting through what rational thought I had managed to gather. He was so far away. I needed them all where I could see them all at once. Amir was always too far.

I unraveled under their combined touch, slick dripping down my thighs, my scream muffled by Diego's cock. None of them stopped. I really was going to burst if I didn't get a second to breathe.

I pushed away from Diego, sucking in gulps of air between moaning as Kai and Amir kept up their work of ruining my pussy. Diego's hand fisted around his cock, pumping briskly.

"Eyes closed, precious."

I could do better than that. I surged forward when Amir's hips struck mine and dove around Diego's cock just as he spilled that warm, spiced cum over my tongue.

A shudder raced over my spine and Amir's hips began an erratic pattern, each of his desperate grunts and groans fueling the desire beneath my skin. Kai stroked my clit to one more rise before Amir slammed home, heat spilling deep inside.

I was still dazed from the aftershocks of my orgasm. Amir pulled me up, one hand in my hair, the other on my shoulder, and before my arms could flail for balance, Kai was right there. His hands swept over me, his chest pressed to mine, giving me all the warmth and stability I craved.

"I need to have you," he murmured against my mouth. "Let me."

"Yes," I breathed.

"Both of us together."

Before I could think hard enough to question that statement, Kai's mouth was on mine, his tongue slick and probing, his lips knowing the steps of some ancient dance I could barely keep up with. Every sweep of his kiss had me clenching on Amir's cock, the alpha behind me licking up my throat, his fingers kneading my hips.

51

I let out a pathetic sound when Kai drew back.

"I'm not going anywhere. Don't worry."

He stretched out next to us and Amir withdrew, guiding me with his hands to straddle Kai. My legs were like jelly, but neither seemed to mind having to support me. I huffed and puffed as I sank down on Kai's cock, getting that same delicious stretch as Amir's.

Don't compare.

Don't think about how much better *they feel than—*

"Deep breath for me," said Kai.

He cradled my throat in one hand and kept himself lifted, balancing on his elbow so he could keep kissing me and shutting off my brain. It wasn't until Amir shifted behind us, straddling Kai's thighs and angling my hips, that I had any inclination of what was happening.

My long, breathless keening sound sparked the energy in the room like a powder keg, everyone waiting in silence for the spark to hit the barrel. Amir panted behind me, slowly pressing his cock in alongside Kai's while shudders rolled through me and my pussy stretched to fit both of them.

"Fuck, fuck, ah—"

"Come on, omega," Kai crooned. "You were made to take us. Let him in."

I curled my nails into his chest and Kai's cock twitched inside me.

"That's it, little dove. You make me feel it too. Hurt me if you need to."

Amir was so much more patient than before, working his way in with barely perceptible increments. His thumbs swept a comforting pattern against my back, but it was still *so* much. The pressure was indescribable. I'd never taken a knot before. Was that what this was like?

I'd never been *allowed* to take a knot before. Jerry thought it would be emasculating if I used a toy for it during my heat, so I had made do, but this...

Amir pulled me up so he could get his teeth on my throat, the sharp sting against my scent gland sending a cascade of pleasure through me that nearly had me blacking out. Spots danced in my vision and I'd have collapsed onto Kai if Amir didn't have the grip he did on me.

"Open up, princess," Amir ordered.

I whined, desperate to obey. He pushed deeper while I keened and struggled to stay still until his hips were wedged against my ass. Then Diego was next to us, he and Amir each taking one side of my throat. Once someone touched my clit, I was done for. I screamed to the high fucking heavens, totally unable to cope with everything I felt. Slick gushed from me, coating Kai until all I could smell was my candied apple scent seamlessly blended with all of them. Every breath was like a drug hit, and every single one of my nerves sang a symphony of delight before I exploded.

Kai and Amir moved smoothly together, so slowly I could barely perceive the motion, but the pressure... I was totally delirious, the world warping around me in a flood of light and color as they carefully withdrew and pushed back in as one.

Diego kept me upright while the two of them used my pussy. I surrendered my weight to him, head falling back, my throat dry from panting.

"Me next," Diego whispered. "When they're done with you, that cunt is mine."

I whimpered, a fresh surge of slick dripping out of me.

"Slutty little omega," he murmured against my skin. "So ready to get fucked again while you're still in the middle of being taken. Do you want my knot, precious?"

"Y-yes. I ne—"

Someone pinched my nipple and the trigger of pain while I was so overwhelmed sent me tumbling over the edge.

"Easy, princess." Amir's hands snaked around my body, cupping my breast, his teeth scraping over my throat. "Fuck, you feel as good as you taste."

Diego stole my mouth for a kiss. He kissed like he was hungry for me, which suited me fine because I was fucking *starving* for these men. His fingertips walked down my body before grinding gently against my clit. That was all it took, the three of them snipping every thread that tethered me to this world with their cocks buried in me, their hands everywhere at once.

Too much, too much.

Darkness swept into my vision. They lowered me down onto Kai and I nuzzled against his throat, trying to regain my balance. He smelled so good. I needed that taste on my tongue. Needed *him*.

I didn't think twice about seizing his throat with my teeth. His cry melted into the air, his hips bucking hard. A hand in my hair wrenched my head to the side and then teeth were on me too. I sang for them, for the crowd watching, all of those eyes like fire on me. Everything that Kai was poured into me, filling up the bottle of my soul until it was overflowing. Lust and panic and affection tumbled through me so strongly I couldn't breathe.

Then I was craned up, Amir growling in my ear. "Did you just fucking *bond* him?"

"Fucking hell," Diego breathed. "And he bonded her right back."

Mmm. *Bonded*. I was so high I couldn't figure out if that was a bad word. They sounded upset, but all I could feel was

Kai in my chest like a toasty balloon of affection. Too much thinking to figure it out. All I wanted was for the alphas to keep touching me. I pawed my way out of Amir's grip and snuggled against Kai.

Sweet cinnamon.

All mine.

Chapter 8
Miles

F uck. Fuckfuckfuckfuck.

James, the control room operator, turned to me. "Did I just see what I think I saw?"

"Yep. Keep rolling. Jesus Christ. I'll be back."

My teeth ached with the urge to bite Callie. She and Kai had bonded. My packmate and my omega had just put their teeth into each other on stage. That was *not* supposed to happen.

Diego and Amir looked at a loss for what to do, and Kai clung possessively to Callie, his growl radiating over the speakers, punctuated by her sweet whimpers. Amir was still balls-deep in her when I arrived in the wings. Every cell in my body wanted me to strip down and join them, but that wasn't how this fucking worked. I *couldn't* touch her. All I could do from here was watch, and while that was generally one of my favorite activities, every moment that passed with her and my pack made me want her more.

It was very stupid of me to be down here. I had followed my instincts to where I was still out of sight from the stage. Now that they were all off their blockers, I could smell their scents wrapped around one another, and even though I was still on my own blockers, I was bordering on desperate, scenting Callie in heat. My cock fought a valiant battle against my pants and I ground the heel of my palm against it.

There was nothing I could do. I had already been daring to hope Callie would stay with us, but now she definitely didn't have a choice. We couldn't let her go after this.

Amir slid free and Diego backed off, Kai flipping Callie and thrusting back into her glistening core. She writhed beneath him. That bite of hers must've sent him into a rut. The others wouldn't be able to safely touch her until he knotted her.

I was going to die standing in the shadows. Every sound she made was like a siren call drawing me toward her. I sank down to my knees, as if bracing my hands against the floor could anchor me to the spot and stop me from following the urge to go to her.

Her body jostled with every thrust, the spotlight high-lighting the bounce of her breasts and the graceful arc of her throat, teasing out a rainbow of golds and reds from her hair.

Diego and Amir slipped offstage and into the shadows next to me. They both had widely blown pupils, their cocks rock hard.

"Miles, what do we do?" Diego hissed.

I didn't have a single fucking answer to give him. That bite they had given each other cracked them open down to the

57

foundations, letting the essence of the other fill up those empty spaces. She might be our mate, but Kai was first bond, and whatever traces of their rational minds they had been in possession of before were replaced with the primal nature of alpha and omega that had reigned supreme since the dawn of time.

"Just get her through the heat." I swallowed hard. Fuck.

My cock was so hard it hurt, and my jaw ached from grinding my teeth.

The tips had already been pouring in for her. Each dollar was a reminder that all the people watching both here and on the livestream were getting to see my mate fucked every which way. Usually watching my pack fuck omegas was satisfaction enough, but not this time.

I savored each moan and groan out of her, almost able to pretend that she was making them in my ear with how loud they were over the speakers.

This was fucking torture.

The notifications on my tablet went absolutely wild, tips pouring in when they realized what had happened. Most people would never see a bond and rut unless it was their own. Callie bonding on camera and sending Kai into a rut was raking in *thousands* every few seconds from the livestream. The tips from the audience in person came in a bit slower, but the amounts were considerably bigger.

Holy fucking shit.

If that kept up, Callie was going to make twice her earnings just on tips.

Diego sat next to me, his eyes wide and fingers flexing like he was trying to stop himself from leaping right back in there. Ruts were too unpredictable to risk it. Once Kai got Callie on a knot, they could go back on stage. In theory...

Amir paced behind us like a caged tiger, his growl a steady

hum that accompanied the soundtrack of Callie coming undone.

Diego glanced over at my tablet screen. "Are you fucking serious? We've never gotten tips like that."

He grabbed it out of my hands and scrolled back, his gaze flicking between the numbers and the pair on stage.

My eyes kept being helplessly drawn to Callie and Kai. All of her nerves from earlier had long since departed, smoothed away by the heat high. As the platform slowly rotated, I got new views, her tipped-back face disappearing to show me the length of their bodies, the arch of her spine, the way her nails dug into Kai's ass as he fucked into her. Watching the descent of his cock inside her was weirdly hypnotizing. I had seen my pack fuck many omegas, but I'd never paid such particular attention before.

Callie was different, though. Every sound she made was burned into my brain. I knew without a doubt they would live in my memory forever.

I took measured breaths. If I hadn't been on scent blockers, I'd have absolutely voided the contract the second I smelled her. I was glad a million times over that I hadn't gone off them, even if it did prevent my body from properly being able to acknowledge that she was a scent match. I wanted to inhale her, to let it sink into my bones and fill me with that perfect knowledge that she was mine, but I couldn't do that until all of this was over.

How many people had walked right by their fated mate simply because they had chemically altered their scent? I hated how close I had been to never knowing. If she hadn't changed her mind about doing the heat, I'd have let her go and been none the wiser. In all likelihood we never would have crossed paths again and my pack would have been without its omega forever. Even the concept had my hackles up.

Once we got out of this, I was going to make sure she wanted to stay, over and above the fact that she would remain because she was our mate.

"These fucking numbers," Amir hissed. "If I were an even bigger asshole than I am, I'd consider bonding her just to see if we got the same numbers as her and Kai."

My fingers locked around Amir's wrist. "Don't. It's fucking bad enough one bonding happened. We can't let another one happen, not until she asks for it."

Normally it wasn't an issue for our performers. The audience liked the risk of having no cuffs or collars to protect bonding sites, and for the most part the alphas weren't as affected by an induced heat as they were by a natural one. They would never lose control and bond a typical omega during these shows, but Callie was a scent match, and that was a whole different ball game.

I should've thought of it and I didn't. It was my fault this had happened, for not thinking far enough ahead, for not thinking how different things might be with a mate instead of any other omega.

I had to dig through several boxes backstage before I finally found what I was looking for. I put the cuffs and collars on Amir and Diego myself just for the assurance that it was done correctly and I wasn't risking Callie further.

Amir pawed at his. "I hate these fucking things."

"We don't have a choice."

"I don't know." Amir shrugged. "She's definitely stuck with us now. What difference would a couple more bonds make if we could all quadruple our income?"

Diego whacked him in the shoulder. "Don't be a dick. She

might be stuck with us, but that doesn't mean we don't have to court her into wanting our bonds too. Kai lost that entire opportunity with her and we both know it's not going to sit well with him that he bonded her during this."

"Kai and I have different sensibilities," Amir countered.

"You don't even *want* a mate," said Diego.

"I don't," Amir snapped, "but I fucking have one anyway, don't I?"

"Both of you, shut up. We're not making a single decision on further bonding until Callie is out of the haze and we can have an actual discussion. At least let her say what she wants."

"She won't *know*," replied Amir. "That omega is high as a kite right now and she can only get so lucid in an induced heat."

"*That omega* is our mate," I growled. "She has a name."

Amir rolled his eyes. "My point still stands. Whenever she's out of the haze, she'll be asleep. We can't ask her until this is over and then our opportunity is gone."

I checked another growl. He wasn't wrong, but he could definitely do with speaking a little nicer about it. The money was a fantastic opportunity, and if Callie decided she didn't want to stay with us, it would more than set her up for a comfortable life, but there was no fucking way I could let it happen without at least asking her.

"What if she still wants to leave?" Diego asked quietly. "What if she takes Kai with her?"

That thought hadn't even entered my head, but Diego's words sent panic spiraling to choke me. Kai would have to go with her if she chose not to stay. This whole thing was a fucking mess. His entire career was compromised. We had so much we needed to talk about and it was genuinely impossible right now. I had never regretted my career choice more than at this moment.

Callie's shriek of pleasure had all of my little hairs standing up, my cock aching. Kai's answering groan was a pretty good indication that he was knot-deep in her. More tips poured in. The audience loved knotting.

As the platform finished a full rotation, more dollars trickled in. No one had as good of a view as they normally would with Kai completely draped over her, but he wasn't thinking about any of them. Putting Callie on display was the least of his concerns. Usually they would knot the omega with their back to the alpha's chest, thighs spread to give everyone the best view, but not today. Kai wanted to keep Callie all to himself, or at least as much as he could while being onstage. I didn't blame him one bit for that.

Her soft whimpers and the way she clung to him had pleasure lancing through me. My hands itched to touch her.

Tips continued to trickle in. Every subtle shift of Kai's hips prompted the most delectable tiny sounds out of Callie. Knots meant minimal movement, but it was always a treat for audiences when the omegas were unraveled with nowhere to go.

I shouldn't be down here anymore. I had made sure precautions were in place, made sure Callie wasn't going to get any more surprise bonds, and I needed to get back to the control room. Moving from this spot was akin to climbing Everest. I didn't want to move one inch further away from Callie.

A message popped up on the tablet from management.

KYLE - MANAGER:

What the fuck happened out there, Miles?

JEFF - OWNER:

That omega could sue us to hell and back

MILES:

It'll be fine

She's Kai's mate

We didn't find out until the serum was already administered

KYLE - MANAGER:

Fix this fuckup

MILES:

I will

I wasn't actually sure Callie *wouldn't* end up suing, but that made it even more important we showed her life with us could be what she wanted. I, at least, would take care of her even if she sued the company into the ground. I could find another job. Maybe... I wasn't entirely certain how well I would be able to find new employment after inadvertently recruiting the mate of a performing pack, but at least now I knew to always get the scent blockers neutralized before anyone signed a contract. It was good, in a way, even if Callie was the sacrificial lamb for us to figure it out.

Sweet bliss covered her features, looking as beatific as a saint blessed with the light of the heavens. I wanted her to look like that *for me*. And damn if I wasn't going to do every single thing I could to make that happen.

Chapter 9
Diego

I was the first one to risk going back on stage, testing Kai's response now that he had knotted Callie.

"Hey, Alpha," I said softly, crooning gently so he'd understand I wasn't a threat. "You know me. Your mate is safe."

The tension in the air was so thick I could barely breathe, everyone waiting to see whether they would have a brawl as well as an orgy to watch.

"It's okay, Kai." I reached out as slowly as I could, tracing my fingertips over his cheek, ready to yank my hand away in case he turned to bite. He growled at first, but recognition flashed in his eyes for a half second and he leaned into my touch. "That's it. You're both safe."

Kai growled again when I reached for Callie to do the same, but he stayed still. He wasn't entirely there, not yet, but every moment that passed would bring him closer to coherency. Callie whined softly when I made contact, tilting her head to expose her throat.

One side was still bare and my teeth ached to leave my own mark there. I traced over it, too focused on her to realize Kai's growl was getting stronger. An arm wrapped over my chest and yanked me back, Kai's teeth snapping at empty air.

"Pay attention to him, not her," Amir ordered. "She's not going to take a chunk out of you."

Amir maneuvered me out of the way and wrapped his hand around Kai's long black hair, locking his other hand around Kai's throat. "Stand down, Alpha. No one is going to hurt your mate."

Kai bared his teeth. He'd *never* done that with us before, and I didn't like it one fucking bit.

"Touch her," Amir told me. "Show him she's safe."

I dropped to my knees at the head of the bed, where I could reach Callie easily but Kai would have to crush her to get to me. "Hey there, precious."

Callie offered her throat again, and I gave into the moment of weakness, not to bite, but at least to taste her. I dragged my tongue up the length of skin, sucking softly at the scent gland. Kai groaned. I wished I was the one knot-deep in her right now, feeling every delicious squeeze of her cunt while the others touched her.

I turned her face to me, devouring that perfect pink mouth, melting as her tongue sought mine out. I drank down her impatient mewls. Amir kept Kai secured, their foreheads together while Amir whispered to him. I snuck my fingers down Callie's body, teasing the curve of her breast and the softness of her belly until I could stroke through the thatch of hair between her thighs. I knew the second I brushed her clit because Kai grunted and Callie squeaked.

Taking her apart was a new pleasure I had discovered. Playing with omegas was always an enjoyable time, but playing with my mate? Un-fucking-paralleled. I stroked her clit, delighted by her squirming, at the way she reached for Kai, but also for me.

Amir kept a steady hold on Kai to let him bend toward Callie. Was I fucking jealous when he took over her mouth, consuming all of the sounds I was prompting in her? Absolutely. It was a tight fit with their bodies pressed together, but Callie made no complaints as I continued sweeping my fingers back and forth over her, the pitch of her moans growing.

"That's a good girl. Come for your alphas." I moved faster, Callie's strangled cry sneaking free as she snatched breaths between tasting Kai's mouth.

The audience released a collective sigh of relief when Callie came with Kai's knot in her and my fingers between them. Some of the tension in Kai's body relaxed, clarity filling his warm brown eyes. He settled back on his knees, pulling Callie onto his lap, leaving her back bowed.

"Ready for my cock, precious?" I asked.

Callie's only response was a whine that rocked me down to my toes, a sound of omega desperation that demanded I act upon it.

I rose up, tapping the tip of my cock against her lips. She opened eagerly, and I stroked my thumbs down her throat, working my way in slowly. Her tongue lapped at me, wandering hands reaching for me to lock around my waist.

Fucking Christ.

If I had been a beta, I'd have come down her throat instantly.

Amir kept hold of Kai's hair, his hand replacing mine to keep Callie climbing up to the peak and tumbling over. The heat of her mouth, her voracious lips and tongue, and the contraction of her throat nearly had my eyes rolling back in my head. I'd never had anyone be quite so hungry for me before.

"That's a good fucking girl," I gasped out. "Taking your alphas like the perfect omega slut you are."

I pulled out enough for her to get a good breath when the next wave of pleasure washed over her, her muscles twitching and sweat making her skin glisten. I couldn't mistake her moan for anything else when I fucked back into her throat. Being as rough as I wanted was out of the question. I could wait until I was in Kai's position to really drive home my craving for this woman.

When I pulled out again, Callie wasn't having it. She brought her hands to wrap around my cock and stroke it while it lay across her face, and her tongue flicked along the underside and over the tip.

Fuck me. That was a sight I was never going to forget. The warm ghosting breaths of her panting was a curious play of temperatures against my skin. Kai dragged her closer and Callie groaned, tilting her head back and pulling at my hips.

Who was I to refuse?

If we could bottle the feeling of Callie's mouth on my cock, we'd be billionaires.

Pleasure built at the base of my spine and as much as I wanted to hold back, to drag this sensation on into eternity, Callie was far too voracious to allow it. I dropped forward, bracing my weight on the bed, hips bucking helplessly as I came down her throat. I jerked back before my knot could swell behind her teeth. I had no interest in accidentally suffocating her.

"Fuck!"

Callie grabbed hold of my knot, not content to let me go just yet. Her grip had me delirious as she forced me to come again, shooting across her breasts.

"Jesus fucking Christ." I was held totally immobile as Callie's fingers explored my knot, teasing and squeezing until I thought I might faint from hyperventilating.

Amir finally dragged her hands away to take pity on me. "That's enough, princess. If you're that eager for a cock, you can have mine."

Kai was clear-eyed by the time I stumbled over to him and parked my ass on the bed. Thank god for that because I did not have the fortitude to restrain an alpha in rut right now.

Amir wasn't quite as gentle with her as I had been, but Callie didn't seem to mind one bit. I shouldn't have been thinking about forever, but there was a certain sort of pleasure in knowing we were matched with an omega who wanted us this much. She was going to be fucking excellent to play with when the heat was over.

Part of me knew she was likely only this exuberant because of the hormones and the serum, but it was impossible not to wonder what she would be like behind closed doors. Would we be able to coax her to the same fervor? I wanted to try so badly, to get my hands on her in other circumstances and see what heights I could take her to. I wanted to make her fly.

One of Callie's hands reached toward me and I took it in mine, my heart giving a squeeze when she held on tightly.

Fuck. I had been so distracted watching her that I'd

forgotten I had a job to do down here. I nudged Kai to angle back and tucked my face down so my tongue could reach Callie. It would only be fair if I was as enthusiastic with her as she was with me. She tasted so fucking good. Sweet and tart, candied apple coating my tongue and filling my nose. I didn't even mind how strong Kai's cinnamon scent twined with hers. This sweet, beautiful omega was all I craved.

"That's it, princess," Amir crooned. "Your throat was made to take cock."

I couldn't help but rock against the bed, knowing exactly what she looked like right now with Amir using her perfect mouth. Callie's grip tightened and she arched up with a cry. I licked her through that rise and the next until she sank to the bed and Amir pulled out, his cum decorating her alongside mine.

She looked good enough to eat.

Kai pulled out of her, his knot finally gone down enough to allow it, and I immediately pushed him aside to properly get my mouth on her. We all got pretty fucking close during these shows, but there had always been relatively clear boundaries; apparently where Callie was concerned, I didn't give a shit. I wanted to taste her and if Kai was included in that, then so be it.

Callie shuddered and squirmed, writhing against me now that she was free to do so without the others holding her down. I wrapped my lips over her clit and sucked, drawing out all her luscious, desperate noises. Her soft thighs pressed against my head as she came, silencing the world around us except for the blood rushing in my ears while twitches rippled through her, making her shiver against my mouth.

Then she was quiet, languid and exhausted. We had taken her enough, given her what she needed to break the haze, and now she needed to rest. I carefully peeled her thighs open and feasted my way up one leg and back down, nipping her clit before lavishing attention on her other thigh. Her sweet shudders were all the encouragement I needed to continue. She might have needed to rest but that didn't mean I had to stop exploring. If all went well, I would have a lifetime to do that, but for the moment I was too eager to stop. She deserved all of my attention, deserved every ounce of pleasure she could grab in this life, and I planned to deliver it to her in spades.

Kai nudged me over, taking hold of one of her ankles and kissing his way along the length of her leg until we were both nestled at the crux of her thighs, alternating teasing licks and nips that had her squeaking and jerking. Callie's sounds changed once more and I looked up to see Amir indulging himself on her tit, her fingers locked in his hair.

I scraped my teeth over the softness of her thigh, cradling it over my shoulder. It was entirely unfair how lovely she was. I didn't know what to do with my craving for her except to pour it out and let her take everything she could hold.

"Diego." My name was broken on her lips.

I climbed up to loom over her. "Yes, precious?"

"Please," she begged. "Please, I need—"

"Of course you do, darling." I pushed Amir out of the way so I could settle my weight on top of her and nuzzle her cheek. "Of course you need. Beautiful, slutty omegas as desperate as you always do. Don't you worry; we're going to give you everything and more."

A simple shift in my hips was all it took and I sank into the scorching heat of her cunt.

"Yes," she whined. "Knot. Please, please, pl—"

The first snap of my hips had her choking off her words

and I settled into a rhythm that had a soft cry bursting out of her with every thrust.

All mine.

I didn't care that I had to share her, didn't care that someone else had the honor of bonding her first. Callie was mine—ours—and soon she would know it.

Chapter 10
Callie

Every inch of me was inflamed, aching to be touched even as hands were everywhere. None of it was enough to drive away the heat that clawed at me, that demanded I be soft and open. I had lost track of who was where multiple times, only concerned that someone was inside me at all times.

Clove and nutmeg saturated each breath.

Diego.

The slick warmth of his skin had me close to overheating, but I didn't want him to move, didn't want him to stop driving his hips against mine, plundering my body to satisfy the demands of the heat. He felt so good I wanted to cry. Honestly, I wasn't far off as I sobbed my release and melted, completely depleted.

"One more, little dove."

I turned to Kai, his chin resting on the bed next to me. He was so pretty. I reached a lazy hand toward him and tucked my fingers into the sweaty strands of his hair.

"One more what?"

"One more knot and then you can sleep."

"Sleep good," I murmured.

Kai chuckled. My eyes flew wide as Diego ground against me, his knot swelling and setting off the first domino of my orgasm, pleasure cascading through me.

"I'm never going to get over how fucking delicious you look coming on a knot," Kai said playfully.

I could only whimper, sucking in minuscule breaths, each tiny shift in Diego's hips sending a fresh spasm of desire through me.

"Come for me." Kai's fingers swept over my clit and Diego moaned as I squeezed hard around him. I was already so primed it took only seconds for Kai to break me.

I let delirium take me, coming back to clarity only when Diego eventually slid free and Amir flipped me over, hoisting up my hips, fingers spreading my tender flesh.

I whined, my thighs shaking. "What?"

"They need to see how much cum you took." I turned to see Amir, his arm wrapped around my waist to keep me upright, and then I felt the warm drip sliding out of me. "There we go, princess. Everyone gets to see what a little cum slut you are."

My cheeks burned and my pussy clenched at his words, more warmth dripping free.

He chuckled. "You like that, don't you? You want all of them to see how well you were used."

I didn't. Did I? Instead of thinking too hard about it, I let

73

my cheek rest against the blankets until Amir was finally done showing me off.

I drifted in and out.

Someone scooped me up.

Cinnamon.

Kai.

Warm water sluiced over me, gentle hands cleaning up the absolute mess they had made of me. I clung to the nearest body, keeping my eyes closed because I was too fucking tired for anything else. I purred under the attention. Hands were everywhere, but my body wasn't craving ruination right now. I just wanted to be held, to sleep, to feel safe.

Cinnamon and cedar, clove and nutmeg wrapped around me. I sank into oblivion with those scents in my nose. They were so cozy around me, holding me like a treasure, but even so I slept fitfully. I woke often and fell asleep just as quickly, unused to the bodies around me and the scent of alpha despite how deeply I had been drenched in it lately.

My dreams twisted and turned, full of flashes of all of their faces, Jerry's sneaking in to send my heart pounding when suddenly it was him taking Diego's place to fuck between my spread thighs.

"Little whore," Jerry whispered. "Giving it up to anyone who gives you a bit of attention. Did you wish it was me? Did you cry? You're not good enough, Callie."

Every time I tried to close my eyes, he appeared again, sometimes murmuring hateful things in my ear, sometimes bending over some faceless woman.

"Fuck," Jerry groaned. "She feels so much better than you. No wonder you were so easy to leave."

I hated seeing it, hated hearing it, but it wouldn't go away. The truth of his words rang through me like the clang of a church bell, vibrating me down to my bones. I should have listened to my mom and my friends. I never should've believed he loved me. It was agony to know how much more I had loved him than he had loved me. I turned to run, the floor slippery beneath my feet. Escaping him wasn't an option. Every step I took away only dragged me closer, forcing me to listen to each grunt of his satisfaction as he shoved his dick into the faceless woman.

I screamed and no sound came out. Then hands were everywhere and eyes popped into existence until it was a wall wrapped around me. Nowhere to hide. I couldn't breathe, salt-water pouring in to sting my eyes and fill my mouth, to drown me in all of my misery.

I swung my fist and woke myself with a jolt, staring around in confusion with no recognition of where I was. The walls were gold and terracotta wallpaper, the ceiling white with fancy molding around the overhead light. Where the fuck was I?

My head swam and I sank back into the blankets. They were deliciously soft, the only comfort at the moment. Every bit of me ached, but in a pleasant, well-used way. The way I knew I was supposed to feel during a heat but that Jerry had never let me experience. As a beta, Jerry had never been equipped to handle my heats, especially not alone, but he'd tried. Or at least I'd assumed he did, since I was delirious for most of it.

Everyone around me was asleep on a bed that was piled with blankets. I counted their faces. Kai next to me, Diego on my other side, Amir on the other side of him and Miles stretched out on the couch across the room. I was totally naked and blessedly clean.

The world felt wobbly when I moved. I sat up carefully again, delirium pawing at the edges of my consciousness. A blush suffused me head to toe. Had I really let them do whatever they pleased to me? Had I let everyone see?

Shame and desire clashed so fiercely nausea turned in my stomach. Was the heat over? I could only hope it was. I needed to get out of here. I knew I could stay, that Miles had said the suite was mine for a couple of days after, but I couldn't bear to see their faces, not knowing if I would find judgment in their eyes.

And Kai... some instinct urged me to touch him and I curled my fingers into a fist just to thwart it.

Mine.

The word echoed through me. Kai had a bond mark on his throat and I followed the compulsion to check my own, finding a tender spot. I climbed off the bed and slipped away into the washroom, staring in burgeoning horror at the mirror. I grabbed one of the folded towels and screamed into it.

There was a fucking bond mark on my throat. That was why Kai felt like mine. Except he wasn't. None of this was right. None of this was my life.

I braced my hands on the sink, not daring to turn on the water in case it woke one of them. I leaned my cheek against the porcelain, just trying to breathe. As much as I wanted to tell myself it was fine, it really fucking wasn't. I had done something colossally stupid during that heat.

I didn't regret doing the heat. It would give me a new life, but I couldn't just fall into the one they were all expecting. I might not have a fiancé anymore, but I still had a job, an apartment, and a life that had nothing to do with Sin City. Expectation threatened to swallow me whole.

They hadn't told me they wanted me to stay, and I didn't want to be around if they did.

How the fuck was I supposed to ever introduce a mate to

my family? Just show up at their door and be like *oh, hey, so my fiancé dumped me in Vegas and I decided it would be a good idea to fuck these alphas in front of a live audience and now I'm mated to one of them.* That wasn't the sort of meet cute any family would accept.

My fingertips turned to ice, the sensation slowly crawling up my arms, my chest going tight and my breath like shards of glass in my throat.

I couldn't do this.

The world warped, everything turning floaty, flickers of light dancing at the edges of my vision. Reality slipped away beneath my feet, everything from the dream rearing up even though I was awake.

I shivered, searching for something to use to dress myself. I wasn't even sure where my purse was. I tiptoed around the room on wobbly legs, seeing a wallet on the coffee table in front of Miles. Urgency clawed at me and I grabbed it, yanking on a robe I found in the closet before I rushed out of the suite, panic so thick in my chest I could hardly stand it. I didn't understand the sensation, why I felt like there was a predator chasing me, but my rational mind said to run even while my instincts screamed at me to find someplace safe to hide.

Kai stirred. Could he feel my panic? I couldn't risk him waking and seeing me.

Home.

I need to go home.

I had a nest waiting for me and if I could just get to it, maybe everything would be okay. If I didn't get my fucking disaster of a life back on track, I would never be able to face my family again.

I swallowed hard, bringing a hand to my spinning head. Everything was so warm. The robe was soft but it itched against my skin and the fabric of the hotel carpet felt prickly against my bare feet. Colors melted like wax around me, the world losing its cohesiveness.

Keep going.

Keep running.

Yes. Running was good. Away from all of my mistakes. Maybe if I ran far enough, I could leave them behind.

A sob worked its way free when I leapt onto the elevator. No one was on it, thank god. I didn't want to see anyone. I would use Miles's card to get a bus ticket, and mail it all back to him when I got home.

When the elevator opened again, I was assaulted by a wave of noise and flashing lights. A casino. Of course it was a fucking casino. I felt a thousand eyes on me as I fled. It got harder to breathe with every step, and when I wrenched open the door to the outside, it was like crashing into a wall of heat.

Run.

I was trying. The concrete was like stepping into a frying pan but I couldn't stop. The screaming inside my head made me dizzy, one voice yelling at me to continue and the other ordering me to return to Kai.

Not mine.

Never mine.

I only knew how to be miserable. That was all I deserved.

Chapter 11
Amir

I woke sharply at the click of the door and sat up, disoriented. Callie was no longer on the bed and the air was filled with burnt sugar, a sure sign she was in some sort of distress. Kai was still asleep, his brow pinched, his eyes moving rapidly beneath his lids like he was having a nightmare.

Climbing out of bed, I poked my head into the hall just in time to see a robed Callie jump onto the elevator.

Absolutely fucking not. I retreated just long enough to grab a pair of lounge pants before taking off after her. She was still in the middle of her heat and I was *not* going to let her go traipsing around Vegas in that condition. It didn't matter whether I wanted a mate or not because she was here and she needed me.

The elevator was too slow. I slammed my fist against the metal doors and took off around the corner, barreling down the concrete steps until I reached the main level. The obnoxious pinging and bells from the machines had me growling as I ran through the casino floor.

What the fuck was she thinking? She couldn't just run off. Even beside the fact that we still had a show to complete, anyone could grab her and soon she would be begging them to take her. I couldn't let that happen to her. If she was going to be fucked by a stranger, she needed to at least look them in the eye and agree beforehand.

I hissed as I stepped out into the blistering Vegas heat. Even in the shade it was too hot and the second my bare feet hit the pavement I was filled with an ungodly fury. But then I saw Callie, running down Las Vegas Boulevard, also barefoot and only in a robe.

"Jesus fucking Christ."

I took off after her. I had done firewalking in the past, and racing over the sun scorched pavement was uncomfortably similar, except this wasn't a ten-foot stretch with people encouraging me. This was a blacktop nightmare.

"Callie, will you fucking stop!" I yelled after her.

She didn't slow, but she did stagger. I pushed forward with as much speed as I could manage. I needed to overtake her quickly and get her back inside.

She shrieked like a goddamn banshee when I grabbed the back of her robe and wrenched backward.

"What the fuck is the matter with you?" I hauled her over my shoulder, hissing as her additional weight ground my feet into the little gravel bits at the edge of the road.

"Let me go! I need to go home," Callie insisted. She

squirmed and when I almost dropped her, I cracked my hand against her ass, making her yelp.

"I'm not letting you go." The way back was so much slower and every step I took was like stepping on shards of glass that were on fire. "If you're gonna be a pain in my ass, I'm gonna be a pain in yours. Stop fucking squirming or I'm going to spank the shit out of you the second we get back inside."

Callie whimpered and let her weight properly sink against me. "Please."

"You don't have to finish the heat with us but you can't fucking run around like this. It's not safe."

"I have to go home."

I adjusted her so I was carrying her bridal style, letting me see the tear tracks down her face. I couldn't afford to let it get to me right now.

The second there was an ounce of shade, I moved us into it. "I'm gonna be really pissed if I burned my feet chasing after you."

Callie didn't answer, only curling up in my arms, sniffling quietly against my chest. Her tears turned to hiccups a couple of minutes later when we reached the entrance to the hotel.

Anyone within our line of sight was staring at us as we walked through, but I was pretty sure I looked ready to murder someone, so not a single one of them approached us.

Callie looked up at me with shiny eyes when we were in the elevator. "I'm sorry. I panicked and I don't—"

"We'll discuss it later." She wouldn't be able to go back onstage like this. I needed to get her settled quickly.

The suite was in chaos when I kicked the door and Diego opened it. "Holy shit, where were you two?"

"This one was running fucking barefoot down the road."

Diego gaped at Callie and quickly took her from me, transferring her to Kai a second later when he realized we were back. Callie and Kai dropped down onto the couch and she burst into sobs. I slammed the door behind me and beelined straight for the bathroom, shucking my pants and sitting on the edge of the tub so I could wash my feet. They were tender as hell, but not as bad as I'd expected beyond being filthy. I took my time scrubbing them for the opportunity to calm down. I could understand that Callie wasn't in her right mind when she fled. No one who fled barefoot in a robe was. The only issue was I didn't have a clue what had set her off.

We'd never had an omega run off on us before. The omegas we played with were more than happy to indulge during this experience. They took advantage of the spa and the room service and the suite, filling up their bank accounts with a few short days of getting railed.

Callie was still sobbing away on Kai when I emerged. He wasn't in his right mind either with a fresh bond chafing and fucking with his rational brain.

"Give her to me," I ordered when I approached the two of them.

Kai clutched her to his chest even tighter.

I sucked my teeth and stared at the ceiling, praying for the strength to deal with these two. She wasn't going to get her feet tended crying on the couch.

"Give. Her."

Kai only growled in response.

"We should let them rest for a bit," said Diego.

"No, she needs a bath. And Mr. First Bond over there isn't going to get anything fucking done while he's in that state."

Diego sighed. "Okay. Let me try."

Miles stood at my side. "This is all a fucking mess."

"That's basically what a mate does to a life," I snapped.

"They're like a bomb going off, and all you can do after is sift through the rubble."

Miles frowned, his eyebrows pinched together. "That's not very fair."

"But it *is* accurate."

"Callie, precious," Diego crooned. "Why don't we get you in the bath? We can order you some room service."

I wasn't sure what else he said, but it took a few minutes of pandering to the two of them on his knees before Kai finally let her go and Callie allowed herself to be scooped up.

I went into the bathroom ahead of them and turned on the water so it was lukewarm, carefully stripped off Callie's robe, and helped Diego set her in the bottom of the tub.

She stared at me with wide eyes, shivering as I got down on my knees and grabbed one of her ankles, angling the foot into the stream of water. Callie hissed at the contact.

"Yeah, that's what fucking happens when you sprint barefoot down the Boulevard. You should've stayed with Kai. What spooked you so hard that you ran off?" I dipped the bar of soap under the water and scrubbed it gently over her feet.

"I don't belong here. That became painfully clear while I slept. I know it was stupid..."

"It was," I agreed. I rinsed her foot and repeated the scrubbing process until it was clean and tiny cuts and gouges were visible.

"I can't be a mate. I can't even be a fiancée right."

"First off, anyone who abandons anyone in a fucking strange city is an asshole. You might be a beautiful pain in the ass, but I haven't seen any good reason for running off on you." I scrubbed up her other foot, focusing on it instead of the plaintive and pitiful look on her face. "And second, you don't have to do anything right. Kai is your mate and we are his pack.

That means something, and it's not something you can run away from."

That only got her crying again.

Christ, I was not good at this. Luckily, I was saved by Diego coming in with a plate of snacks and a bottle of water.

"Drink this," I ordered, passing her the uncapped bottle.

She sniffled her way through consuming it, and then I filled the bath with water just on the warmer side. She was already going through a heat and didn't need anything to raise her temperature, but I didn't want her shivering.

I didn't like seeing her like this. Not because she was my mate, but because she was a fucking person. Her fiancé had hurt her and her financial situation had driven her to us before she'd had time to grieve and heal. Unfortunately for her, she would have to do that while navigating her way into our lives.

"Kai," I called out. "Get your ass in here."

Once he was in the water with Callie, I turned it off and left the two of them to tend each other.

"You saved her," Diego said quietly.

"Someone had to."

"You could've woken us," he pointed out.

"I wasn't going to give her any extra seconds to be out there. Who knows who the hell could have found her if I had waited?" Huge swaths of the city weren't particularly safe even if you knew where you were going. A heat-high omega panic-fleeing would have found trouble sooner rather than later. All it would've taken was one car pulling over with an alpha who had shit motives. She'd have been dragged into that car and we'd have never seen her again. Just the thought of it made me nauseated. Too many people out there couldn't be trusted in general, let alone when it came to the vulnerable.

"Thank you." Diego pulled me into a hug. "I know you

don't love the situation but Callie is lucky to have you in her pack. We all are."

I shrugged and slipped out of his embrace, heading over to the tray of food that had been delivered. Most of it was scooped off the buffet downstairs, but they also kept trays ready at all times so we got our food as quickly as we needed it. That was the helpful thing in working where we did. Even though our jobs were usually part of the underground in most places, this city had such a thriving underbelly that anyone could get whatever they needed in short order.

Miles dropped down onto the couch, looking like he was one inconvenience away from a full-blown crisis. "I don't know what to do," he said.

"Well, I don't have any answers for you. You're the brains of this operation; I'm just a dick."

Miles snorted and chugged down one of the glasses of juice. "I'll fix all of it."

"I genuinely don't know how you can."

He wilted and I felt a little bad, but it was still the truth. Nothing was ever going to be the same again.

I could hear Kai and Callie purring from out here. He had some magical power to soothe her I didn't possess. I didn't want that power either. It was way too much fucking hassle to feel someone else's emotions, to be connected to them that way. Kai could have her. We might be a pack, but Callie was never going to be mine.

Chapter 12
Kai

Relief at having Callie in my arms was so strong I could barely breathe. I had woken in a panic straight from a nightmare to find her gone and feeling like I was on the verge of cardiac arrest with all her emotions thundering down the bond. But now she was safe. Holding her was the only thing that kept the panic at bay.

"You're okay, little dove," I told her, though it was as much to reassure myself as her.

"I'm so sorry," she whispered.

"No need to apologize. Hormones do funny things to a brain. The important thing is that you're safe."

I focused on breathing. There was still a whole mess of

shame and anxiety filling up my chest, and it felt foreign enough that I knew it had to be from her.

"Talk to me. I'm the one person in the world right now who can intimately understand what you're feeling."

Callie took a moment to collect herself and I did my best to purr despite everything swirling around inside me. She needed the comfort, and if we could take the edge off those worries, then we could start nudging her toward healing.

"I didn't mean to bite you. I'm sorry, I'm sorry, I—"

"Shhh. It's all right. It likely would've happened sooner rather than later with the scent match. We just got a bit ahead of ourselves. I promise I'm not upset with you about it."

"I'm upset at myself." Callie sniffled. "I took away our choice."

"It could have just as easily been one of us biting first." I'd felt my resolve weakening every second I was with her. If she hadn't bitten me, I wouldn't have lasted long regardless.

"I'm still sorry. For the bite, and for running. The nightmare felt so real. I freaked out."

"Tell me what it was about?"

She relayed her fractured memories of it, mostly consisting of the hateful things her ex-fiancé had said.

My body tensed with every word. "Were those things he's said to you?"

"In bits and pieces over the years," she confessed. "Never quite a tirade like that."

I was ready to strangle her ex just for thinking those things, let alone saying them to her face. I had never really endured vitriol about what I did for a living. In part, that was likely because my family had no idea, and all of my friends now were in similar industries. We knew and understood. From the sounds of it, Callie wasn't so lucky.

"I know none of this is ideal," I said carefully. "Hell, I'm scared shitless about it myself, but I want you to understand that I've got you now. I mean, I hope we've got each other, but it's okay if you need time."

Her heart pounded against my palm, and I purred as loud as I could until hers kicked on in response and her heartbeat slowed bit by bit. Everything was still chaos, but the undeniable truth was that this omega was mine, and I was her alpha. I didn't know her yet, but I wanted to. I craved every detail that would let me make her happy. I couldn't undo any of the harm that had already come to her, but the fear that flooded down the bond toward me from her was intolerable, and I intended to fix as much of it as I could. Not for my sake, but for hers.

I wanted to quiet that whole storm of negativity inside her and replace it with the immutable knowledge that she had someone on her side now. I gathered up every ounce of calm I had and tried to project it toward her. No one was 100% certain how bonds worked, only that they did, and if I could feel everything coming from her, then surely she could feel everything coming from me. It wasn't only calmness I wanted to share. I thought of how beautiful she was, how brave she had been, how completely delicious she was, and her scent sweetened, the chaos inside her ebbing.

"That's my good girl. We belong to each other now and I'm going to take care of you. I don't know what that looks like yet, but we'll figure it out together."

Callie tipped her head and I boosted her up so I could lick over the bondbite sitting on her throat. "I don't know how to be a good omega."

"You're my perfect omega already," I promised.

She sniffled. "You've been a really good alpha, Kai. I'm sorry I'm such a basket case."

"We were definitely both basket cases. You just weren't here to see me freaking out. Besides, you've been through a shit ton of things, and I would say you're entitled to a little freak-out."

Her laugh was broken, a sob sneaking in to shatter it. "It's been way too much."

"Will you come stay with us after the heat is over? Or should I plan to move somewhere?"

She squirmed, her discomfort made manifest. "I don't know where else I would go."

"Please stay. At least while we figure things out. I don't even want you out of my sight. I don't think I would be able to cope if you left us."

I would have no choice but to follow if she did go. Keeping Callie close felt necessary, like one of the fundamental laws of the universe I simply couldn't break. She was meant to be with us, with me, even if fate had an unconventional way of bringing us together.

Closing my eyes, I breathed her in and stretched us out in the bath, purring away until she melted against me and the bond settled. It wouldn't always work, nor should it, honestly. Sometimes feelings just needed to be experienced even if they were uncomfortable as hell. Right now she needed soothing. She wasn't going to process anything truly meaningful in her healing journey during a heat anyway, so I leaned into what she required from me: safety. I had to show Callie I could protect her even if I didn't know how.

I had no clue what the future held for us. At the moment this was enough. I had my own instincts to quiet down, and the only way that was going to happen was if she stayed exactly where she was.

At some point I would have to tell my family that I was bonded, but I was in no rush to do that. There were a million other things about my life they had no idea about. This could be on that list for a little while longer.

"Tell me everything about yourself," I prompted. "I want to know all the details."

"Like what?"

"Favorite color?"

"Pink. You?"

"Orange. Favorite food?"

"Thai green curry. You?"

"Spam musubi for childhood classics. Shrimp pho otherwise."

Callie wriggled around to face me. "Siblings?"

"Only child."

"I have a younger sister. She's definitely the favorite."

"Parents aren't supposed to have favorites."

"Tell that to my mom." Callie snorted. "She never got that memo."

"Does it help if I say you're my favorite omega on the planet?"

I caught the ghost of a smile on her face. "A bit, yeah, even if you're obligated to say that."

"Excuse you, I'm obligated to say nothing. Take the compliment."

She leaned forward and snuggled up against me, tucking her forehead against my neck. "Okay."

We picked our way through an introduction. I learned bits and pieces that helped me make sense of her. Her ex had roped her in when she was only eighteen and living in a foreign city, ground her down over their years at college and convinced her to move to LA with him, where she didn't know a single soul. Once he had gotten her good and trapped there, he had weaned more and more bills over to her, forcing her to take on additional hours to compensate until she was too exhausted to do much of anything. No wonder she had stayed so long.

At least she was free now. I was ready to fistfight every insecurity drilled into her by her ex and her family. She didn't have to worry about any of that with me, but I knew it wouldn't be that easy. I knew I would support her, but that didn't mean she could believe me with a lifetime of trauma between her and the truth. I could work on it, though. Every day I could knock out one brick, prove to her that my pack and I were whom she belonged with. I had avoided in-depth relationships for ages, between med school and the job I did now; maybe the universe thought it was funny to send me from zero to mated in a heartbeat.

"I never thought I would have an omega."

"I never thought I would have an alpha. I don't really know what it means yet, but it's nice so far."

I swished warm water up her back. "Definitely nice. I still hoped for you, even if I didn't think I could have you."

"Me specifically?"

"From the moment you got tangled in your seatbelt."

Callie laughed quietly and squeezed me in a hug.

"Should we make a promise, you and I?"

"What kind of promise?" she asked.

"I will be your alpha in any way you want me to be. I will do anything I can to support your transition into this new life, but I want you to promise me that you'll be open to it. I know you're scared, and you have every reason to be, but you have a secret weapon now. You're always going to be able to tell what I'm feeling, so even when your anxiety is screaming at you, I want you to check what you're getting from me. Let the bond show you the truth of whatever situation you're questioning. We can't hide from each other. That's nerve-wracking as hell, but I also kind of like it. I've never been able to be that vulnerable with anyone."

"The anxiety does get pretty screamy."

"I bet. Tell me what you feel right now coming through the bond."

I felt the scrunch of her forehead against my skin. "I don't really know what it is."

"Good or bad?"

"Good. It's soft, kind of warm."

"That would be affection."

"Well, now I feel dumb for not knowing it."

Shame bubbled up in the bond and I intended to squash it immediately. "It's not your fault you don't recognize it. It doesn't sound like you've experienced much of it in your day-to-day. I fully plan to change that."

Affection from her flickered, and when I lifted her chin to place a delicate kiss against her lips, it flared along with whispers of lust.

"I know you have no reason to trust me, but the second you put your teeth in me you became mine, and I will *always* take care of who's mine. If you can't trust anything else, trust that."

She snuggled up against me. "I promise I'll do my best."

"That's all I ask, little dove."

Chapter 13
Miles

I had never been so scared in my entire fucking life. Waking up to find Callie and Amir both gone, the stench of her panic thick in the air... I didn't want to think about what could have happened. I didn't think Amir would hurt her but he was definitely someone who spoke his mind and Callie was so fragile right now. Amir could be tough to handle even when you were totally on your game.

I had immediately called security and they told me Callie was most likely the omega that had burst through the doors a moment ago. Staring out the windows and seeing her race down the road with Amir hot on her heels had plunged my stomach down to my toes. I should've done something more, should've gone after them, but I had stood frozen at that window watching them through the glass.

Diego had done his best with an inconsolable Kai who had all of Callie's panic pumping through him from the bond, along with what I'm sure was a hefty dose of guilt that he hadn't woken up in time to stop her. I couldn't imagine what either of them were feeling.

The moment I had assured myself that Callie was all right, I let myself sink into my own little pit of despair.

How the fuck was I going to fix this? I had promised everyone I could but I had no actual confidence in my ability.

I dialed the lawyer who handled the shows, trying to figure something out.

"Go for John," he said, answering the call.

"We have a problem and I'm not entirely sure how big it is yet."

"Walk me through it," he ordered.

I told him everything from my first meeting with Callie all the way up to her bolting out of the suite.

John whistled when I finally finished. "The omega bit first?"

"She did, yeah. We have it on video."

"That might be the only thing that can save your asses if she does try to go after you. My concern would be her blowing up the entire organization. It's not like we're operating totally on the up and up."

"We try," I argued.

"Yeah and trying won't fucking fly in court. The heat serum isn't legal."

"They're working on approving it," I groused.

"Again," John sighed, "that won't hold up in court. You're gonna have to convince her not to do anything. Smooth talk her, get the bosses to pay her off, whatever shit you have to do to get her under an NDA."

I swallowed hard. I didn't want to pressure Callie into anything. If it wouldn't cost jobs, I wouldn't give a flying fuck, but our pack couldn't take care of her if she nuked our employment. But then I suppose if she went that route, she wouldn't want us to be her pack anyway.

There were still laws on the books in a lot of places, including here, that turned a bonded omega into property, for all intents and purposes. Kai might be able to legally force her to stay, and sign a contract to protect us, but then she would hate us. Just because the law allowed us to do certain things didn't mean I was remotely comfortable with pursuing that option. It was far better for everyone if Callie was excited to stay with us. I felt like a slimeball for even going through all of these choices.

"Is a contract really necessary?" I asked.

"That depends on how much you like your kneecaps intact."

I cursed quietly. He was right. We wouldn't get out of punishment if we let Callie leave here without signing a contract. I didn't want to force her, but Kai would absolutely get in deep shit if we didn't. The flip side of the situation was that Kai also had some legal responsibility for Callie and if our employers and the people who funded them thought she was running amok, they might take it out of his hide.

When had everything gotten so fucking complicated? Our chances of successfully courting Callie seemed to be plummeting by the minute. I could take one for the team, resign myself to her never wanting anything to do with me if it meant protecting the others.

I fucking hated that. I loved my pack, but if the only way to keep them safe was to deny myself a chance with this bright and beautiful omega, then I would do it and be in misery for the rest of forever if they didn't kick me out of the pack outright. I wouldn't blame them for that if they did.

"Send me the paperwork."

"Already on its way."

"You didn't put in anything fucked up, did you?"

"I feel like we have very different definitions of what *fucked up* means. You'll have to read it and let me know if I did."

Jackass. "All right, I'll be in touch."

I sat back, shoving my fingers through my hair, and opened the email. I pored over it line by line. There was indeed bullshit nestled in there. I struck out as many clauses as I dared, mostly ones that made no fucking sense if she was going to be part of the pack. Her family should be allowed to know us and we were absolutely not going to put in anything that was near a restraining order. The company was too fucking concerned with shuttling omegas through the system to ever consider ones that might get caught in it. I couldn't, in any circumstances, allow her to sign a contract that restricted her so heavily in how she wanted to pursue her life afterward.

"Do you want to talk about it?"

I looked up.

Diego was staring at me, his dark eyes soft with worry.

"Not really."

"You look wigged out. We always talk through it. What's going on?" Diego sat next to me and tried to peek at the tablet, but I turned it away from his gaze.

"Just paperwork. Honestly it's probably better if you don't know."

That only made him frown instead of leaving me be.

"Come on, Miles. I know things are kind of fucky, but we'll figure it all out."

"We will."

Callie's whine from the bathroom had all of us snapping to attention.

"I'll send an alert to everyone that Callie's going back out."

"Do you think she should?" Diego asked.

"She's still in heat and she's still under contract. Doesn't seem like she notices the audience during it. I need her to have the best chance at a future with or without us, and that involves her having a full bank account."

"I guess that's fair," Diego said with a sigh. "Okay, we'll see you during the next break."

Kai came out of the bathroom, carrying a naked Callie, and I couldn't help but trace the curves and dips of her body with my eyes. Amir and Diego joined them and tossed a blanket over Callie for some semblance of modesty while they traveled back to the stage.

I followed them a few moments later, taking up my place in the control room. Callie had already succumbed to the next heat spike by the time they got her out on stage. I had memorized so many things about her, and I wasn't surprised when the breathy sound of her begging all of them to take her etched itself into my mind.

While they tangled around one another, I quietly made plans for a life without any of them. Looking at apartment listings fractured something inside me, but I had to be prepared. If they wanted to remove me from the pack for what I had to do, I needed somewhere to go since I had no choice but to stay here to work.

"What are you doing?" James asked.

"None of your business."

"I don't know how you can look anywhere else when you work up here."

I huffed out a breath. It wasn't disrespectful to look at someone on stage, but it felt wrong nonetheless. Callie deserved so much more than me.

Kai, Amir, and Diego would take care of her. She liked Diego; maybe they would bond next. Amir might kick up a fuss, but that didn't mean he wouldn't take care of her. She didn't need me. None of them truly did.

"Fuck, that's hot," James murmured.

"I swear to god, if you take out your cock right now, I'm going to hit you with this tablet."

"Chill out," he said with a laugh, tapping his forehead. "It's all stored in the spank bank for later."

I hit him with the tablet anyway.

"Ow, fuck. What the hell was that for?"

"You can at least pretend to have a little respect."

James only shrugged. "If they didn't want me to look, they wouldn't be out there right now."

He might be right, but I didn't have to like it. It was correct, in a way, for me to be separate, to only ever have Callie at a distance, through glass. It would be easier this way when I had to leave. If I was able to get a taste of her, I wouldn't be able to let her go.

"Be nice anyway," I ordered.

"Miles..."

I froze at the sound of Callie's voice on the speakers.

"Did she just call for you?" James asked. "You lucky asshole."

"Fuck off. I can't touch her until her heat is over. She only agreed to the three of them."

"*Miles.*"

That voice was going to be my ruination.

"You're really going to make an omega beg for you?"

I didn't have a choice. I didn't have to stay up here, though. I left the control room and made my way down to the stage. How strong could I actually be? Who knew? Hearing her whine my name in person instead of through a speaker had me cursing every god I'd ever heard of.

She caught sight of me as the platform spun her slowly, and she reached a hand toward me. Fuck me, I was not strong enough to resist that.

I had no clue how people would react to me walking onto the stage fully dressed and with no intention of fucking the absolutely gorgeous woman spread out with my pack, but it was so hard to care when her fingers curled around mine.

"I'm right here, sweetheart." I got on my knees so we were eye level with each other.

Callie gasped, gripping my hand like it was her only lifeline while Diego ruined her. "Fuck," she breathed. "It felt weird for you to be gone. I don't like it."

Goddamn, it was going to hurt like a bitch when she changed her mind about me. I kissed her knuckles. "I can't stay. This is your show, not mine, but I'll be just offstage, okay?"

The pout she gave me made me want to nip it right off her face.

"Be a good girl for your alphas for me. I won't be far."

Prying her fingers out of mine was an agonizing effort in self-control, but staying would put her at risk, and that was something I simply couldn't allow. Her whine of dismay was a kick in the chest, but I kept removing her grip and stepped off the platform and offstage.

I could already feel how easy it would be for her to dig in

her sweet little claws and rip me apart. She might not do it on purpose, but she could if she wanted to. And I would let her. If it would make things better for all of them I would lay myself out and let her cleave me open.

Callie was a dangerous woman and she didn't even know it.

Chapter 14
Callie

"Open up, princess." Amir spread my ass cheeks while I was sprawled across Diego, his knot wedged deep.

I was already so fucking full I couldn't imagine taking more, but Amir kept insisting I could. He coated himself with my slick and dripped lube between my ass cheeks, working it into me with his thumb while I keened against Diego's skin.

The pressure when he replaced his thumb with his cock had my eyes rolling back in my head. "Amir, I can't."

"Yes, you fucking can."

I panted as he worked his way in, the slow, incremental pushes getting him deeper and deeper.

"That's my good girl, princess. You know how to take a cock. Your body was made to take me, to take all of us."

I dug my nails into Diego and he had his eyes closed, his fingers gripping my thighs, his whole body shuddering with each squeeze of my pussy around his knot. Kai was waiting so patiently to make use of my mouth, but that wasn't going to happen until Amir got his way.

"Oh god." The stretch had every inch of me shaking. I wanted to be good for him and give him what he wanted. I wanted to know what it felt like. The sounds he was forcing out of me weren't quite human anymore and I felt the tension in the air, all of those eyes watching me. Most of the time they were easy to ignore with how well the alphas distracted me, but right now I couldn't help but think about them. What had been nerves at the start was now a pleasant simmer in my blood. They all wanted to see me do this. They were paying for the privilege.

The me of a few days ago would never have dreamed of feeling desirable in this situation, but I did. I felt like I was glowing under the spotlight.

Amir rocked his hips and pulled me up by my hair, cupping my breasts and teasing his lips over my throat. He felt so good I could've died on the spot. His teeth ghosted over my skin. I hadn't forgotten how life-changing it had felt to bond Kai. Even with the heat haze stealing my senses, that lingering knowledge had remained. What would it feel like for Amir to claim me right now?

Diego would only have to move a few inches to bite my wrist, but both of them were in the cuffs and collars to prevent me from doing the same to them. Whoever had thought of them was a godsend, because during the spikes I was consumed by the desire to drive my teeth into their skin and take them for my own. That was the ridiculous thing about my panic, because I wanted them as much as I wanted my old life back, and none of this was fucking fair.

"Get out of your head, princess, and let me in. One big deep breath and push out a little."

I followed the instruction and his cock finished its journey through the ring of muscle.

"Fuck yes. You're so tight. Your little ass has such a grip on me." He nipped my shoulder. "I would tell you to hold still, but you're not going anywhere on that knot."

I quivered as he moved, a smooth glide out before he drove back in. Desperation burned through me.

"More," I demanded.

Amir chuckled in my ear, pinching my nipples until I keened, and then he bucked. "Such a good little cock slut. I knew you could do it. Now be our best girl and let Kai use that pretty mouth."

My jaw dropped obediently and Kai moved closer to cradle my head in his hands, my tongue popping out to flick the head of his cock.

The heat in his eyes had me squirming. No one had ever looked at me like that before these men. Maybe it was secretly a good thing that we had accidentally bonded because there was no fucking way anyone else would ever be able to compare.

I was pretty sure if I had to face the aggressively mediocre dating pool outside this room, I would melt into a puddle of despair. I could embrace my spinster era if I had to, I loved cats, but this unfairly gorgeous alpha was my future, and at least right now, that didn't seem so bad. Honestly, I was going to give myself whiplash with how chaotic my emotions were about everything.

But then Kai slipped past my lips, and Diego and Amir moved, and it was impossible to think at all.

Sweet mother of god, everything was so fucking much. I was filled to bursting and steeped in bliss.

"Your mouth feels so fucking good, little dove."

I whined around him, struggling to catch my breath while Diego flexed his hips to shift his knot inside me and Amir wrapped his arm snugly around my waist to snap his hips against my ass.

"So sweet, princess," Amir growled in my ear. "Tell me how much you love it."

Kai pulled back to let me answer and I huffed and puffed, trying to gather enough coherency to string two words together. I groaned long and low when he slowed his pace and pulled almost all the way out to drive back in.

"F-fuck, f-feels so good," I choked on a breath when he stilled. "Don't—don't stop."

He chuckled in my ear and drove home; the strangled sound I made was muffled as Kai pressed back into my mouth.

The world seemed to flow in slow motion, seconds dripping by like molasses in winter. Every glide of Amir into me, every subtle shift of Diego, every thrust of Kai over my tongue went through the control panel of my brain, flicking off switches as they went until nothing in the fucking world mattered except the way they touched me. They supported my weight when I melted against them, Diego's hands bracing my ribs to assist.

I let go. Sliding down the dark and slippery path in my head was so easy. Detaching from my body until just one little thread tethered me to it felt like the most natural thing in the world. Pleasure still snaked up that thread to me, but the sheer overwhelm stayed down with my body, letting my mind float freely.

So light.

Here there was only peace, only quiet and softness.

When Amir bucked into me and the pressure of his knot filled me to overflowing, I screamed around Kai, dropping away entirely when he pulled away, his fist stroking until he splattered warmth against my skin.

I sank under the darkness.

Gentle touches and quiet whispers tried to disturb me, but I had no interest in emerging from where I was just yet.

Rest.

Sleep.

Quiet.

I needed those right now.

The touches and whispers didn't cease, but eventually they were accompanied by warm water enveloping me and the press of skin.

"Come back, little dove."

Talking was far too much work, so I stayed silent. Cinnamon infused every breath. I needed that too. Controlling my body through that tiny thread was so much effort I couldn't be bothered, even though I wanted to turn, to press my face to the source of the cinnamon.

"Callie, precious, wake up."

No. I was far too comfy to engage with reality again.

Hands smoothed my hair and traced delicate patterns on my skin, over and over. The thread connecting me to my body grew a little with each repetitive motion. Gradually, the thread thickened into a rope and began to inch me back down.

Someone dug into the bottom of my foot, working out the tension until I was groaning.

"Found the Callie comeback button," someone said with a laugh. Their voices were distorted, slowed down, but not so much that I couldn't understand the words themselves.

More hands touched me, insistent, digging into my muscles, and twisting both relief and discomfort as knots released.

Bit by bit those hands coaxed me back, forcing me into reality again, but when I opened my eyes everything was dimly lit and I was so cozy. Kai cradled me to his chest, the firm length of his body along my back in the bath. Diego worked the tension out of my hands, and Amir was at my feet.

"She lives," Diego said with a quiet laugh. "Welcome back, precious. How are you feeling?"

Speaking was still too much effort even though I was at least awake now. I let out a contented hum as my response, closing my eyes again, the flickering candlelight along the vanity too much right now.

Something hard and plastic pressed to my lips and I turned away from it.

"Not a chance, sweetheart."

I peeled open one eye to see Miles with a bottle of juice and a straw.

"Drink it, princess," Amir ordered. "We need to get your blood sugar up a bit."

I opened my lips just enough for Miles to slot the straw through and sucked obediently. The flavor was distinctly tropical and just shy of too sweet, but I drank until I couldn't anymore.

"Good girl." Kai nuzzled my cheek. "We'll get you fed soon, too. Any requests?"

I shook my head, the motion feeling like water sloshing around inside an inflated balloon.

"Start with ice cream, the high-protein ones," Diego suggested. "No chewing required."

"I'll put in the order," Miles replied.

They were all tucked into the bathroom with me. I was totally naked and plastered to Kai, but I couldn't work up an ounce of self-consciousness. My purr slowly rolled to life and Kai's kicked on in response, the vibration in his chest making me even meltier.

"Comfy?" Diego asked, his smile coloring his tone with amusement.

"Mhmm."

I lounged there in total bliss. Eventually they insisted on feeding me, Miles wedging himself alongside the tub with the others and spooning me delicious bites of creamy chocolate. By the time I got to the last mouthful, I was feeling considerably more human and much more tethered to reality.

"Sleep?" I murmured.

"Anything you want, sweetheart."

Arms lifted me out of the bath and held me upright while someone toweled down every inch before bundling me under insanely soft blankets. Bodies tucked up against my front and back, a glorious amount of skin-on-skin that had all my instincts happy as a clam.

The next time I woke, I was trapped beneath a tangle of limbs, with cinnamon, clove, and nutmeg thick in my nose with whispered hints of cedar. I groaned, my exhausted body protesting, shifting and stretching. The room was dark so I could only tell who was where by scent. I snuggled closer to the person in front of me, getting a good whiff.

Diego.

My rustling around woke him, his hands sliding up my body from my waist to cradle the back of my head. "Hey there, precious. Feeling better?"

"That depends on your definition of better." Fucking hell, I sounded like I was smoking two packs a day.

Diego chuckled quietly. "Let me get you some water."

As soon as he climbed off the bed, someone moved to take his place. There was hardly any scent, which told me it was Miles. His T-shirt was soft beneath my fingertips. Kai wasn't wearing a stitch of clothing behind me, but then I supposed I had gotten a lot closer to Kai than to Miles in that regard. I hummed softly and rooted my nose against Miles's throat, growling when it didn't reveal what I sought.

"Miles?"

"Yes, sweetheart?"

"I don't like your scent blockers."

"I can go off of them," he promised. "I had to wait until your heat was fully over."

"It's over now?"

"It is. Now all you have to do is rest and let us take care of you. Whatever you need, we'll handle. No request is too extravagant."

Kai woke enough to pull me tighter against his chest before his breathing evened out again.

I liked the idea of them taking care of me. I wasn't entirely certain I could stand at this point, so it was probably better if they managed everything for me anyway. My whole body felt like a bowl of overcooked noodles, and forming sentences was still an uncomfortable amount of work.

I curled my fingers in Miles's shirt. "Go off them right now. I want to know."

"I haven't taken today's dose. You'll have to give it some time to process out of my system, though." His thumb brushed over my cheek. "I'll toss the whole bottle away just for you."

Just for me.

Fuck if I didn't love the sound of that.

Chapter 15
Kai

I couldn't stop looking at her. Mate. *My* mate. Her dark hair haloed her while she slept, pink lips softly parted. She'd been sleeping a lot since the heat ended, not that I blamed her. My joints were creaky from staying horizontal, but I couldn't bring myself to leave her side. At least two of us were always in the bed with her, the others trading off whenever they ate or showered.

"She needs to eat." Amir sat down where I could see him with a bowl of food. "Wake her."

I didn't want to disturb her, but he was right. She hadn't consumed nearly enough calories to recover from the heat. I threaded my fingers through her hair, scratching lightly until she stirred, blinking those beautiful brown eyes at me. "Time for a meal, little dove."

Callie groaned and rolled closer to snuggle against my chest. "Sleep."

"You can sleep after you eat. You're only going to get more exhausted if you don't," I reasoned.

Amir tapped her ass and she squeaked, my hand whipping down to cradle her butt cheek. He rolled his eyes. "I didn't hit hard enough to hurt. Get up, princess. You're going to grow roots if you don't move more."

Diego appeared at the foot of the bed and reached out his hands to her, wiggling his fingers. "Come on. I'll help you up."

Callie lifted one limp hand and Diego hoisted her up, giving me enough motivation to join her in the land of the vertical. The two of us got Callie settled on the couch, wrapped up in blankets. Amir fed her bites of macaroni and cheese, her mouth popping open like a little bird to receive each forkful while her arms were buried beneath the blankets.

I inhaled my own bowl sitting next to her, Diego at my side, and Miles on the loveseat across from us. Miles kept frowning at the tablet in his lap.

"What's up?" I asked.

"I'd say not to worry about it, but I actually should discuss it with you."

"With us or just with me?"

"You to start," Miles replied.

I didn't want to leave Callie, but she would be in good hands for a few minutes at least. I set down my empty bowl, pulled on just enough clothing to be acceptable, slid on a pair of slippers and followed Miles into the hall.

"What's going on?" I asked.

"I've been fighting with management on some paperwork

they want Callie to sign to protect everyone from liability over the bonding."

My spine stiffened. "But she already signed paperwork before we started. Doesn't that protect them?"

"Not entirely. Not with so many witnesses and a recording. Every time I strike something out and send it for approval, they send it back with a refusal."

"What's so bad about what they're asking for? Do we really think Callie would sue?"

Miles deliberately avoided my gaze, a sure sign that he was feeling guilty. "It's too early to tell. They said if she does sue, they're coming after *you*, which means they're coming after the pack, and I can't let that happen. But I also can't let her sign this paperwork with what they're demanding. All of it's a fucking mess."

"How do we get around it?"

"I've talked to the lawyer multiple times now and they're refusing to budge. I don't want to have to go old school with the situation."

Old school? "What do you mean?"

"You're legally responsible for her now."

"And what does that have to do with her suing?"

"Obviously you could stop her from doing that."

Bile rose in my throat. "I don't want to control her like that."

"And I don't want you to either. If they would just fucking cooperate with me and let me adjust this contract, it wouldn't be an issue. We also have to have a meeting with management because you still have shows contracted and I highly doubt you're going to be able to do that now that Callie is involved."

"Can *any* of us?" I asked. We were all Callie's pack, even if I was the only one bonded. She would never feel comfortable with us fucking other omegas even if it was a contractual obligation.

"I haven't talked to the others yet." Miles shrugged. "A lot is up in the air right now and I don't know how to fix any of it. We can't lose three-quarters of the pack income and still give her the life she deserves. Hell, we might lose the *entire* pack income at this rate because they are *not* happy with me either."

Fuck.

We hadn't paid off the mortgage on the pack house yet, and continuing to do that relied on us having steady work. All of our financial opportunities had ground to a halt the second Callie's blockers had worn off; we just hadn't known it. And by bonding her I had totally eliminated my ability to financially care for her.

"I know it's a lot." Miles set a comforting hand on my shoulder. "Trust me, I've been turning this over in my head for days while you were all occupied. I'm going to try for one more negotiation. If I thought storming the castle would accomplish anything, I would suggest it and have all of us go there right now, but they're being a bunch of stubborn assholes."

"They're not usually this difficult, are they?"

"We don't usually give them this much trouble." Miles swallowed hard and shoved a hand through his hair. "I'm going to tell them that I'll bear the burden of any actions Callie takes against the company. As long as they have someone to blame that's not them, I hope it'll be enough."

"Can't we just talk to Callie about this?"

"She'll have *years* to be able to take action against the company if she wants to. They want security before she leaves the hotel."

Frustration built, radiating like heat off embers in my stomach. "That's not fair."

112

"No, but we're not the ones with the power here. I just wanted you to know before I throw myself under the bus."

"Miles, you can't do that."

"I can and I will. *I* recruited our mate; *I* was a dumbass who didn't think about cuffs and collars. Let me protect the pack. Callie needs you all way more than she needs me."

I growled. "Don't fucking do that, Miles. We are *all* her pack. You don't have to be a martyr. Tell them Callie can sue all of us instead of them. If we fuck up in taking care of her, and in making her want to be part of this pack, badly enough that she wants to take legal action, then that's our own fucking fault at that point."

"Kai..."

"Don't be a dumbass. We're in this together. I'll take responsibility for my own actions. Not a fucking one of us thought of cuffs and collars even after scenting her. We've done this long enough we should've known it was different just as much as you. So, you tell those fuckers if they want to be cowards, they can be, and we'll take care of our own."

Miles hesitated, but eventually nodded. "Let me adjust the contract and send it back. Go back to Callie for now. I'll take care of it."

I stared at him for a long moment. "If I find out you took sole responsibility for this, I'll kick your ass."

His smile was small, but it was there. "Noted."

I felt bad leaving him in the hallway while he made the phone call, but I was already itching to touch Callie again. She was comfortably inside her blanket burrito and immediately started purring when I sat down next to her, tilting the whole mountain toward me so she could lean against my shoulder.

"Feel better after eating?"

Callie nodded.

Amir fished out a fruit tray from the cart the staff had brought to us and stabbed two chunks of watermelon onto a fork, holding it out for Callie. She ate both obediently.

I didn't want to think that we could fuck up so badly she might come after us, but she had every right to do so if that was how she felt. I wanted Callie to be happy for a million more reasons that didn't involve the risk of being sued. She was our forever now, and that meant we would take care of her one way or another.

"Can you come in here?" Callie asked.

"I'll have to unburrito you to do that."

"That's okay."

Amir helped me untangle her. I stretched out across the couch and Callie draped herself atop me.

"You are wearing *way* too many clothes. If I have to be naked, so do you."

"In all fairness," I said, "you don't *have to* be naked. If you would rather have some clothes, we can get some for you."

She pouted and I followed my instinct to nip it.

"If we both have clothes, it feels weird."

I stripped off my shirt, which was a task and a half because she refused to get off of me first. "Better?"

Callie shook her head. "More."

I wrestled my way out of my pants, and when I was bare, she settled her weight completely on me, her face tucked against my throat.

"Perfect." She immediately started purring again when Amir piled on the blankets we had removed before.

Having her this close soothed my worries. I struggled to keep the contract Miles was dealing with in my mind while I had a content omega in my arms.

"What do I do about all of my stuff?" she asked.

"What stuff?"

"My apartment." She yawned and snuggled closer. "In LA."

I had almost completely forgotten she still had a home somewhere else. She would have friends and family we would all need to meet, and a shithole ex-fiancé we would have to navigate. "We can pay for a company to pack up your things and ship them here if you want to stay with us."

"Stay with *you*," she mumbled, sinking closer to sleep with every second.

I caught Diego's eye, noting the worry pinching his brows and the frown turning down his lips. "Only you?" he whispered.

"She probably doesn't mean it," I said quietly, not wanting to disturb her. "It's too early to decide anything for sure."

That didn't seem to assuage any of his worries. Our home would fit Callie just fine. Honestly, it was probably far better than what she was living in now with all of our combined incomes going toward it. It wasn't a huge mansion, but we hadn't skimped on luxury.

Fuck me.

If she didn't want to stay in Vegas, I couldn't stay either. I didn't want to think about leaving my pack, but Callie was my bonded mate, and that took precedence on both a legal and instinctual front.

LA wasn't unfamiliar to me. Diego and I had both grown up there, but our work was here. Or at least his was, for as long as it lasted. I wouldn't be able to continue. If I had my way, I would never touch another omega again. The sweet, beautiful omega in my arms was it for me, and no matter how much agony it would cause me to leave here, if that was what she wanted, I would make it happen.

115

I *could* make her stay, but just the idea of using my power like that made my stomach twist. I had to let go and let Callie choose what was best for her. If she thought that was LA or anywhere else on the fucking planet, I would follow her to the ends of the earth, heal myself with her presence, and try not to think about the heartbreak of leaving the others behind.

Chapter 16
Callie

"I made sure the contract has as much as possible in your favor," Miles told me as I pored over the paperwork in front of me.

While I was considerably more human than I had been the last couple of days, I still wasn't all there. Miles went over each section with me, explaining the terms and conditions. It didn't seem like there was anything drastic to worry about, and the other alphas listened carefully through the spiel. I didn't know them well enough to assume they would speak up if there was something wrong with the contract, but I didn't *think* Miles would actively let me get screwed over.

I signed my name everywhere he told me to and initialed

the rest. He blew out a relieved breath when I got to the last page. "I'll get this filed and then we can be on our way."

I cringed internally. On our way back to Los Angeles, where my fiancé—my *ex*-fiancé—was probably snuggled up in our apartment with his new wife.

Even if I wasn't sure about a permanent move-in with these alphas, I sure as hell couldn't stay at my old apartment anymore. Unless of course we got there and found it empty because he was mooching off his new partner instead of me.

"The moving van in LA will meet us there in six hours," said Diego. "I had the kitchen pack us up a lunch and cooler for the drive."

What the fuck was I supposed to talk to these men about on a five-hour road trip? I didn't know the first thing about any of them, and for the last few days the only real communication we'd had was about sex or making sure I didn't shrivel into a raisin during the heat. Talk about awkward as hell.

I had dressed in a pair of booty shorts and a tank top with flip-flops to accommodate the heat, the rest of them dressed similarly, albeit with longer shorts.

Kai took my hand in his as we departed the suite to head down to the van. It was so weird to crave touching him the way I did when I knew nothing about him. Why was sex easier than talking?

Miles slid into the driver's seat and Amir was next to him, which put me in the back seat between Diego and Kai. Amir passed the cord back so I could plug in my phone and control the music. Jerry had never let me play what I wanted to in the car... My music taste was so varied but I hoped at least one of them liked something that popped up over the next five hours.

Diego offered his upturned hand on top of his knee, and I took it. Touching them made the entire situation a little easier to bear somehow. I really hoped Jerry wasn't home when we got there. I could only imagine what he might say about me showing up with four men, one of them my new mate.

As soon as we got out of Vegas, the silence grew to an unbearable level. Diego was the first one to break it. "Have you always lived in LA?"

"I moved there about four years ago. I grew up in Seattle."

"We just missed each other," Diego replied. "Kai and I went to high school and college together before we moved out to Vegas around the same time you moved to LA."

"You moved to Vegas for work?"

"Sure did," answered Diego.

"I...moved for my fiancé. *Ex*-fiancé, fuck. I'm sorry; it hasn't been long enough for me to get used to that."

"Don't apologize, precious. He was an important part of your life for a long time. None of us expect you to forget him." Diego squeezed my hand, lifting my knuckles to his lips.

That was a bit of a relief, even though I wished I could just forget Jerry.

"Where are you two from?" I asked the ones up front.

"I'm from Seattle, too," said Miles.

"Oh my god, shut up! Really?"

"I moved around a lot, but that was the longest stint. Born there, stayed until kindergarten, and back briefly for college."

"Army brat?"

"Unfortunately. I hated moving. Every time I felt settled somewhere, we'd get notice it was time to go."

"That's so hard on kids. I'm glad I got to stay in one place growing up." I poked Amir's arm. "What about you?"

"New York," he replied.

"NYC or the state?"

"Albany, but I did go to NYU."

"Okay, this is fucking weird. I went there too."

Kai leaned over and nuzzled my hair. "Red thread."

"What?"

"The red thread of fate. It's a folklore tradition that fated partners were connected by a red thread the gods tied to them so they would remain connected until it was time for them to meet."

I couldn't exactly deny it. Trading home cities with Kai and Diego, being born in the same place as Miles, studying at the same place as Amir. "That just makes me want to check all the dates to see how close we got without ever meeting. Amir, what did you study?"

"Physics."

"Okay, we probably didn't have any intersecting classes then. I was there for cinematography. How the fuck did you go from physicist to live sex show performer?"

Amir snorted. "I don't know how much you know about physicists, but it's not the most highly paid profession in the world."

"I guess that's fair." I nudged Kai and Diego. "What about you two?"

"I made a go of med school but decided I liked sleep and sanity a lot better. It was absolutely not for me," said Kai.

"Honestly, same for me," Diego replied, "but with pharmacy. By the time I got close to finishing my first degree I was about ready to have a panic attack every time I walked into a pharmacy. Kai and I dropped out at the same time, decided to fuck around in Vegas like two little dumbasses who weren't even old enough to drink. Rang in our twenty-first birthdays there and decided to never leave."

"And how did you all end up doing the shows? Do your families know?"

"Absolutely fucking not," Amir said with a snort. "I got a job right out of college, recruited by a company in Vegas, and my parents still think that's what I do for work. I started escorting when I realized I hated my socially acceptable job, and that's where I met the others."

"*Escorting*? I need everyone to back up. There's a lot going on in these backstories."

"After I graduated university," said Miles, "I moved to Vegas. Mostly I just needed to get away and Vegas seemed like a good place to lose myself. I was the first one of us to get recruited into escorting. Did that for about four years before I ran into Kai and Diego."

"We were both working miserable retail jobs," added Kai. "We escorted for about a year before Miles got his job in recruitment for the company that does the shows and he dragged all of us with him so we could have way better paychecks."

"I guess I'm kind of ruining that." Guilt sat like a stone in my stomach.

"You're not ruining anything, little dove." Kai draped his arm around me. "The point is that we've all pivoted in our careers pretty hard, so it's not the end of the world if we have to do that again."

I leaned into Kai, getting as comfortable as I could with the seatbelts in the way of me draping myself across his lap. "I wish that red thread thing would just tell you you have fated people out there so you could avoid all the stupid ones before that."

"In fairness," said Kai as he traced patterns on my arm, "we never would've met you at all if your jackass of an ex hadn't insisted you come to Vegas to begin with and then fucked off. Things line up a certain way and a million building blocks go into creating the unique circumstances. If we all knew beforehand, the world would just be at a standstill. And to answer your earlier question, none of our families know exactly what we do."

I wouldn't want mine to know either, so I didn't blame them for not telling their loved ones. People could get so weird about sex. I had mostly been intending on just forgetting the heat had ever happened when I started. I knew things on the Internet didn't disappear, and obviously there was no going back now that I was bonded, so my original plan was out the window.

I stared at Kai, still trying to figure out how I felt about him in a way that wasn't influenced by all the hormones. He had been nothing but kind to me from the start, so I could at least be somewhat reassured that liking him wasn't purely hormonally based. I just didn't *know* him, but that would change with time. Warm sweetness flowed steadily down the bond from him, little flickers of worry in the background that were all but drowned out by surges of that sweetness whenever I touched him or he looked at me.

Through the rest of the drive, I learned more bits and pieces about them. They had been an official pack for a little over three years, had a pack house on the outskirts of town in a district I could never hope to afford. Their families knew they were a pack, but never came out to visit.

At some point I would probably have to meet their families and they would have to meet mine, but right now I was not remotely emotionally equipped for any of that.

I fell asleep on Kai shortly after our mid-trip snack and woke when the vehicle stopped in front of my apartment building. I groaned, half-ready to indulge myself in a full petulant tantrum as if I were a child. I didn't want to go in there after everything that had happened, even though I had to.

"Deep breath, precious." Diego helped me sit all the way up. "You're starting to smell like burnt sugar."

"I don't want to be here."

"We won't be here long," said Miles, checking the time on his phone. He passed back a pair of skin patches to cover our fresh bite marks. I didn't want to answer unnecessary questions if Jerry saw the bondbite. "The moving company is only about fifteen minutes out. Let's go start grabbing your essentials."

I pouted, using the fob to let us into the building, and the four of them followed me with duffel bags slung over their arms. When I got up to the actual apartment, my door code didn't work, and neither did my key that I tried afterward. "Motherfucker."

Locked out of my own apartment was not how I'd expected this to go. Jerry always left the tasks to me, but maybe his new woman had thought of this and done it for him. He'd been good at the start, competent enough that it hadn't raised too many red flags, at least until I'd moved here with him, and then that had all changed.

One of my neighbors, Mrs. Frisk, poked their head out across the hall. "Hello, Callie dear. I never expected to see you again. Jerry said you moved out."

"That's what I'm *trying* to do, but he changed the locks before I could get any of my stuff."

Mrs. Frisk chewed her bottom lip before dipping back inside for a second and returning with a key. "He gave me this for emergencies. Try to be quick."

"You're an absolute angel. Thank you so, so much."

"You are so welcome, dear. You were such a lovely neighbor to have and I'm so sorry things didn't work out."

My bottom lip wobbled as the realization of everything struck me again. An eight-year relationship down the drain.

123

Meeting Jerry when I'd started university, latching on to him immediately, never taking a chance on anyone else, and following him across the country had been the biggest mistake I ever could have made. My family hadn't liked him, but they'd tolerated his frat boy attitude. I'd been trapped with rose-colored glasses, so in love I'd ignored all the issues, and then I was in a new city and reliant on him until I got a job. At that point he'd pushed more and more bills onto me, and at first it had felt like I was just making up for him having to support me those first couple of months, but...then it had never stopped.

"Who are these lovely gentlemen?" Mrs. Frisk asked, startling me out of my thoughts.

"Friends," I said before any of them could tell her otherwise. "They're helping me move out."

"How sweet. Be sure to say goodbye before you head out."

"I definitely will. Thanks, Mrs. Frisk."

I could do this. I could face this. I'd built a life in this apartment and just because Jerry had lit it all on fire didn't mean I had to simply let him push me out. I didn't want *him* anymore, not really, but I was still nervous about what I'd find on the other side of the door to what had once been my home.

I shoved Mrs. Frisk's emergency key into the lock, both relieved and terrified when it turned.

Chapter 17
Amir

Callie shrank into herself, her hands shaking as she pushed open the door to the apartment, and the sight filled me with rage. *She shouldn't feel like she has to hide.* That asshole had ruined her home for her, and even though we were determined to give her a new home, I knew that didn't take away the pain of losing this one.

The apartment smelled wrong when I stepped into it, my nose wrinkling. It was like a hoarder had taken over, with stuff covering every surface. Was this how she'd lived?

From how wide her eyes were, and the way she walked with her fingers pressed to her lips as she took everything in, I could only assume this was a new state of affairs. Had it taken so little time for her ex to ruin the place they'd shared together?

Callie picked her way through the chaos toward the master bedroom. We followed closely behind, ready to fill the bags with her clothing. Her brows pinched when she opened the closet doors, her expression turning from confusion to fury.

"Fucking fuck!" She ripped her way through the closet, shoving at the clothing with tears pouring down her cheeks.

I stepped up behind her, wrapping my arms over hers to still her movements. "Breathe."

She did, though it hitched, and she leaned back against me.

"Just tell us which things are yours and we'll pack them."

"None of them." Her voice broke. "All of my things are gone."

"Maybe they've only been packed away into another closet," Diego suggested. "Let's look before we panic."

I let him take her from me. He and Kai walked her around the apartment to check the closets and dressers while Miles hung back with me.

"How did he move so fast?" Miles asked. "We haven't even had her a week and he's already tossed her things?"

"Maybe he planned it in advance?" I couldn't imagine why he would. I might not want a fated bond thrust onto me, but Callie's ex had *chosen* to have her in his life. If he'd had any affection for her at all, it seemed impossible to me that he could have stripped the essence of her out of this place so quickly.

Callie's cry reached us, setting both Miles and me on edge. Primed for danger, we raced toward the second bedroom, where Callie was on her knees. "My nest. It's—" She broke off with a wail.

The room contained only a simple double bed covered in cheap plaid fabric. Did this fucker actually have the audacity to get rid of an omega's nest? He might as well have ripped the

126

pacifier out of an infant's mouth if he wanted to cause that much needless anguish with his casual cruelty.

I didn't want coming here to be a failed endeavor, but it was quickly feeling that way. They must have found some things of hers because one of the bags on Diego's shoulder looked about half-full.

Kai wrapped her in his arms, his expression twisted. I didn't entirely know what a bond felt like, but I knew emotions were shared through it, and feeling even a fraction of the pain she felt right now had to be agony. "We'll make you a new nest."

We would, too. We weren't going to have an omega in our home and deny her that basic comfort. Fury twisted in my chest on her behalf. The fact that her ex trashed something so sacred made me want to push him off the roof.

"It's not *fair*. I paid for all of the furniture in here. All he got rid of were *my* things."

"Then take back everything you paid for," I said. "If he's going to be a jackass, he doesn't deserve any of the things you've shared with him."

As if on cue, the movers arrived, ringing the buzzer to be let in. Miles headed down to let them in and guide them to the apartment.

While he was gone, Kai helped Callie stand and rested his chin on the top of her head. "You won't need any furniture at the house, but if you want to keep it, we'll pay for storage."

"I don't really want it."

"Take it anyway," I insisted. "Donate it if you don't want it."

Callie perked up a bit. "That's actually a good idea. I'm sure a shelter or something could use it."

When Miles returned with the movers, he was tasked with

finding a domestic violence shelter that was equipped to take the same-day donation of furniture while the rest of us stripped down the bed to take the frame and mattress, removed clothing from dressers, and emptied out any piece of furniture that Callie had purchased for the apartment so the movers could take it away. Some people might think it was a bit petty, but it was really fucking satisfying to know we would force that asshole to see the void of her absence. He couldn't just take everything from her and have no repercussions.

Callie found a few more items tucked here and there as we worked, tossing them into the bags. She even took her partially used toiletries out of the bathroom, and meals she had pre-cooked and frozen from the freezer, taking them across the hall to give to her neighbor. A petty move I was truly proud of.

"What the fuck is going on?"

We all turned to the voice in the doorway, a totally average asshole standing there with a beet-red face, a brunette woman on his arm, and an older version of that same woman standing behind them.

I knew immediately who it was, given how sharply Callie's scent switched to fermented apples and scorched sugar.

The ex.

"I'm taking my stuff," Callie snapped, her face still pink from crying.

"Like fucking hell you are," the asshole growled.

"Jerry, who is this?" the brunette asked.

"Just a bitch," he replied.

I moved without thinking, stalking toward him with murderous intent. He shrank away.

"Watch your fucking mouth. Callie's entitled to take her things, which it seems you were very quick to get rid of, and all the things she paid for are no longer your problem."

The two women with him looked both confused and angry.

"Mom, why don't you wait outside?" the brunette said.

"No," Jerry snapped. "This isn't Callie's home anymore. Katrina and I live here with her mother, and Callie is no longer welcome."

I glanced back to Callie, seeing her little fists clenched, fury vibrating her whole body. Jerry slipped right past me and got up in her face.

"You broke into my fucking apartment?"

"*Our* apartment!"

"No, it's mine. We broke up."

"I pay the fucking rent! And we only broke up because you got drunk-married and fucking *left me* in another city, you goddamn selfish fuck! How could you do that to me? I can't believe I almost had a baby with you! How can you replace me so quickly?" She choked on a sob before saying much more quietly, "I don't understand what I did wrong."

My anger with her ex was far easier for me to deal with than Callie's pain.

Kai put himself bodily between Callie and Jerry. "We've gotten all her things and we're heading out. Let's just leave it at this."

"And who the fuck are you?"

"Her—"

"Friend, Jerry. Maybe you would fucking recognize it if you had any. Not everyone is a selfish jackass."

"I see why he left her," the mother whispered to her daughter, and it took all of my self-control to not spin around and tell them both to fuck off.

"I'm gonna call the cops," Jerry said. "You robbed my fucking apartment."

"I didn't take a single thing I didn't pay for. Buy your own shit. You don't get to use me for anything anymore. Did you really think I would have no reaction to what you did?"

"I hoped you would take the hint but apparently not."

"Yeah, I got the hint about the fucking relationship. That doesn't mean I'm going to abandon everything I own. And don't bother calling the cops because I have all the purchase receipts in my emails. I know you don't have purchase proof for all my stuff that you threw away."

Jerry shrugged. "It was all trash anyway."

Callie let out a shriek, diving for him before Kai or Diego could stop her. I was close enough to snatch her out of the air, earning a snarl, and her little nails dug into my arm, but I wasn't about to let her get charged with assault, as much as he would deserve a feral omega ripping him apart.

"Here's what we're going to do," I said firmly. "Assholes in residence are going to wait in the fucking hallway. Callie is going to get the last of her things and we are going to leave. Hopefully none of us ever see one another again."

Callie was fuming in my arms, and while it was pretty easy to see that Jerry wanted to say something, he wasn't willing to take on all of us to do it.

"Fucking fine," he snapped. He and the two women stepped into the hall and we picked up what Callie had already packed, the five of us slipping out of the apartment. I kept my arms firmly around her and made sure she was facing away from him the entire journey.

By the time we got her down the hallway, she was sobbing, her whole body shaking. I scooped her up bridal style and kept walking. Kai helped me secure her in the backseat of the van when we got downstairs. She curled into his arms crying so hard she was gasping for breath.

"I don't know what I did wrong. I don't know how he could…"

The fucker was lucky I didn't go straight back upstairs and clock him. I didn't know Callie that well, but no one deserved what he had put her through.

The moving truck was already gone, taking the furniture to someone a hell of a lot more deserving than Callie's ex. I wasn't entirely eager to climb back into a vehicle that was going to be filled with the scent of distressed omega. Rolling the windows down wouldn't be seen as polite and I didn't want to upset her more, but smelling that scent on her made me want to punch something.

Kai was doing his best to soothe her, Diego too, when he climbed in next to her, but she had just had years of her life thrown back into her face by someone she had thought she could trust, and there wasn't a hug long enough in the world to change that.

While Miles navigated us out of the city and I tried not to choke on Callie's despair, I flipped through listings for private investigators. Everyone had skeletons in their closet, and I was willing to bet Jerry was no different. In all likelihood we would never see him again, but just in case, it wouldn't hurt to have some ammunition in case he decided to make Callie's life worse.

The drive home was an experience in misery. Callie cried for a solid half of it before she exhausted herself. Kai and Diego rearranged her so she could stretch out in the backseat, but she continued whimpering in her sleep like she couldn't escape her pain even in her dreams.

I turned over the things we had learned in my head. She had been entirely blindsided by the break in the relationship. Based on her statement that she had at one point been trying to have children with him, I could only assume she had been happy before everything had gone down. And if not happy, at least comfortable.

"I think I should be allowed to hit him," I said quietly, not wanting to wake her.

"If you get to, so do I," said Miles.

"There's four of us," Diego pointed out. "We could take turns making him suffer for making her cry."

"Better revenge would be giving her a good life," said Kai as he stroked her dark hair. "One where she never feels the need to cry like this again."

That revenge might be better, but it would certainly be less satisfying than feeling the crunch of his nose beneath my fist.

Chapter 18
Callie

I was exhausted and miserable by the time we pulled up to the pack house. It looked like a mini estate, the house more reminiscent of a castle than any home I had personally been in before, with tall rounded windows, sweeping roofs, and skinny trees dotting the yard in front of it. Even if I felt brittle enough to fall apart in a strong breeze, I could still appreciate the beauty of the building before me.

We pulled over a brick drive and disappeared into the double set of garages. I didn't protest when Kai offered to carry me in, unsure how steady I would be on my own feet.

He took me in through a spacious, tidy pantry and into the prettiest kitchen I had ever seen with brick archways, three glowing chandeliers hanging above a long island that could easily fit a dozen people around it. Gold fixtures and hardware popped against the white cabinetry. A large arched window on the other side of the kitchen opened into a courtyard that was full of neat hedges, numerous cacti, and red stones nestled around the plants.

"We'll give you a proper tour tomorrow," Kai told me. "You can pick any room you want and we'll figure out everything later."

He carried me straight upstairs and I tried not to gape at the twenty-foot ceilings in the foyer or the gorgeous curve of the stairway with decorative wrought iron swirls beneath the railing. At the top of the stairs Kai set me on my feet, keeping a steadying arm around me.

"My room is at the end on the right, Amir across from me, Diego and Miles down the other side. There's a guest bed downstairs too if you don't want to stay with any of us."

"Yours," I managed to say.

Kai showed me to his own room, the air thick with muted cinnamon when he opened the door. The scent was a bit stale, but then I supposed they hadn't been here for a little while. I staggered out of his arms and crawled onto the bed, burying myself beneath the blankets.

"Do you want company?"

"No." It was a lie, but I just wanted the space to cry in peace. I had already cried too much in front of them and I could only bear so much humiliation in one day.

"All right," Kai said softly. "Sleep if you'd like. Or I can get you something to eat."

My stomach growled, but I was nauseated too. I would worry about food in the morning. "Just sleep please."

He kissed the top of my head before leaving me and I clutched his pillows to my chest when the door closed, leaving me in darkness. My whole life was fucking ruined and they had all seen me at my worst. I'd almost gone feral on Jerry for destroying my nest on top of everything else he had done. I was absolutely certain I had ruined the pack perception of me with my behavior, but my only regret was that I hadn't taken a chunk out of Jerry when I had the chance. Amir had stopped me, and logically I knew that was for the best, but I was also really fucking pissed and aching. My chest was scooped out, hollow, and I didn't know what tomorrow would bring.

I burrowed under Kai's blankets and cried myself to sleep.

I woke up feeling like a truck had run me over, backed up, and run me over again. My body was stiff and my throat was dry, my eyes burning and my skin itching with the need to be touched. I had spent the night away from a fresh bond and my body was punishing me for it. Maybe all of the symptoms of agony would have been cured by Kai's presence, but I couldn't have handled it just yet.

The cinnamon in his room smelled wrong. I needed him to freshen it. I peeked out into the hall, finding the house silent. I didn't dare approach Amir's door, and turned down the hall to Diego's, finding it slightly ajar, with him and Kai fast asleep in the massive bed. Nutmeg, clove, and cinnamon filled my nose when I poked my head in, teasing all of my instincts to life.

I was still humiliated from yesterday, but I needed them right now. Hopefully they wouldn't turn me away.

I crawled up the bed and wedged myself between them on top of the blankets.

Diego cracked open one sleepy eye. "Good morning, precious."

I pressed my face to the blankets and mumbled a *good morning* back.

"Are you wanting to start the day already or can we have a cuddle first?"

"Cuddle is good," I said, still not daring to look at him.

"Climb under," he said quietly, nudging back the blankets as I navigated to get beneath them. He sighed tiredly and drew me closer until he was curled around me, my back to his chest. Diego's purr rumbled, almost too soft to hear, but I could feel it nonetheless.

Kai rolled toward me, his eyes still closed, like he was seeking me out in his sleep. The two alphas sandwiched me together and even my embarrassment couldn't stop my purr.

This was exactly what I needed, but had been too stubborn to accept the night before. The room was drenched in the scent of their spices, the bed warm with the heat of their bodies.

So comfy.

I need to pull them into my nest.

My purr stuttered as I realized I didn't *have* a nest anymore. Kai had promised me a new one, and realistically my old one would've been tainted anyway, but I had built it over years, creating the perfect sanctuary for myself in the apartment.

Kai groaned and shifted closer, lifting his hand to cup the back of my head. He kissed my forehead and sighed. "I'm sorry you're so sad, little dove."

I set a palm over his heart, feeling the steady beat beneath my fingers. I hated that he could feel what I did. Kai didn't deserve any of what I was going through.

"Did you not like my room?" he asked softly.

"It smells funny."

He chuckled. "I'll wash all of the bedding for you."

"No, it just needs you to refresh it."

He blinked slowly at me, his golden brown eyes tired but gentle. "Is that your way of saying you missed me?"

My cheeks heated. "I—"

"Don't tease her." Diego dragged me closer, making me all too aware that certain parts of him were much more awake than others. Desire curled in my belly, but things were different now. The heat was over and I didn't know how to approach anything of that nature with them.

"I'm not teasing," said Kai. "It's pretty early. Are we getting up for the day?"

"I was trying to get her to sleep more, but apparently we're all awake," Diego huffed.

"Breakfast? I can cook if you give me a quick tour of the kitchen."

"You're only cooking if you desperately want to," said Kai. "If it's something you enjoy, that's fine, but if it's not, I want you to let us take care of everything."

"I mean, I *can* cook, but it's not necessarily my favorite chore."

"Then you don't have to worry about it here," Kai insisted. "What can I make for you?"

"Chocolate chip pancakes?"

"I'm pretty sure we have everything for that, and if not I'll dip out to the grocery store. Are you okay to stay here with Diego or do you want to come down with me?"

The bed was extremely comfortable, but I was also very curious about the pack house. "Can Diego show me the house?"

"I absolutely can, precious." He sat up slowly, as if reluctant to move away from me, stretching his arms above his head. The movement highlighted the muscles of his torso and I couldn't help but stare.

He slid out of bed, leaned over to scoop his arms beneath me, and dragged me over to the edge. I squeaked, wrapping myself around him so I didn't fall when he hoisted me up.

"I'm going to run you a bath and I'll go get your suitcase so you can change into some fresh clothes for the day. Unless you would rather wear something of Kai's."

It took a half second for my brain to process the statement, initially wondering why I would want to, before my instincts caught up, screaming *yes!* in the back of my brain.

"Does that delicious scent of candied apple mean you would like something of his?" Diego asked.

My cheeks warmed again, and I nodded as small as I could while still being perceptible.

Kai dug through Diego's dresser and pulled out an over-sized T-shirt. "I'll wear it while I cook and bring it up for you before you get out of the bath."

Kai kissed the top of my head before departing and Diego turned me toward the bathroom. An enormous bath sat beneath an archway with a copper chandelier above it and copper mosaic covering the alcove where the bathtub was nestled. A separate shower with warm brown stone and matching cabinetry filled the rest of the space. It was better than any hotel I'd stayed in before.

Diego got the water running and added a splash of pumpkin spice bubble bath.

"You take bubble baths?"

"You think omegas are the only ones allowed to be luxurious?"

"No, it's just a little unexpected."

He politely stepped out into the bedroom while I stripped off my clothes from yesterday and slid into the warm water. Diego let me soak, and I could hear him bustling around, but

138

he didn't come back in until I was thoroughly relaxed and my fingers were pruney. He set down two fluffy towels on the edge of the bath along with the shirt Kai had gone downstairs in. Then he brought in my suitcase, leaving it next to everything else.

"I'll be in the bedroom when you're ready."

The towels were like clouds and I dried myself off slowly to enjoy them before locating fresh underwear in my suitcase and pulling Kai's shirt on over top. It smelled deliciously of his cinnamon scent and hung to my mid-thigh, making it more dress than shirt. I debated for a moment whether I should wear shorts beneath it, but I had worn dresses this long with just panties. The light was wavering outside the windows, a tell that the day was going to be blistering hot. No need to add more layers than necessary in that case.

Diego's gaze swept over me and my whole body reacted to his attention, goosebumps raising down my arms and my stomach clenching. "No one's ever looked so good in my clothes before. Come on, precious; let's get you acquainted with your new home."

We started with the balcony outside his room that overlooked the pool. It was so tidy, cut in a perfect rectangle with white tile around the edge and centered in the courtyard I had seen bits of yesterday.

"Kai's room has the same view as mine," he told me. "Miles and Amir face the front lawn."

"I don't know how so many people can have grass in the desert."

Diego leaned down, whispering conspiratorially, "Don't tell anyone, but the grass is fake. We weren't going to waste that much water out here. The few plants we do have are watered by an underground irrigation system so they use way less water and they were all picked for their ability to thrive in drought conditions."

"Well, that's a relief. I was about to judge you guys."

Diego laughed and looped his arm around my shoulders, taking me back inside and down the gorgeous rounded staircase. There was an old-timey movie theater tucked behind it, with red velvet stage curtains, plush leather seating, and a popcorn machine ready for use.

"You can pick whatever we watch for your first movie night with us," Diego told me.

The scent of chocolate filled the air.

"Smells like breakfast might be ready." Diego ushered me into their exquisite kitchen, where Kai was flipping pancakes shirtless, looking more like a snack than the food he was preparing.

"Perfect timing." He smiled at me, depositing three stacked pancakes on a plate with multiple others. He had also prepared another plate with bacon and a bowl of cut fruit along with a pitcher of juice.

"I'll go wake the others," said Diego, leaving me with Kai.

"Come pick anything you want," said Kai.

I moved slowly around the island to stand next to him, and he wrapped his arms around me, pressing me to his chest. "I know we can't fix everything, but I hope you'll let us try. I really want you to be happy here." Heat sparked in his gaze that dropped to my lips.

I wanted his kiss but I was frozen, looking up at him, unable to bridge that gap.

"Can I?" he asked quietly, his thumb brushing against my bottom lip, sending shivers through me.

I nodded, closing my eyes as he descended toward me until a rush of cinnamon on my tongue unlocked my limbs. I wrapped my arms around his neck, gasping against his mouth when he scooped me up to set me on the counter.

He tasted so fucking good.

"As delicious as her cunt was, I don't really want it all over my breakfast."

Every inch of me locked up with embarrassment, pulling away from Kai to see Amir, Miles, and Diego descending the stairs.

"Don't listen to Amir, little dove." Kai dropped a quick kiss to my lips before helping me get my feet on the floor again. "He's just jealous he's not the one you're kissing."

Chapter 19
Diego

Seeing Callie walking around in my shirt made me want to eat her right up. She'd been so fucking cute this morning when she climbed into my bed so delicately like she was too embarrassed to wake me, but couldn't help herself.

Callie had come into *my* room. She'd have had no reason to think Kai was staying with me so he could be nearby, and my instincts were fucking *preening* over being chosen. And now she was stuffing her face with pancakes and strawberries, her cheeks as full as a chipmunk's like she couldn't eat fast enough.

It was fucking adorable.

Watching her go through so much pain yesterday had been utterly heartbreaking and not an experience I had any desire to repeat. If I had my way, she'd never cry another day in her life.

We'd sat down as a pack after she'd gone to bed, trying to sort out the best way to make her happy here. We had never planned for an omega, and while the guest room could easily be converted into a space for Callie, our hope was that most of her nights would be spent with at least one of us in our rooms until she settled.

Everyone at the table watched her discreetly, stealing glances at the sweetheart in our midst. Our omega.

How long would it take for her to bond me too?

I craved that connection with her. In some ways I was glad Kai was the first of us to be bonded. He was the best choice to ease her in, far better than Amir with his quiet temper or Miles with his anxiety. Callie had enough of her own stress to manage right now without having to directly feel how either of them had reacted to yesterday.

Before breakfast had finished, the order I'd put in after leaving her apartment arrived. I probably should have discussed it with Callie first, but everything in me yesterday had been screaming *fix it!* so I'd jumped the gun a bit. Hopefully she would like it.

I got up to answer the door and accepted the stack of boxes. She'd said her favorite color was pink during the drive when we'd worked on learning about one another, so I'd taken that knowledge and run with it.

Callie perked up, staring at the boxes as I carried them into the kitchen one by one to set them down on the free space on the island. "What are those?"

"Presents for you."

"For me?!" she squeaked.

"I may have gone a touch overboard, but—"

She was up and out of her seat, crashing against me, her arms locked around my waist. "Thank you."

"You don't even know what the presents are yet."

"Doesn't matter." She pressed her face to my chest, squeezing tighter. "You thought about me."

"Precious, I don't think it's possible for me to *stop* thinking about you."

I fetched her a box cutter out of our utility drawer, lowering the first box so it was properly in reach for her. She stared at the contents, lifting a plastic-wrapped, vacuum-sealed pink pillow.

Callie looked at me curiously and found three more like it, the next box containing twenty different throw blankets, all shades of pink in various fabrics and textures.

"Diego..." she whispered reverently. "Are these *nesting* supplies?"

"All of yours got thrown away. I thought—"

Callie burst into tears, burying her face in the first blanket on top.

Panic lanced straight up my spine that I had managed to make her cry. "I'm sorry. I should've talked to you first."

"No! I *love them*. Everything is so beautiful."

Kai was already on his feet, kneeling behind her to drag her onto his lap. Callie reached for me and pulled me down so she could awkwardly loop her arms around my neck, the blanket wedged between us while she continued sniffling away. It wasn't a comfortable position, but my omega wanted me close and I wasn't going to deny her.

"Thank you." She hiccuped, clutching me tighter.

"You're more than welcome, precious. I wasn't sure what all you would like so I picked a bunch of everything in your favorite color. Anything you don't want we can ship right back."

"Can you open the rest for me?" she asked, looking at me with watery eyes.

"Of course." I brought the final box down and sliced through the tape, revealing novelty pillows and plushes. She picked out the apple cider plush. It was in the shape of a paper cup with a bright red apple in the center, and a little smile above it with a plush cinnamon stick poking through a swirl of faux whipped cream. Not exactly accurate for how it was usually consumed, but the aesthetic was cute. I had chosen it for her and Kai, a combination of both of their scents since they were first bond in the pack.

"It's so cute. Jerry never let me have stuff like this in my nest. He said it was too childish."

I growled before I could stop myself and Callie leaned back into Kai's embrace. "Sorry, that was *not* for you. I can't believe he would dare dictate what an omega is allowed to have in their nest."

Miles and Amir hovered nearby, observing but not interfering.

"Do you want to set up your nest, sweetheart?" Miles asked.

"I can have one here?" she asked.

"Of course you can have one here," I insisted. "It wouldn't feel like home if you didn't have a nest."

Kai helped her stand and showed her the guest room that we were fully prepared to turn into her space, but she hesitated in the doorway, her apple cider plush squeezed in her arms before she turned and trotted directly up the stairs.

Where was she going?

The four of us followed after her and I found her back in my bed, looking at me with wide, plaintive eyes when I stepped into the room. Seeing her in there smoothed down the rough

145

edges of my worries. "Precious, would you like my bed to be your nest?"

She squeezed the plush harder. "I don't want to steal your space."

I joined her on the bed, threading my fingers through her hair, gratified when she closed her eyes and leaned into the touch. "You're more than welcome to turn this into your nest. I can move downstairs if you'd be more comfortable here."

She brought the plush up until it was covering everything but her eyes like it could shield her. "I don't want you to move."

"Then I'm even happier if you want to share this with me."

"The other rooms don't smell right. This one smells like you, me, and Kai."

"You don't have to explain. If you want it, it's yours."

That got her eyes watering again and she tipped forward, curling into a ball with her head on my lap. I didn't take a bit of her trust for granted, knowing how vulnerable she had to be feeling right now. She felt comfortable touching me and having me close, and I recognized that for the gift it was.

"You're all being so nice I don't know what to do with it."

"You have to get used to being treated well because that's your future with us."

Kai joined us, kneeling on the floor so he was at eye level with Callie. "We'll still take you shopping for more nesting supplies if you want. We need to take you shopping for clothing too. Until you're ready to go out, you can use anything in the house to build up a spot that's perfect for you."

"You can order online too," said Miles. "I'll get you my credit card and you can pick out anything you want."

The doorbell rang again and Amir disappeared to answer it, returning a moment later with another box.

Callie lifted her head, staring at both box and carrier. "What is it?"

"You gave all of your toiletries to your neighbor. I figured you would need new options and wasn't sure if you would like what we have here."

Callie let out a quiet sound of distress, getting to her hands and knees to cross the distance to Amir, where she pulled him into a hug he didn't seem to know what to do with. He did put his arms around her, but he looked at me over the top of her head like he wasn't sure what to make of her. I knew she was just overwhelmed. Our omega had been through a lot this week. At least Amir rolled with it instead of denying her that basic comfort. He had made it clear he didn't want a mate, but I was grateful that didn't mean he was going to be unkind to her.

Miles looked like he was desperate to hold her too, but I could see the anxious tension in his body and I was pretty certain he wouldn't reach out to her unless she came to him first.

"I'm sorry I'm such a fucking mess." Callie sat back, wiping her eyes.

"You're not," Kai insisted, pulling her close again. "You're in pain."

I was so curious to know what she felt like through the bond. Maybe by the time her next heat rolled around, she would be ready to do that with me. Even if the first bond with Kai had been an accident, she would be used to it by then and maybe it wouldn't feel so strange to consider.

"Would it be okay if I made my nest and had a nap?"

"You can do anything you want, precious. We'll bring the boxes up."

Kai stayed with her, while Miles, Amir, and I headed downstairs to bring up everything Callie needed.

"I should've gotten her something tangible," Miles lamented as we swept down the stairs. "You two thought ahead."

"We also ordered while you were driving. You were in charge of getting us safely there and back. The rest of us had time to worry about other things," I pointed out. "Besides, there won't be any shortage of time for you to get gifts for Callie."

Miles chewed his lip as we gathered up the boxes. "I worry she won't like me."

"Give it time."

Amir snorted. "Easy enough for you to say when you're already one of her favorites."

"She's just more comfortable with me right now. You'll get there. And maybe she would like you better if you would pull that stick out of your fucking ass."

"I like my stick right where it is, thanks."

I rolled my eyes and turned back to the stairs with the box of pillows. Callie and Kai were in the same position we'd left them in, but she perked up when we rejoined her. I unwrapped the pillows from their vacuum seal, letting them fluff back up. Amir handed her each of the numerous blankets in turn so she could make sure the texture was appropriate for her nest before he undid the packaging. She rejected four of them but kept the rest. At least I had mostly chosen correctly.

Watching her set up camp in my bed, arranging pillows and blankets, was like the fulfillment of a dream I hadn't even known I'd had. She looked so happy as she tucked blankets this way and that until they met her satisfaction.

Callie frowned. "It's still not quite right." She climbed off the bed and stopped in front of me, curling her fingers in the waistband of my lounge pants, sending every nerve to attention. "I need these."

Oh. She was full-throttle nesting then.

"I'm not wearing anything under them."

Her cheeks flushed hot pink. "But I *need* them."

"Okay, one second. Close your eyes if you don't wanna see the full moon." I pulled another pair of pants out of my dresser and traded them for the ones I was wearing, turning to see Callie still watching me, her lips softly parted and her pupils wide. I passed her the pants she had requested. "Anything else you need from me, precious?"

Callie bit her lip, her sweet candied apple scent in a thick cloud around her. "Get in the nest. Please," she added.

"That's my cue to leave," Amir announced. "I'll take Miles with me. Take your time."

Callie pouted as Amir departed, but didn't tell him to stay.

I followed her back into the nest where Kai was waiting. It was blatantly obvious that Callie wanted us, given the state of her scent and the extra sweetness of her slick tinting the air, but I could feel her heart pounding beneath my palm when I reached out, and saw the panic in her eyes.

"It's all right, little dove," Kai crooned. "Only as much as you want. I'll be able to feel if you need to stop."

Callie whimpered as she stretched out, reaching one hand to me and the other to Kai, drawing us close. I was determined to go at a pace that she was comfortable with. It didn't matter that I had already had her every way possible, because that was under contract and during a heat. Now this was just her, asking for us despite her nerves. There was no fucking way I was going to make her regret that. I wanted her to stay forever, and maybe if we made her happy enough, she would.

Chapter 20
Kai

Callie's heart hammered beneath my lips, her anxiety and desire twisting through the bond. Diego was so gentle with her, tilting up her chin and kissing her until she was shivering head to toe, her worries melting away. I kept all of my movements slow to give her time to react and hit pause if she needed to. The collar of Diego's shirt only went so far so I switched to the hem, lifting it up with a slow drag of my fingers over Callie's stomach. Her muscles twitched beneath my fingers, the scent of slick growing stronger by the second.

She arched her back and cried out when I wrapped my lips around the pebbled tip of her breast. They were so sensitive, and she squirmed like I had my tongue on her clit rather than her nipple. I took my time there, relishing the taste of her and the way she writhed under me. I switched to the other breast, her whimper sneaking out against Diego's lips.

He walked his fingers down her stomach and waited at the waistband of her panties until she bucked her hips. Diego glanced briefly at me, and I nodded, silent encouragement for him to give her exactly what she was wanting.

"Greedy little omega," Diego mused as he kissed his way from her lips to her throat. "Do you like having two alphas to play with?"

"Y-yes."

His hand sank deeper and Callie shifted, spreading her thighs to give him more space. I slipped my hand down to join his, working her clit while he fucked his fingers into her. I could have happily drowned in her scent; sweet candied apple mixed with our spices. She already smelled a little like me from the bond, but I liked being close enough to her that I could coat her skin with it.

Everything about her was perfection. The way she bucked against our hands, the beautiful whimpers she made as we slowly overwhelmed her, the smooth warmth of her skin pressed against me.

Bit by bit, her nerves in the bond were silenced in favor of desire. At least I knew we could calm her this way. If she needed a break from all the shit of the last week, I was only too happy to provide that. Putting her into subspace like we had during the heat was probably too much for her while she was fragile, but we could still give her much better things to focus on.

I claimed her mouth for myself while Diego was busy at her throat. Her nerves prickled back through the bond, so I switched to her throat, immediately feeling her discomfort melt away as I sucked on the spot where I had left my bondmark. Maybe kissing me was an intimacy she still struggled with?

"Fuck me," Diego groaned. "You're squeezing my fingers so tight."

I already knew she was close with how much she was squirming, her hips rocking frantically, and her fingers digging into my arm.

With nothing to muffle her and nowhere to go as we played her body like a violin, Callie came with a cry that had me preening. I knew how to take care of my omega, to give her what she needed.

Diego and I traded places, her cunt swallowing up my fingers while he took over her clit.

"You're so wet for us, little dove. Such a perfect omega coming for her alphas."

Callie was already so primed it was easy to send her into a spiral where she broke apart in a cascade of pleasure, one orgasm after the other, as we both kept up a steady rhythm until she was whining and nudging at our hands.

"Too much."

Diego pulled his hand away, dragging Callie into another kiss but this time no nerves bubbled up, only bliss. I eased my fingers out of her, enjoying the shudder that rolled through her.

I was hard as a rock next to her, but I wasn't going to mention it and make her feel an ounce of pressure. Even so, her nerves wormed their way back to the bond.

"I don't really know what to do with more than one person outside of a heat," she confessed quietly.

"I can leave," Diego offered.

Regret shot through the bond. "I don't want you to leave. I just don't know what I'm doing."

"In fairness," I said, nuzzling her cheek, "if you want any of us, you don't have to have a clue what you're doing. You might have noticed we have a fair bit of experience in our pack."

Callie let out a nervous laugh. "I *may* have noticed that."

"Whoever you want and whenever you want us is your choice. And it's okay if your choice is no one right now. We're more than capable of taking care of ourselves as needed."

She pouted. "That's very sweet but also unfair because I want about six billion different things."

"Pick one of them. You can always change your mind later," I insisted.

I hoped she would say she wanted me, but just because I wanted to sink into the heat of her body right now didn't mean I couldn't control myself otherwise.

"I don't know how to word it and I don't know how to make it not weird."

"Try."

Whatever she could possibly think of, we'd probably done it before. I couldn't conceive of anything she would come up with that would be new territory for anyone in the pack.

Callie closed her eyes, refusing to look at either of us. "I don't want Diego to go anywhere, but I don't know if I'm up for both of you right now. It feels unfair to only ask for you."

Diego chuckled softly and kissed her cheek. "That's not unfair, precious. If you want me to stay while Kai fucks you, I can do that. We took turns during the heat and this is no different. If my turn comes days, weeks, or later, or even *never*, that's okay. I would honestly rather stick my dick in a cactus than to have you only be with me because you were trying to be fair."

Callie curled one hand around his cock, her cheeks so brightly pink I was surprised they didn't start glowing. "No cactus. I like it right here."

Diego hissed, groaning as she gave him a tentative stroke.

153

"How do you want me, little dove?"

"On top? I want to be squished."

I rearranged myself, lifting her knees and settling between her thighs. Diego inched over to give me enough room to brace my forearms on either side of Callie. When she tipped her head up for a kiss, I met her in the middle, relieved when only quiet satisfaction simmered in the bond. Her fingers curled at the back of my neck and her hips rocked, urging me to get a move on.

It only took one shift for me to line up with her dripping core, and I about died and went to heaven at the squeeze of her cunt as her muscles eased to allow me entrance. She moaned against my mouth, her fingers trembling and getting a good grip on my hair.

"Fuck, you feel so good," I breathed.

Callie whined, pulling me close so she could tuck her face against my throat, her panting punctuating each thrust into her. It took only a couple of seconds for the glide to be smooth, her body ready and willing to handle me. I fucked in hard just for the pleasure of the strangled sound she made in my ear.

Diego moaned. "Fuck, she grabbed on so tight when you did that."

I rode her slowly until she got impatient, her heels pressing into my ass cheeks in a demand for more. That was what I had been waiting for, for her to crave a firmer touch. I picked up my pace, driving in hard and fast, setting both her and Diego off as she reacted to me and he reacted to her. I glanced down, seeing Callie's hand work over him at the same pace my hips drove into her.

My world narrowed down to the contents of this nest, to Callie writhing beneath me, every delicious whine begging me without words to give her as much as she could handle. My own pleasure at having her, and hers at being taken, ricocheted through the bond. She clung so sweetly to me. I had never dared imagine how good it would feel to take a bondmate to bed, to be able to read them perfectly so I could give them the best possible experience. I knew every angle to work, how and when to tease, both from the reactions of her body but also from the bursts of surprised delight that struck me when I found something new.

"Fuck, Kai, I—"

Her pussy locked down with a rush of slick.

Hearing her say my name like that scratched an itch deep in my brain. I had made my omega happy. I had done my job as her alpha to give her pleasure and unravel her in her nest.

"Almost there, little dove. Do you want my knot?"

"*Yes*," she gasped out.

Diego was rapidly coming undone alongside our omega, his hand clenched around hers, his hips fucking himself through their combined grip.

A few more thrusts, and the tension that had been slowly building at the base of my spine released. I plunged into Callie's cunt, my knot swelling and setting off the cascade of a full-body orgasm in her. Every bit of her twitched, hips rocking helplessly against me, panting cries filling the room as her sweet pussy adapted to the pressure.

She was shaking like a leaf in my arms, but no distress was coming down the bond. Diego cursed next to us, finally spilling over their fists, cum splattering against Callie's side.

"Dead," she whispered when the twitches finally calmed down. "I think I died."

"You definitely didn't." I coaxed her into a luxurious kiss before a plaintive sound out of Diego had me pulling back so he could kiss her himself.

"Feels like it," she said softly when he settled back and she melted against the blankets. She wiggled her hips and hissed. "It feels bigger than during the heat."

"I assure you it's the same size. Your body is just in a different state during a heat. Everything loosens up a little more during it so you can take all the alpha dick you want."

Callie giggled and I felt the ripples of it all the way down her body. She turned to Diego. "Was that okay?"

He hummed happily. "I got to come with my omega's hands on me. It was more than okay."

"Good." Callie pulled me closer, letting out a bone-deep sigh, tugging until my full weight was compressing her into the nest.

She felt so small like this. I'd have worried I was crushing her if not for her purr vibrating against my chest and the smooth satisfaction I felt from the bond. I tucked away this knowledge for later. If my omega enjoyed being squished, I would at least make sure the others knew. They didn't have the same advantage I did with the bond telling me what Callie couldn't express with words, and I wanted her to be comfortable with all of them.

I could already see that she was with Diego, but her interactions with Amir and Miles since we had come home were too infrequent for me to judge. We came as a package deal, or at least I had always thought so. I wanted Callie to know them and come to love everyone in the pack, but if she didn't... I didn't want to think about what would happen if she never liked them.

I had heard of packs cleaved apart because the omega picked favorites and rejected certain members. If I could prevent that from happening, I would. I could encourage her to spend time with them, and while I was pretty certain Miles would be down for that, it was hard to tell where Amir sat with things right now. I couldn't hold things together on my own, but Diego being in the nest with us right now gave me hope it would all work out.

"You look so happy to be smushed." Diego gave her a soft smile, tracing his knuckles over her cheek.

"It feels so good," she said, her voice breathy and quiet. "Kind of like it squeezes out all my anxiety so there's no room for any of it."

"I would offer to help with the squeezing," Diego said, "but Kai isn't going anywhere with his knot in you, and I think if I climbed on top you would lose the ability to breathe entirely."

"Unfortunately." Callie sighed and I lifted myself up just enough so she could get a full inhale before melting back down. "Stay, though. If you want to."

"Of course I want to, precious. There's not another spot on the planet I would rather be than right here with you."

Diego's sentiments echoed mine exactly. She was it for me. This sweet, beautiful omega that welcomed me into her life and her body. My mate.

Chapter 21
Callie

Kai and Diego followed me around the pack house like a pair of pups. It was cute as hell, and I felt almost ridiculously safe to have them flanking me wherever I went.

We had stayed in the nest most of yesterday, emerging to eat, but otherwise I was too ridiculously comfortable with them to consider doing much more. I still had to figure out a lot of my life, but at least I had a nest that made me purr just looking at it and two alphas who were all too willing to attend to my every whim.

When we came down for lunch, Miles was sitting at the island with his tablet, his brow pinched as he stared at the screen.

"Something wrong?" I asked.

"Just trying to figure out the schedule. I can't officially take the pack off it right now, so I've just been pushing their shows and communicating with other performers to make sure all the slots get filled."

I frowned. "I made things harder on you."

Miles's gaze snapped toward me. "No." He sighed. "No, Callie, you didn't do anything wrong."

I inched closer, turning back briefly to discover that Kai and Diego had vanished. Apparently I was spending time with Miles now. A refreshing crispness hung in the air around him. It reminded me a bit of the forests around Seattle where I'd grown up, with the conifers and moss-covered ground, moisture thick in the air. I got nearer, trying to discreetly sniff, realizing his scent blockers must have finally vacated his system.

Warmth rippled down my torso when he turned more fully to me, sending a cloud of that clean, mountain air scent toward me.

"Everything all right?" he asked.

"You smell nice." My cheeks toasted as I said it, but it was the truth.

Miles glanced down at himself like he hadn't quite realized the scent was coming from him. "Oh, yeah, my scent finally came back during the night. I take a pretty hefty dose of the blockers so I can be clearheaded to manage the heats."

"Do you have to go back on them?" I glided toward him like I was magnetized, stopping mere inches away. "For work?"

"Ah, no. There are other methods I can use."

I sat down on the barstool next to him. "Good."

"Are you hungry?" Miles asked after a beat of silence. "I can make you something. Or we can order in?"

"What's your go-to?"

"If I'm not making it, Thai food. If I'm in the kitchen, then, um, grilled cheese?"

He was *so* stiff, nerves practically radiating off him. It was strange how different he was now than when I'd met him and we'd talked together so easily. Maybe he didn't know how to handle me when I wasn't in crisis mode.

"I *love* grilled cheese. With tomato soup for dipping, of course. Can't separate the food sisters."

"We only have canned soup," he said carefully. "But I could pick up fresh tomatoes."

I snorted. "Miles, I'm not above canned soup. Why are you being so weird?"

"*Because.*" He shoved a hand through his hair. "It's my fault you're in this situation and frankly I'm worried you're going to hate me forever for it."

I tapped my fingers on the counter. "Listen, it's not ideal by any means, but, Miles...my life was pretty fucked before you got your paws on it. You gave me a new future to work toward right when I thought there was nothing left for me. Besides, you didn't do it on purpose, right?"

"God, no."

"Then I could never hate you. We're all just doing our best, I think."

Tension leaked out of him like a punctured balloon. "I just want everyone to be okay, and there's still a lot we need to sort and fix, but I'm glad you don't hate me."

I nudged him with my elbow. "Should we get started on that lunch, then?"

"I suppose we should." He offered a tentative smile. "Can't have our omega going hungry."

I was put in charge of keeping the soup in motion while we warmed a handful of cans on the stove to feed everyone, and

Miles sliced cheese and buttered bread, arranging them neatly on the electric griddle.

"That's so handy to make enough for all of you at once."

"Takes a few rounds with it to satisfy all the appetites, but certainly quicker than a frying pan."

We chatted about nothing of consequence, mostly the touristy bits of Vegas I had seen before everything had gone to hell. He didn't entirely relax, tensing up at odd moments, but it felt *almost* like the first time we'd met.

Miles stacked the completed sandwiches on five plates and moved the soup pot off the burner for me. "Why don't you collect the others and I'll set the table?"

"Yes, sir." I grinned at how easily he flushed.

I had no clue where the rest of the pack were in the house, but figured it would be safest to start with their bedrooms. Diego and Kai weren't in the nest or in Kai's room, so I stopped outside Amir's door, knocking and waiting for a response.

It swung open and I froze in place as his bare torso filled my vision, a light dusting of black hair on his chest, and then dragged my gaze up to his face, where his eyes were narrowed.

"What?"

"Um, Miles and I made lunch, if you wanted some."

He looked me over, head to toe, heat ghosting over my skin. I was only in one of my tank top and booty short sets I'd packed since we hadn't gone clothing shopping yet and I didn't trust anything I couldn't try on. I couldn't quite tell if he liked the outfit or not with the sharpness in his eyes, though with the way he lingered on my curves I could only assume he didn't hate it.

"I'll be down in a minute." He shut the door without another word, a gust of delicious cedar wafting over me.

Well, that was one very confusing alpha down at least. Now I just had to find the other two. I wasn't totally familiar with the floor plan of the pack house yet, but I reasoned if I got lost for too long, someone would eventually come looking.

I plucked open one of the doors to the balcony overlooking the courtyard and poked my head out. "Are you guys out here? I'm not coming out to look; it's too hot."

"We're here, precious," Diego called back.

I whimpered as I went downstairs and stepped out in the heat, weaseling myself into the strip of shade along the wall. I skirted around until I found the two of them sitting at the patio table, a bottle of water in front of each.

"Why are you guys out here?"

"Giving you time to hang out with Miles," Kai replied.

"Could've given me a bit of warning instead of vanishing into the night."

"We vanished into the *morning*." Diego stuck the tip of his tongue out at me before lapsing into an easy smile.

"Did you two have fun?" Kai asked.

"I feel like he's even more nervous than I am," I confessed.

Diego chuckled. "Yeah, Miles is like that. He finds a thousand things a day to worry about."

"All the more reason it'll be good for him to have an omega in the house," Kai added.

It was too fucking hot out here, so I grabbed each of them by the wrist and dragged them up. "The grilled cheese is going to get soggy if you don't hurry up."

"You're not supposed to be cooking for us," said Kai.

"Miles and I made it together. All I did was stir the soup."

Kai scooped me up bridal style and I squawked as my feet left the ground. "Since you put in effort on that, you're not going to put in any effort to get to the food."

162

"You're gonna make me so lazy. Treat me like one of those little purse dogs and I'm gonna get all yappy and bitey."

"You can bite me anytime you want, precious." Diego grinned, pulling open the doors to the kitchen so Kai could navigate me inside.

Amir was already at the dining table, his arms crossed as he waited for us. Why the hell was he so cranky today? He pushed the chair out next to him with his foot so Kai could set me down.

A bowl of soup sat at each spot and a stack of grilled cheese cut diagonally—the only correct way to cut it—was in the middle of the table. They all watched me, waiting until I had taken the first piece before helping themselves. I almost never had grilled cheese made with real cheese. The cheap plasticky stuff that melted down into cheese-flavored glue was more my speed, but I couldn't deny that having a proper cheddar was fucking delicious. I dunked every bite in the soup, wiggling happily.

I was pretty sure at one point Jerry had known how to cook, but as soon as we'd moved in together it was like he had forgotten the skill entirely, leaving the meals to me. He had never been very happy with meals like this, but they were so nostalgic for me that they were my immediate go-to whenever he was out of town.

I inhaled three of the half-sandwiches before finally sitting back, patting my food baby with a deep breath.

"How did you fit all of that in there?" Amir asked, amusement coloring his tone. "You're so tiny."

"I need the fuel. Besides, I can fit three cocks inside me and I don't think the sandwiches are any bigger than that."

Diego choked on his soup, laughing between gasping

breaths. Kai had luckily not been eating when I said that, and had his mouth covered with his hand, his shoulders shaking.

I beamed at them. Sure, maybe the joke was a little bit crude, but I liked that I could make them laugh.

"My cock takes up more space than a sandwich," Amir grumbled.

"Do you still want to go shopping for new clothes today?" Miles asked, changing the subject.

"I wouldn't say no to some fresh clothes. What I brought with me is going to get old fast, and I can't exactly be running around in your shirts in public."

"Sure you can," said Amir. "Add a belt and it's no different than any other dress."

"Tell me you don't know anything about fashion without telling me you don't know anything about fashion." I stuck my tongue out at him. "I need at least a few more basics."

The whole pack took me to the outlet mall. I didn't want to keep them for too long, so I mostly stuck to brands I already bought from to grab a few easy things that were replicas of what I used to have.

"We should definitely go through here," said Kai, pointing out one of the lingerie stores.

"Sure, pick out anything you want and I can try it on."

That was the wrong thing to say because Kai took off like a kid in a candy store. Diego followed after him, leaving me with Miles and Amir.

"Pick some things for yourself," said Miles. "We both know they're not going to choose anything practical."

He wasn't wrong. It was more than a little awkward to dig through the on-sale panties with the two of them hovering and Amir looking like he would rather be anywhere else.

"You can leave if you want to," I told him.

"We're supposed to make sure you're safe."

"Well, if you're going to stay, could you at least not look like you're being held at gunpoint to be shopping with me?"

"You're supposed to be looking at the clothes, not at me."

"I would love to do that but you're walking around over here with a little storm cloud over your head."

"Don't worry about me."

"Seriously, just go do whatever you want. Miles is with me, and Kai and Diego are, like, ten feet away."

Amir considered for a few moments before nodding. "One of you text me when you're ready to go."

He disappeared, leaving me with Miles, and I tried not to feel the cut of his rejection. Easier said than done.

I put on every item Kai and Diego picked out, but refused to show them in the store, knowing that if I caught sight of the heat in their eyes, we would end up doing something that would get us kicked out. They could wait until we got home to see the items before they ripped them off.

By the end of the afternoon, I had a decent start at a proper wardrobe. Miles had insisted on paying for my clothes. The second I had tried to pull out my own card to buy anything all day—lunch, lemonade, soft pretzels—one of their hands would whip out to replace it with their own.

Hot damn. A girl could get used to that.

Chapter 22
Miles

C allie's eyes were on me all evening. I wasn't sure why she was watching me, but whenever I looked over at her, she would glance away.

"Movie night?" I suggested once we'd finished the pizza we'd had delivered.

"I like movies," Callie replied.

"Pick something," said Kai. "We have a million DVDs, or see what's on streaming."

I got the projector going while Callie combed through the movie choices and the others prepared all the snacks. She settled on an action-packed historical Cinderella retelling I remembered loving as a kid.

The others joined us while Callie was picking out the second movie for our double feature.

"Where do I sit?" she asked since we'd taken the front row of four chairs.

"Pick a lap, precious," Diego said. "Or we can shuffle around if you want your own seat."

Callie looked at each of us in turn, and I expected her to immediately go to Kai or Diego, but her gaze lingered on me. "Can I?"

She wanted to sit with *me*?

When I didn't immediately answer, she shrank back.

"Yes, sorry, of course you can sit with me. I just didn't expect you to want to." I patted my knee. "Come here."

I scooted over, making space for her to plant her butt and curl her legs over my lap. Every inch of me was taut as a bowstring, unsure what to do with the omega in front of me. Was I supposed to put my arms around her? The others had all been intimate with her, and I had no idea what she wanted or expected of me. I should probably ask, but this didn't feel like the appropriate moment to do that.

Callie wiggled around to get comfortable, tucking her head beneath my chin and wedging a bowl of popcorn on her lap. Kai and Diego both looked over longingly. Maybe we should take out the theater seating and replace it with a giant nest so more of us could touch her at once. Diego scooped up her legs by the ankle, propping them on the armrest between us so he could lay his hand over them.

Her candied apple scent was sweet in my nose, her body warm, and my hands shook when I settled one on her waist and the other on her shins. She didn't tense and didn't tell me off, only relaxing a little more. Amir got the movie going, transporting us to medieval France with its rolling countryside and misty mornings.

I couldn't focus on the film at all with Callie so close. She smelled like heaven, and the more time that passed, the more she melted against me. I got bolder, mindlessly stroking her hair until she was purring. Amir's gaze on us was like a tangible thing, but I couldn't quite decide if he would prefer to drag her out of my arms and into his or if he was upset that she was there at all.

When we moved on to the next movie, another fairytale retelling turned action movie, Callie stretched out, still cradled on my lap, but with her legs across Diego, the tips of her toes reaching Kai's armrest and her head resting on the one between Amir and me. Luckily the armrests were low and padded so it wasn't too far off from a bed with laps to support her between them.

Amir's fingers flexed like he was trying to stop himself from reaching out to her. I had nothing stopping me. Callie's breathing turned shallow when I curled my fingers over her waist, resting my palm on her stomach in the gap between her top and shorts. Goosebumps prickled down her legs and her scent sweetened.

"Are you cold, sweetheart?"

Before she could answer, Amir was on his feet, grabbing blankets out of the storage bench at the back of the theater and tossing them over her.

I tried not to think of the great many things I could do unseen to Callie with a blanket over my hands. I glanced back down at her and found she wasn't watching the film at all, but rather *me*, her lips slightly parted. My fingers twitched against her and she bit her lip, turning back to the movie. Did I imagine her thighs parting a little further?

I wanted to know what she felt like, to press my fingers into her and coax out some of the delicious sounds she had made during her heat. God, what I wouldn't give for this omega to fall apart in my arms.

I wouldn't *take* anything from her, not until everything was sorted, but I could give her something if that was what she wanted.

Callie wriggled restlessly, her ass grinding against my already hard cock, her scent rising by the second.

Amir snaked a hand over her throat, her scent exploding at the first contact, and he tilted her chin to look at him. "Use your words, omega. If you're angling for attention, just say so. You're going to drive poor Miles crazy, squirming on him like that."

"It's not my fault," she said quietly. "Everyone smells really good."

Amir stroked her jaw with his thumb. "I never said it was your fault; I said to use your words. Tell us what you want and who you want to touch you."

"Miles," she gasped out.

Oh, fuck. She really *did* want me.

Amir kept her pinned by the throat and Diego lifted one of her legs, letting her ankle rest on his shoulder to open her up for me. Fuck me. My hands were sweating like I was a nervous teen. I wiped my palms on my shirt. Callie's shorts had a stretchy waistband and barely came to her mid-thigh, so I could easily access her.

She whined when my fingertips hovered for too long, trying to work up the courage to touch her. I swallowed hard, diverting in the other direction to sweep under her tank top and tease the soft curve of her breast, sweeping my thumb over her nipple. All of my muscles were so tense I could barely

169

breathe, my hands shaking and desperate to stay on her. I couldn't get my mouth on her in this current position, not without readjusting her.

Callie whined again, rolling her hips in a silent request.

"What did I tell you about words?" Amir tapped her cheek.

"Miles, *please*. I need more."

Hearing her say that made me *very* glad I was an alpha and not a beta, or I'd have embarrassed myself coming in my pants.

I held my breath as I moved my hand beneath the blanket, under her waistband, and into her slick folds.

"Jesus Christ," I whispered. "You're so wet."

Callie shuddered as I explored, squeezing her clit until she bucked against me. I teased lower, sliding one finger into her. Her pussy clenched around it and she immediately begged for another.

If I were struck dead in this moment, I would die the happiest fucking man on the planet. Listening to Callie pant and moan because *my* hands were on her was a gift I had never expected. Unlike the others, I didn't have the benefit of sharing her heat and learning how her body worked, but I paid attention to every squeak and every caught breath, adjusting incrementally until I found a rhythm and angle that had her cries pitching. Her legs trembled and her hands dug into me wherever she could reach, her pussy clenching frantically. A few more circles around her clit with my thumb had her shattering, and pride filled my chest like a balloon.

I had made our omega come.

I eased her down slowly and when her breathing had recovered, she looked up at me with wide eyes and pink cheeks just visible in the light from the screen. Amir and Diego helped her sit up, all of us watching her. I rearranged her carefully, settling her on my lap so her back was to my chest.

"Watch the movie," I instructed.

I kept my hands on her, doing a slow exploration of her body, tracing the softness of her thighs and stomach, down her arms, over and over until she got squirmy enough that I explored where she actually wanted my hands to be. I slipped down the straps of her tank top and bra, leaving her exposed, but her arms tangled.

Touching her was like being half-drunk. She made tiny sounds when I cupped her breasts and teased her to my heart's content. As much as I would've loved to bury my cock into her and feel every squeeze of her cunt while I did this, I had to be patient.

When I did slip my fingers back into her, I kept my touch deliberately slow, too gentle and leisurely to make her come this time. I fully intended to work her into a frenzy and then let Kai and Diego take her up to the nest.

By the time the movie ended, Callie was a desperate, squirmy mess, and her slick had soaked into my lounge pants.

When the credits started to roll, I turned to Kai. "Come get your mate. She's going to need a little bit more than I've given her."

Kai scooped her up and Callie turned back to me. "You're not coming?"

"Not today, sweetheart. Go have fun with Kai and Diego. We'll get our time together."

She pouted but didn't protest as Kai absconded with her, and Diego followed behind him.

Amir nudged my shoulder. "What the fuck was that about? She was putty in your hands."

"I just don't feel comfortable taking more from her until everything with the company is settled down and I know nothing is going to come back and bite us in the ass."

"It doesn't have to be that deep, Miles," Amir insisted. "This isn't the old days when fucking a woman irreparably damaged her future. You're allowed to just have fun."

"So why aren't you?" I countered.

"Mind your own fucking business." Amir crossed his arms over his chest, glowering at me.

"Don't look at me like that. You've already had her, so why aren't you tripping over yourself to get back into her bed?"

"She's Kai's mate, not mine."

"She's *our* mate, Amir. Kai bonding her first doesn't change that."

"Can we cut down a little on the pot calling the kettle black here? We both have our own logic for not fucking her. Let's just agree not to dig into each other's reasons."

"But now you've made me curious."

"Sorry to disappoint. You're gonna have to stay that way."

He swept out of the theater, and I followed him for lack of anything better to do, turning off the projector on my way. He beelined for the courtyard, shucked his clothing down to his boxer briefs, and rinsed off under the deck shower before plunging into the pool. Maybe Amir had the right idea. Cold water would do me good right now.

I could hear Callie being taken apart upstairs, and my options were to get where I couldn't hear her so I could calm down, or go upstairs and take care of myself, listening to her like an awkward stalker.

"Want some company?" I asked Amir.

"Not particularly," he replied before dipping beneath the surface again.

Looked like *awkward stalker* was going to win. I took my walk of shame up to my room, leaving the door ajar just enough that I could still hear her. I stripped off the slick-soaked pants and dropped them by my pillow so I could get her scent all over my bed before stretching out, adding a bit of lube, and wrapping my hand around my cock.

I bucked my hips, fucking through my fist, the scent of her making me dizzy, and the distant sounds of her pleasure winding me up until the tension was simply too much and I exploded across my chest, her name on my lips.

I was so fucking gone for her it was ridiculous.

Chapter 23
Callie

"Here." Amir set a crisp white box in front of me at breakfast the next day.

"Um, thank you? What is it?"

"Open it and see."

I grabbed hold of the top and the bottom slid cleanly out, revealing a brand-new smartphone. "I already have a phone, though?"

"That thing is at least five years old and it's always half drained every time I see it. You need something newer and more reliable."

My chest warmed at the thoughtful gift. "Thank you. This is really sweet. Do any of you know enough about phones to help me get it set up? I usually just get the store to do everything when I get a new phone."

"I can do it," offered Amir. "Give me your old one and I'll get the process started."

I watched, absolutely fascinated, as he navigated his way through both phones with lightning speed, and soon enough everything on the old one was syncing to the new.

"Give it about ten minutes and it's all yours. I charged it last night for you."

Why was he being so sweet when he was so fucking cranky with me all the time? It didn't make any sense.

"I should've thought of that," said Kai. His cheek was resting on his hand, observing the two of us.

"I'm sure you would have eventually." Amir shrugged. "I got to it first."

"Do you want to hang out today?" I asked Amir.

"You don't want to spend time with me, princess. Kai is right there. You don't need me."

I pursed my lips. "Yeah, I can see him. I asked *you*."

"And I'm saying no. I have plans."

The rejection shouldn't have cut as deep as it did, shouldn't have had a squeak of distress escaping or tears pricking my eyes.

Kai pulled me against his chest. "Don't be rude to her."

"I'm not allowed to have plans now?"

"Just watch your tone."

Amir sighed and turned away from us, heading up the stairs.

"Why doesn't he like me?" I turned my face against Kai's chest. "I don't understand. Sometimes I think he wants me and then he just shuts me down. It feels like before."

"With your ex?" Kai asked.

I nodded. I didn't want to think about Jerry, but Amir was triggering my insecurity, making me want to try to make him happy without knowing if I could. I *hated* that feeling.

"I'll talk to him," promised Kai.

"You don't have to talk to him. I'll get around to it. I'm just so confused."

If Amir didn't like me, I had to accept that. I couldn't, *wouldn't* allow myself to fall into the same trap with him that I had with Jerry. The other men in the house liked me plenty and I could put my focus into building relationships with them.

"What happens if he never likes me?"

"That won't happen," Kai assured me. "He doesn't have to *be* with you, but he's pack, and he needs to check his attitude. I don't want you to be uncomfortable here."

"I don't know what's up with Miles either. They're both so frustrating."

"Miles is...honestly, I don't really know. It's obvious to anyone that he wants you, but he holds on to guilt for a long time."

"He did tell me he feels like my being here is his fault. I told him it was fine, but..."

"Ah, yeah. It'll take him a while to sort that all out in his head, but I'm one hundred percent certain he'll come around. He likes you; he just has to feel worthy before he's all in. He was the same when we were forming the pack because he felt guilty taking a recruitment job while the rest of us stayed in sex work. Doesn't matter how much you tell him you're comfortable with something. If it hasn't clicked in his head, he's going to be riddled with anxiety over it."

"So what's the best plan of action, then? Do I just keep telling him things are okay?"

"Well, that probably won't hurt, but mostly you have to let it run its course."

I groaned, dropping my forehead against his chest. "You and Diego are making this so easy."

"That's usually how things go around here," Kai said with a laugh. He stroked soothing hands up and down my back until I was purring. "I think it's easier on me too, to accept this is our life now. I don't want to fight it when it feels so nice to have you here."

I sighed and snuggled in closer. So much was still up in the air, but I appreciated that Kai wanted to smooth the path for me.

"I'm not entirely sure what to do about my job," I said after a few moments. "My clients are back in LA."

"You can go back and finish the work for them and we can look at finding you clients here. I know you went to school for cinematography. Is that what you do for work too?"

"Yeah. I work with a lot of indie producers."

"Given how many shows there are here, how many performers, I can't imagine you would be short on clientele if you wanted to transition to finding people in Vegas instead." Kai kissed the top of my head. "Obviously the connections I'm going to have are in the live sex shows, and I don't know how interested you would be in doing cinematography for those, so I'm just gonna throw it out there and if you want to pursue it, let me know."

"I was going to say I feel like I'm too much of a prude for that, but I don't think I can actually say that anymore."

Kai scooped me up, perching my butt on the counter before leaning down for a luxurious kiss that had my toes curling. "I would definitely say you're a lot more adventurous than you give yourself credit for."

"I've never thought of myself like that before."

"That's probably because you were with an inconsiderate asshole. Having the right partner for things like that makes all the difference. Really hard to let your freak flag fly if you don't feel safe."

I burst into giggles and pulled him down for another kiss, delighting in the cinnamon sweetness and the way his arms snaked around me. In a lot of ways it felt weird to be so comfortable with Kai, and maybe it was the bond, but he was also so lovely with me. He wanted me to feel safe and comfortable and went out of his way to make sure that happened. How was I supposed to hold on to my anxiety when this alpha seemed ready to fall at my feet to make me happy?

I never would have casually made out with Jerry while sitting on the kitchen counter. With Kai I was tempted to lie back and let him take anything he wanted. I inched closer, locking my ankles behind his hips.

Kai wrapped his fingers around the back of my neck, tipping my head so he could get his mouth on my throat and I melted instantly at the sweep of his lips on my skin and the rock of his hips between my thighs. Completely pitiful sounds escaped me when he settled on his bondmark, sucking at the sensitive skin until my brain was mush and my panties were damp with slick.

"I'm curious how many times a day I'll have to have you before I stop craving you every second." Kai nipped my earlobe. "I feel like there's no actual number. As soon as I have you, I want you again."

I didn't truly give a fuck if it was the bond that caused that to happen, because it felt so fucking good to be wanted that much. Even if I was drawn to the others, Kai was a safe space.

"What do you think about letting me have a second

breakfast on this counter?" His nose trailed up my throat and one of his hands dipped between us to grind against my pussy.

"I think I'd let you do anything if you asked like that."

He pulled away with a wicked smile, heat in his eyes as he nudged me back to lie across the stone. Kai set my ankles on his shoulders and tapped my ass so I could lift it and he could peel down the tiny shorts and panties, leaving them on the floor before sinking to his knees. He wasted no time at all, seeking out my clit and sucking hard until my hands were clenched in his hair and every bit of me was shaking on the precipice of release.

"Kai, fuck, that's too much."

He turned his head to lightly bite my inner thigh. "It's not too much, little dove. I'm well aware of how much you can take."

I whined when he went immediately back to my clit, locking one arm around my thigh to keep me spread as he thrust his fingers into me. I never thought I would be spread out on the countertop, back arched like a cat and trying desperately to keep my grip on sanity while an alpha tried to suck my soul out through my clit.

I was breathing so hard I was almost dizzy when I shattered for him. I wanted to rock against his mouth but he held me so tightly I could barely move. He just continued his attention as I crested one peak, and before I could even drop, I was already scaling another.

"I feel like we could make an absolute fucking fortune in porn," Diego said as he joined us in the kitchen, still dripping from his time in the pool. "I've never seen anything that hot, precious."

I whimpered, barely coherent as Kai continued his mission.

Diego swept around the other side of the island and dropped to his knees by my head.

"Such a naughty omega," Diego whispered in my ear. "Do you like your alpha eating you out where anyone can see?"

"Ye—" My answer broke off as I came, breathing hard through the surge of pleasure, squeaking and panting until Kai finally pulled away to kiss up the inside of my thigh, letting me sink back against the cool stone.

"Do you want me to touch you too, precious?"

"*Please.*"

Kai went back to work after giving me a moment to breathe, and Diego turned my face to his. I felt his kiss down to my toes. He snuck his hands down my tank top, caught my nipples between his thumbs and forefingers, and pinched until I arched against his hands with a moan. His mouth dragged down my throat and settled on the curve of my neck and shoulder, cupping my breasts and teasing me while Kai rapidly undid me.

Desperation burned through me. Neither of them gave a flying fuck about their own pleasure, pouring all their attention into mine until I broke apart in their hands, whiny, squirming, and breathless.

"Right here." Diego kissed my throat. "In your next heat I want to put my mark right here."

I shuddered as Kai withdrew his fingers and stood up to hover over me, rocking his hard, but still clothed, cock against my core.

"Would you like that, precious?" Diego asked.

"Yes, Diego, please," I gasped out and pulled his head closer. Kai ground harder against me. "Fuck, Kai, if you don't get that in me immediately, I might explode."

Diego laughed quietly, still slowly teasing my breasts. "I

already knew you were greedy for cock, but it's even more fun when you beg for it outside of your heat."

Kai shoved down his shorts, firm hands gripping both of my thighs as he angled himself and eased his way in. Diego drank down my whine. Kai's hands shook and his breathing was ragged by the time our hips met.

"I'm never going to get used to how good you feel."

"Beg him," Diego crooned. "Tell him how desperate you are for him to fuck you."

"Kai, please, *please*." He pulled out and thrust back in, stealing my breath. "Fuck, yes, again. Harder."

The next buck would have slid me across the stone if he didn't have such a grip on me. It struck exactly like I'd hoped, hitting the sweet spot inside me that had pleasure rippling through me.

"More, please. I want to feel it all day."

Kai moved in earnest this time and I surrendered to it entirely. Between the two alphas, I was utterly overwhelmed. I reached back for Diego, trying to unravel his towel, push down his swim trunks, and drag him closer. I needed him too.

Pleasure and contentment flowed through the bond from Kai, watching me pull at Diego until his cock was in my mouth, his hand cradling the back of my head so I didn't hit it on the counter while Kai jostled me. I purred between thrusts, Diego using my mouth while I moaned around him. Old Callie would have had an aneurysm to see me right now. New Callie was desperate for these alphas and eager to catch all the pleasure they could give her.

"Fuck, precious," Diego gasped. "That tongue is wicked."

I had never been wicked before them, and if this was what it felt like, I never wanted to stop.

A low growl to the side caught my attention. I could just

barely see Amir out of the corner of my eye, standing there and watching us, his fists clenched and his brows pinched. "I can't go anywhere in this damn house without the two of you having her bent over every surface."

Diego slid out of my mouth and Kai stilled between my hips. I bit down on the whine of frustration at having them both pull back. I wanted to reach out, to ask Amir to join us, but if he was going to be an ass about it, I couldn't afford to let myself. I have been down that path before and I was *not* going to do it again.

"You weren't home," Kai pointed out. "I thought you had plans. You made that pretty damn clear earlier."

"I forgot my wallet."

"I'm sorry," I said before I could stop myself.

Kai's gaze whipped back to me. "Don't apologize to him. I'm the one who asked you to do this, and he wasn't supposed to be home to see it."

I sat up, feeling too awkward to lie there with Kai inside me and Amir glaring at the three of us. Kai gathered me close, letting me use his arms to shield me from that disdainful look.

"Do whatever the fuck you want." Amir turned on his heel and left. "Don't wait up."

Kai hissed and I realized I had been digging my nails into him. I released my grip on him, my chest aching and the start of tears clogging my throat. "Sorry."

Don't wait up... People said that when they were going on dates. Was that where Amir was going, why he wanted nothing to do with me?

"*I'm* sorry. I don't know what's gotten into him." Kai grimaced. "I'm going to punch him if he upsets you again. I hate feeling you hurting."

"Sor—"

"*Don't* fucking apologize," Kai said exasperatedly. "It's helpful for me to feel it so I know, but I hate that *you* have to feel it. I want our whole pack to be together and I don't know how to bridge this gap with him."

"He'll come around or he won't," Diego said with a sigh. "I guess fun time is over for now. Do you want to go steal some of his things for the nest?"

I *did* want his scent in there, and Miles's too. It was kind of cruel how their scents gave me comfort when I was pretty sure it might break my heart to have them so close when they didn't seem to want to be mine. I could only hope they changed their minds eventually.

Chapter 24
Amir

G etting out of the pack house was my only option. I was going to lose it if I stayed there. Sexual frustration wasn't all that familiar to me. Between the heats and casual partners, I had never been without. But things were painfully different now.

Having a mate threw off the entire flow of my life. I knew it threw off the others too, but they were too blinded by Callie's scent to realize how deep that disruption went. I didn't want an omega. I didn't want fate dictating who I had in my life and when. All I wanted was a carefree life with my pack, and the freedom to do anything I chose.

I had friends up and down the Strip, performers of all varieties, and I was itching to see one in particular, to know exactly how different my life was now.

Farrah already had the door to her place open, waiting for me after I'd messaged her my ETA before leaving the pack house. She waved excitedly to me as I pulled to a stop in her driveway. The pretty omega had her brown hair tied in a braid, her freckles more pronounced than the last time I'd seen her. "Hey, cutie, long time no see. You usually pop up sooner after your shows."

I hovered by my car, half-afraid to get closer.

"Everything okay?" she asked. "I was expecting to be up against a wall already."

I flexed my fingers on the car door, working up some courage before closing it and moving toward her.

"Okay, you're kinda freaking me out. Can you say something?" Farrah tipped her head, examining me.

"Sorry. Things have been fucking weird lately."

"Wanna talk about it? I know that's not really how things work between us, but if you need to, I'm right here."

She held open her arms, offering me a hug, and just for a moment I let myself accept it...just to see. Touching Farrah, which had once been second nature, an ease I had shared with lovers, felt strange now. Farrah's scent—strawberry—was as sweet as it had always been, but I had no reaction to it, or the warmth of her, or the big doe eyes she was giving me.

"I shouldn't be here."

"Hey, it's okay. Tell me what's going on."

"The pack has an omega."

"Oh, whoa." She stepped back. "When were you planning on telling me you guys were courting someone?"

"We're *not*. We didn't—"

She looked at me curiously. "I'm gonna need a little more info here."

"She's a scent match. Kai bonded her during a show."

"Oh, shit," Farrah breathed. "So we're done, then?"

I crossed my arms over my chest, letting my petulance win. "I didn't want to bond her."

"And you still don't now?"

"Fuck if I know, Fare. I just wanted to keep doing what I was doing."

Farrah raised one eyebrow at me. "Well, you can't."

"I'm aware of that." I sat down on her concrete stairs and she tentatively joined me.

"Sucks for me. We had a lot of fun." She sighed, resting her chin on her palm. "What's wrong with the omega that makes you not want to bond her?"

"Nothing," I growled out. "I wish there was something so I could justify being annoyed. The others love her, and there's just so much fucking *pressure* to fall into line."

"They're pushing you for it?"

"No." My eye twitched. "They're being chill, but I know my choices are to accept her or leave the pack, and I don't want to leave. Feels like the walls are closing in and forcing me to choose one or the other immediately, and it's just making me feel worse. Fuck. If I could have gotten to know her outside of this, maybe I'd feel differently."

"Go to therapy," Farrah stage-whispered. "Give yourself a break. This is a huge change and it makes sense to me you'd feel that pressure. Maybe you should chat with a professional about it all? Either way, I'll say that she's probably feeling the exact same as you."

"What do you mean?"

"You're part of the pack. She's hopefully not wanting to

cause issues with an established unit, and so I'd bet you anything she's looking at you and feeling the same panic. I'm sure if you asked, she'd tell you she's worried about things working out between you two so it doesn't cause friction with the others."

"I..." I hadn't thought of it like that. Maybe Farrah was right and Callie felt those same shackles closing around her throat.

"Take some time to breathe," Farrah offered. "Obviously we're not going to play now, but if you want to hang out, I'm fine with that. I can call some friends to join us so you don't feel weird with it just being me."

"That would honestly be great. I need a few hours of space before I go back to the pack house."

Farrah patted my shoulder and popped to her feet. "Well, I'm honored you picked me for that space. Let me see who I can rustle up."

A handful of her friends joined us over the next half hour. I knew a few of them, other performers who called the city home. As much as I needed the time away, it also grated on me. The minutes ticked by, slowly ratcheting up the tension in my shoulders.

Maybe I should try to start over with Callie. We could go on a first date instead of staring down the barrel of the *together forever* gun. I knew I wasn't being fair to her, but my mouth kept running faster than my brain and my pride was too fucking strong to backtrack when I said something stupid.

I sat there for hours, watching people enjoy themselves around me, participating in conversation when someone thought to include me, but otherwise mostly stewing.

Farrah passed me a bottled water. "You look miserable and I can't use my normal method of fixing that."

I gave a bitter laugh. "I have one source for that method now and that tap isn't flowing."

"Pity for her. She's missing out on the best head this side of the Strip." Farrah grinned at me. "Go be nicer to her. You're a hard man to resist when you're relaxed. Take her out dancing. Ooh! Take her to my show! On a night I'm not performing so it's not hella weird," she clarified. "The show is so fucking hot. No way she'd be able to resist you after that. Spend time with her and enjoy yourself."

"You really think I should?"

"Of course you should." Farrah sat down next to me with her own drink. "Just because you feel like something is inevitable doesn't mean you get to take it for granted. At least try for Kai. He's a sweetheart, and if you're wigging out an omega he's bonded to, you're passing that along to him. Now, I'm not kicking you out, but I *am* going to point out that you look just as miserable as when you arrived, so I dunno that the space is helping."

She was right. I'd wanted to breathe air that didn't smell like Callie so I could have a clear head for half a second, but now that her scent was nowhere to be found, I was craving it. "I should probably go home."

"Not a bad plan. Or invite your omega out." Farrah shrugged. "Either way, you need to quit moping."

With a sigh I got to my feet and accepted her goodbye hug, probably the last one we'd have. "You're a good friend, Fare. Thanks for today."

"You're more than welcome."

"Someone better hurry their ass and snap you up."

"I think that regularly," she said with a laugh. "Good luck with your omega."

I took the long way home, looping the city and blasting

188

music to settle myself. I'd fought so hard to get away from the weight of expectation that had choked me all my life, and every time I thought about Callie, it was like crashing myself against that wall on repeat.

Instead of going straight home, I diverted into Red Rock Canyon. There was nothing much to see in the dark, but it would be quiet and I wasn't eager to face any of the pack quite yet. When I'd first come out here from New York, I'd gone to the canyon a lot simply to get away from the city. On occasion I'd actually hike, but more often I'd pick one of the overlooks and sit, watching the light play over the stone. It looked so unlike where I'd grown up, and that had always been a comfort, a reminder that I was far enough away that I could create the life I wanted instead of the one expected of me.

I'd have to go home eventually, and I did, turning onto the road back only when I was reasonably certain the others would be in bed, if not asleep, by the time I got there.

The pack house was dark when I arrived. Small blessings.

Tomorrow I would work on making amends.

The moment I stepped inside I was confronted by Callie's scent. It was *everywhere*. Her stress, her desire, her mere existence coating every surface and snaking through my system like a venom I couldn't stop. I hadn't realized how strong it would be after hours without it. All of my nerves primed, cock tenting, and heart pounding to be submerged in her candied apple scent again.

Fuck me.

I pushed ahead until I hit the doors to the courtyard and stepped out into the night air to get my head on straight.

A sharp inhalation drew my attention, and I turned to see Callie sitting in one of the wicker egg chairs with her phone in hand.

189

"What are you doing out here?" I asked, trying very hard not to focus on the way the screen light accented the curve of her lips and the barely there nightgown that dipped entirely too low for my brain to manage.

"I couldn't sleep. It's so nice out tonight I thought I would read out here for a bit."

"The others weren't successful in tiring you out?" I regretted the words the moment her lips pursed. "I'm sorry. I've been...on edge."

Callie snorted. "Is that what you're calling it?"

I flexed my fingers, trying to dispel the desire to touch her, even though her scent hung in the air like a lure, calling me.

"Why do you always do that?" she asked, tilting her head like it would give her some insight into my internal workings.

"I thought it would be better to do that than to touch you when you don't want me to."

Candied apple reached across the distance to me. "Oh."

"I should go to bed. It's been a long day."

"Wait." Callie set down her phone and padded over to me, bringing that maddening scent with her.

Every instinct tuned to her. I should've ignored her and left, but her simple request had me rooted to the spot. "For what?"

"Did you, um, have fun tonight?" She was looking at me with enormous eyes, her breath quickening.

"Not particularly, no."

"Oh. Why not? I thought you had a date."

"Something of the sort."

Her scent turned sharp, her lips bowing into a frown. "What does that mean?"

"It means I went to a lover's door and couldn't fucking

bring myself to touch them because all I was thinking about was *you*."

"M-me?" Candied apple filled my nose, a sweetness I couldn't escape.

"Yes, *you*. I can't even breathe or think in my home because you're *everywhere*." I knew I sounded frustrated, perhaps bordering on angry, but it kept coming out regardless. "Even when you're not around, you linger, and when I leave, you follow. I have carved out my entire life after suffocating under the weight of expectation from my family, moved across the damn country so I could stop doing what others expected of me, and then *you* appear. A mate, decreed by fate, and solidified into our lives with a bond none of us had a choice in. I refuse to fall in line with you."

"I'm not asking you to," she said softly, her arms wrapped around herself. "I just want us to get along. You don't have to like me as a mate, but we're still pack and we should be friends. Is that so hard?"

"*Yes*," I hissed. "Because I don't know *how* to. You provoke every desire and I refuse to follow that path because it's what fate decided. If things were different, if—"

"I provoke your desire?"

Those fucking perfect lips were parted, her breath coming fast, only drawing my attention to her breasts, to how they'd been pressed together when she'd crossed her arms. Her scent was trying to drown me, to steal my senses and coax me to give in. "I don't know what you want me to say."

She swallowed hard. "Maybe I don't want you to say anything. Maybe I want you to prove it."

Fuck. Me.

Callie surged up on her toes the second I leaned toward her, putting that perfect, delicious mouth to mine in a kiss that had me backing her up against the wall. The moan out of her melted what little resistance I'd been clinging to. When her hands dragged me closer, inviting me to take, I listened, scooping her up until she was pinned and kissing me with a desperation I'd thought only *I* had for *her*.

Apparently I was wrong about that.

Chapter 25
Callie

I had taken a chance. A desperate one that was against my better judgment but also made my instincts sing. Confirmation that he wanted me had snuck into the heart of me and lit a match to the buried embers there. Even if I wasn't sure of his mind, his body certainly left no question. Amir touched me like he craved me down to the depths of his soul, and for all that his confusing rejections and reactions twisted me up, I knew for certain Jerry had never touched me the way Amir was now.

His hands cradled my thighs, trapping me between his body and the wall while he devoured my kiss like he couldn't get enough. I clung hard, hooking my elbow behind his neck and whimpering against his lips, trying to keep up. Something about having my feet off the ground and a warm alpha body pressed to me reduced me to my base form. Just an omega who needed her alpha, nothing more, nothing less.

He nudged my head to the side with his and arced down to get his teeth on my throat, sending a cascade of pleasure sliding over my nerves. Slick dampened my core with every delicious grind of his hips against me. Relief poured through me at knowing he still wanted me without the influence of the heat or the urging of the contract.

Amir set me on my feet and dropped to his knees, hoisting the hem of my nightgown. "Are you seriously running around with no panties?"

"They get in the way."

He looked up at me and I braced one hand on his shoulders just to stay upright with the amount of fire in those eyes. "Tell me to stop right now if you don't want me."

"But I *do* want you." The words felt thick on my tongue. I'd never been particularly good at voicing what I wanted, but I knew Amir wouldn't let me get away with that.

A second later, my thigh was propped on his shoulder and his mouth was buried against me. I made an absolutely feral sound when his tongue flicked my clit, and slid my hands into his hair as he lifted my other thigh. He kept me pinned like that, his hands holding my ass while his mouth ruined me. I only remembered bits and pieces of having him during the heat, but my body apparently kept the knowledge of every touch stored away; I felt like I was going to burst into flames.

If I had told past Callie she'd have had two different alphas in the same day eating her out, she probably would've fainted.

I mewled and squirmed, holding onto him with shaking hands and quivering thighs. His thumb stroked through my folds before pressing into me. I leaned my head against the wall, trying to catch my breath while he seemed entirely intent on making that impossible. Amir alternated sucking on my clit with rapid flicks of his tongue until I broke apart in his grip in a rush of slick. He groaned and kept lapping at me until I was half-delirious.

Amir got to his feet, folding my legs with the movement to brace against the wall, my knees hooked over his arms, leaving me totally exposed.

"Be a good girl and undo my pants for me."

I opened the button and zipper with shaking fingers and extracted his cock from the confines of his clothing. He wasted no time getting it inside me, choking off his name on my lips as he filled me in one swift motion.

"Fucking hell, princess."

I grabbed tight to his hair and dragged his mouth to mine, his sun-baked cedar filling my senses. "Give me everything," I demanded. "I can take it."

I only half believed my own words when he fucked in hard and I saw stars. Clinging desperately for some sort of anchor barely helped as Amir drove into me with every ounce of friction there had been between us since Kai had bonded me.

I knew sex wasn't the answer to everything, but it probably wouldn't hurt the situation. He needed to get out his frustrations and I would much rather he do it this way than how he had been.

My core tightened with every thrust, and when he turned his head to bite my wrist where I was holding on to his hair, I came all over his cock in another gush of slick and a scream I couldn't muffle. Pleasure sparked up my arm and straight to my clit as Amir sucked at the scent gland there, his hips still grinding against me.

Helplessly pinned, I could only let myself be open to everything he wanted to pour into me. My brain was going to melt out my ears at this rate. The glide of him sinking into me on repeat soothed the deepest parts of my mind. My alpha wanted me and he was taking me. I couldn't breathe well enough through my panting to purr.

Amir released my wrist and I whimpered at the loss of his bite.

"Again," I gasped. "Please, god, fu—"

He turned and bit the other wrist, sending me spiraling all over again, clamping down so hard on his cock his movements stuttered, and he moaned against my skin, bucking hard one more time before heat burst from the tip of him and his knot swelled between us. My eyes rolled back, mouth dropping open in a silent scream as he overwhelmed everything.

"That's my good girl, princess." He licked my wrist. "Taking everything your alpha wants to give you. Your cunt feels like heaven."

I whined when I regained the ability to breathe, my muscles twitching as I floated down from the high. Moving was still next to impossible with him holding me, but I wasn't sure I'd have the strength to try anyway. I focused instead on taking long, deep breaths while I trembled in his arms.

"You okay?"

"Yeah, just...you're a lot to take outside of a heat." I wiggled, a moan sneaking out. My body was still getting used to knots.

"I'll take that as a compliment." The kiss he dropped to my upturned mouth was softer than I expected out of him. I sighed into it, scratching softly at his scalp and pulling him closer. He very carefully rearranged me so my legs could wrap around his waist in a more comfortable position. "Should I take you inside or do you want to stay out here for a while?"

Going inside felt like it might break the delicate spell we'd woven. "Out here."

Amir carried me to a lounge chair, stealing the blanket from the chair I'd been reading on, and flipping it over us after he'd stretched out.

I plucked at the fabric of his shirt. "Off."

His eyes gleamed. "Does that mean you're taking off that nightgown too?"

I lifted my arms in response and he sat up, pulling it over my head and catching one of my nipples in his mouth the second it was bare. The sweep of his hands up my back pressed me closer. I'd thought he'd have had his fill, but he acted like a man starved for the taste of me.

My pussy went wild under the attention, squeezing his knot so hard I was right back to my desperate clinging. The quick snap of his teeth had me squeaking, the sharpness giving way to a warm ache, and he pulled away with eyes full of mischief. "I remember *everything* you liked during the heat."

"I suppose it's helpful that at least one of us does." I traced the planes of his face, wondering what was going on inside his head.

But then I caught the scent of strawberries on him, faint but distinct, and I froze instantly. A growl leapt out of me.

Amir scrutinized me. "What's wrong?"

"I can smell her on you." Agony boiled in my chest. I had no claim on him except the scent match, but it hurt nonetheless. The mystery woman had been a hypothetical before I caught her scent, far easier to push out of my mind.

"We didn't do anything."

I believed him. Her scent would've been a lot stronger if they had. "Why did you go?"

Amir's growl was low and smooth, raising the little hairs on my arms. I couldn't go anywhere while he was knot-deep, and truthfully, I regretted asking as soon as the words had left my mouth.

"Because I had a whole life before you. She deserved an explanation. More than a text message that she was never going to see me again."

I dropped my gaze, setting a palm on his chest and feeling the thunder of his heart against my hand. Desire for him still burned strongly in me, but mostly I wanted to sink my teeth into his skin so the whole world would know he was mine. I couldn't do that until the next heat, and certainly not without his permission, but smelling another omega on him was turning my insides into a tangled mess. I followed the compulsion—not to bite, but still to claim him—and dragged my cheeks and wrists over his skin to scent mark anywhere I could reach, and he let me. It wouldn't change anything, but it made me feel better at least.

"She's a good person and she was a good friend," he said softly. "I needed to see her, to know..."

"To know what?" I asked quietly, barely daring to form the words.

Amir let out a sigh, tracing his fingertips up my arm until he was cradling my throat, his thumb sweeping softly down the length of it. "To know how tight a grip you have on me. It doesn't seem fair."

It *wasn't* fair, and I knew that, but instinct didn't care about fair. "And what did you find?"

"I could barely make myself get to her door. I spent all of this week wanting to get your scent out of my head so I could think, and as soon as I did, the only thing I wanted was to breathe you in again."

I stared into his dark eyes, and even in the dim light I could see the vulnerability there. It wrapped itself up with heat and anger. "I don't want to keep you from her if she's who you would rather be with."

It was only a half truth. I didn't want him to be with me only because he had to be. Would I be devastated by him pursuing another omega? Absolutely. But I wasn't so cruel that I would stop him from pursuing someone else who already made him happy.

I had Kai and Diego, and they were wonderful, but this whole pack was mine, and I was theirs, even if it was fated and not choice. I'd had the luxury of my previous partner destroying everything before I'd scent matched this pack. What would I have done differently if my relationship had been intact and I'd met these alphas under other circumstances? I genuinely wasn't sure, and I held on to that, trying to understand why he had gone to someone else.

"I don't want her," he said stiffly. "I used to. I thought maybe I could evade fate by trying to go back to her, but that obviously didn't go as planned."

"And—" I swallowed hard. "—when you came back here? Did you have me just because you couldn't have her?"

"No," Amir growled. "I might be struggling with everything, but I'm not *that* much of an asshole."

"Why *are* you struggling so much with it?"

He sighed, leaning back on the lounger and bringing me with him so we were chest to chest, breaking our eye contact. "I grew up desperate to please my parents. I did everything they asked, adhered to every single expectation, and cleaved away whole parts of myself to ensure I fit into the box they created for me. They dictated my friends, what I studied, all my extracurriculars. I don't even *like* physics, but I made sure I was the best at it to get their approval.

199

"When I got offered a job at a company in Vegas straight out of university, I jumped on it. They were much more forgiving of my going far away because they wanted my career to be a success. They still think I work for that same company. I quit before my first year there was over because I hated every second of it and I couldn't stand imagining the rest of my life looking that way."

I listened in silence, absorbing the words, his heart racing against my ear.

"And then you appeared when I had finally settled into a life that felt like one of my own making, where *I* got to make my own choices. But I didn't get to choose you. Fate dropped you into our laps and it all just whiplashed me right back to the feeling of being backed into a corner, slowly cutting away the pieces of me to follow a path someone else had picked out for me."

I curled my fingers over his shoulder. "I think I know a thing or two about cutting away pieces of yourself. It's not the same, but I absolutely did that with my ex. I made myself smaller, more palatable, trying to win approval I don't think I ever actually got."

His growl rumbled in my ear. "I'm going to push that man off a bridge the next time I see him."

"I don't want you to go to jail."

"I could be stealthy about it."

I laughed quietly, something inside me finally settling now that I knew what he was thinking. "I feel like I understand you so much better now. I won't like it if you don't want to be with me, but I'm never going to force you."

"I do want you, but wanting to *be with* you in some ways feels like betraying my younger self."

"Did you know that four months from now I was going to get married?"

His grip on me tightened.

"I understand what it's like to look at who you were and know that person would be upset seeing you now, but I'm trying to adjust. I want to build a life that makes me happy, and I don't *know* if I could make you happy, but I hope I could, one day."

Amir didn't speak for a long while, only stroked my hair. Eventually, he said very softly, "Is it enough if I try?"

Was it? "I think so. I suppose that's all I can expect from anyone, given how weird this situation is." Honestly, I never thought I'd get this far with him at all. Trying was a blessing I hadn't expected.

His sigh lifted me and we settled together. His knot had gone down enough for me to slip off, but I didn't go far. He lifted his arm for me to tuck myself at his side, ensuring the blanket covered all of me, though I really only needed the warmth of his body.

"I'm sorry I've made things difficult for you." His voice was quiet, but felt so much louder when I was this close. "If it's any consolation, I promise I've made things very difficult for myself too."

Chapter 26
Callie

"Good morning, little dove."

I peeled open one eye to see Kai, Diego, and Miles with soft, amused smiles on their lips, the brilliant blue sky behind them.

"I see you and Amir sorted out your differences."

It took me a second to process the words, to realize where I was and *whom* I was wrapped around. Amir was stretched out on the lounge chair, one arm pillowing the back of his head, the other wrapped around me. The blanket covering us had slipped down a considerable amount and Kai adjusted it for me.

"I'd have let you sleep, but you're a bit lacking in melanin and the sun is going to pop over the roof soon. I'd hate for you to turn into a lobster because you didn't wake up in time." He dropped down next to me, pressing a kiss to my bare shoulder. "Are you all right? It felt like you had fun, but a lot was going on and I wanted to be sure."

"Worried I took advantage of her?" Amir's voice startled me and I jerked against him.

"If I thought you had, I'd have already drowned you in the pool," Kai said sweetly, but there was an edge in his eyes. "I felt everything through the bond, by the way. Don't think I don't know you upset her."

"We worked it out," I assured him. "I think, anyway?"

Amir sighed, his fingertips gliding up my side. "As much as can be worked out in a single night."

"I think breakfast is in order," Diego said, offering me the slinky robe I had purchased on our shopping trip. I really had no reason to feel uncomfortable running around naked, except for the fact that I hadn't been with Miles yet, though I was still feeling a little vulnerable with Amir. Once the robe was cinched around my waist, I let Kai usher me inside.

A bowl of sliced fruit was already on the table and a bowl of batter was sitting next to the waffle iron ready to go.

"You were busy this morning."

Kai shrugged. "Gotta make sure my omega is well fed."

I couldn't quite bring my eyes to reach Miles's questioning gaze. I wasn't opposed to being with him, but he seemed intent on keeping distance between us. It wasn't the same sort of rejection I had felt from Amir, but I still didn't like it.

"Sweetheart, while you're here, I've got a form for you to fill out." Miles slid his tablet over to me.

"Form?"

"To register your bond with Kai. Just a formality. I already had Kai fill out his."

203

"Oh, sure." The form was simple enough since it was just to collect information and we were already bonded, so they just needed to document it.

Amir joined us a few minutes later, dressed in his pants from yesterday and carrying the rest of the clothing that had been scattered around the courtyard. He disappeared upstairs to get dressed before seating himself at the table.

I tried to focus on my waffle instead of staring at him like I wanted to. My thoughts turned as I sliced into each crispy square. "Do you ever think about how I'm not the only one who was fated to you guys?"

Amir lifted one questioning brow. "What do you mean?"

"You're all fated to one another, aren't you? What are the odds otherwise of the four of you finding each other and all being a scent match for me? Maybe fate put all of you on the path to one another in hopes that when you met, you would all love each other enough to form a pack."

"I never thought about that part," Amir confessed.

"That's because you were too busy freaking out over me."

He gave me an exasperated smile. "You're not wrong about that. I don't know if I like that concept either, that all of my life was actually predetermined? From the degree I took to the company that offered me a job where I had the opportunity to meet everyone?"

"But you're happy, aren't you?"

"I am," he sighed. "For the most part, anyway."

"I think," said Diego, "that even if fate is responsible for dropping us in front of one another, we still had a choice after that. Fate gives us opportunities, but it can't force us to do anything about them."

"Plus, we're never going to know what's actually fate and

what's not," Kai added. "Seems stressful to worry about that part."

"I think it was fate that I ran into Callie exactly when I did," said Miles, "but I don't think it forced her to accept my offer."

"I think so too. If I'd made a different choice, we'd all be apart right now." I nudged Amir with my toes beneath the table. "If I ask you to hang out again, are you gonna be weird about it?"

He hesitated for a second. "No. I mean, we can hang out, but I can't guarantee I won't be weird at any point."

"I'll take it. We can be awkward weirdos together."

Kai and Diego laughed.

"I love how she's managed to distill down your core elements," Diego said. "The rest of the world might think you're suave and smooth, but we know the truth."

Amir flipped him the bird, focusing on me. "Let me take you out somewhere later tonight. I would take you now, but we'd be trapped in the car with how fucking hot it is outside."

"Where are we going?"

"If I told you, it wouldn't be a surprise."

"Maybe I don't like surprises."

"Do you not?" Miles asked.

"Honestly, I don't really know. I feel like most of my experience with them has been negative, but I'm sure there could be good surprises."

"Well, I'll tell you that it'll be outdoors and we'll head out a bit before sunset. Is that enough detail for now? I won't make you hike."

"I don't mind hiking when it's a reasonable temperature. Drag me out all you want in the spring or late autumn, but in summer I'm an indoorsy girl."

"Can I take you somewhere, too?" Miles asked. "I have to go into the office today, but maybe tomorrow?"

"Sure, that sounds good. I've got to pick up a decent computer since mine got tossed. Thank god I can access all the projects on the cloud because I have client work I'll need to start on soon. Could I borrow one of the cars?"

"I can take you," Kai offered. "We'll pick you out some kickass hardware. My treat."

"You can't treat me on *everything*."

Kai narrowed his eyes and booped the tip of my nose. "Watch me."

"I haven't had to touch a single dollar in my account yet. I'm itchy to spend some of my own money."

"And you'll get to," Kai promised. "Later."

"What am I supposed to do all day if you're being hogged?" Diego asked.

"What did you do all day before me?"

Diego sighed dramatically. "Fine, I'll go work out so I can keep this rockin' bod."

I laughed so hard I snorted, covering my face with my hands. "Don't make me laugh when I'm eating. I'll die."

We poked fun at each other all through breakfast and it was so wildly different from all my mornings with Jerry, and even my family growing up, that I wasn't entirely sure what to do with it. They felt like a family, one that was happy to welcome me in, and I liked it more than I expected to.

Kai wasted no time in sweeping me off to the electronics store. I tried to be economical about what I was choosing while also not sacrificing performance because video editing software could be hard on the machines. Kai made me do at least one step up in quality for every piece I chose, and he took me for lunch while they put the PC together for me.

"You're a very stubborn man, you know that?" I told him over our shawarma.

"You need nice stuff to do your work," he insisted. "No sense in getting something shitty and then having it sound like it's going to take off into outer space every time you have to do anything."

"You're not *wrong*, but it was still a lot of money. I could've paid for at least some of it."

"Consider it a courting gift."

I pouted, but I couldn't argue with a courting gift.

"And now that I've gotten you alone and some food into your stomach, how are you feeling about everything?"

I stared into my shawarma. "A lot better than I have been, and honestly a million times better than I was expecting to be."

"I'm glad." He laid his hand over mine, stroking his thumb over my skin. "If I need to kick anyone's ass, you just let me know."

I laughed softly. "No ass kicking required, or at least none since Amir and I are doing better."

"You have no idea how glad all of us are that he pulled his head out of his ass about you."

"I think it might still be up there a *tiny* bit, but more like a little ass hat instead of living all the way in there."

Kai started laughing and immediately choked on his food.

"No dying. I just got you." I patted his back and nudged his water bottle closer.

He slurped down some water and recovered himself. "I'll do my absolute best not to die. We have one more stop to make today."

"Where?"

"Furniture shopping. Unless you'd rather live in Diego's room forever?"

207

I frowned. "I'm totally hogging his space."

"Do *not* feel bad at all for that. He's been so fucking smug that you picked his room to nest in. I think he'd rather light himself on fire than ever ask you to move out of it. But I figure at a certain point living with us, you'll want a space that's exclusively yours. We're all totally down for sharing and you can sleep in any bed you want at any time, but you deserve your own space, too."

My bottom lip wobbled, emotion clogging my throat. "I've never actually had my own space before. I shared a room with my sister growing up, I had roommates in the college dorms, and then I shared a room with Jerry. I mean, I had the nest at the apartment, but that was my office too since Jerry didn't like my work stuff around the apartment, and he kind of went in and out as he pleased, and he didn't like me to spend too long in there or have too much stuff."

"All the more reason we need to outfit you with the perfect space. We'll get you a lock on the door so you can kick us out, get whatever furniture you want, any decorations. This will be coming out of the pack joint account so we're all in on it. I promise we have enough to cover anything you might need, so don't be afraid to point out anything that catches your fancy."

I sniffled, trying to wrap my head around the fact that these alphas really did want to take care of me, wanted to give me the world. I could already feel the tears working themselves up and I was desperately trying to hold them back.

"You're sitting too far away." My voice shook. Kai dragged his chair over until the edges of it were touching mine, and I locked my fingers in his shirt, curling my legs over his.

"Come here, little dove." He scooped me all the way onto his lap, wrapping his arms around me. The sweetness of the gesture had tears streaking down my cheeks. I'd expected him to tell me to stop being a baby in public, the way too many others had told me in the past, but he just purred softly and said, "Cry all you need."

Was I going to question their kindness forever? I was only starting to see the damage Jerry had done to me, and I wasn't sure how long it would take me to shake it, if I even could.

I had lived so long in that state of complacency and I had to relearn myself in this new context.

Kai continued to hold me until my tears had dried themselves out, his purr carefully untangling the knots of my stress until I could breathe easy. "If you're not feeling up to shopping, I can take you home."

Home. It really was starting to feel that way.

"I'm okay," I promised.

"If you're sure." He kissed the top of my head. "Are you done with your food?"

"I'm stuffed."

"How about a nice lemonade for the road? It'll keep you cool enough you won't melt when we step outside."

I nuzzled the underside of his chin. "I like lemonade."

After dealing with the remnants of lunch, we got a pair of drinks and headed off to the furniture store.

An absolutely gorgeous sleigh bed caught my eye the moment we stepped inside. It was easily big enough for the whole pack and I ran my fingers over the glossy wood. It had optional steps and a railing that could be brought up on both sides to turn it into a proper nest.

"Want me to ask if it's in stock?"

"It's so much."

"Anything that fits a pack is going to be expensive, but it's an investment. We need enough space for you to be comfortable regardless of how many of us you have in there with you."

209

I chewed my lip. I really did love it, but I still wasn't used to anyone wanting to spend money on me. Kai worked me around to it, and once we learned they had one bed left in that style it hadn't taken much more to push me over the edge to say yes to the bed.

"It's going to be so weird having a fresh bed. I need to get all of you rolling around on the sheets ASAP."

Kai laughed, drawing me close and tipping up my chin so he could kiss me. Jerry hadn't kissed me in public since the days of college parties, and here Kai was, broadcasting to the whole world in this store that we were together. Like he was proud to be seen with me...

Apparently I was just going to be all up in my feelings today. Kai kept his arm wrapped around my shoulders as we checked out more items in the store. Diego had stocked me up on a lot of nesting supplies, but I picked out some sheet sets that would fit the new bed, and Kai and I sprawled out on half a dozen mattresses to test if I liked them before I settled on one that felt like rolling on a cloud.

I would have to wait for everything to be delivered, but each piece we ordered, even though I wasn't very good at accepting how much money they were spending on me, definitely helped me feel more grounded.

They really were investing in me. I didn't get the sense that any of them would twist it around into me owing them like Jerry had done anytime he actually bought me some kind of gift.

I really needed to stop comparing them to him, but I couldn't help it. The differences were so drastic I couldn't quite believe what I had tolerated for so long.

"You're going to look so beautiful spread out on that new bed, little dove," Kai told me as we slipped back into the car to head to the pack house. He slipped his fingers into my hair and drew me close, devouring my lips until my perfume saturated every molecule of air around us. "I suppose I should get you home so Amir doesn't accuse me of hogging you."

"I do love being hogged, but I'm also very, very curious what his plans for tonight are."

Maybe this would be my first good surprise.

Chapter 27
Callie

The handoff was almost instantaneous once we got back to the pack house, Amir waiting in the shade for our arrival. He opened my door for me, let me take a quick bathroom break and give Kai a goodbye kiss, and then had me bundled into his vehicle, the AC already on full blast.

"You're getting to know me so well," I said, leaning into the chilled air flowing from the vents.

"Don't want you sweating all over my seats."

I turned to stick my tongue out at him, relieved at the playful smirk on his face to know he wasn't actually serious.

"Don't stick that out unless you're going to use it, princess. Might give me ideas."

I sucked my tongue back in and pressed my thighs

together, wiggling to get comfortable before putting on my seatbelt. "Do I get to know where we're going now that we're in the car?"

"We're going to one of my favorite places," he replied. "At some point we'll get you out to all of the national parks around here, but we're going to start small with Red Rock Canyon."

I immediately tried to snoop on my phone and Amir put his hand over the screen.

"Quit that. The view has to be a surprise."

I pouted at him and closed the page, turning my phone face-down.

"If you don't put that pout away, I'm going to pull over and bite it."

My perfume filled the car. "That's terrible motivation for me to stop."

He looked so pleased with himself. Amir swung us onto the road out of the city and settled comfortably in his seat, calmly reaching across the space to gently hold the back of my neck.

"It won't take long to get there. I make this trip whenever I need some time for myself."

It warmed me down to my toes that he wanted to include me in a place he kept to himself. The sun ahead of us was a little bit blinding, but we swooped into the shade of the mountains quickly, passing a sign that said *Red Rock Canyon National Conservation Area*.

"Close your eyes."

"Okay, but I'm trusting you like me enough that you won't leave me out here," I said with an awkward laugh. Probably not the best attempt at teasing...

"One, I wouldn't do that even if I *didn't* like you, and two, the others would toss me off a cliff if I even thought about it, which I never would. I just want the view to be a surprise."

I dutifully closed my eyes and waited. The radio was playing the top forty quietly and I allowed myself to relax into my seat until Amir pulled to a stop.

"Keep them closed."

I did so, waiting while he turned off the car and a moment later my door opened. Amir unbuckled me and scooped me right out of the seat. I koala-clung to him and buried my face against him.

"I'm going to put you on your feet now. Just let me get you angled before you open your eyes, okay?"

"Yes, sir."

My feet settled on top of gravelly ground and Amir shifted me just so, pressing up against my back with his arms around my waist. "Open."

The expanse of stone in front of me looked like it was lit ablaze by the sun, a rainbow of red and gold spilling over the undulating rock in a brilliant display of light and shadow. I couldn't breathe for how beautiful it was. Like art come to life.

"Oh my god," I whispered. "How is it real?"

Amir purred behind me. "It might be my favorite spot on the planet. I know bigger and grander places exist, but this one feels like mine. I've never even come out here with the pack. Not this spot, anyway. We've gone for hikes during the day, but they've never been to this particular viewpoint with me."

"Thank you for sharing it with me."

I leaned back against him, held awestruck by the view while he purred away. We didn't speak for a while, just watched the sun slowly sink and the shadows slant to add darker shades to the rainbow. When the sun was finally behind the top of the mountains to the west, Amir sighed and squeezed me to him.

"Do you like it?"

"I've never seen anything so beautiful."

"It looks like the exact opposite of where I grew up, and when I moved out here, when I'd wake up in a cold sweat from the pressure of expectation, or even the memory of it, I would drive out here. It's so alien compared to the forests of the Catskill Mountains, and that difference was the best anchor I could have to know I had escaped the person I used to be."

"I'm glad you had somewhere to come that made you feel better. You didn't like who you used to be?"

"More that I don't recognize that person. I love my parents, my family, and I was good at what they chose for me to do, but I never felt like me until I met the pack and could finally breathe."

"You keep surprising me by how alike we are. I'm such a short time away from my old life and I still don't even recognize it when I turn it over in my head. Like a story someone else told me instead of something I had lived."

"That's exactly it." His hands swept down me and back up, settling on my arms. "This isn't the best place to see stars, but if you want to stay for a while, we still get a pretty good view."

Encouraged by him sharing this place with me, I spun and hooked my arms around his neck, standing on my toes for a kiss he readily gave. "Keep me out all night if you want. I like having a chance to get to know you."

"I didn't pack for an overnight, but we can enjoy it out here for a while."

He tucked me back into the vehicle and we drove further in until we reached a valley with some tables. I hovered in the shade of the mountain while he unpacked what he had brought with us. Amir set two neatly folded blankets on the

215

edge of the picnic table, and spread a third over the top before putting the cooler and two flashlights on top of it.

While we waited for the light to disappear entirely, we wandered through the shade while the air was still warm but rapidly cooling. There wasn't a ton of plant life, but we did see a few adorable lizards and I got to touch the beautiful red stone. Once it was dark enough to haul out the flashlights, we settled back in at the picnic table. Amir sat cross-legged and patted his lap for me to climb into it.

"Now we wait," he said.

I was cozy as hell in his arms. "Did you bring us snacks? What's in the cooler?"

"Water, cola, gummy bears, chocolate bars, and mini cheese."

"You monster, those gummy bears are gonna be hard as fucking rocks." I tried to reach for the cooler, but he held me fast.

"I like them with a bit of chew."

"The allure of gummy bears is that they're *soft*." I whined and he finally let me grab the edge of the cooler to free them to come up to the outside temperature.

"At least let me have some while they're cold."

I fed him the gummy bears myself, popping them between his lips while I asked questions about his life, finding out that he had two brothers, had broken his arm falling off the monkey bars when he was eight, was allergic to horses, and never turned down a dumpling.

"I feel like you need to take me on a dumpling crawl so I can taste all of the best ones the city has to offer."

"That would take us at least a week of eating them for every meal."

"Oh no," I mock gasped, "more time with a beautiful alpha. However will I survive?"

He nipped my earlobe, making me squeak. "Are you turning into a brat now that you feel comfortable?"

"Maybe." I shrugged. "I'm figuring out who I am around people who want me to be happy."

I never would have dared to sass Jerry.

Amir was quiet for a long moment before pulling me even closer and resting his chin on my head. "Every time I learn something new, it makes me want to push your ex off a cliff and give you the fucking moon just to prove a point."

"I don't need the moon. I'm just glad I have room to breathe. I think what I'm quickly learning is that it's been a long time since I felt safe."

"If I have my way, that's the only way you'll feel until we all die."

I turned my head, drawing him down for a kiss as the first stars winked awake in the sky. I didn't know what to do with a future like that stretched out in front of me, but if the days ahead were anything like today, I was going to be the happiest omega to ever live.

Chapter 28
Miles

Amir had brought Callie home late, so I let her sleep as long as she needed, waking early and getting as much work done as I could in the meantime. When Callie finally made her way downstairs, looking sleepy, beautiful, and content, she floated straight across the kitchen to where I was sitting at the table and draped herself against my back.

"Good morning."

"Good morning, sweetheart. Did you have fun last night?" I took one of her hands hanging in front of me and brought the back of it to my lips.

"Mhmm." She nodded and slid into the chair next to me. "We're going out today?"

"If you still want to, yes."

"Yes, please. I'm feeling so fancy with four men to take me out on the town."

"Would you rather eat breakfast here or go out? There's no wrong answer."

"Could I have a tiny breakfast here and we get something out when I've worked up an appetite?"

"I'm fine with that. I'll be here when you're ready to go. No rush."

Diego was the first of the pack to join us, immediately moving to put together some toast and fruit for Callie while she sipped her orange juice.

Once Callie was fed and dressed, I popped her in the car. "I know if you're staying with us you'll have plenty of time to explore everything the city has to offer, but it sounded like you saw so little on your vacation, and I can't let that stand. Take your pick between the gondolas, zip line, or Ferris wheel."

"I've wanted to go on the gondolas forever. I know they're super cheesy, but they're so cute." She looked so sheepish as she said it, and I wanted to immediately grant her wish.

"Gondolas it is."

The trip into the depths of the city was pretty short, even with traffic. I parked as near as we could get to the Venetian, but Callie still wilted going from the car to the hotel, instantly perking back up when she stepped into the air-conditioning.

"You'd think for how long you've lived in LA, you'd be a little better with the heat."

Callie pouted. "I can't help it that I still have the blood of a Seattle girl."

"I'm only teasing, sweetheart." She let me take her hand while we walked, making our way into the Venetian.

"I asked Jerry if we could go on them, but he said they were a waste of money."

Just hearing that made me wish her ex were still around simply so I could wallop him with the gondolier's pole and then drive the boat over him. "Nothing that makes you smile is a waste of money."

I was indeed rewarded with her beautiful smile when we got onto the gondolas. She leaned into me the whole ride, grinning as we were serenaded in Italian in a little boat beneath a fake sky. I didn't do a lot of tourist things in the city, but with Callie I loved every second of it.

"I was on the real gondolas on a high school trip," she told me, "and I have to admit, the inability to get sunburnt on these boats here is a huge perk."

"You and I can be sunburn twins if we ever go to Italy."

"I'm sure one of the others will bully us into wearing sunscreen to avoid that fate." She snuggled into my side, a soft rumbling from her buzzing against the arm I had looped around her.

"You're purring," I pointed out.

She snuggled closer as the boat spun around at the halfway point to head back, our gondolier singing his heart out. "I'm happy."

Those two words got my purr going as well.

The tension leaked out of my body bit by bit. She was so sweet and pleased next to me that when she drooped as we arrived back, I immediately paid for another round just to bring her smile back.

"You're way too cute," she commented.

"You're having fun. I don't want it to end too early."

"You don't have to spoil me, Miles."

"But I *want* to." I lifted our joined hands and kissed her knuckles. "I'm the only one of our group who gets to court you in the traditional sense. I'm not going to waste the opportunity."

"You don't have to court me. I'm kind of a done deal."

I shook my head insistently. "I'm never going to take an omega for granted, and I will kick the ass of any pack member who leans in that direction. Just because you're bonded to one of us doesn't mean you don't deserve all the fun of courting."

"I've never been courted before."

"Why not? You were with your ex for years and he never courted you in the beginning?"

Callie shrugged. "Jerry and I met in university, and things were casual until they weren't. I think I was just convenient, to be honest. He didn't put effort into much, and I never really thought to question it, I guess."

"And what about your crush you had on your twenty-first birthday? That was within the timeline of you being with your ex, isn't it?"

"We were on a break," she explained. "We'd been split for about two weeks, and as soon as this classmate found out I was single, he started to lay it on really thick. I think I was just really depressed, thinking about spending my birthday by myself, so I didn't say no when he asked me. Jerry showed back up in the picture about a week after that and I went back to him like an idiot."

"You are *far* from the only person to stick around in a lackluster relationship." The gondola came to a stop and I helped her out of the boat, wrapping my arm over her shoulders as we started to wander. "Did you have anyone in your life to show you what a good relationship actually looks like?"

Callie was quiet for a moment. "Not that I can think of. Everyone had friction or terrible taste. No one had relationships I'd consciously wanted to emulate, though I guess I did anyway."

"It's hardly your fault when you fell into the same pattern everyone around you was also in, right?"

"You're making me feel a lot better about wasting eight years of my life on an asshole."

"I prefer to think of it as a learning opportunity rather than a waste. Mostly, I just want you to accept that we're going to give you better."

"I'm not sure I know what to do with better."

"You'll get used to it in time," I promised. "I plan on giving you plenty of practice."

We spent a lovely couple of hours wandering the hotels along the Strip, sticking mostly to the ones that connected so I didn't have to take Callie into the heat. I'd forgotten how exciting the city could be for people who didn't experience it every day. Watching her marvel at the art exhibits and sumptuous decor, dragging me excitedly into selfies whenever she found something she loved, was cute as hell.

My phone rang and I sighed, seeing Kyle's name on the screen. "I'm so sorry, sweetheart, but I've got to take this call really quick."

"You go right ahead. I'm gonna check the shark reef times while you're busy."

I answered the call, immediately regretting it.

"Miles, what the *fuck* is going on with the schedule?"

I didn't have to guess what he meant. I'd been rearranging things to push the pack further and further down the calendar to keep them off the stage while we figured everything out. "I had to reschedule some things."

"Yeah, I can fucking see that. Why is Kai still on the payroll?"

"Because he's still contracted? Or were you planning on firing him for bonding someone?"

"Well, he sure as hell can't do the rest of his contract, can he?"

"It's illegal to fire someone for taking a bondmate," I pointed out, voice firm and the edge of a growl sneaking in.

"Fuck off. You know half of what we do isn't legal."

"I'm just trying to give everyone time to figure out what's happening."

"We don't *have* time. Amir and Diego need to stay on the schedule. Stop playing favourites and fucking around everything for your pack, or you'll be on the chopping block instead."

"They're a team," I insisted. "All the alpha groups are a team."

"If they can fuck a new omega each time, there's no reason in the world they can't add a new alpha to the mix."

Jeff and Kyle didn't have omegas or a pack. They didn't understand what they were asking and I was pretty sure they didn't care either. Their only concern was the money. "All the spots are filled. Why is this an issue?"

"You're abusing your power, and we're not going to let that little tramp fuck with everything."

A growl ripped free before I could stop it. Callie stared over at me with wide eyes.

"This is what we're talking about, Miles," Kyle said with a sigh. "Bringing her in was your fuckup and now you're trying to cover your ass, but we see what you're doing. Stop working things around her and do your job."

He hung up on me and I stared at the screen, trying to control the urge to hurl my phone against the marble floor.

"What's going on?" Callie asked, approaching me tentatively.

"Nothing you need to worry about, sweetheart. My boss is being a jackass."

She chewed her lip, scuffing the toe of her shoe against the floor. "Because of me?"

It technically *was* because of her, but it still wasn't her fault. "Management wants Diego and Amir to continue performing."

The growl that leapt out of Callie had every eye turning toward us.

"It's okay, sweetheart. Take a deep breath for me."

She did so, but I could see the words turning themselves over in her head, see her waging war against her omega instincts. "I know it's their job," she eventually said, "but they're mine."

"We should probably discuss all this at home and make a decision as a pack," I said.

Callie nodded sadly. Of course Kyle and Jeff would ruin my date with her. We couldn't work around this. Callie was our omega, and as much as her rational brain might be fine allowing her alphas to continue with their work, instinct didn't give a shit about that. The others would struggle to put on a performance, and it would probably push her to the edge of a breakdown to think about her alphas with another omega. If it were a case of having two omegas in our pack, that might be different, but we all knew that wasn't what this would be.

I cursed my job as we made the trip home. The others looked like they had recently arrived as well when we pulled up.

"Pack meeting," I announced.

Callie went straight to Kai, tucking her face against his chest.

"What's wrong?" Kai asked us.

"Let's all sit down first." We gathered around the breakfast table and I laid it all out as clearly as I could.

"And we can't do a wrongful termination suit if they fire me?" Kai asked.

"We could try, but I'm not sure we would win. You're not able to continue the job."

"This is fucked," Amir growled. "They can't force us."

"No, they can't, but if you can't fulfill the terms of the contract, you need to buy it out and if we do that, we might risk losing the pack house. We'd be out all that money and have all those streams of income cut off."

Callie whimpered. "This is all my fault."

"No," Diego snapped and immediately reined himself in. Much more quietly, he said, "No. This is management being a pair of dicks. They could work with us if they wanted to, but they don't."

"I don't want you to get in trouble." Callie looked around the table, her dark eyes luminous. "I don't want to be the reason you all lose your home. I would hate every single second of it, but if you need to keep doing your work, then I'll just suffer."

Chapter 29
Callie

They all stared at me like I had grown a second head.

"I could barely touch someone I've fucked multiple times," Amir pointed out. "I'm betting odds are extremely fucking slim that I could still perform the way they want me to."

"We'll figure something out, precious," Diego assured me. "Miles, hold them off for as long as you can, and we'll all see what else we can get for work."

"Let us worry about it, little dove. In the meantime, your room is ready if you want to look at it."

"Are you trying to distract me from despair?"

"Is it working?" Kai asked with a smile.

I pouted. I really did want to see the room.

They ushered me over to what had previously been the guest room. All the furniture had been changed out, the walls painted a warm sunrise pink with blackout curtains the same shade so they blended into the wall, and the beautiful sleigh bed I had admired was front and center. The bed itself was empty beyond the new mattress and sheets I had purchased; all of my nesting supplies were still upstairs in Diego's room.

"It's beautiful." I laid my hands on the smooth wood. I had wanted a pink room for as long as I could remember, but my sister hated pink, we weren't allowed to paint in the dorms, and Jerry certainly hadn't been amenable to the idea. Tears pricked my eyes, and I climbed onto the bed, spreading out to see the ornate ceiling rose they had added around the light.

Was this what it felt like to start healing your inner child? I had been working on reparenting myself before everything went down, letting myself have the treats and small experiences that had been shamed out of me my whole life. A pink room was beyond indulging myself, and I'd never thought I would be able to feel loved because of a paint color, but here I was, sprawled in the start of a new nest and ready to start bawling.

"Everyone get in here."

Kai was first in, Diego tucking up against him and Amir on my other side while Miles hesitated.

"I said *everyone*."

Miles joined us, stretching out next to Amir. "I'm pretty sure this is the best mattress in the house."

It honestly felt like a cloud, and even though everything was fucked up, I couldn't help my purr at all the alphas being in here with me. I was trying not to feel guilty over how much money they'd spent on me since I'd come to stay with them. We hadn't known how precarious things were at the time, and the thought of returning everything had my instincts twisting me into knots.

I loved this beautiful house they called home, but if we needed to move, I was pretty confident I would be happy anywhere as long as they were with me. I might not be able to pull as much income as they could, but I would be handing in some big projects soon and getting paid. Hopefully that would be enough to offset things while they looked for work.

Being with someone unemployed did make me nervous after I had supported Jerry, but I kept trying to remind myself that these alphas were different. They had been going out of their way to take care of me since we had met, and even if they needed some financial support, I didn't think it would stay that way.

It wasn't like Kai was going to lose his job and hide it from me. The pack seemed like they were pretty good at open communication and that helped.

We decided on a quiet night. The last project I needed to work on had finally finished its download and the alphas were going to start looking for other work. In a sense, it was nice to fall into this sort of rhythm. I had been neglecting my own work in favor of getting to know my new partners, but it would be better to ensure my clients were happy and hopefully they would hire me again or refer me to others.

An email popped up in the corner of my screen after I'd been working away for a few hours.

Notice of nonpayment.

What on earth? I clicked into it and found a notification from my phone company that payment for my bill this month hadn't cleared. That didn't make any sense. Miles had assured me that all the payments for the show had gone through already.

I logged in and felt the same dread as when Jerry had first abandoned me, seeing zero dollars in my account. I clicked into the account history and found no record of any money coming into it.

What the fuck?

I locked my computer and wandered through the pack house in search of Miles, finding him in the courtyard on his tablet.

"Hey, sweetheart. Is everything okay?"

"Not really."

He sat up straighter. "What's wrong?"

"None of the money from the heat is in my account."

Miles paled. "*What*?"

"No payment and no record of it in the account history. I thought you said everything would be paid out by the end of the heat?"

"It should've been. We've never had a problem with payment going through before."

"Glad I get to be the first problem for a lot of things lately," I said bitterly.

"I'll look into it," he promised. "Let me contact the accounting department."

"Please do." My bottom lip wobbled and I was trying very hard not to start crying. I didn't know if the company was scamming me or if I had a problem with my account, but what mattered was that I had gone through all that, turned everyone's lives upside down, all to end up in the same financial situation.

Couldn't the universe cut me a fucking break?

I didn't want to wait there and start crying in front of

Miles, so I turned on my heel and zipped back to the workstation they had set up for me, forcing myself to get things accomplished while tears slipped down my cheeks. Maybe it would be a quick fix, something that only took a phone call to resolve. I was still way too raw from the first time being fucked over, and my brain kept screaming that it was happening again.

Soft tenderness flowed down the bond toward me from Kai, and a moment later a text popped up.

KAI:

Need me to come home?

CALLIE:

I'll be fine <3

But thank you

I wasn't going to make him cancel his plans to babysit me. Realistically there were a bunch of things I still needed to do to protect myself. I needed to get myself off the apartment lease so my credit score wouldn't get fucked if Jerry didn't pay. I needed to cancel everything we'd booked for the wedding. I needed to decide if I really was going to stay here with the pack, and if the answer was yes, I needed to update my documents, find a handful of professionals in the city like a new doctor, dentist, and who the hell knew what else. I would probably have to set up mail forwarding because if Jerry was willing to throw out all of my things, I could basically guarantee any mail that showed up with my name on it would go straight into the trash.

Why wasn't there someone I could hire to think of every single thing I needed to do and they could do it for me? Not that it would matter since I had no money to pay anyone to do anything.

I hadn't been financially insecure growing up, at least not in a way that I had noticed when I was young. Facing it as an adult had been a steep learning curve. I probably should've chosen a more practical degree, but I hadn't and I'd had to compete with everyone else in LA who wanted to make it as a cinematographer. I had plenty of other skills I could put to use to make money if I wanted to work myself to the bone. It wouldn't be the first time I'd had to do so in the past few years, but for now I would focus on getting the two jobs ahead of me finished as quickly as I could.

I took a break for a couple of hours and worked down my list. Mail forwarding was blessedly easy to set up. After that I contacted my old landlord and told him what went down. He agreed to take me off the lease and would speak to Jerry about adding the other people he had moved in without permission.

Next up was canceling all the wedding things. I didn't have a lot to worry about since we couldn't afford a big wedding. We lost the deposits, but that couldn't be helped. The worst was telling the guests, not that we'd intended to have many. I opted for a mass email, dreading any responses that might come through.

My phone rang not two minutes later. Mom's name and number floated across the screen.

Great.

With a sigh, I answered. "Hello?"

"What did you do?"

I flinched at the immediate accusation. "I didn't do anything."

"Callie," she sighed, "don't be obtuse. What happened?"

I didn't want to give her details, but I knew if I didn't, she'd be up my ass about it until I caved. "He married someone else."

Another sigh. More dramatic this time. "*What* did you *do*?"

"Nothing!"

"Darling, people don't throw away that many years of a relationship for no reason. Were you not servicing him?"

"*Mom!*"

"It's a reasonable question."

Reasonable to whom? "I don't want to talk about this."

"How else can you avoid failure in your next relationship if you don't examine your flaws?"

I ground my teeth together, already drained after a minute of her. "Why are you assuming I'm the one who failed here?"

"Are *you* the one married out of the two of you?"

"I don't think his marriage really counts when he got drunk and dragged the first woman he found to the chapel."

"So argumentative. Men don't like that, darling. Of course it counts. The documents were filed, right? Unless he gets divorced, it counts. Should I assume you're coming back home then? You'll have to sleep on the couch. I turned your old bedroom into my craft room."

"I'm not coming home."

"Don't be silly. What are you going to do in LA without him? He's the only reason you moved there."

God forbid she assume I have a job and friends and other roots tying me to the city. I didn't, but that wasn't the point.

"It's all right to admit defeat and come home to Mama."

"I'm not doing that. I'm going to stay in Las Vegas with friends."

Mom tutted. "Well, don't stay too long. You know what a burden you are on people."

"That's really unfair to say. Just because you think I'm a burden doesn't mean I am to everyone. They're really excited to have me stay. I don't expect you to understand, but things ending with Jerry was not my fault, and I'm not going to come back to Seattle. I'm sorry that your first instinct was to blame me for how everything went down, but I think it would be best if we didn't speak anymore."

"What on earth do you mean? You can't just stop speaking to me."

"Actually, I can. And I've kind of been wanting to for a while. I put up with how you speak to me because I didn't see that it was out of the ordinary before. I do now. I'm not gonna force myself through that anymore. I don't expect you to understand, but I hope you'll at least let me have peace, though we both know that's not your strong suit."

"Callie..."

"I really did love you. I'm sorry you could never love me the same way you did Tanya. Have a nice life."

"Cal—"

I ended the call and blocked the number before she could call back, though I wasn't even confident she would.

Numbness settled over me. I had thought about cutting that tie for years; I'd known I wouldn't feel good doing it, and I didn't, but it felt right. I might not have had much experience with being treated well, but now that I'd tasted it, submitting to casual cruelty was so much harder than it used to be. Maybe one day we would talk again, but her response to my split showed me that I would never be good enough for her and that she would never put aside her own feelings to be there for me when I was in crisis.

I deserved better than that even if I had never been good at grabbing it before.

I avoided the pack the rest of the night, too close to the edge to let myself get comfortable. I had cried all over them too much already.

While Diego was in the shower, I slipped upstairs and extracted a few blankets from the nest to take downstairs. It made me a little queasy to dismantle my nest at all, but I just needed a bit of space to cry in peace.

Chapter 30
Diego

I had expected Callie to be curled up in the nest with Kai when I emerged from the shower, but the room was empty, and the nest looked a little sparser than usual. I pulled on a pair of lounge pants and went to check Kai's room, hearing his shower running, but saw no sign of Callie. Checking with Miles and Amir as well, I found both of their rooms also devoid of our omega.

I paused outside her room on the main level, finding the door closed and the soft sounds of her crying coming through it. The door was locked, so I knocked and waited.

"Go away."

"Precious, what's wrong?"

She didn't answer, and I wasn't about to pick the lock if

235

she didn't want to see me, as much as that would've been my preference. Since I couldn't comfort Callie, I backtracked toward Kai's room. He looked absolutely miserable when we crossed paths at the top of the stairs.

"She's so upset," he said quietly.

"Her door's locked. She doesn't want to see anybody."

"What happened?"

"I have no idea. She was totally fine the last time I saw her."

"It feels wrong to think about going to sleep when she needs us." Kai pulled a hand through his damp hair with a sigh.

"She might *need* us, but she doesn't *want* us right now."

"I have to try before I can go to bed," he insisted.

I followed him back down on the off chance that she would actually open the door for him.

"Little dove, what's wrong? What do you need?" He knocked and waited.

"*Please*, go away."

Kai looked over to me and I could only shrug. If she wasn't going to let us in, we couldn't do anything until she wanted to come out. Theoretically we could break into the room, but I wasn't sure if we would recover from that breach of trust. She needed a space that was safe and belonged to only her, even if she was going to use it to lock us out.

"I hate this," said Kai.

"Same. She took some of the nest in there with her. At least it wasn't the entire thing, but that can't be a good sign, can it?"

"Definitely doesn't feel like a good sign."

"Well," I sighed, "our choices are to wait up to see if she emerges, or go to sleep right now and wait for her to come out in the morning."

Kai stared longingly at the door, his palm on his chest. "I

guess it might be overstepping if I just grabbed some couch cushions and lay down right here?"

"Considering we don't know what kind of mood she's going to come out in, probably. Let's get some sleep and hope everything looks better in the morning."

Kai reluctantly agreed and followed me up to the nest. "Can I stay here tonight?"

"Of course you can. Until all the nest is gone, this is communal sleeping space."

Kai blow-dried his hair before climbing in, stretching across the pink expanse that held Callie's rich candied apple scent. It was weird as hell to sleep in the nest without her, but it was better than sleeping somewhere I couldn't smell her. Kai was staring up at the ceiling, moving his palm in a slow circle over his chest.

"Is that where you feel her distress?"

"Yeah. Just a dull ache right here."

"If you want, we could spoon a bit. Shove your face into the nest to breathe her in and pretend it's her hugging you."

Kai laughed quietly. "I wouldn't say no."

He got himself comfortable, wedging some pillows against his chest and put his head beneath one of the blankets before I tucked myself against him. We had gotten much closer plenty of times, and since Callie had joined us, we had ended up in some manner of tangled up multiple times, so it felt like the most natural thing in the world to offer him this comfort. I nudged his hand out of the way and replaced it with my own, feeling the beat of his heart against my palm.

Eventually his breathing evened out and he fell asleep. It took me a while longer, and I woke to Miles kneeling on the nest, his hand on my shoulder.

"Pack meeting in the courtyard," he said.

"Okay. I'll go see if Callie wants to join," I mumbled sleepily.

"No. This one is just for us."

I raised one questioning eyebrow, but Miles was already leaving. I nudged Kai awake and he groaned, burying his face deeper into the nest.

"More sleep."

"We have a pack meeting. You have to wake up."

"Why can't we do that in the afternoon?" Kai grumbled and sat up slowly with a yawn.

I didn't bother getting fully dressed, heading downstairs in just my lounge pants and stopping to see that Callie's door was still closed and firmly locked. Kai looked longingly at it as we passed, and I pulled him along to grab our coffees before joining Amir and Miles in the courtyard.

"Why are we awake so early for this?" I asked.

"I wanted a chance to discuss everything with you before Callie woke up," said Miles.

"What's the meeting about?" Kai took a sip of his coffee.

"Callie came to me yesterday and said her account was empty."

"What do you mean?" I asked.

"Why would her account be empty?" Amir asked. "She hasn't had to pay for a single thing since the bonding."

"It shouldn't be," replied Miles. "I looked into everything with the company. Everything she was owed was deposited into the account she gave us, but she's telling us she never got paid."

I frowned. "That doesn't make any sense. Why would she lie about that?"

Miles shrugged. "I don't know."

"That's such an easy thing to check, though. If she were lying, shouldn't she know we would be able to tell?"

238

"As someone who has dealt with a lot of liars in my life," said Miles, "not all of them are that smart."

"Watch it," growled Kai.

"I'm not calling Callie stupid, and I'm not saying she's lying," Miles defended. "But the fact remains the company did pay her."

I could practically see the walls Amir had lowered around her snap back into place, and Kai looked lost, eyes unfocused as he stared past us.

"Have you talked to Callie about this yet?" I asked.

Miles shook his head. "Not yet. I wanted to talk to all of you."

"I'd like to look her in the eye when she tells you she didn't get paid," Amir said.

I couldn't wrap my head around why Callie would lie about something like this. If she was trying to get more out of the company, she had to know they weren't going to pay any more than they had to. Financial records said they'd paid what they owed, and that was that.

The four of us slipped back into the kitchen, and at some point during our meeting, Callie had emerged and was making herself a cup of tea. She looked rough with purple shadows under her eyes.

Callie turned toward us, immediately clocking that something was wrong. "Why are you guys looking so ominous coming in here like that?"

"Callie," Miles hesitated.

"Okay, the vibes are seriously off. What's going on? Is this because I locked everyone out last night?"

"No," I said, though I certainly hadn't enjoyed that part. "You're more than entitled to your own space whenever you want it."

Miles stepped forward. "The company records show all five payments going through and being deposited."

She stared at him for a long moment. "Well, their records are wrong because nothing's in my account."

"They contacted the bank to make sure. All the payments cleared."

Her hackles went up. "Well, they're lying, then. Or there was a glitch." Callie snatched up her phone and poked at her screen before eventually turning it toward Miles. "Nothing's there! And there's nothing in the account history, so wherever they sent it, it wasn't to me."

"Can I have a look?" I asked.

She leveled a glare on me and slid her phone across the counter toward me. "Loving the level of trust here."

"Sweetheart..." Miles began.

"Don't you *sweetheart* me. If you think I'm trying to swindle the company, just say it."

"It's not...that. But there's only so many explanations."

Fury radiated off her. "Well, here's another explanation for you." She flipped him the bird, spun on her heel, and stalked back into her bedroom, where she slammed the door, the lock audibly clicking.

"Fucking hell," Miles lamented quietly.

"It had to be asked," Amir said. "Either Callie or the company is lying, and we've never had anyone come back saying they weren't paid."

"Can I see the deposit info on your end?" I asked.

Miles pulled it up on the tablet and set it on the counter. I read through everything on both screens and then laid her phone on the tablet, carefully comparing the account numbers.

"Oh, shit."

"What?" Kai asked, leaning over my shoulder.

"They're both telling the truth. The company paid out into the account she gave, but that account number isn't hers. One second." I risked knocking on Callie's door, and even though she told me to fuck off, I asked anyway. "Precious, do you know the account number of your joint account?"

The door whipped open. "Why are you asking?"

"Come sit with us, just for a moment. The account number you gave the company isn't the one that you're showing us on your phone."

"What are you talking about? What other account would I have given?" Her face blanched, all of the color leaching out of her cheeks. "Oh my god."

She raced out into the kitchen and grabbed her phone, opening an account statement record and holding it up next to the payment record that was still open on the tablet.

"Son of a bitch!"

Kai was at her side in a second. "Did the money go into the wrong account?"

Callie dropped her face into her hands and started sobbing.

"Precious, is the money not in your joint account either?"

"I don't know!" she sobbed. "I don't have access to it anymore."

"How the hell would you not have access to it?" Amir asked.

"Your guess is as good as mine. It's not listed under my accounts anymore."

"Okay, let's all take a breath," I suggested. "Callie, you need to get in contact with your bank and find out why you don't have account access anymore. The company isn't going to pay out another dollar, but maybe we can still get you back onto that account."

She made the most miserable sound, sinking all the way to the floor. "He probably took everything."

"We'll cross that bridge when we get to it," I assured her. "For right now, we need to find out what happened."

"Maybe breakfast first?" Kai offered.

"No." She shook her head. "The sooner I figure it out, the better."

I wrote down both of her account numbers for her so she didn't have to worry about flipping through screens while on a call, and we got her situated at the table. The bank itself wouldn't be open just yet, but they had a twenty-four-hour line she could call in the meantime.

Amir fetched her cup of tea and got fresh coffee for the rest of us while we hovered awkwardly around the kitchen, waiting for her to get through the automated menus and electronic voices until finally a person answered.

"Hello there, how can I help you today?"

"I'm not able to access my account and I'm not sure why. It's not listed at all anymore."

"Oh dear. Let's see what we can uncover. Do you have your account information?"

Callie gave the woman everything she was asked for, and eventually we got the answer.

"It looks like a few days ago you came in and authorized the transfer of the joint account into the sole possession of Jerry McIntosh, which is why it's no longer visible for you online."

"Excuse me?" she hissed. "I did no such thing."

"That's what our records say. There's paperwork on file about the transfer."

"Well, that's impossible because I never authorized anything."

"Transfer us to the fraud department," I ordered, taking up a seat next to her. "Please."

"Of course. One moment."

It took a few minutes more before we made it to another human and Callie shoved the phone toward me, spilling into tears once more.

"We need to initiate a fraud check on the following account," I told them, giving them the account number. "We were told Callie Price authorized the transfer of a joint account into the sole possession of Jerry McIntosh, and that is *not* the case."

"Let me get a file set up."

We gave them as much information as we could and told them Callie had not been in Los Angeles at all except for when she was in our presence, and hadn't visited a bank or discussed any paperwork with anyone. I wasn't under any illusions that it would get resolved immediately, but they promised to look into it, interview the bank associates who had approved everything, and check the on-site cameras.

Callie screamed into her hands when the call was over. "This is so fucking fucked. I went through all of that just for Jerry to steal everything?"

I didn't know how to fix anything, but we had taken the steps to start. First we had to rebuild some of the trust we'd broken by not believing her from the start.

Amir growled and sat down across from her. "I know you don't know me that well yet, but I'm not going to let him screw you over twice. I've never gotten to tell someone that they would rue the day before, but that fucker is absolutely going to."

Chapter 31
Callie

I hated everything. That money was supposed to help me start my life over. At the very least, it could've held us over while the pack figured out how to support themselves after I had steamrolled their jobs.

All the security I'd felt from knowing I had that money was gone. Jerry really was committed to taking everything from me that he possibly could. And the worst part was that he was entitled to everything in the joint account, so there was a possibility I would never see that money again no matter what the bank uncovered.

I was trying to feel grateful for what I had been given instead of focusing on everything that had been taken away, but it was hard. I hated how I had reacted to the pack not immediately trusting me. I'd still been raw from my conversation with my mother, and having one more thing stacked on top of my already fragile emotions had been too much to handle.

The pack had the numbers in front of them, so it wasn't a surprise they would've been skeptical, and they didn't know me that well, but it cut all the same.

It wasn't the first time I had encountered a guilty-until-proven-innocent situation with the people in my life. Maybe it was unrealistic to expect the opposite with the pack. Even a hint of my old life rearing its head with them had taken me out at the knees.

I tried to work, but it was slow going. Without the option to push the deadlines, I had no choice but to continue no matter my emotional state. It wasn't hard to tell that the pack felt bad for how the discussion had gone, both in how they had approached me and in the realization that all the money I had earned was in the hands of someone else. Kai's guilt through the bond sat like lead in my chest. We were probably feeding each other's anxiety in a cycle at this point.

They didn't seem to know what to do, and I didn't know how to approach them, so we spent most of the day tiptoeing around each other.

Kai set down a tray with a sandwich, blueberries, a glass of water, and a can of cola for me. "You have to eat."

"I don't feel like eating."

"Callie, look at me."

I tore my gaze away from the screen and focused on him.

"I'm sorry, little dove. I know you can feel that's true."

I could. The dull ache from him was obvious through the bond, sadness wrapped in anger. The anger wasn't directed toward me; that much I knew.

"We should've trusted you."

"Yeah, you should have." I wore my bitterness like armor. "Do you have *any* idea how shitty it made me feel to have the four of you come at me like that, like you'd already decided I was in the wrong?"

"I—"

"*I'm* talking right now," I snapped. "I have been through a lot of hell with the people in my life, and maybe I stupidly thought things would be different, *especially* with you, when you can feel what I'm going through, but *no*. That didn't matter. And you know what? It fucking sucks to see so clearly that you don't trust me and wouldn't even give me the benefit of the doubt."

"Cal—"

My glare lapsed him back into silence. "I've realized how unhappy I was in my relationship with Jerry, and with my family. You've all shown me things don't have to be that way, but I will *not* put myself in a position where that behavior becomes the norm again. You trust me or you don't, and if you don't, I can't stay."

The anguish from him twisted in my chest, but I hadn't said anything that wasn't true. I'd never have said anything like that to Jerry, but I felt safe enough to speak my mind here. I hadn't a fucking clue where I would go with no home, no money, and no car, but I'd figure it out somehow, even if it was a few miserable months staying with my sister, paying with my sanity instead of paying rent.

With a sigh, I said, "You can talk now."

"Callie...I'm so sorry. I should have trusted you. *We all* should have trusted you. Please, please don't leave us. Give us a chance to make it up to you."

It would be so easy to agree, but I'd lived so fucking long in complacency, staying quiet because I didn't want anyone to be *upset* when they didn't give a shit if *I* was the one upset. "And what if you can't?" I held my breath at the sharp pain coming through the bond.

"If you want to leave, I'll go with you and spend the rest of my life making sure you never feel that way again. I know talk is cheap, and the only way this can be fixed is if you give us the time to implement actions that prove it. You're my mate, and I fucked up. I want to fix it."

I really, really wanted him to fix it too. I was so fucking trapped and I didn't know what to do. Even leaving here meant him following because we were bonded. Wanting the life they offered didn't change the fact that I had very little choice in the matter. Bonding was bigger than marriage, older and deeper, winding souls together, and I *couldn't* leave Kai. I didn't want to think about how much pain I would be in every day for the rest of forever if I tried. For the sake of saving us both a lifetime of pain, I had to let them try.

"Can I hold you?" Kai asked.

I slipped out of my seat and let him take me in his arms, relaxing against the warmth of his chest, his purr rumbling to life beneath my ear. I knew it was just a biological response, alpha to omega, but it felt like maybe everything would be okay if I could just stay right here.

"We're going to get everything figured out," he promised. "And we won't lose faith in you again."

I wanted to believe it.

"Eat your food, and when you're done working, we'll spend some time in the pool to relax, okay?"

"Okay."

I didn't protest when he lifted my chin and dropped his mouth to mine. Rising on my toes to hook my arm around his neck, I let myself sink into the taste of him, drowning in the sweet cinnamon that soothed all my worries.

I consumed everything he had brought for me after he left me in peace, and I put in a few more solid hours of work before I rejoined them for the day.

They all looked so contrite when they noticed me. I could only assume Kai had told them about our discussion.

Kai was the first and boldest to approach me. "We're making dinner. Can I get you something to drink?"

I shrugged, still exhausted from earlier and half tempted to lock myself in my room.

"Alcoholic or virgin?" Amir asked.

"Virgin is fine. I'm gonna sit outside, if you guys don't mind. I'm not very hungry."

The four of them frowned, but no one made a move to stop me. It was uncomfortably warm outside, but I found a corner of the pool that was shaded and stuck my feet in it, stretching back across the tile to stare at the wide sweep of blue above me.

Why wasn't there a two-stage bonding? Do the initial bond when you're out of your mind from the hormones, and then, like, two weeks later, a biological notification pops up to ask if you were actually sure about that. I knew it wasn't possible, but a girl could dream. It would certainly be saving me a lot of grief right now.

A flash of pink out of the corner of my eye caught my attention. Amir was approaching with a pool float and a fancy drink.

"At least lie on this and not the tile." He laid out the float next to me and set down the drink. "Virgin piña colada."

I readjusted myself, too proud to admit that the float was much more comfortable than the tile.

Amir sat down unbidden. "In fairness, both you and the company were telling the truth."

"I don't want to hear it right now. If you don't want me to pour this drink on you, you'll leave."

He moved it out of my reach. "I'm just saying. No one has ever complained they haven't been paid before and the records were right there. Yes, we should've discussed with you before making up our minds, but the facts really were saying one thing."

"If you're not going to leave, I am." I tried to get up, and his hand wrapped around my wrist. "Let go."

He did immediately. "How long are you going to be upset for?"

I leveled a hot glare at him. "You are *really* reminding me of my ex right now."

That statement seemed to shock him into reality. "Fucking hell. I'm not good at this."

"No shit."

"I made a choice based on facts, and I'm sorry it hurt you. In the future we'll talk to you first." Amir sighed. "I want you to feel safe here, whether or not you want to stay."

"You know, I can't think of a single time in my life where someone just believed me immediately. With my mom, my sister could do no wrong, and even when *she* had fucked up, it took one little lie from Tanya for me to take the blame. With Jerry, I never felt I could do anything right, but I had grown up with that, so I just assumed that was how I would feel forever. I had *just* started to feel like things would be different here, and then I was right back to square one, the girl getting blamed for breaking something she didn't touch." A sob snuck up on me and I hastily wiped away the tears that slid down my cheeks. "I never *saw it* before. I didn't know I could feel any other way, and I can't go back to that."

Amir looked like he might be sick. He crawled up next to me and pulled me into his arms. "I'm sorry. Fuck me. I know what that feels like. I won't do it again."

I held on to his shirt and let everything pour out. He held me without speaking, squeezing tightly until it felt like his arms were the only thing keeping me together. I felt like a pup that had only ever known scolding and then learned what a loving pet was, only to be scolded again and have all that pain rear its head.

"I'm sorry I'm crying on you," I mumbled. I'd been doing way too much of this since Jerry abandoned me. Grief was tiring, and it wasn't even grief for *him*. Just realizing I'd lived a lifetime of pain was overwhelming.

"Cry as much as you want. As long as you hydrate afterward, it's all good."

He passed me the drink and I swirled the contents, sipping the cool, fruity coconut mixture. It was a relief against the heat, and it tasted sweeter because he had made it for me. I finished the entirety of it in his arms until my whole body ached from crying and my eyes burned.

"I thought I had communication figured out," Amir said quietly. "Turns out I'm shit at it."

I laughed softly. "I see that. I don't need you all to blindly believe me, necessarily, but please don't assume I've done something wrong from the start."

"I'll do pretty much anything to never get compared to your ex again. All of us coming to a conclusion before talking to you was a shit move, and it probably sucked a lot to feel like it was four against one."

"Yeah. Did not enjoy that part." I told him about my mom, breathing in his cedar sweetness to keep myself steady.

"I'm just going to say it—your mom sounds like a cunt."

I let out a strangled laugh. "You're not wrong. At least I don't have to worry about talking to her again. It's kind of freeing even though it's really fucking sad."

"I'm sorry you had to take that step." Amir gave me another squeeze. "I'd say I can't speak for everyone, but I think in this I can. We'll do better. I can't promise we won't fuck up on occasion, but there's not a soul in this house that wants to hurt you."

"I know." It didn't fix everything, but it was a bandage over a wound that needed time to heal, and for the moment it would have to be enough.

Chapter 32
Kai

Callie seemed slightly better when we brought dinner outdoors. Amir was still sitting with her, and she leaned heavily against him, her eyes closed. I'd felt all of her tears but didn't want to interrupt the two of them. I'd already had a chance to speak to her a bit and needed to leave space for the others. Callie and I had the bond, and it was a constant tightrope balance between letting the rest of the pack get to know her and wanting to keep her all to myself.

Maybe that was a disservice to both of us. Maybe it would be easier for her to feel comfortable with the entire pack if I monopolized her a little more, made her feel more secure in her connection with me? I had never been part of a pack with an omega before now, but it felt like learning as we went wasn't good enough. Callie had been hurt, almost a decade of her life had been thrown back in her face, and as her bondmate I had to ensure she would never worry about that with us. That was probably an impossible task. She might never truly get over her past, but at the very least we could work on creating a strong foundation to move forward.

"Where's Miles?" she asked.

I thought he had followed us out, but he wasn't in the courtyard. "Not sure. Let me go check."

He didn't respond when I called for him indoors, so I fished out my phone to text him.

KAI:

Where the hell are you?

MILES:

Be back soon

I thought of something

KAI:

Are you going to tell me what it is?

MILES:

Only if if I'm successful

"He stepped out," I told them upon my return. "He'll be back."

Dinner was a mostly silent affair. I was just grateful Callie was eating and hadn't retreated to her room. Of all of us, I hadn't expected Amir to be the one able to comfort her.

I had no idea what the hell Miles was doing, but I had a distressed omega to focus on.

"Do you want us to move the nest properly down into

your room or are you going to keep the one in Diego's?" I asked.

Callie shrugged. "I like it where it is, but I'd like to have a proper nest instead of one split in two. I just... I don't know if I can stay here."

The words sliced through me. "We want you to stay."

"Sure didn't feel like it," she grumbled.

"It was a lapse in judgment," I promised.

Callie sighed. "That's what makes me nervous. There were a lot of those with Jerry in the beginning. A lot of promises to do better, and then once he was sure I wouldn't leave, he stopped trying."

"I know saying we're not him won't make a difference," said Diego.

"You're right," she replied. "I can't help how I feel when I see what could be the start of a new pattern now that I finally recognize what he was doing."

"You don't have to change how you feel, little dove. It's up to us to break that pattern before it forms. This is new for all of us too, and that's not an excuse; we're just used to doing things as a unit."

"I know that. And it feels like shit to be on the outside of it. You guys have had years to figure out how everything works between you, and I just get thrown in the deep end. I don't know how to do any of this either."

"Can we do anything to help you feel more comfortable going forward?"

"Maybe start with a *whole* pack meeting for anything that comes up instead of ganging up on me."

"None of us will make that mistake again." I reached out for her hand, grateful when she didn't withdraw it. I linked our fingers and kissed the back of her hand. "No more pack meetings unless everyone is involved, unless it's to plan awesome surprises."

That last bit got a small smile out of her. "I might be starting to like those. Do you think we could move to the nest? I'm tired."

"Up or down?" I asked.

"Down. I'm not climbing stairs unless one of you is carrying me."

"That's very easily arranged," said Diego. "Pick the one you want either way."

"Hmm, maybe still down. My room smells wrong with no one's scent but mine in there and that needs to change. Plus, I need to drown out all the stress scents or I'm going to trigger a cry the next time I lie down in there."

Amir and Diego got the dishes back into the kitchen and I took Callie to her nest, my omega dragging me straight into it with her. She curled up instantly in my arms. The action loosened a knot in my chest, even though the scent clinging to her pillows had my instincts on edge. Tears and stress saturated her nest. Our fault.

I got my purr going and snuggled as close to her as I possibly could, pleased when she relaxed. Diego and Amir joined a few moments later, and I could see on their faces the moment they caught the same scents I had. We wedged her between us, all three of us purring until Callie was boneless and purring in return. Amir dragged one of the blankets over us, cocooning the four of us and trapping the scents that were infinitely preferable to what we'd encountered upon arrival.

Slowly the burnt sugar was replaced by crisp apple and sweetness, mingling with each of our scents. And bit by bit that sweetness began to overwhelm the confines of the nest, Callie's breathing shifting and her hips pressing closer. My body responded to it instantly, cinnamon filling the air and my cock hardening against her ass. The others noticed too. Soon her wiggling brought on whimpers and she tipped her head up to Diego, dragging him into a kiss that had my nose filled with candied apple and spices.

Our omega still wanted us. Being able to hold her, to give her what she craved, helped bridge any gaps that formed between us. I would let her take the lead here; if she only wanted Diego, Amir and I would leave. If she wanted us all, we would stay and indulge in the pliant warmth of her body.

Her movements grew more frantic, the most delicious sounds escaping her as Diego kissed her.

Amir pried their heads apart and flipped the blanket back, bringing a gust of fresh air to us. "Before you get too lost in the sauce, tell us who you want to be involved in this."

Callie blinked rapidly in the light like she was waking out of a dream. "Um, everyone?"

"Fair enough." Amir tucked the blanket into the end of the nest so it was out of the way. "Quit hogging her."

"Fuck you. I can hog her all I want. Both of you have fucked her since the heat and it's my turn to give her some loving."

"All three of you can fuck me if you get a move on," Callie said, dragging Diego closer again.

Their mouths met once more and Callie tossed her leg over his hip, where Amir slid his palm up her calf. I couldn't help but rock against her ass, tracing the curves of her body before carefully working her shirt off. Her sound of protest lasted only a moment before she was pressed up against Diego again.

Callie grew more frantic by the second, and I wasn't sure if it was her own desire getting the better of her or if she was using the excuse of her response to us to bury her hurt from earlier. Not the healthiest coping mechanism, if that was what she was doing, but we could talk more later. All the tension and anxiety through the bond was muted by her desire.

The taste of her skin was sweet on my tongue. Her desire ricocheted in the bond, stoking mine that flowed back to her, a feedback loop cycling between us.

The three of us were so used to managing one omega between us that it was no hardship for us to tease Callie into a frenzy while Diego buried himself in her. Every sound she made was like a drug, and as much as I wanted to get my own cock into her, I could be patient. Diego propped her ankles on his shoulders to give us more space to work, his fingers digging into the softness of her thighs. Her nipple puckered under my tongue and I nudged my fingers between her thighs to stroke her clit. Amir held her by the throat while he sucked diligently on her other nipple.

Callie broke so easily for us. Diego groaned as she cried out, his hips stuttering. I knew exactly what he would be feeling, the clench of her muscles around him that was enough to undo any man. He didn't still or slow once she was breathing normally again, and Callie reached for Amir and me, her fingers locking in our hair as her eyes rolled back and she cried out again. All the worry and discomfort I had been feeling from her melted away, replaced entirely by desperate need.

It wouldn't be difficult between all of us to keep her in this state, but then none of us would get anything done ever again.

A breathless chant of *fuck*, interspersed with each of our names in turn, was a symphony I never wanted to stop hearing. The next wave of pleasure that crashed over her finally dragged Diego along with her. The sharp arch of her back and the shift in her breathing was enough for me to know he had knotted her.

I dragged my tongue up her throat and whispered in her ear, "How do you feel about getting fucked everywhere else while Diego has you on his knot, little dove?"

Callie nodded frantically. "Please."

We carefully rearranged the two of them until Diego was on his back and Callie was sprawled over him.

"Do you want it rough, princess?" Amir asked. "Or should we be more gentle?"

"I'll take anything you want to give me. Shut my brain off. I don't like it up there right now."

Amir looked to me for guidance. I would be able to monitor her pretty easily to keep her safe, so it wouldn't hurt to try giving her what she wanted. I nodded and Amir threaded his fingers through her hair. I picked out a bottle of lube I had stashed in her bedside table and got to work on easing her ass open to me. She squirmed and moaned as I worked in one finger, then another, rotating carefully, but there was no sign of pain through the bond, as if her body was just waiting for us.

The first glide into her was slow, testing to make sure everything was slick enough and nothing was hurting her.

"More," she demanded.

The whine out of her when I fucked in next was absolute perfection. The one after that was muffled as she got her mouth on Amir and the two of us rode her from end to end while she was trapped on Diego's knot.

It was so hard to focus between the hot, slick glide of her body and everything that was projected to me through the bond. Overwhelming pleasure and desire turned my brain into mush and I kept a firm grip on her hips to keep myself steady.

It was the first time we had all gotten to be with her since the heat, and while the actions were similar, the circumstances couldn't be more different. I didn't have to pay an ounce of attention to an audience, focusing only on my omega, who was so keyed up she couldn't even manage to beg. Her own need blended with mine, simmering in my blood. She needed us, and fuck if I wasn't going to give her everything she asked for.

Chapter 33
Diego

Watching Callie fall apart was fascinating. Watching my pack ruin her while she squeezed the life out of my knot was *transcendent*. My omega was draped across me, getting fucked in every hole, and her scent was the sweetest I'd ever smelled it. I could get drunk on it. Tart, sweet, candied apple that made my mouth water and my cock hard.

Amir tugged her closer until her nose brushed his stomach, and I knew from the choked-off sound he made that he was spilling down her perfect throat. It was ridiculous to be jealous of him when I was knot-deep in her, but I still craved having her every way at once even if it wasn't possible.

I wanted all of her, every way, every day. I couldn't get enough. The tension of the last while had been unbearable and

I had no idea how to fix it. Fucking her was no hardship. Giving her pleasure was the easiest thing in the world, but I knew things went deeper. Wounds took a long time to heal, and even if someone else had inflicted them to begin with, we'd poured some salt into them. If this was what she wanted to clean it out, I was happy to oblige.

Tomorrow I planned to take her out, spoil the shit out of her, and get to know her more. In the meantime, I intended to get in my cuddles once she'd gotten everything she needed.

My knot was going nowhere fast with the way the others gave and took in equal measure until Callie's perfume was drowning me. I felt the second she surrendered and Amir carefully extracted himself, arranging her on my chest while Kai came to his own finish and pulled out before his knot got him trapped in her too. She melted perfectly against me, and the others stretched out on each side, both taking one of her hands to lay on their chest. Callie hummed, the sound content and sleepy.

"How are you feeling, precious?"

"Hmmm, okay, I think. Nowhere near as deep as in the heat, but a little floaty."

"Floaty is good. We've got you."

"Really?"

"Absolutely. You're our omega, our Callie."

She rooted against my neck and pressed a soft kiss to my skin. "I really want to stay. Don't make me go."

"Callie, we would never make you go," promised Kai.

"I can't do my old life again."

Amir ran a hand down her back and she sniffled against me. "Eventually we *will* prove that lapse in judgment won't happen again. We have to give each other a chance. None of us want you to leave."

I threaded my fingers into her hair. "We love you being here, even if we haven't figured everything out yet."

"Can I have more people cuddling me, please?"

Kai and Amir tucked closer, each draping an arm over her waist and wedging the pillows so we were one big pile.

"Better?" Amir asked.

Callie nodded, taking a big breath and letting it go slowly. "It's really scary liking all of you so much. I think you're the only reason I survived what Jerry did, and I hate being scared that it could all go away."

"You're stuck with me forever," Kai said with a touch of humor in his voice.

Callie wriggled around to face him. "I don't want any of us to be *stuck*."

"If I weren't comfortable being bonded to you, I already would have discussed how we could separate out of each other's lives once the bond wasn't fresh anymore and we could stand to be apart. I think we'll all fit well together; we just need time to grow and learn how to make this work for everyone."

"I personally can't wait to be bonded to you," I told her. "I've been thinking about it since you sunk those pretty little teeth into Kai."

Callie shifted again, the others lifting their arms so she could rise up enough to look down at me. "You really want to be bonded to me?"

"I would do it right now if we didn't need a heat for it."

A bond sounded so mystical. Being able to know another person that deeply, to sense their emotions and connect with them in a way that was unlike anything anyone else would know. I wanted that. Plus, bonding Callie would connect me to anyone else bonded to her. If Amir and Miles bonded her too, we'd have that unbreakable connection between all of us. A pack forever.

My omega's kiss was the sweetest yet, soft and tentative. It was a bit of a marvel how she could go from desperate to fuck us to tentative as hell. In time that dichotomy should ease. If she and I were bonded, she would be able to feel how much I wanted to be with her. Maybe with all of us bonded, she would be surrounded with all the love she needed to feel secure forever. I wanted that for her.

Callie rolled her hips and when it became clear that my knot was no longer keeping her pinned, she slid off and settled back down against me. "Purrs?"

I didn't have to be asked twice.

"I'm not ready to bond you yet," said Amir, "but I think we're growing on each other, and I definitely want the opportunity to get to know you better until we're both ready to take that step."

Callie nodded, drawing Amir in for his own kiss before she snuggled against me once more.

I lost track of how long we lay like that until a knock at the door alerted us to Miles's return.

Callie adjusted only to drape the edge of a blanket over her exposed pussy. "Come in."

"I see the four of you had fun without me while I was saving our asses."

"That was your fault for leaving," I pointed out.

Miles held up a handful of envelopes. "I have gifts for everyone."

"Gifts?" Callie asked.

"The tips from the shows are run through a separate system from the regular pay, and with all of the chaos I never authorized the payout."

Callie sat up sharply and twisted around, not seeming to mind in the least that she was naked around Miles. That probably boded well for the future. Miles passed her an envelope and she tore it open, pulling out a payment statement.

"*Miles*! Oh my god."

"Like it? After the house took its cut and we accounted for taxes, you made $112,000."

"Holy shit. How much does the house take?"

"20%. And that's just *your* cut. You get as much as the performers combined."

That meant our statements had around $37,000 on them. We hadn't made tips like that on one show in our entire career.

"I don't understand. Did they pay me again for the performance after the confusion?"

"No, sweetheart. That's just your tips. People got very generous over the bonding."

Callie burst into tears, clutching the paper to her chest. Amir, Kai and I gathered her close, her sitting on my lap.

Miles sat on the end of the bed. "We have enough to buy out both contracts if we want to now," he said. "Or I can keep working on them while we figure everything out."

"Push them for now," I said. "I know we're not going to do the contracted performances, but I hate the idea of letting them win. We'll pay out the contracts when we're good and ready."

It was pure fucking villainy how much we had to pay to get out of our contracts. I would much rather we be able to figure out something sustainable before having to fork over that much cash.

"This made it into the correct account this time?" asked Kai. "The ex doesn't get a fucking dollar of this?"

"I triple-checked the account numbers myself," Miles promised.

We were all so careful with her the rest of the night, settling in for a movie that she fell asleep halfway through. We had a tentative path forward, she was more financially secure for the moment, and we were all dedicated to making this work.

By the time the morning rolled around, Callie was in a much better mood and the whole house felt infinitely more relaxed.

"Are you feeling up to going on our date today?" I asked.

"As long as part of it involves keeping me fed and hydrated," she replied.

"Like I would ever let my omega go hungry." I grinned at her. "I have a lot planned, so we should get going if you're ready to rock."

"I'm all yours." She was dressed in a pair of hot pink shorts and a shiny, drapey white tank top.

"Hold up." Amir marched in with a spray can of sunscreen in his hand. "Step outside so I can protect your pale ass."

Callie pouted but obeyed, moving to stand on the front step, eyes closed and arms extended for Amir to coat her in the sunscreen.

Then he passed it to me. "Every two hours. If you bring back a lobster, I'm gonna kick your ass."

"I'm not that bad," she protested.

Amir raised a skeptical eyebrow. "You and Miles are pasty as hell. If you had been blessed with at least a little bit of melanin I wouldn't have to worry, but here we are."

"I'll set a timer," I promised. I did that right then so I wouldn't forget, and Callie tucked the sunscreen into her purse.

Once we were in the car, I turned the AC on full blast and Callie preened in the cool air.

"You'll notice he didn't give a shit if *I* get sunburned," I said with a laugh. "He likes you a lot more than he's willing to say."

Her cheeks flushed the prettiest shade of pink. "At least that's not one-sided. What are we doing today?"

"Important things first. I really want you to stay, and the only way that's going to work is if you feel at home here. Might take us a few hours, but I'm pretty sure by the end of the day you'll be a lot closer to that."

She looked at me curiously, but I didn't elaborate.

The first stop was the dreaded DMV, but I had made an appointment and greased a few palms so we could get Callie an updated license. She would have to get a new one anyway since she was no longer living at her old apartment.

"Are you serious?" she asked.

"As a funeral," I replied.

The whole affair was blessedly short thanks to my preparations. Most of the tasks today were tedious—getting her photos taken for a passport application so we could travel if we wanted to, stocking her up on any missing essentials, getting her signed up with the best omega clinic in the city that would handle all her medical needs, taking her for a trim and blowout at the salon Kai frequented to see if she liked it, and finally stopping by the local library so I could get her a card.

I watched her soften through each task, and she scanned the city with greedy eyes as she started to learn her way around it.

"I can't believe you thought of all this," she said between sips of the enormous sweet tea in her hands.

"The only way for a place to feel like home is to make it

one. This way you have a bunch of services you're familiar with."

"It's not very date-like," she said, "and even though I am exhausted from people-ing, I actually really loved today. I think it's probably the first time I've felt normal for weeks."

"I'm glad. I know we won't be in the 'getting to know you' honeymoon phase forever, and I want you to feel comfortable with the city. I hope it takes at least a few things off your plate."

She laced her fingers with mine. "It absolutely does. A lot of it was things I was dreading doing by myself, but it was actually a little bit fun having company for it."

"Well, I hope the rest of the evening is much closer to date territory for you."

"What's next?"

I turned into a parking lot, pulling to a stop in front of an enormous bookstore. "Next we spend as much time here as you want. I'll buy you as many books as I can carry."

Callie gave me an excitable kiss. "You guys really don't play around with this courting thing, do you?"

"Absolutely not. If I could buy you the entire store I would, but we'll start small and work our way up."

Watching her move reverently through the aisles was a rare treat. She gravitated toward the fantasy, romance, and travel sections, flipping through pages and tracing her fingers down the spines. It took her a while to actually pick anything out, and I started adding anything she touched to the pile before she finally got with the program and added a few series to the stack. It was a damn good thing I worked out so often, because hauling that many books around was like clutching a bag of bricks.

"Do you have a top favorite of all time?" I asked.

"Not really. I've loved lots over the years, but I feel like my answer changes depending on what phase of life I'm in. Do you have a favorite?"

"I read one series as a kid about a little girl in an all-omega family who wanted to be a knight. I loved that one."

"Oh, I read that one. I don't think I ever finished the whole series, but I'm pretty sure it got, like, twenty books long by the time it was done."

"It definitely did. I still read every single one. I used to stop by the bookstore on allowance day every week and see if there was anything new yet. I still have all of them in storage at my parents' place."

"That's so cute."

We talked while she perused, discussing different books we had both read when we passed the shelves containing them, or sitting on the floor in the travel section and looking at photos of places we both wanted to go. A lot of today had been mundane, but a lot of days in our future would be, and I liked knowing we could be just as happy on those days as the ones filled with excitement.

When we had traversed the store twice over, we finally made our exit with a grand total of twenty-three books. Before I took her home, we grabbed some drive-thru and drove to the outskirts of the city to watch the sun disappear behind the mountains, chatting and eating in the air-conditioning.

"You know, I was kind of skeptical about this place ever feeling like home. It's just so sensationalized that I sometimes forget people actually live here." She pulled me close, kissing me slow and deep as sunset gave way to night. "Thank you for today, for helping me put down some roots."

"You're more than welcome, precious."

I would help her lay down all the roots in the world if it meant that she would stay with us.

Chapter 34
Callie

I was up to my eyeballs in video editing when the phone rang, the name of my bank flashing across the screen.

"Is this Miss Callie Price?"

"This is she."

"Excellent." After a couple of quick identity confirmation questions, the caller said, "I'm calling to let you know that we've concluded our fraud investigation into your account."

"Oh?"

"It does appear that the staff member who handled the authorization and transfer of the account did not in fact check the identification of the woman who was impersonating you. They have subsequently been fired and we have reinstated your access to the account in question. However, because this is now a criminal fraud matter due to the impersonation, the assets within said account are frozen until the criminal investigation is complete."

Of course.

"And how long does a criminal investigation take?"

"I'm afraid I can't give you a timeline. Your personal accounts will remain entirely unaffected during this process. Do you have any questions at this time?"

"How can I access the money when the investigation is over?"

"The bank will be in contact with you and provide instructions. I'm very sorry for all the trouble. We'll be sending you an email shortly with all of the relevant information, and law enforcement will handle things from here."

"All right, thank you."

I hung up with a sigh. At least things were moving forward even if I still couldn't access the money. I logged into the account out of curiosity to see how much damage might've been done.

"Motherfucker."

"What's happening?" Kai asked, appearing in my doorway. "Felt you getting twitchy through the bond."

"I got the account back, but I can't do anything with it while they investigate. It looks like Jerry's already spent about forty grand."

"What an asshole. I would ask what the hell he spent that much money on in such a short time, but we did leave him with a pretty barren apartment after taking out all the things you bought." Kai sat down next to me, wrapping an arm over my shoulders. "How are you feeling about all of it?"

I shrugged. "Mostly annoyed. It was my own fuckup, but

any decent person would've contacted me before spending the money."

Kai kissed my temple. "I'm sorry to say it, but your taste in lovers before us has not been the best."

"You're not wrong." I updated him on everything I had been told.

"They could get in some serious shit over this. It's pretty hefty jail time for bank fraud and identity theft."

I didn't necessarily want Jerry and Katrina to go to jail; I just wanted them to get out of my fucking life and give back the money they stole. They could've just screwed me over emotionally and left it at that, but apparently Jerry wasn't content with that.

My phone rang again, his name appearing.

Speak of the devil.

Kai and I watched it ring and I made no move to answer it.

"What do you think he wants?" Kai asked.

"Probably pissed he doesn't have free access to everything. Honestly, he has bigger things to worry about now."

A moment later, there was a voicemail.

"Should I listen to it?"

"Only if you want to. Want me to listen for you?"

"I am too morbidly curious for that."

I played the voicemail on speaker.

"Callie, you fucking cunt! Where the hell is the car? Did you just appear in the middle of the night and drive off with it? Call me back. Jesus fucking Christ."

"Oops."

I turned to Kai. "Oops?"

"So, I hired a company to pick up your vehicle and bring it out here since it's in your name. I figured it would have arrived here before he noticed and I could surprise you."

I burst out laughing. "You stole back my car for me?"

"Well, you weren't exactly in any condition to deal with it when we went to get your stuff, and I thought the easiest option would be to tow it here and then you never have to go back. We'll probably have to get it re-keyed to be safe."

"God, he's so pissed." I let out another chuckle. "I'm actually very glad you went for that option because I might have run him over if we'd gotten me behind the wheel and he was talking to me like that."

"Always happy to keep my omega out of jail for vehicular manslaughter."

I let myself sink against him, reaching out for the warm steadiness that pulsed through the bond from him and wrapping myself in it. "How long 'til it gets here?"

"Maybe about an hour. I was going to see if you wanted to drive to our lunch date so you could start learning the city a bit more."

"You gonna be my passenger princess?" I teased.

"I will be whatever you want me to be. If you feel more comfortable driving, I'm happy to be a passenger, and if you don't actually like driving and you're just doing it out of necessity, one of us should be available to take you where you need to go."

"I like it as long as it's not rush hour."

"Entirely fair. Luckily, it's off-season and lunchtime, so we should skip the bulk of the traffic."

"How do you even cope with all the tourists coming here during peak season?"

"We suffer through it because we make a lot of money. Shows are more frequent and there's higher demand, so the tickets are pricier since there's a limited number of seats."

"Oh, I guess that makes sense. I should get a little more

work done before we take a break. Come get me when the car is here?"

"Can do." He lifted my chin, kissing me until my perfume filled the air and I was regretting saying I needed to work. His hand slipped down my throat, stroking the column of my neck with his thumb. Just as I was about to cave and ask him to stay, he pulled back. "Enjoy your work."

I pouted as he departed and took my horny self over to my workstation. It took me a little while to get my focus back, but I was fully in a groove by the time Kai appeared again, my car keys dangling from his fingers.

"Your carriage awaits."

I closed everything down and hopped up. "He didn't fuck with it, did he?"

"Not that I could tell. It looks pretty clean, but we can drop it off to get detailed if you want that done first."

"Let me snoop first."

The whole vehicle reeked of Jerry and what I could only assume was Katrina's scent—sage and lemon, with an undercurrent of tobacco.

I wrinkled my nose. "I think a detail is probably a good idea. That smell would stick to my hair."

"We can have someone come do it here. Take out anything you need."

I checked the glove compartment and extracted the insurance and registration, both in my name. Nothing else of mine had survived the purge, not that I kept a ton in the vehicle.

"You really do think of everything."

Kai preened. "I'll ask Diego where he suggests we take it. He was actually the one who thought of this, but I'm the only one with the legal pull to make it happen."

"I keep forgetting about that."

As convenient as it was that Kai could handle so many things for me, I still felt a little queasy that those laws were still on the books to begin with. If I had simply left without getting bonded, then Jerry might have been able to make some kind of legal claim against anything of mine, but Kai's claim would supersede everything else. A lot had changed over the years to give omegas more authority and control over their lives, but a bonded alpha could slide right in there and take a controlling hand in any of it.

"I do really appreciate everything that you've done, and I know it was meant to be a surprise, but maybe a heads-up next time?"

"Absolutely. Shit, did I fuck up again?"

I shook my head and snuggled into his arms. "It was genuinely really helpful of you to do. I'm just a bit nervous about the legal aspect of the bond."

"Oh yeah, that totally makes sense. What if we did up a contract or something? We could put a flag on anything in your name so whoever handles those accounts knows that they're not to let any of us do anything without your consent."

I brightened, some of the weight of my worries slipping off my shoulders. "You would do that?"

"Of course I would. I want you to feel comfortable and in control of things that belong to you." He sighed. "I forget sometimes how biased the laws are toward alphas in these situations. I can't change the politics of the world, but if you would feel better about it, I am more than happy to do whatever paperwork we need to give you exclusive control over as much as we can."

I rose up on my toes and threw my arms around his neck, pulling him down to meet my mouth. He kissed me breathless until I was half tempted to drag him straight back inside instead of going out for lunch. "You're a really good alpha, Kai."

He smiled down at me, tucking my hair behind my ear and cradling my head. "I have to be so I can be worthy of the best omega. And in the interest of continuing to be a very good alpha, I need to make sure you get fed."

"I like food."

"Italian, tacos, or barbecue?"

"I *love* tacos."

We took his vehicle to a food truck on the outskirts of downtown and ate the most delicious tacos in the blistering heat until I was sweating as much from the weather as from the spice in the food.

"This is so fucking good, but I think if I eat one more, I might pass out."

"Let's get you into the air-conditioning."

Once I was back in the car, I shoved my face up against the vent and let the icy air ghost over my sweaty skin.

"Feeling better?"

"A million times better, thank you. I am a well-fed omega."

"Perfect. Wait here just a couple minutes so I can pick up some tacos to go for the others."

I closed my eyes and relaxed, comfortable as hell in the cool interior. Kai didn't take long to return, passing me over a horchata I sipped happily all the way back to the pack house.

"Working for a living is really putting a damper on me dragging you into the nest," I complained as we returned home.

"You are entirely too full of tacos for me to fuck you like I want to."

Heat flushed through my body. "Give me a couple hours to digest and you can have me any way you want."

Kai grinned. "I'm definitely going to take you up on that. Get some work done. I'm going to feed the others."

We parted ways, me to my workstation and Kai to hunt down the others with our bounty. I was oddly peaceful as I settled into work for the afternoon. I still wasn't one hundred percent certain what to do with anyone who was so dedicated to my well-being, but it was a welcome change nonetheless. All their grand gestures have been wonderful, but it was the little things I was looking for now, like getting my library card with Diego, and Kai being happy to take me out for tacos. Those were the moments that would build a life, and right now those little moments were looking really fucking good.

Chapter 35
Amir

"Y ou'd never fucking survive out there. Don't even try to pretend."

"I could survive out there better than the people walking in the river when it's about to freeze overnight," Callie defended.

She was snuggled up against my side while the two of us watched an adventure survival show. After flipping through countless options, she had perked up when I found it, so that was what we were watching.

"Do you think they have secret space heaters?" she asked. "They wouldn't really just leave them out there like this, would they?"

"Depends on if you believe the players or the production team."

We were still feeling one another out, but it got a little easier every day, finding things we had in common, and if the awkward silence stretched too far, it was easy enough to fill with the physical.

"I've never been to Alaska," she said. "It looks so pretty, though. I'd love to go one day."

"I think we would both freeze our asses off even in their summer."

Callie snorted. "That's what sweaters are for."

"We could go on a cruise," I offered. "Spend our nights and evenings in luxury, and then dip into the wilderness during the day."

She wedged herself even closer, her arm draping over my chest, where her fingers curled in the fabric at my waist. "That sounds fun. Alaska for beginners."

I had been doing so well keeping myself under control around her while we were watching this, but that light grasp of her hand sent all of my nerves into overdrive, my scent erupting like a fucking cloud around us.

Callie's perfume echoed mine and she turned her face against my throat, breathing deeply. "What did I do?"

"You don't have to do anything for me to react like this," I reminded her.

"Want me to move over?"

"Absolutely fucking not." I set the popcorn aside and dragged her straight onto my lap. "I want you right here."

It took all of my willpower to stay quiet and still, to not tell her exactly how much I wanted her right now.

She wiggled around to get comfortable, and I couldn't quite tell if she was deliberately grinding against me or if it was just a happy byproduct of rearranging herself. Once she was exactly where she wanted to be, she sighed and melted against me, dragging up one of my hands to wrap around her, her purr quietly rumbling.

"Do any of the others watch reality TV?"

"Not really. It's my guilty pleasure."

"Twinsies. This is the quintessential experience, you know?"

"What is?"

"Harshly judging the people on-screen from the comfort of our own home, knowing we would be just as stupid if we were there."

I barked out a laugh. "You're so right about that. It's my favorite part."

"Mine too." She grinned and critiqued someone's fire-starting skills, and I added commentary on how inadequate their shelter building was. It was stupid as hell, but I loved every second of it. We watched for a few hours, snuggled exactly like that, judging the participants between bites of popcorn and stolen kisses.

One kiss in particular spiraled into her straddling my lap, her hips rocking against my hard cock, while I drank in her whine. It was unfair how good she tasted. Her fingers dug into the leather on either side of my head when I squeezed her ass cheeks and pulled her closer.

I broke away, taking in her flushed cheeks just barely visible from the glow of the screen. "Should we turn off the show?"

"That's an unfair question because I like doing both of these things with you."

"All right. Turn around, then."

Her perfume exploded. Callie carefully climbed off my lap to spin around, and I stopped her just long enough to tug her little shorts and panties down to her ankles before nudging down the waistband of my lounge pants and pulling her to sit down on my lap. Her groan at the first bit of contact had me painfully hard. I balanced most of her weight in my hands so she could lower herself slowly.

"Oh my god." Her panting breaths were punctuated by deliciously desperate sounds until she had sunk all the way onto my cock, her ass touching the top of my thighs. She shook in my arms and I held my breath, adjusting to the hot, slick feel of her.

"Go on," I coaxed her, tracing my fingertips along the soft sides of her thighs. "Tell me everything they're doing wrong."

"You really expect me to be able to focus on the show?"

"Only if you want me to touch you."

Callie whimpered, her cunt squeezing me as she put her attention onto the screen. "Can't we take a break and then go back to the show?"

"Where's the fun in that?" I continued tracing patterns on her inner thighs, breathing in the plumes of her perfume, my cock twitching inside her at the richness of candied apple in my nose. So fucking sweet.

She rocked her hips, leaning her weight against my chest. "They don't know how to tie knots to save their lives."

I chuckled, planting a kiss against her shoulder, and let my fingers slide against her pussy. "What do you know about knots, princess?"

"Not much, but I hope you'll give me one." She giggled at her own joke.

"Wrong kind, but I'll give it to you soon enough. Have some patience."

"That's not fair. Do you know how many years I had to wait for good sex?" She adjusted, trying to press against my fingers. "I shouldn't have to wait anymore."

"A valid argument." I stroked her clit, loving her sharp

intake of breath. The moment I withdrew, she whined. "Counterpoint. You sound fucking incredible when you beg."

"*Amir.*"

"Mmm, say my name like that again, princess." Nudging her thighs further apart, I worked two fingers into her cunt alongside my cock, savoring the shake and shiver of her body.

"Fucking fuckity fuck. *Amir, please.*"

"Getting closer."

I took my time with her, pressing against the textured spot that had her gasping, and teasing her clit with my thumb while she slowly broke apart in my arms. When she got too unruly I took hold of her throat, not squeezing, just grasping enough to keep her attention.

"Don't forget your task."

"I can't—fuck. How am I supposed to focus when you're trying to ruin me?"

The grip of her cunt was wicked strong and I couldn't wait to feel it on my knot. "You're a capable woman. You can do it."

"Fuck," she gasped, "you."

"You will very shortly." I nipped her shoulder and pressed my thumb to her clit until she groaned. "Play the game one more time and I'll let you come."

"So mean." She turned back to the screen, where contestants were lashing together small trees to make a raft. "Fuck's sake. That's not how you tie a raft. There's too many gaps; it's totally going to sink."

"That's my good girl." I set a steady pace, firmly grinding my thumb on her clit while she twitched on my lap, her breathing shifting the longer I teased her. The delicious flutter of her cunt let me know she was close, so I kept doing exactly what I was doing until she let out a breathy squeak and spilled over the edge in a flood of candied apple, my name a long, low moan on her tongue.

"That's my new favorite sound."

Callie let out a broken laugh. "Of course it is."

I slid my fingers free and wrapped my arms around her waist, resting my chin on her shoulder.

"You're not going to come too?"

"Unlike you, I actually have some patience. Maybe I just want to enjoy being inside you right now."

She relaxed against my chest, tilting her head back to settle on my shoulder. "I don't think you meant that to be cute, but it feels that way."

"Whatever keeps you where you are." We finished off the episode exactly like that, Callie half-asleep on my lap while I drew patterns on her skin with my fingertips, her surprised clenches when I hit a sensitive spot keeping me plenty hard. It was like regular cuddling but jacked up to eleven, and something I hadn't really indulged in with previous lovers. Her perfume remained sweet and steady, more comfortable than sexually charged as the minutes passed.

"Why are they so fucking bad at making fires?" Callie laughed.

"Where would the stress and drama be if they were actually good at the things they were tasked at doing?"

"Fair enough." She wiggled around, her breath shifting when she gave her hips a slow rock. "You can't say I haven't been patient. It's been at least a half hour since you made me come."

"Have you just been thinking about that this entire time?"

"Do you think I can spare thoughts for other things when there's a cock inside me? I get, like, two seconds of brainpower at a time like this."

"I could always keep you needy and distracted." I slid both hands beneath her tank top and cupped her breasts, teasing her nipples.

She started squirming immediately. "But if I'm needy, you're gonna be needy too."

"Like I said, one of us has patience, and it's not you. My desperate little omega. Consider this practice."

"For a whole lifetime of this?"

The idea wasn't as distasteful as when she had first come into our lives. I could certainly be content with how things were evolving with her. "If you'd like."

"I would." She said it so quietly I could barely hear it.

My chest constricted. Her near-silent confession made it easier for me to admit, at least to myself, that I was starting to see an actual life ahead with her in it. Countless things were still up in the air. Money, jobs, family—that would have to be dealt with, but this right here, having her in my arms, was easier than I'd ever expected.

"Can I turn around?" she asked.

"Sure." I let her climb off my cock just long enough for her to turn and settle back down, wrapping her legs around my waist. Her smile was soft before she drew me in for a kiss. She was sweet on my tongue, her fingers tender on my cheeks.

"Do you mind I'm watching you and not the show?"

"Do I mind being more interesting to a beautiful omega? What do you think?"

"Well, I don't *know* what you think most of the time." Callie chewed her lip and I tugged it from between her teeth with my thumb.

"I like your attention on me," I confessed. "I like *you*, but I'm taking the time to learn about you and figure out if I like you because of the scent match or because we're compatible outside of that."

"Or both." She shrugged. "The scent match part definitely makes the rest easier."

She wasn't wrong. I had a stubborn streak I was well aware of, and it was holding firm about this. I wasn't opposed to falling for her, but I wanted to know it was *her* I was falling for, and that I wasn't simply being led around by my hormones twisting reality. We both deserved more than that.

Chapter 36
Callie

I paused to watch the pack, taking them in as they huddled around their laptops before they noticed me. They were all so sweet, wonderful really. The sort of men I'd fantasized about in my younger years, ones I'd never dreamed I'd actually find, and so I'd settled for the charming smile of a man who ended up caring nothing for me in the end. But these men? They cared. And I...well, the word for what I was beginning to feel was far too early to say. They were a unit, but I wasn't with each of them in the same way.

At some point that was a conversation we'd need to have. Kai and Diego seemed perfectly happy to grow a relationship with me, and Amir was giving it a chance, but Miles made no sense at all. Even if he wanted me, he'd made no move to

285

pursue anything. He was a scent match too, but that didn't mean we had to be together.

I leaned against the archway, staying silent to observe as long as I could. I'd never really felt at home anywhere, not with the people or places surrounding me, as a child or adult, but I had simply compressed myself to fit the way I needed to. Now I had no box holding me in and I had a craving to learn who I was, who I could be with these men by my side.

We had time for a lot of things, but some issues were closing in quickly, and as much as I'd love to court forever, and coax Miles out of his shell to see if he wanted to court too, it would have to wait.

Kai noticed me first, and the second he locked eyes on me, it broke the spell and all the others looked over as well.

"How are the job hunts going?" I asked, crossing the kitchen toward them slowly.

"Really fucking hard when we can't say what we've actually been doing the last few years." Amir dropped his chin into his palm, staring bitterly at the screen.

"I know a lot of helpful freelance skills if anyone wants lessons in something," I offered.

"I feel like starting from scratch with something like that would be even better than trying to go back to a job at my old company," Amir said with a sigh.

"Too bad we can't just start our own company," I said with a laugh.

They all stared at me with an unnerving intensity.

"What?"

"Okay," Diego said, "I know you said that as a joke but we do actually have all the skills we would need to do that. We would just need an investor."

"Whoa, whoa, whoa. We can't actually do that... Can we?"

"That would probably depend on what we want this company to do," said Kai.

"Are you suggesting we create a company that does live shows?" Miles asked.

I swirled the idea around in my head a bit. "I do have a degree in cinematography. And we have a house full of performers, though I'm not entirely sure how that would work because I super do not want any of you fucking other omegas."

"I'll look into some things," promised Miles. "The seed is planted, at the very least. I know how everything runs and it would be a pretty simple matter to secure everything we would need to do it ourselves. It's only the financial side of things that might make it difficult to get off the ground."

"It was silly anyway," I added.

"Not really," said Amir. "It's something that uses all our skills and experience. Just because it's not easy to start doesn't mean it's a dumb idea."

I sat with the concept, trying to sort out how I actually felt about it. If they were going to do it, I would have to do it too, and that would put me front and center again in a live show. I wasn't an actress by any means, but I could do a killer video edit, and the live shows were livestreamed. There were bound to be people who wanted a more tailored version, but then maybe part of the allure was that it was completely unfiltered.

"We still have to figure out the contracts," Miles reminded everyone.

"How much would the contract buyout be?" Kai asked.

"About three times as much as we have in the pack account right now."

"Give us an actual number," said Diego.

"Hundred grand for each of you. Well, I guess only two

hundred total is needed since they want to terminate Kai, so we don't have to buy out that contract."

"That's still bullshit," Kai grumbled.

"How many heats were you contracted for?" I asked.

"Six per year with options to fill in as needed," Miles replied. "Yours was their fourth of the year."

"It's ridiculous they can charge that much when we only had two heats left. We don't make fifty grand each during those," Amir huffed.

"So you have enough to buy out one contract in the pack account right now, and I can buy out one with my tips. That would cover everyone?"

Miles frowned. "We could do that, but then we would have no assets at all."

"What other choice is there?" Kai asked.

"Not much of one," Miles conceded.

As nervous as I was about them losing their income, knowing it would be impossible for me to support all of us, I laid it out anyway. "Miles and I both have jobs. Mine doesn't pay incredibly well, but I can contribute. Maybe with some strict budgeting we'll be fine."

"I don't want to have to budget during your courting period," Diego said sadly. "You should be spoiled."

"I've already *been* spoiled. Now we have to take a serious look at making sure our little family is going to make it."

"We're supposed to be taking care of *you*," Kai insisted. "That's what alphas do."

"And you can still take care of me, but once we're no longer staring down the barrel of this particular gun."

None of them looked too happy, but we would have to work together on this, and that included me helping however I could. Before we looked at moving into a cheaper home or making any drastic choices, we needed to find out what all we could afford.

The monthly mortgage payment on the pack house was outrageous. Right now they could cover it for about a year, well, significantly less with the contract buyouts. Miles and I could cover the necessities outside of the mortgage, but if we didn't get some steady income flow, we wouldn't be able to keep this house.

We poked briefly at the real estate market, and it was a huge relief that we had options big enough to suit us that were much more viable financially.

"Why don't we take a break and discuss?" I offered. "We could float in the pool for a bit and see what ideas we come up with."

"Might as well make use of the pool while we still have it." Amir sighed.

We broke apart to get changed and reconvened in the courtyard, rinsing off beneath the deck shower before slipping into the water. Miles passed me one of the numerous floats and I clung onto it, lazily swishing my feet.

"Do you think we could do anything to get them to release the contracts without a buyout?" I asked.

"It's hard to say," replied Miles. "Plenty of people have left over time. Most just finish out their contract, but a few left early. They're just going to be reluctant because the last heat was the most lucrative the company has ever had with that bonding."

I perked up. Maybe the solution was staring us in the face.

"What if we gave them another one just like that?"

All four of them stared at me.

"My next heat was due in about two months when I was given the serum. I'm not sure if it throws off the schedule, but it's not like management would have to wait a year to get us back on stage. They want you to keep performing. If I offered to do another heat, then you would be able to, and Diego already said he wanted to bond me in the next heat."

I watched each of them process the suggestion.

"Anecdotally, the serum only pushes back an omega's regular heat cycle about a week, so you'd still be due in a bit over a month," Miles told me. "Do you actually want to do another performance?"

"I...I don't really know. I had fun with the last one, and it would be less chaotic if we did another."

"A natural heat could be more intense." Amir's gaze was hot on me and I was grateful for the pool so I could get out my nervous energy with fidgeting he wouldn't notice. "You've never had one when you've been around alphas beforehand and the serum doesn't trigger it to the same degree."

I squeaked, warmth suffusing me when I forced my gaze to match his. "How could it be *more* intense?"

Diego floated up behind me, pulling me against his chest, my nerves buzzing at his nearness. "You'll definitely find out. Your preheat phase will probably be a bit wild now that you have a bonded alpha, plus the rest of us in the house." His lips on my ear had me perfuming, my whole body tightening.

"We would be prepared for everything this time," Miles pointed out, and I struggled to pay attention to his words while Diego nipped along my shoulder. "You wouldn't get bonded out of the blue again."

Diego licked over the curve of my throat. "You want me to bond you in public?"

"You're making it so hard to think."

"That doesn't answer my question, precious."

"Do *you* want to bond *me* in public?"

290

His purr rumbled against my skin. "Do I *want* to claim you in front of everyone, put my mark on your skin, and show the world you're mine? Hmm, let me think *really* hard about it."

Diego bit right on the spot he'd told me he wanted to mark me when he and Kai'd had me stretched across the kitchen island. My brain turned into pure mush, my head tipping back to rest on his shoulder as his hands swept up my body. I wanted to have the same connection with him that I did with Kai, to feel all that desire of his pounding through me alongside my own.

"We're supposed to be discussing, not fucking." Amir whacked Diego with one of the pool noodles. "Let her have a clear head for this."

"Fine," Diego sighed, but he still didn't let go of me.

"To clarify," said Amir, "do you want to be bonded in public, or are you only offering this because you want to get us out of our contracts?"

"Um, I mean, obviously everything would be more comfortable in private, but once the heat hit onstage, I forgot to be nervous. If you all want to, I'll do it. I might be suggesting it to get us out of a desperate situation, but I did that once and I can do it again. At least this time I know all of you and what to expect."

Diego purred quietly, the sweetness of the sound settling my worries.

"What do you expect from me?" Amir asked.

"I know you're not ready to bond. I'd never ask you to do that before you want to, let alone to get out of your contract."

He lapsed into thoughtful silence, staring at me with heat again. I felt his gaze like the blistering rays of the desert sun, sliding over my skin, ready to burn me if I let it touch me too long.

Kai snatched my ankle between his feet, pulling me through the water toward him, Diego trailing beside me. "I'm not opposed to the idea of having your next heat on stage. At the very least it would give us more time to sort out a long-term plan."

"Question."

I turned to Amir. "Hmm?"

"Totally tell me to fuck off if you're not into the idea, but I was thinking about something you said when we were getting your stuff from LA. To be clear, I don't want you to think what I'm about to say has anything to do with the fact that the management would be all over the idea. It's just something we should all consider."

"Well, spit it out," I said with a nervous laugh. "What is it?"

"You said you almost had a baby with your ex, and a natural heat with no birth control would draw a massive crowd, spike the ticket prices, and make you the hottest commodity in the city."

I tensed, and the rest of the pack froze, staring at Amir.

"Do you want to have children with the pack?"

"Oh god. Uh, well..." A confusing mix of emotions flowed down the bond from Kai. "I do want to be a mother. I've wanted that since I was little, thinking about how I would give my child a life where they never had to wonder why their mother didn't like them as much as their sister."

Kai crushed me between him and Diego.

I continued quietly, the words sticking in my throat, the pack moving closer to hear. "I'm really glad I didn't end up getting pregnant during my last heat with Jerry. That was the first time we'd tried. Looking back, I can't believe we tried at all. I don't know why he'd have even wanted to when he ended things so easily." I huffed out a shaky breath. "Enough about

292

him, though. I don't need to have a child if you all don't want one."

I glanced at each of them, and Diego looked like he was ready to eat me.

"Precious, the hot second you give me the go-ahead to bond and breed you, I'm going to fucking take it."

Kai's cock rose to full attention against me. "Before we talk kids, I think there's one more thing to add, because as much as I absolutely want to breed you like the perfect omega you are, I also need you to know that I love you. I need that to be clear before anything else."

I barely dared to breathe. "You *love* me?"

"I'm surprised you've never felt it through the bond, but yes." Kai smoothed my hair behind my ear.

I hadn't heard those words for a long time.

"I love you, I want you to stay with us, and I'd love any child you brought into our family."

"Well, if we're going for love confessions, I'm going to join," said Diego, "because I love you too, precious."

My eyes burned as I looped an arm around each of them. I wasn't entirely certain I'd ever *felt* love before. I didn't trust myself with my history, but I did feel affection pulsing in the bond, and I saw it in their eyes.

Be brave, Callie.

"I love you both, too."

Diego's purr was like thunder in my ear.

"I don't have a confession of my own," said Amir, "not yet, anyway, *but* I have no opposition to you having kids with the pack. I actually like kids."

That admission shouldn't have surprised me, but it did. "You like kids?"

"I might not have a gaggle of them around me anymore,

but I babysat a hell of a lot through high school. I can handle anything from infant to teen like a pro."

His words gave me the cutest mental image of his arms full of small children, with more clinging to his ankles. If I did have children with the pack, as nice as it was that Kai and Diego were very on board with the idea, I needed *all* of them to want it.

"Miles, you've been so quiet. What are you thinking?" I asked.

"A hell of a lot more than I should be thinking, considering we haven't even had sex yet," he confessed with a laugh.

"Does that mean you'd be on board with breeding our precious omega?" Diego asked.

The look of longing and desire that swept over Miles's face had hope surging in my chest. He'd been keeping himself so separate since I'd come into the picture, and maybe before, for all I knew, but he was my scent match too. I wanted all of them to want this, to want *me*.

"I don't want you to feel rushed or pressured when it comes to an important decision like this," Miles said. "I'd never forgive myself if you pushed yourself to do this because of something I did to fuck all of us up. We'll work something else out if we have to."

"*Miles*," I said firmly, "I'm ready if you're ready. I don't want you to feel pressured to agree with it, though."

"I don't," he promised.

He and I really needed to have a long private conversation about everything. If we were going to do this, I needed him to accept me and stop pulling away. "There's no guarantee I would even get pregnant during this heat. I didn't during my last natural one."

"In fairness," said Kai, "that heat was with a beta asshole

who probably didn't give two shits about your pleasure, and everyone knows you're much more likely to conceive if you have the best time of your fucking life."

I choked on my laugh. "You're not wrong."

"Plus," Diego added, "you're going to have four extremely motivated alphas trying to breed you. I'd say the odds are a lot higher in that case."

"Four?" I squeaked.

"I assumed Miles would be part of that. Am I wrong?"

Miles was red as a beet, and I was sure I looked about the same.

"Are you suggesting I perform onstage with all of you?" Miles asked.

Diego nodded. "I think it's only fair that if the pack is going to breed Callie, you get a chance too if she wants you there. Besides, wouldn't management be more into the idea if we had at least one newbie? Half the fun for the audience is all of those authentic reactions to brand-new stuff. You would be perfect. What do you think, precious? Do you want Miles there for your heat?"

How was I supposed to answer that when I hadn't even kissed him yet? "Theoretically yes, but I don't really want all my first times of the entire pack to be on stage."

Amir chuckled. "Pretty sure if Miles had to wait until then, he might have blue balls so bad he couldn't even use his dick anymore. Either that or he would spill the second he gets his hands on you."

"Okay, let's get back to the actual conversation at hand," Miles said in a strangled voice. "I have no issue if Callie wants to have kids with our pack. If she wants me to be a part of her heat onstage, I'll make it work."

"Miles, you don't have to if you don't want to," I assured him.

"Oh, trust me, I want to. I might change my mind when confronted with the stage fright, but I don't want you to mistake that and think that I don't want *you*."

"I kind of thought that anyway," I murmured. "Feels like we've been playing a game of tag, and you don't wanna be caught."

Miles swallowed hard. "That has nothing to do with you. I'm just trying to figure things out in my own head, and there's a lot of mess up there."

"Can you come here, please?"

Miles swam over, and Kai and Diego released their holds on me. I wasn't tall enough to touch the bottom of the pool here, but Miles was. I let my forearms rest on his shoulders, his hands moving to my waist automatically.

"We have to figure things out between us, okay? You're my scent match as much as the others, and I want to give us a chance, so please stop running away."

"Okay," he said it so quietly I could barely hear. "I'm sorry."

"Don't be sorry. I was a wrench thrown into all of your lives. I just don't want to bring a child into things, or try to, if I'm not confident in the direction things are moving with all of you."

Miles nodded, his thumbs sweeping softly against my skin beneath the water. "Can I take you away before the heat? A weekend that's just the two of us?"

"I would love that." I leaned in to kiss him and he didn't retreat, his mountain air scent thick around us even with the water diluting most of it. His mouth was tentative, but I felt the hunger simmering there, barely held back and betrayed by the shake of his hands.

When I pulled back, he still looked nervous, but he kept me close anyway. "Don't offer everything to management at once. Offer one term to start, and only add if they don't agree. Hopefully getting you bonded is all they need, but it's good to know we have other options in our back pocket to sweeten the deal."

"I can do that. So, to reiterate," I said, glancing between my mates, "we're on board with a heat onstage, and we're all happy with a potential pregnancy coming out of it?"

My alphas all nodded.

"All right, then. Miles, get me a meeting with management. I have some assholes to persuade."

Chapter 37
Callie

"And why would we be interested in a repeat performance?"

I fought the urge to roll my eyes. Miles had told me they would try to play it cool and wear me down to give them as much as they wanted while giving me as little as possible in return.

"Because I am *well* aware of how much money my show produced."

"There's no reason to think you would make that much again. People have already seen you." Jeff and Kyle were a pair of pissy pants. Their sour expressions matched their too-sharp citrus scents.

"People have already seen my pack before too, and they still show up. You don't think new people are going to buy tickets who have never seen me before? Besides, I can offer you something your other performers can't."

"Oh?" Jeff raised one eyebrow. "What's that?"

"Another live bonding during the show."

The two of them exchanged a look.

"You can't pretend it didn't get results for all of us when it happened the first time. How many people are ever going to get the opportunity to see an omega bonded during a heat unless it's their own? Market it. Sell the experience."

Kyle narrowed his eyes at me. "It's not enough."

All right, then. Let's add the next layer of sugar to sweeten the deal.

"What about a new alpha? I know people like the omega to be the inexperienced ones, but I think it would be fun to have an alpha experiencing everything for the first time."

"And you're just going to let some random alpha join your heat?"

"Not a random one," Miles stated from behind me from where he was supervising the meeting. "Me."

Jeff burst out laughing. "Are you fucking serious? You finally got tired of standing on the sidelines?"

"No need to be an ass," I snapped. "There's also no need to pretend you don't want the money you know will come from this. I know you're both smarter than that, and you can play this game all you want, but if you don't want me, I can take my talents elsewhere."

Kyle snorted. "Talents? Is that what we're calling it now?"

"If the two of you think it's so easy, maybe you should take a turn onstage in your own show. But I can understand why you might not want to. I doubt either of you could keep it up

299

that long, and I know you prefer to leech off the labor of others instead of doing actual work yourself."

"Callie," Miles said quietly, his voice laced with anxious warning.

I only shrugged. "I'm only giving them this opportunity because of you, Miles. If they don't want me, I'll head right over and sign my other offer."

"Whoa, wait. What other fucking offer?" Jeff asked.

"You can't take our performers," said Kyle. "They're under contract."

"I'm sorry, do you think we can't read? There's no non-compete clause anywhere in their contracts."

"Jesus Christ." Jeff crossed his arms over his chest. "It's still not enough. What else can you offer?"

I shared a look with Miles. I had only been bluffing about the other offer, but the management didn't need to know that. "Tell your patrons it's a breeding heat. I won't take the birth control beforehand."

That seemed to get their attention. I had already laid out the terms: all pack members would be released from their contracts with no buyout required, and everyone would continue to get paid at their same percentage rates, plus tips.

"I'll help with the cinematography this time. I think if you took down the option of a livestream and turned tickets into an auction, you'd make just as much."

"The livestream brings in half the income," Kyle pointed out.

"Start the ticket price at triple."

"You're awfully fucking confident you can pull this off." Jeff's gaze swept over me head to toe and Miles stepped up against my back.

"If you market it properly, and you don't see the results

you're looking for in the first few days of sale, we can bring back the livestream. We can also sell portions of it recorded."

"You don't want to livestream, but you're fine with it being recorded?"

"They would pay for each portion. Give them all the button and when they hit it, it'll mark out thirty seconds prior and record for the next five minutes. They can choose their favorite pieces of the heat as a keepsake."

If anyone actually paid for the entirety, we could probably all retire early.

"Get out while we discuss," Jeff ordered. "We'll come get you when we've decided."

Miles and I slipped through the doors and sat down on the chairs outside.

"How do you think I did?"

"You've got them hooked like fish."

"You think so?"

Miles nodded, pulling me in for a hug. "I know those bastards very well. They'll make us wait a bit to try to make us sweat, but they're both totally into the idea."

I snuggled against him, breathing in his crisp mountain air scent. "You're still okay being part of the heat?"

"I think so. It's nerve-racking, but I want to be there for you and it has the bonus of getting our pack into a much better situation. You'll have to give me tips for handling it as a first-timer."

"I don't think you'll be able to use my tips, considering I'm high as a kite off heat hormones during the show."

My phone buzzed and I pulled it out to see if one of the pack had messaged, but it was Jerry's name on the screen. I hit ignore and a few seconds later a call came in again.

"Fuck's sake." I ignored it again and the call came through a third time.

"What do you think he wants?" Miles asked.

"I guess I'll find out since he's not giving up." I answered with a sharp "What?"

"What the fuck did you do, Callie?"

"What did *I* do? What did *you* do?"

"Why is the bank account frozen?"

I took a deep breath, rubbing my fingertips on my temples, where a headache was already brewing. "I'm *sorry*. Did you think I wouldn't ask the bank what was going on?"

"It's a joint account. I'm just as entitled to the money in there as you are."

"I know that. But you know what you're *not* entitled to?"

"What?"

"Impersonating me and signing it over to just you. That's bank fraud and identity theft, dumbass. You know, things that are federal crimes?"

Jerry growled on the other end of the line. "Give me the money."

"I couldn't even if I wanted to."

"Callie, I'm not fucking joking. If you don't give me the money, I'm going to call your family and tell them where it came from."

Ice poured down my spine.

Miles leaned close to whisper in my other ear. "The company name that deposited the money won't lead to the shows. He's bluffing. He can only guess where that much money came from."

"Fuck off, Jerry. I'm not the one who froze the money, and it's not getting unfrozen until the investigation is over."

"In-investigation? What the fuck are you talking about?"

I rolled my eyes, looking skyward. "You fucked up *legally*. This isn't about screwing me over. You committed multiple crimes. Did you seriously not think this through?"

"Shut up."

Miles made a grabby hands motion for the phone and I passed it over. "I sincerely hope you're not considering continuing to speak to my mate that way."

I leaned close so I could hear Jerry huffing and puffing.

"*Mate*?" he squawked.

"Yes. Callie has four of those now who actually give a shit. I think any further communication with her should go through us, since you can't be bothered to treat her with any respect."

"Callie, you stupid slut!" Jerry shrieked. "How long were you cheating?"

Miles ended the call and turned to me. "I'm sorry he spoke that way to you, sweetheart."

It wasn't very often that Jerry hauled out language like that, though it certainly wasn't unheard of. "I'm used to it, mostly."

Miles's frown was so deep it etched lines in his face. He cupped my cheeks and pressed a soft kiss to my forehead. "You never have to be used to that, and I will personally make sure no one ever speaks to you like that again."

I tipped my face up and kissed him at a luxuriously slow pace, pleasure making my toes curl as my body woke up. The door to the office opened, and we pulled apart as Jeff and Kyle joined us.

"Come back in," Kyle ordered.

Once the doors to the office were closed again, they both faced us.

"We accept the terms," said Jeff. "We'll have the contracts drawn up and the current ones nullified."

"Thank you."

"When is your natural heat due?" Kyle asked.

"About six weeks."

"And what's your plan if it doesn't start on time? We use the serums for a reason."

"I'm told preheat with a bonded alpha will be just as entertaining for an audience as a heat. Warn them that it's a natural heat so they can plan accordingly."

"Fair enough. That's all for now. Miles, we'll be in touch and your job will continue normally in the meantime."

Once we were dismissed, I threw myself into Miles's arms. They locked around me instantly and I drank in the taste of him. He was still a little hesitant, taking a second or two before he melted, but this was much better than him seeming like he was afraid to touch me at all.

"Do you want to get in some practice?" I asked when my toes hit the floor again.

His cheeks flushed bright red. "I absolutely do, but..."

"But?"

"Would you think less of me if I said I wanted it to be special?" He gave a nervous laugh. "I'm the only one of the pack to get that opportunity with you for the first time."

As ready as I was to climb this man like a tree, I could understand where he was coming from. "I think it's sweet."

"Oh, thank god." He laughed in earnest this time. "I was worried you would think it was lame."

"You're much too cute for me to think that."

"Well, that's good." He took my hand as we walked, diverting to get some iced coffee before we would head back to the pack house. "So, full confession, I'm not a virgin by any stretch of the imagination, but I definitely fell into the habit of watching more than doing the last few years."

Heat rolled through me. "That's a little bit hot, Miles. Probably a great start for you too."

"Start?"

"Yeah, for our practice. We can't get you any of that on stage before the actual heat, but if you're nervous about participating, I have no opposition to you watching me get railed until you're ready to rail me yourself."

"Not sure how long I'll last doing that."

"Figure out our special first time fast and then you can join the fuck puddle."

He immediately pulled out his phone and scrolled.

"Whatcha doing?"

"Booking us a place near Lake Mead for next week."

"Hell yes." I swung our joined hands and we fell into line at the coffee shop. "The pictures I've seen are beautiful. I can't wait to go there with you."

He kissed the top of my head and looped his arm over my shoulders. "And I can't wait to get to learn every perfect inch of you."

Chapter 38
Miles

"I want to be clear that there's no pressure for this trip," I said as we pulled out of the driveway to head to Lake Mead. "If you just want to hang out this weekend, that's totally fine."

"I mean, same goes for you, but, Miles, I've wanted to fuck you since I first scented you."

Heat erupted head to toe, and from the grin on Callie's face, I could tell she absolutely noticed my scent going haywire. I'd never had to worry about it before she was around since I was on heavy-duty scent blockers so I could keep a clear head while monitoring the heats. Now, all bets were off and Callie would be too close the next couple of days for me to hide a single reaction from her.

We weren't going far from home. There wasn't much on Lake Mead itself aside from camping, but the edge of Boulder City had some cute rentals, and we were easily within a mile of the lake. I'd briefly thought about offering Callie a glamping experience, but those were neither soundproof nor in possession of air conditioning, and I didn't want my omega to melt.

Callie watched the city disappear past our windows. The drive didn't even take an hour, and I let her absorb the scenery instead of trying to push for conversation. She and I hadn't had a lot of that. I wasn't particularly worried, especially knowing I was the very first of the pack members she had opened up to. Circumstances had been different at the time, but I liked to think that we were closer now than we had been.

I parked next to the little cabin we were renting. If I squinted, I could see the lake from here, though it was warped from the heat rising off the ground. Callie bounded from the vehicle and into the already blessedly cool interior of the cabin. She paused in the foyer to take in the Southwest decor of terracotta shades, patterned carpet, exposed beams, and cacti.

"It's so cute." She disappeared to explore, snooping through the kitchen cupboards before diverting to the bedroom, where a king-sized bed occupied the bulk of the space. Callie flopped backwards onto it. "Not quite as comfy as my nest, but I'll take it."

I took a tentative seat next to her. "What would you like to do today?"

"Is it an inappropriate answer if I say *you*?"

My scent went wild and my cock immediately tented in my pants. "Um, not inappropriate, no. I just thought you might want to eat, or go check out the lake."

"We can do those first if you want." She sat up and tilted her head. "Are you nervous? If you don't wanna have sex while we're here, you should probably tell me now so I can get it out of my head."

How was I supposed to explain to her that I hadn't had meaningful sex in years? It wasn't that I didn't know *what* to do, but I'd never had so much riding on my ability to connect with someone. "It's not that. It's just... Callie, when was the last time you had sex with someone you cared about?"

"Last night." She eyed me curiously.

"I haven't had sex with an actual partner since my early twenties. I started escorting at twenty-two, did that for five years, and then was on scent blockers so strong I didn't even give a shit that I wasn't fucking anybody. I'm basically re-learning to function with my normal biology and I don't want to ruin anything."

"You're not gonna ruin anything." She wiggled over until she was touching me, resting her head on my shoulder. "I said there was no pressure and I meant it."

"I want to be with you—" I took a deep breath trying to collect my thoughts. "—as a proper part of your pack and as a partner. I just get these giant fucking walls in my head and it takes me a while to climb over them."

"Take all the time you need to climb. I'll be waiting on the other side when you're ready."

"Why don't we go swimming for a little while to work up an appetite and then I can make you some of the best white-people tacos."

Callie giggled and kissed my cheek. "Sounds great. Can you help me with the sunscreen so Amir doesn't yell at us for coming back burnt?"

"Absolutely." I changed into my swimming trunks and unloaded the groceries we had picked up into the kitchen while Callie changed into her bikini.

She approached me a few minutes later in barely there triangles of hot pink fabric, holding a bottle of sunscreen. "Ready to be slathered."

I swallowed hard at the sight of her. She passed over the sunscreen, a lotion this time rather than the spray. Goosebumps rose under my touch when I worked it over her shoulders and down her arms, sliding between each of her fingers in turn. I covered her stomach and made sure to get the sunscreen beneath all the little straps. Callie looked at me like she was ready to devour me, but stayed dutifully still while I completed my task.

I had gotten my hands on her before, but somehow her declaration of no pressure only ratcheted up the tension, turning the simple action into a silent foreplay. She watched me without speaking as I got down on my knees and propped her foot against my chest. Candied apple with a hint of cinnamon filled every breath, sweetened to new heights as my hands swept over her thighs and cupped her ass to make sure no spots were missed. By the time I was finished, I was hard as a rock and the scent of her slick was obvious.

"Return the favor?" I asked quietly, unable to tear my eyes away from hers. "I'm afraid I'm just as prone to sunburns as you."

Callie nodded and dragged one of the kitchen chairs over for her to stand on, bringing her a little above eye level with me. Her touch was impossibly tender as she carefully coated my face, taking extra time with my ears, before hopping off the chair to stroke her fingers over my chest while I tried very hard not to breathe deeply. She looked way too fucking adorable, the tip of her tongue sticking out of the side of her mouth in concentration. There wasn't a white streak to be found once she had completed my chest and arms before dropping to her knees just like I had done.

Fuck me. Seeing her down there was pure torture. My hard-on was painfully obvious, but Callie ignored it, working the sunscreen into my thighs. I was shaking with the effort to keep still when she swept her hands under the hem of my trunks to get the first few inches of skin hidden beneath it. By the time she was done, I thought I might pass out, or drag her straight into the bedroom and ruin all of our hard work. If nothing else, the sunscreen checked the urge to taste her, knowing I would get a tongue full of chemicals and coconut fragrance.

Callie fetched us a pair of towels and I packed up a quick cooler with drinks before we set off to one of the swim areas.

"It's like a bath," Callie commented when she dipped her toes in.

"It gets pretty warm in the summer, but still better than the air temperature." It was hot as balls, and while the water certainly wasn't cooling, it did make the experience tolerable. I set aside our supplies and followed Callie into the water. When she was waist-deep, she dove under and popped up again with her hair slicked against her head before launching onto her back with a splash.

She was unfairly cute.

"Enjoying yourself?"

"Hell yes. I love swimming."

I settled on my back next to her, my sunglasses blocking the blazing glare of the sun.

Callie laced her fingers with mine while she slowly kicked, swishing her other hand to stay level. "We should've brought some floats."

"I feel like that would encourage you to stay out long enough to get burnt."

"Spoilsport."

"I don't think either of us want to piss off Amir."

"Fair point."

She got bored of floating after a few minutes and slipped away, sending a wave splashing against me.

"That's a declaration of war."

Callie grinned and dove under, kicking erratically to get as much splash going as she could. Her swimming away triggered my predator drive and I launched myself in her direction. She didn't have much chance of evading me, considering how much taller I was, but she was pretty fucking agile in the water.

Callie tried to glide past me like a seal and I caught her by the ankle, dragging her close so I could scoop my sodden princess out of the water. Her arms locked around me and she wiggled until her legs could do the same, her giggles muted as she laughed against my skin.

"Is that you conceding?"

"Absolutely not." Her arms released and she fell backward against the water, swinging them like angel wings to send a massive splash straight at my face. I released her legs so I could wipe my face and she took the opportunity to get into shallower water to sprint away.

I raced after her, heart pumping excitedly, instincts sliding to the surface. My fingers caught the string of her bikini, and when she jumped forward, it unraveled the bow holding everything in place. Before anyone else could get an eyeful, I took a flying leap, wrapping my arms around her top half and sending us both crashing into the water, twisting so I landed first.

It was shallow enough here that she could get her head out of the water while bracing her fingertips on the bottom, and she was laughing heartily when I swept my hair off my face and sat up, my shoulders peeking out of the water with my ass on the ground.

"Trying to expose me to the world," she teased. "You already did that."

I dragged her onto my lap and she sat on her knees, straddling me while I tied the top back up, adding a double knot to be safe before sweeping my thumbs over the curve of her breasts. A saint wouldn't have been able to stop touching her right now, and I had certainly never claimed to be saintly. Callie shivered as I adjusted the fabric to cover her, though the peaks of her nipples pressed against it, betraying her arousal to anyone who might get close enough to look.

Callie walked her fingertips up my chest and linked them together behind my neck. "Are kisses off-limits too?"

I shook my head, barely daring to breathe. Then her perfect mouth was on mine, lips sweeping and tongue searching. I locked my hands around her hips and pulled her down. Callie only wiggled closer, every inch of our chests touching, the heat of her cunt pressed against my cock with only those thin layers of fabric separating us. I was absolutely *not* going to fuck her in the water. Who knew what the hell was in it?

The only thing in the world that mattered was the taste of her mouth and the feel of her body against mine, at least until a golden retriever came racing past us.

"Cockblocked by a cutie." Callie laughed as the dog retrieved its toy and went splish-splashing back to shore. Then Callie turned back to me, her pupils still dilated, and her candied apple scent thick around her. "Sorry, did I go too far?"

"My body would say you didn't go far enough."

"But it's your nervy *brain* I'm worried about, Miles."

"I think if you kiss me long enough, my brain could be persuaded of just about anything."

"Take me back to the cabin and I will persuade all the nerves right out of your head."

"You're so dangerous for my self-control."

"Then I guess it's a good thing I don't want you to control yourself."

Chapter 39
Amir

"You guys want to go to LA and beat up an asshole with me while Miles and Callie are away?"

Diego and Kai lifted their sunglasses, both of them stretched out on the lounge chairs under the baking sun in the courtyard.

"Who are we beating up and why?" Diego asked. "I mean, I'm pretty sure I know the answer, but I want to be extra sure."

I dropped the manila envelope on the little table between them. "Callie's lucky that guy bolted when he did. He's been up to a lot of shit."

"What kind of shit?"

"Money laundering, insurance fraud, and a warrant for his arrest in New York State."

"Oh, shit." Diego sat up straight.

"There's hardly anything in his name directly. The PI thinks he was using Callie's name to hide himself, and he's already convinced his new wife to open another joint account so he can start doing shit under her name."

"So he's already set up to fuck up this woman's life too?" Kai sighed.

"Exactly. The investigator also found evidence of five different affairs during the timeline that asshole was with Callie, plus another since he got married."

"Jesus Christ." Diego perused the documents. "We should probably tell his wife too, shouldn't we?"

"I had the investigator do up a point form report for her, and he included his contact information for her if she wants additional details."

"When did you even do all of this?" Kai asked.

"I hired him on the way home from LA. Hardly took any time to dig up all this shit."

Kai looked at me, his eyes soft. "You know, you might not be ready to bond her, but I like knowing you were so ready to protect her from the start. I think you might be in deeper than you realize."

"We're not talking about that," I huffed. "Focus on the task at hand."

"All right. How do we manage this without his wife getting caught in the crossfire?"

I could only shrug. She could only avoid so much when she'd married a criminal, however unknowing she might have been when she'd signed the papers. "She impersonated Callie to commit bank fraud, so my sympathy for her only goes so far."

"Yeah, I guess that's true," replied Diego. "She can get a divorce and face her own justice."

"When do we leave?" Kai asked.

"As soon as you put on shirts. I already have the cooler in the car for driving snacks."

The two of them bolted upstairs to get dressed, and I was waiting in the driver's seat when they joined me.

They read over the report while we drove, and we discussed the best way to tackle everything. The plan of attack was to corner Jerry and make sure he stopped bothering Callie, make sure his wife knew exactly who she was married to, and then give the investigator the go-ahead to report all the uncovered crimes to the appropriate law enforcement. Before Callie had left, we had set up call forwarding. Anything Jerry sent her would come to my phone so she could enjoy her time away with Miles. Part of the reason I'd suggested it was morbid curiosity, but it had also firmly solidified that I was ready to kick this man's ass over the way he spoke to Callie.

I was a bit reckless on the freeway between Vegas and LA, bringing the trip down to three and a half hours so that we arrived a little before noon.

Kai pushed the button for Callie's old apartment when we arrived. A woman's voice crackled over the speaker.

"Yes?"

"We're looking for Jerry McIntosh. Is he available?"

"He's out," the voice replied.

"Is this Katrina or her mother we're speaking to?" I asked.

Silence hung in the air for a few heavy seconds before the voice answered back. "Her mother."

"Can we please talk to you for a few moments? We have reason to believe Katrina's not safe with Mr. McIntosh."

More silence. Then the buzzer on the door sounded and Diego pulled it open before it could lock again. No more came from the voice, so we took that as her acceptance and made our way up to the apartment. She had the door cracked open when we got there, the chain keeping it locked.

"You're the horrible people who took everything." She slammed the door.

With a sigh, I knocked. "I'm going to slip a paper under the door, and after you read it, if you still don't want to talk to us, we'll leave."

I slid one of the summary report copies beneath the door and watched as the edge of it disappeared as she picked it up. We waited awkwardly in the hall and then I heard the scrape of metal from the chain being removed and the door opening fully.

"How do you know all this?" she asked.

"I hired a private investigator to see how much damage he had done during his relationship with Callie. It appears his behavior in that regard didn't end when he got together with your daughter."

The woman's face was a mixture of fury and tears. "He's lucky he's not here right now. I warned my daughter. I knew something wasn't right."

"Are you aware he convinced your daughter to commit bank fraud?" Diego asked.

She paled. "What?"

"The bank has video evidence," I told her. "If she doesn't already know that she's under investigation, she'll find out very soon."

She sat down hard on the end of the couch, likely a brand-new one purchased with Callie's money. "There's nothing that can be done? Can't you tell his ex-girlfriend not to press charges?"

The fucking *audacity* of this woman. "Your daughter committed a federal crime. Even if I thought it was remotely appropriate to ask Callie not to press charges, it wouldn't matter. Katrina fucked with the bank, and they show no mercy. We just wanted to let her know who she married. If you could tell us where we could find Jerry McIntosh, we'll be on our way."

"He's at the casino by the airport."

Fucking Christ. "Tell your daughter to empty the joint account while she still can."

We left her standing there with her mouth open. Rage pulsed through me. I understood her compulsion to protect her daughter, but that woman had fucked over my mate. It might not be as much as Jerry had done himself, but she had been an active participant and the duty of a decent human being ended at letting her know she'd married a complete snake. Now she could lie in her own fucking bed.

Diego got us the address for the casino and we went straight there, finding Jerry losing spectacularly at the blackjack tables. I sat down next to him and it took him a few moments to recognize me.

"Shit. What are you doing here?"

"We came for a little visit," Kai said behind us and Jerry whipped around, going immediately pale when he realized he was surrounded.

"Let's go for a walk," said Diego. "It's much too nice a day to spend inside." It was a bald-faced lie, considering it was over ninety outside.

He swallowed hard. "Let me finish this hand?"

We agreed so security wouldn't get involved on someone walking out in the middle of a bet, and we watched him lose two hundred dollars before he finally got up and followed us. His gaze darted around like a panicked fox when we herded him into the car where he sat between Kai and Diego.

"You're not going to hurt me, are you?"

"That entirely depends on how well-behaved you are," I replied. "We need to have a little talk."

I got us on Highway 1 heading north before I spoke again. Jerry's stench was sharp and panicked, filling up the car. "Would you like to explain the last text you sent to Callie?"

"I...I don't recall."

"Let me refresh your memory, then. You called her a vicious cunt for looking into a missing account you stole from her. You also included some rather colorful language about how much of a cheating slut she was for getting involved with us. The irony on that one was particularly potent."

The pathetic jackass looked like he was ready to faint.

"Not that it matters," said Diego, "but we didn't even meet Callie until you had already abandoned her and married Katrina. I just don't want you thinking your actions had any justification."

"I'm sorry. I shouldn't have—"

"You're damn fucking right you shouldn't have." Kai growled. "You say something about my mate like that again and I will personally remove all of your teeth. I didn't make it to the end of med school so I never took any vow to do no harm. I know *plenty* of ways to make you suffer if it comes down to it."

Jerry flinched.

"Maybe we should talk about the arrest warrant they have out for you in New York," I added.

"How...?"

"Oh, Jerry," I sighed dramatically. "Did you actually think you were hiding?"

"We know all about your little string of robberies in college, not to mention the money-laundering scam you ran a

319

couple years ago, oh, and insurance fraud for the truck you claimed was stolen but you actually sold?"

"Jesus, what, are you guys stalking me?"

"Feeling vulnerable, Jerry?" Diego asked. "Maybe a bit like how you made Callie feel for years? We haven't even gotten to the multiple affairs."

While we navigated LA traffic, Kai and Diego grilled Jerry about his various sins in excruciating detail. I took us all the way to Topanga State Park, nearly an hour away from where we'd started. I parked at a rest stop no one else was at.

"Jesus Christ, you're not gonna murder me in the woods, are you?"

"No," I replied calmly, getting out of the driver's seat and waiting for the others to step out. Jerry glanced nervously between the three of us before exiting as well. "If it wouldn't mean going to prison and being away from Callie for years, I would break your kneecaps and push you into a ravine. But, since we know so many fun details about you, I do get to do one thing I've been wanting to without worrying about you going to the cops."

My fist flew too quickly for him to react or dodge. Pain shot through my arm, but I knew it wouldn't be anything compared to what he'd felt when his nose crunched beneath the impact.

"Son of a bitch!" Jerry clutched his bloody face.

"If I see one more call or message from you to Callie, I *will* make good on my threat about the ravine. Am I clear?"

"Jesus, fuck. Yes, you're fucking clear."

"Good. Let's go."

Kai and Diego slipped back into the car.

"You're just leaving me out here?" Jerry shrieked.

"Yep. Kind of like how you left Callie in Vegas with no car

and no money. Hope your phone is charged. Maybe you should call your wife and see if she'll come get you." I climbed into the driver's seat and locked the doors while he was busy gaping at us. I rolled down the window nearest him. "I wouldn't count on that, though. We let her mother know everything you've done, so you might want to start walking. You only have so much daylight and plenty of things in those woods might want to take a bite out of you."

Kai and Diego waved to him out the back window as I tore out of the lot, gravel flying beneath the tires, forcing Jerry to dodge the projectiles.

His echoing *FUCK!* was one of the most satisfying sounds I'd ever heard.

Chapter 40
Callie

The second we got back to our rental, Miles ushered us into the spacious bathroom and got the water running. Still damp from our time in the water, and barely clothed, I shivered from the air-conditioning. Miles pulled me close and I savored the warmth of his skin.

"Go as slow as you want, and don't be afraid to hit the brakes," I told him.

He chuckled. "Aren't I supposed to be saying that to you?"

"I don't think I've really hit the brakes for weeks. All my omega instincts are loving me getting railed regularly." I stood on my toes and hooked my hands behind his neck, pulling him down for another kiss. He tasted like breathing on a mountain-top, or like when I used to chew peppermint gum on the walk to school in winter and inhaled what felt like pure ice. Hints of spruce and pine laced his scent, reminding me a bit of Amir, but without the sun-baked sweetness.

Miles got me under the hot spray, the dual showerheads making sure both of us were toasty.

"Are we getting naked during this shower or are we keeping the swimsuits on?"

Indecision flashed in his eyes for a half second before he reached around to tug at the knot holding on my top. "Fuck me, I tied this too tight."

I giggled while he wrestled with the knot, letting him spin me around so he could unravel it with his teeth and then undo the knot holding it together at the back of my neck. I tossed the whole thing aside and spun back around to face him. His breathing was shallow, his pupils blown wide as he stared at me.

"You're unfairly beautiful, you know that?"

"Starting to learn that, yeah. The pack is very good for my ego," I said with a laugh.

Miles got to his knees and I felt rather like a goddess with a supplicant before me. I slid my fingers into his wet hair and pressed ever so slightly, just enough to let him know what I wanted without forcing him to do it. He followed the silent instruction, his hands sweeping around my waist and his mouth closing over my nipple. Electricity crackled from his tongue all the way down to my clit. I hadn't even realized before the heat how much I liked their mouths on me like this. It hadn't happened all that often before them.

I squirmed, panting and trying not to yank his hair. "Fuck, Miles."

His fingers fanned over my back to press me closer, his tongue lapping at me like my skin was his first taste of food after starving. My clit throbbed, begging for friction when the best I could give it was a bit of pressure from squeezing my thighs together.

The second of relief as he switched to my other breast had my body shaking before the tension consumed me once more, and I rose on my toes. I dug my nails into his scalp, with pathetic, desperate sounds tumbling from my lips. If this was all he intended to give me tonight, I would savor every moment, even knowing I was likely to die of sexual frustration if he stopped.

Miles ever so slowly slid his hands down until his fingers curled into the strings holding my bikini bottom on. He tapped my back and I realized I'd been squeezing my eyes shut. When I opened them, the question was clear in his eyes.

"Please."

He pulled the garment down with the utmost care, releasing my breast so he could make sure I stepped out of it without tripping. Both of my nipples were tight and dark pink, practically begging for more attention. He traced his fingers back up my legs and I shivered, waiting to see what he would do. His hands swept around to cup my bare ass and he pressed a kiss between my breasts and trailed further down. The shower was a steamy fog of candied apple and mountain air.

Miles rose to his feet and dipped down to kiss me. Without a word, he picked up one of the washcloths and lathered it up with soap, carefully scrubbing down my skin that had been covered in sweat and sunscreen and lake water. His eyes gleamed as he worked, thoroughly taking care of my soaped breasts before his fingers slid down my stomach to make sure the thatch of hair between my thighs was extra clean.

I clung to him to stay upright, rocking my hips against his fingers.

"I think I could get drunk on your scent alone. Maybe also on each of those delicious sounds you make."

"Please. Miles, I need you."

A low, delectable growl rumbled through him and had all of my nerves at attention. "How am I supposed to deny a request like that?"

I shucked his swim trunks to the floor and he stepped out of them with ease, letting me soap up my own hand and take hold of his cock.

"Fuck. Me," he gasped out.

"I'm trying."

His reactionary laugh immediately melted into a moan when I gave him a firm stroke.

"Wash up fast so we can work up an even better appetite for dinner."

"Yes, ma'am."

We both scrubbed down in record time, rushing through the shampoo and conditioner and making sure not a single ounce of Lake Mead remained on our skin. Then Miles scooped me up and carted me back to the bedroom while we dripped a trail behind us. My purr kicked on the moment he hovered over me and I locked my ankles behind him to pull him closer and feel the weight of his body.

"It's not too fast?" he asked, droplets of water hanging on the tips of his hair as he stared down at me.

"If anything, it's not fast enough. Take your time, though, if you need to."

Miles laughed quietly. "I feel like you might burst if I actually took my time. I'll go the speed you want for now, and I'll take my time later when we've worn off the edge of your need."

"What about *your* need?"

He kissed me, slow and deep, before smiling at me. "That's going to be taken care of in about five seconds."

I shifted to get into position, holding my breath as Miles lined up his cock. I'd been ready for him all day, slick practically dripping from me, my pussy eager to get an alpha inside me. *This* alpha in particular.

Miles fucked in slowly, easing every inch and watching my reaction the entire time. Keeping eye contact with him was a struggle when all I wanted to do was close my eyes and throw my head back. He was just a touch thicker than the others, stretching me so perfectly. I adjusted quickly with a fresh surge of slick, my heels pushing against his ass to encourage him to keep going.

This time when he kissed me, it was a dazed tangle of tongues.

"I knew the moment I felt you it was all over for me," he whispered against my lips. His smile was soft when he got far away enough for me to see it. "You're going to have to let me move if you want me to fuck you."

With a whimper I adjusted my legs so they were around his waist instead of keeping him exactly where he was.

"That's my good girl."

His next thrust had me seeing stars. Like a treasure hunt, Miles's cock sought out each spot that would send me over the edge, every drag and thrust unraveling me until I could hardly think and barely breathe with how hard I was shaking.

"How am I supposed to last onstage when you feel this fucking spectacular?"

Then his teeth were on my throat and I erupted. My vision slid to black as Miles kicked off my orgasm, overwhelming sparks of sensation triggering like dominoes tipping over. His hips stuttered and he fucked deep, holding still to wait out the wave. My pussy clenched on him so hard it was probably for the best not to try to move.

"Knot?" I asked between gasping breaths when I finally started to surface.

"All in good time," Miles promised.

I moaned when he pulled back, feeling every inch of his cock leaving my body. "No." I tried to keep him where he was, but my legs felt like they were made of jelly.

"I'm just changing positions. I noticed something in this room that will be extra fun for both of us."

Miles rearranged me and I found myself face-to-face with my own reflection.

"I did tell you I was a fan of watching," he said, another soft smile gracing his lips. "No reason I can't enjoy having you and watching you at the same time."

He pulled me up so my back was to his chest, his hands snaking up my body to cup my breasts. My lips parted in a quiet gasp when he teased my nipples.

"Perfection," Miles purred in my ear. "Look at that beautiful face, losing yourself to pleasure." Miles took his sweet time exploring my skin, at least until he noticed the slick dripping down my thighs. "All that for me?"

"Yes," I whined.

One hand moved up while the other descended, his fingers carefully cradling my throat to keep me looking at the reflection while he slid through my folds to rub circles on my clit. My eyes were so wide, looking back at me. I had never watched myself before, and it was hotter than I'd expected. Miles looked wildly smug and satisfied as he coaxed more pitiful sounds out of me with his slow teasing.

"Miles, I want you to fuck me."

"I will. Let me play with you first."

I whimpered when he slid one finger inside me. It wasn't nearly enough and I rocked helplessly against his hand, seeking more than he was willing to give me right now.

"I've seen you desperate," he said roughly in my ear, "but having you desperate for *me* is a whole new sort of pleasure. Do you know how jealous I was, watching my pack have you?"

"You could have, fuck—" I broke off when he added another finger. "You could've had me anytime, Miles."

"Not during your heat. Damn near killed me when you asked for me, and I couldn't do a fucking thing about it."

"I wanted you then, and I want you now. *Please*."

"So impatient," he chided.

Miles kissed his way from my shoulder, up my throat and down the other side, pausing every so often to scrape his teeth over my skin until I was half-delirious. Every inch of my skin was flushed pink with need, and still he took his time. I couldn't quite decide if this drawn-out rise was better or worse than if he had taken me to the edge and stopped.

"Now, I've seen what your face looks like when you take my cock like the perfect omega you are. This time you're going to see it too."

He settled onto his knees and drew me back. I watched the mirror with rapt attention as his cock disappeared into me. My eyes fluttered half-closed, my shaking obvious in the reflection, and my mouth dropped open to pull in the air I needed to stay afloat.

"That's it, sweetheart. You were such a good, patient girl. Present for me."

Something in my instinctive brain clicked and I slid straight off his cock to tip forward, lifting my ass in the air. Half my face was buried in the blanket, with just enough visible to watch the mirror and see the way his face lit up with feral desire as he fucked straight back into me. I could see the indents in my hips his fingers made from how tightly he held me and I watched, fascinated, by the way he moved until it was all simply too much.

Miles fucked me until my eyes crossed, and nothing in the world mattered except for the glide of him and the impact of his hips striking mine. His fingers brushed over my clit and I was lost to the void, screaming into the blankets as I tumbled over the edge, and Miles buried himself to the hilt, his knot stealing every thought in my head.

Chapter 41
Kai

"Y ou're absolutely sure you're ready?"

"Not at all," replied Miles with a laugh.

He had been a hell of a lot more relaxed since returning home from his time away with Callie, but he still had a lot of new things coming. He had never been part of a heat before, had never coordinated working with other lovers, and thus far hadn't been chilled out enough to get in actual practice with everyone involved.

"I still think we should do a trial run."

I wasn't really worried about him having performance anxiety because Callie's heat pheromones would definitely take care of that part, but we couldn't be tripping over one another on stage.

"You know I've watched you guys fuck dozens of omegas. I know how your system works."

Callie popped her head into the courtyard, where Miles and I had been going over some of the plans for her upcoming heat. She had been showing subtle signs of preheat for the last week, but I still hadn't been sure if it was that or if the entire house had simply settled to a point where she was extra comfortable now that the entirety of the pack was on board with building relationships with her.

Every time I tried to pick apart what I was feeling through the bond from her, I was never able to come to any definitive conclusions. Maybe she wasn't certain herself. We had all come to understand that she had probably never actually felt safe before. Watching her blossom over the last few weeks since returning with Miles had been a special treat.

Callie came straight over to me and plunked herself down on my lap, nuzzling right up under my chin with a contented purr and a cloud of candied apple.

"Hello to you too." I kissed at the top of her head and wrapped her securely in my arms even though it was still August in Vegas and plenty hot.

"I got lonely. Amir and Diego had the audacity to run errands."

"Well, we can't have a lonely omega in the house."

She reached a grabby hand toward Miles and he dragged his lounge chair closer so she could stretch her feet across his lap and link fingers with him. "What're you guys talking about?"

"You."

She popped her head up with a pout.

"We're just making sure we're ready for your heat. Nothing bad," I promised.

"Okay." She snuggled back down.

My scent on her skin grew subtly stronger each day we got closer to her heat, tweaking her candied apple to be more like a fresh-baked apple pie. It eased any worries I might have had about the others going into a rut during her heat. At the very least I would be able to intervene as necessary since they were very unlikely to register me as a foreign scent with the way mine clung to Callie because of our bond.

"You smell good enough to eat, little dove."

She tilted her head just enough to nip at my throat. "I'm not the only one."

Miles watched the two of us with longing in his gaze.

"I think your other alpha might be feeling a bit lonely, too."

Callie shifted over to his lap, and every ounce of tension bled out of him. I couldn't remember a time before Callie when I had ever seen Miles relax like that. He had been so fucking high-strung since the moment I'd met him. If anything was going to help, it would be having an omega snuggled up to him.

The live show was scheduled for six days from now, and not a single one of us had any clue if Callie's heat would trigger at a convenient time. The show had been pitched to previous attendees, and even with the jacked-up ticket price, they had sold out almost instantly.

It was a huge relief that Callie's plan seemed to be working. If the clip purchases and tips were good enough, we would have a decent chunk of change to pay for our next venture. We had discussed investors, but the nature of what we did was delicate, and if we weren't beholden to someone's opinion who was just there for the money, we could tailor everything to make potential performers more comfortable. We had all been putting out subtle feelers to other performers and had a handful who were interested in switching over once we got things up and running.

It was impossible not to think about the future. As much as I tried to focus on the here and now, I was keenly aware that by this time next year we had a high chance of being parents and having our own company. I hadn't been this ambitious since I applied for med school. I couldn't drop out of this plan, though, not that I was worried about that. Now that Callie was comfortable with the entire pack, it was like her essence had spread out and filled up every hidden crack within all of us. I felt whole in a way I had never thought I would experience.

"If you're not working, can we go nest snuggle?" Callie asked.

"We absolutely can, sweetheart." Miles scooped her up and I followed the two of them inside.

Callie's purr was closer to a roar when we settled into the nest on either side of her. It was adorable how happy she was.

"Are you nervous?" I asked her.

"Not really. I like that I'll have all four of you this time. I know what to expect, too. Plus, this time any bonding will be on purpose, and I'm not fresh off a crisis so I'm pretty sure I won't flee down the road this time." She said it with humor, but the last time she'd done that, it had scared the shit out of all of us.

"Yeah, please don't. I want to keep you right where you are now or at least the closest approximation we can get on stage."

We had to be mindful for the next few days so we didn't accidentally trigger her heat early. None of us were entirely certain how responsive her heat cycle might be this close to the start, with her surrounded by scent-matched alphas. It was damn fucking hard, considering how delicious she smelled and how often one of us found ourselves with her curled up on our laps.

Self-control was the worst.

Miles pressed a kiss to her throat and Callie's moan had goosebumps rising all over my body, my cock springing to attention.

"You're making it so difficult to be careful, little dove." My lament was halfhearted at best. Her leg tossed over my hip to pull me closer and she tipped up her face to accept my kiss. I moved as slowly as possible, both to try keeping myself under control and also to avoid spooking Miles.

Going away with Callie had broken some seal, and now that the dam had burst, there was no containing it. Our sweet omega had found herself bent over just about every piece of furniture in the house the past few weeks. Miles tended to follow her around like an enamored pup who had received his first treat. I didn't typically think of my packmates as cute, but it was hard to use anything else to describe the wide-eyed wonder on his face every single time Callie came to him, or *for* him, as was often the case.

We passed the next few hours in the nest, trading Callie back and forth between us, and when Amir and Diego got home, they joined us. At least two of us were with Callie at all times over the next few days, her scent growing sweeter and stronger by the hour until just being in the same room with her had me hard.

The morning the show was due to start, we moved into the penthouse. Callie's heat still hadn't triggered, but she was so fucking close. If someone wasn't wrapped around her at all times, she started to whine, and the last thing I wanted was for that sweet scent of hers to go sour with distress.

Miles started to pace and I headed that off immediately by transferring Callie into his arms.

"Deep breaths," I ordered.

One of the other performers we trusted was our monitor this time since Miles would be with us. Luke poked his head through the penthouse doors. "People are starting to arrive."

I sent Miles with Callie, Diego, and Amir to the bed so I could talk with Luke. "She's not in heat yet."

"Damn close, though, by the smell of it," he replied. "I wouldn't be surprised if it broke during the strip. Latest during the first knot. Do you guys need anything?"

"I think we're okay." We had been carb loading all morning and making sure all of us were well hydrated.

"Super weird being on this side of the door," Luke said with a laugh.

"We really appreciate it."

"You'd do the same for me."

I nodded. He and the other alpha he usually performed with were on our shortlist of interested parties to switch over when the time came.

Hair and makeup came in after Luke, and they made sure everyone was tidy and camera-ready. They put Callie in pink this time—a white-and-rose-checkered dress—with a high ponytail and a matching flower at the base.

"I don't look silly?" she asked.

"You look delicious," I assured her.

"We should head backstage," Diego said.

Amir carried Callie, and in a couple of minutes we were hovering behind the door to the stage. The audience was packed for our sold-out performance. Management had worked quickly to set up the system Callie had suggested to capture timestamps for recorded snippets. Since we weren't livestreaming this time, that would be their only memento of what they were about to witness. Miles had snooped on the audience demographics and found that about half of them were usual livestream consumers who simply refused to miss the show. Almost all of them would be attending for the first time and maybe that would mean a lot more live shows for them. Nothing on a screen would ever compare to the real experience again.

Luke waved us on. Callie would only be alone for a few seconds as the four of us moved under the spotlights. I reached out my hand to her and she took a tentative step toward me, fresh nerves probably hitting her now that we were on the stage, but that nervousness would be battling with her heat hormones and compulsion to come to me. Once she was within reach, I pulled her for an indulgent kiss, the sound of her moan against my lips echoing over the speakers and charging the air with electricity.

Callie was passed among the four of us, each claiming a kiss before we turned our dazed omega toward the audience. She was panting by then, and the scent of her slick hung in the air. I took advantage of her ponytail and curled my hand around it, pulling her head back to expose her throat. Miles and I took immediate advantage, Callie's perfect sounds echoing while we did as we pleased to the sensitive skin of her throat and Diego and Amir worked to strip her down. We moved slowly, leisurely, until Callie was pawing desperately at anyone she could reach, standing on her tiptoes and rolling her hips forward to beg for attention where she needed it.

"So needy, little dove." Just like the first time we'd gotten her on stage, I slid my fingers down her stomach and into the little pink panties they had put on her. She was drenched and nearly feral between my stroking her clit, Amir and Diego tending to each of her breasts, and Miles at her throat. The tension in the air was almost as heavy as her candied apple scent filling my lungs.

She melted when we scooped her straight off the ground and carried her to the bed like a sacrificial offering. The others parted like the Red Sea for me and I slid straight home into Callie's eager cunt. The warmth of her was like coming home and the way she begged, pawing incoherently between me and the sheets, her ankles locked behind me to try to force me deeper, all combined to work me into a frenzy. She took every thrust, the sounds of her pleasure infusing the air around me.

I fucked hard, knowing it was up to me to push her over the edge. Diego and Amir pinned her arms overhead and she writhed beautifully against their grip while Miles put his focus onto her clit. When she came, the squeeze was like nothing else and dragged me straight over the edge with her, my knot swelling. With her scream of completion came a fresh cloud of her perfect, syrupy sweet scent, so thick I could barely think. That meant only one thing.

Callie's heat had started.

Chapter 42
Diego

Her scent was a lure and I was hooked like a fucking fish. We had briefly discussed leaving the bonding for later in the heat, but now that I was faced with the reality of her, my teeth were aching to sink into her skin. I didn't want to wait.

I draped myself over our omega. She was spread out and beautiful, a blush suffusing her skin. Kai's attention wouldn't hold her for long. Callie was already squirming when I let my weight rest on her and devoured her mouth. With the taste of candied apple on my lips, I swept my tongue into her mouth and indulged in every delicious sound she made. I wouldn't make her wait for too long, not while she was in heat, but we had plenty of time.

Her nails dug into my scalp and my back, her mouth eager and desperate. "Please, alpha. Knot." She said the words between kisses, trying to pull me closer with each one.

"I'll give you a knot soon," I promised. "I know you can't be patient right now so I won't ask you to be."

Callie rocked her hips against me, her glassy eyes wide as she tried to encourage me to get a move on. Just like we had pinned her down for Kai, they did the same for me as I kissed my way down her body, dipping to her throat, to the curve of her breast, and teasing her nipples before I nipped over her stomach.

Her muscles twitched beneath my touch and her hips strained, trying to get closer to me. I slid my thumb through her slick, enjoying her shudder as I settled over her clit and moved in a slow circle while I took my sweet time scraping my teeth over the plushness of her thighs.

Amir stretched out lazily next to her, just as slow and deliberate as I was in the way he cupped her breast and lapped at her nipple. Kai sucked at the scent gland on her wrist and Miles settled himself at her head, lifting it onto his lap. Her keening had the audience on edge, their stares palpable.

"*Please.*" The whine that came out of her was long and low, a primal demand that turned my brain to soup.

I growled. "That's a dirty trick, using my instincts against me."

I bit the inside of her thigh and settled myself on the bed so I could comfortably eat her out. She arched with a squeak when I raked my teeth over her clit before fastening my lips over it to suck until she was shaking.

"I know you want a knot, precious girl. Let me play with you a bit more first."

Callie whimpered and turned her head, seeking out Miles's cock as if she could self-soothe on it. I chuckled at the strangled sound he let out when she took him into her mouth.

"My beautiful, needy omega," I purred. "Tell everyone how much you want to come."

The energy in the air was already keyed up from her last whine. She had probably triggered every single alpha in the audience. They wanted her to come just as much as she wanted to. Her cunt smelled like fresh-baked apple pie and tasted just as sweet. Callie rolled her hips against my mouth, desperately trying to get herself off. I let her try for a while before hooking my arms over her thighs and pinning her in place.

"Alpha," she moaned. "Please, please, please."

She tried to buck against my grip, but she wasn't strong enough to get far. Tending to Callie's clit was a gratifying task with the way she writhed beneath me, gorgeous sobbing whines filling the air around us. Teasing her was entirely too much fun. As much as I craved burying my cock into her and sinking my teeth into her skin, I wanted her an absolute mess of desire before that happened.

She cried out as she broke apart on my tongue, the heat making her extra sensitive with a short fuse for her pleasure. With four mouths on her and her pussy empty, Callie was quickly growing belligerent in her lusty demands, those whines sliding into growls.

"I know, precious." I kissed her thigh. "Beg for my knot."

"Please, please," she chanted. "Diegooo. I need it. I need it! Knot!"

I purred, slowly rising up. I teased her clit a little more, waiting until her slick ran clear before sinking my fingers into her. It might have been a tiny bit petty to work her into a frenzy so all of Kai would've dripped out of her before I knotted her, but I was a bit desperate to breed her myself. She would look beautiful rounded with any of the pack's children, but I knew the second her scent came in I would go feral if it was mine in there.

Callie arched like a bow when I notched the tip of my cock and made the slow descent into her body until our hips were flush. She squirmed as much as she was able with all four of us restricting her movements, deliciously trying to encourage me to give her everything she wanted. Lucky for her, it was what I wanted too.

My first thrust into her flipped off the switch on my rational brain, though to be honest I'd been holding on by a tenuous thread already with how good she smelled and how much she was begging for me. The squeeze of her cunt was unreal. Every bit of her quivered as I fucked her up the steep slope of pleasure just to enjoy the spasms of her pussy around me.

The strange confluence of hormones during a heat meant I was more likely to come, but also to stay hard despite that, and my hips stuttered embarrassingly quickly as I gave in to the warm clutch of her body. I didn't want to knot her quite yet and I held it back as much as I could, riding her through another rise.

"Flip her," I ordered.

I pulled out in one sharp motion, and the other three tossed Callie so she was face down, her squeal of surprise drawing a smile out of me before I pulled up her hips and slid straight back in. A couple more thrusts while watching the ripple of her ass from the impact of our hips and I spilled inside her again, burying as deep as I could get before my knot swelled inside her.

Callie sobbed out her release. The rhythmic pulsing of her

coaxed every drop of cum out of me, the combined pressure of her slick and my cum trapped inside her enough to make my eyes roll back.

"Sweet fuck, precious." I groaned, gripping two over-flowing handfuls of her ass cheeks. "That grip is going to wreck me."

Amir carefully coaxed her up from where her face was buried in the blankets and claimed her mouth for his own. I settled back into a kneeling position, letting Callie's spread thighs rest on mine. She moaned into Amir's mouth and Kai worked her clit, sending both of us tumbling off the sharp edge we had been staring over the precipice of.

The surge of pleasure shattered my last connection to reality and I wrenched Callie back, sinking my teeth into the curve of her shoulder until I tasted copper and candied apple sweetness on my tongue. Callie came again while I was half-blind from the pleasure. Her frantic hands grabbed my wrist and brought it up to her mouth, the bond snapping into place as she broke the skin.

A flood of delirium, affection, and delight washed over me. The others scattered as my brain melted out my ears; the only thing in the world that mattered was the omega in my arms. I growled, frustrated that she was already on my knot and I couldn't fuck her straight onto another one. It was a slippery-ass slope into a mindless rut, and one I couldn't help but fall down when Callie was already lost to her own heat.

My knot was too thick to pull out, but Callie rocked anyway, helplessly seeking a fresh release. I rearranged us, curling over the top of her body, my fingers dipping to stroke her clit, my teeth still fastened on her shoulder.

I didn't want to let her go, not for a second.

Callie came with a muffled cry, her tongue lapping over the

bite she'd left on my wrist. I kept teasing her, and by the time I slowly emerged back into reality, she was a limp, sobbing mess beneath me who could've come a hundred times for all I knew.

A firm hand on my shoulder dragged my attention to Kai. His smile was soft as he sat down next to us.

"It's time to give her a break."

I growled, holding her possessively to me.

"I know." His voice was soothing, like he knew exactly how to speak to let me gain footholds in proper consciousness again. "You can keep her, but it's been hours and we're going to take a break, okay?"

Kai pressed a soft kiss to my temple before carefully unlacing my fingers from Callie and helping her sit up as she slid off my knot. We were only apart for a few seconds. Kai let me collect her again and Callie wrapped weak limbs around my neck and waist.

"Dinner will be here soon and the audience swap will happen while we eat. Bring your omega."

I complied, carrying Callie after Kai, the stage lights darkening behind us. He guided us to the vague approximation of a nest behind the stage, where I curled up around my omega. Amir and Miles lounged nearby.

With each bite of food Kai forced past my lips, the rut receded. Callie drifted in and out of wakefulness, Amir keeping a careful eye on her to make sure she swallowed each bite before falling asleep again.

"That rut was worse than Kai's," Amir commented. "Feeling okay?"

Truthfully, I felt fucking amazing. The hormones kept any bit of pain at bay. I probably could've broken my leg out there and I wouldn't have known the difference.

"Probably?" I answered.

Amir laughed and passed me a bottle of water. "The audience definitely got their money's worth."

Good. I looked over the bond mark I'd put on Callie's throat. We'd all gotten what we wanted.

After a brief rest, we went back out to a fresh audience. I couldn't let go of Callie, but luckily she also couldn't let go of me. Amir helped balance her, and when I slid back into her cunt, I felt the ricocheting pleasure of my own body and hers coming through the bond. It nearly sent me over the edge right then and there.

"Holy fuck."

"Intense, right?" Kai grinned. "It's kind of wild, fucking a bondmate."

I nodded frantically, trying to breathe through all the sensations.

Amir chuckled. "Let's put your mouth to good use while Diego takes care of you, princess."

Callie devoured his lips before slowly slipping down his body with a whine to suck his cock. The flow of her body as I fucked her was perfect for this position, allowing her to do nothing more than take the motion and glide between the two of us.

When Miles reached beneath her to touch her clit, the orgasm took me completely off guard, my knot swelling instantly and grinding all my movement to a halt.

"Fucking Christ." I let out a half laugh, half moan as I registered what happened. Callie was shuddering beautifully and still going to town on Amir, who had his fingers clutched in her hair.

I pulled her off him and rolled us over so she was spread across my chest and Miles settled between her legs to lick her while Amir went right back to fucking her perfect mouth. I could hardly breathe with everything surging through the bond, so I simply clutched her to me, hoping each orgasm they gave her brought me a little bit closer to breeding our omega.

Chapter 43
Miles

How the fuck did any of these guys keep it together during these shows? I'd always had the benefit of being on scent blockers, so while the omegas on stage had always smelled delicious, I had never been especially tempted by them. With Callie I was barely holding it together from one second to the next, brushing the edge of a rut with just my mouth and hands on her. Once it came time for me to get my cock into her, I was pretty sure I was going to lose it immediately.

I had done ecstasy a few times at college parties, and being around my scent-matched mate in heat was similar, but about ten times more potent.

"You doing okay, Miles?" Amir asked.

"More or less."

"Confident." Amir chuckled.

Callie had been in heat for a little over a day, and I had been rock-hard the entire time but had been too fucking nervous to take her. It was already tough enough to keep it together just playing with her and seeing the others make her shatter.

"Well, it's easy to be relaxed when she's a fountain of heat hormones during spikes. My anxiety has time to get the better of me in between those."

"You're doing *way* better than I expected," Amir confessed.

I gave him a chagrined smile. "Thanks."

"I'm serious. It's not easy to keep your head during all of this. I have a fuckload of experience with this, and I can feel how close to the edge I am just because it's Callie."

That made me feel a little better, but also even more nervous at the same time. If he was struggling, what hope was there for me?

I took a deep breath when it was time for us to go back out. I couldn't avoid taking a full turn with her for the entire heat. The audience might not notice with the change-out, but management certainly would, and I had to fulfill the basic obligations of being part of a heat show. They would never hire someone who was afraid to fuck the omega on stage, and they definitely wouldn't keep someone on staff who refused to do so.

Callie staggered out ahead of us and a hush fell over the audience. The lights glinted off her skin, every inch of her coated in that delicious candied apple scent that saturated the air. All the eyes watching me as I followed her onto the stage made it more intense. Even with my focus on Callie, I could feel the heat of their gazes.

"Come here, sweetheart." I stalked toward her and she let out a whine that had all of my primal instincts flaring. I walked

through plumes of her scent, her eyes gleaming with excitement as she retreated. I caught Kai's gaze where he stood backstage on the other side, taking his nod as reassurance that Callie
was playing and not actually trying to retreat. It was probably
too early for me to stake my claim on her, but god, I wanted to
feel the bond sink into my bones and blood, to tune me in to
her deepest desires.

I unleashed a low, rumbling growl that spiked her scent and
had her whimpering, the light catching the glisten of her slick
sliding down her thighs.

Fuck me.

One quick step and a leap had me caging Callie against the
bed in the middle of the stage. Her ankles locked behind my
back and she raised her hips to grind only half-successfully
against me.

"Hello, sweet girl. Did you need something from me?"

Callie bit her plump bottom lip and nodded. She curled
her fingers around my cock and tried to rearrange us so I could
slide into her dripping cunt.

"So impatient," I chuckled.

"I'm in *heat,*" she whined.

I purred and stroked one finger from her lips all the way
down her body to slide between her slick folds. "So you are. I
suppose it would be cruel of me to deny you?"

"Yes!" Callie bucked her hips and I withdrew my hand,
smiling at her mewl of protest.

"Now, sweetheart, what makes you think I'm not cruel?"

She whimpered and spread her thighs further. The rustle of
the audience shifting and the swell of their anticipation filled
me up.

"You should let me play with you a little first. Be a good girl
for me, and then I'll fuck you."

I sat down on the edge of the bed and patted my lap. Callie clambered obediently over and I stretched her out over my thighs, stroking my hand over the swell of her ass. She yipped at the first impact of my palm against her skin, a flood of slick dripping down her thighs.

"Sweetheart, did you like that?"

Callie nodded excitedly.

I smacked my hand down on the other cheek before smoothing my palm over the flushed skin. "I wish you could see how beautiful this shade of pink is. Spread your thighs for me."

She wiggled around, doing her best to accommodate the order. The next impact was straight onto her clit. Callie's initial yelp melted straight into a moan and I couldn't help moaning myself at how wet my hand was with her slick when I pulled it away.

"Look at how drenched you are." I reached my hand out to her and she craned her head around to lick at my fingers. "Should we get these inside you?"

"Please," Callie gasped out. "Miles, please."

I plunged my fingers into her, delighted by the sound while she shuddered in my lap. I cradled her throat with my other hand to keep her in place while I had my fun, coating my thumb with her slick and working it into her asshole so she was going nowhere soon. Judging by the tension radiating from the audience, they were enjoying this just as much as Callie. She came hard on my fingers, slick lighting up like glitter under the stage lights as it leapt from her pussy.

I kept her occupied just like that until the muscles in my arm burned and a puddle of slick shone beneath her.

She was as prepared for me as she was going to get.

Now or never.

"Present for me."

Callie moved like a newborn foal on wobbly legs, using the bed to support her as she climbed atop it and raised her ass in the air.

What alpha on the planet could resist that? Not me.

My anxiety clashed with my desire to give her everything she wanted. Every breath turned my brain to mush, whittling down my resistance and soothing my nerves. I filled my hands with her hips and dragged them back, driving my cock into her wet heat in one smooth motion, not giving myself time to think anymore about it. Fuck, she felt like heaven. The grip of her was like a vise, squeezing me, trying to get me to come so I could give her my knot.

Callie rocked against me, all those beautiful desperate sounds a symphony of need that called to every alpha instinct I possessed.

I wrenched Callie up and sank my teeth into her throat, coming instantly at her cry, her pussy convulsing around me. The guttural sound she released along with the swell of slick and a cloud of her scent severed my connection to rationality.

The energy around us was electric as I wrapped one arm around her waist and the other around her throat, letting my teeth sink as deep as instinct demanded. Callie writhed in my arms, panting and dripping slick down my thighs.

With the taste of metal and candied apple on my tongue, I pushed her forward, pinning her by the back of the neck before taking her as hard as I pleased. She took every thrust, pawing frantically at the blankets and tipping her hips back to meet my movements. I couldn't get enough air and I felt like I was half drowning as I rode my omega into the bed.

That was what she was. *Mine*.

A dark halo surrounded my vision, illuminating only the

beauty before me. She was the only thing that made sense right now. I curled my fingers over her hip, digging into the plush softness, and I drove myself harder, deeper, all to the music of her moans.

I fucked her just like that until I couldn't see straight, my throat burning from the constant growl. I couldn't see them, but I could feel the other people nearby.

They weren't allowed to touch her.

She was *mine*.

Slick splashed out of her each time I buried myself to the hilt, and I savored the drip down my skin. She sobbed her way through another release, and I followed the compulsion of her milking cunt, tipping my body over hers one more time before my knot swelled and her teeth ripped into the flesh at my wrist, awareness of her exploding through every molecule of my being.

I ground against her and snapped my teeth back into place at her throat, lapping my tongue over the bite. A disorienting wave of desire and contentment filled me up, my emotions and hers sloshing over the edge of my soul.

Too much.

Not enough.

I wanted to crawl right inside her skin, but being knot-deep would have to do. Even though I couldn't move, I still tried, grinding our hips together while her pussy twitched and squeezed around me. Settling us on our sides, I curled around her. Callie tucked herself close until she was a little ball of omega with barely a patch of skin untouched by me.

She licked my wrist, slow deliberate laps that had me shaking. In the back of my mind there were flickers of light, comforting presences that I only half recognized in my daze. Time warped and spiraled, punctuated by bursts of pleasure.

A soft hand touched my shoulder and I jolted to attention, crushing my omega to me so hard she squeaked and squirmed against the grip.

She had to stay right here.

"You're okay, Alpha," the voice crooned. "She needs to breathe."

I growled and latched my teeth onto her, refusing to relinquish my omega.

More hands appeared, but my gaze was unfocused so I couldn't see who it was. They stroked my hair and carefully unraveled my fingers from where they held onto her, all while murmuring softly and whispering words I couldn't quite understand.

"Miles?" Her soft voice broke through the haze as she nuzzled my hand.

I grunted in response.

"You're squishing me."

I understood those words but couldn't make myself do anything about it. The other hands pried at me.

"Come on, Alpha. Your pack is right here. Your omega is safe."

Safe.

Was she? She only felt safe when I was curled around her.

"You did so well," the voices assured me. "Let our omega go."

Our?

Right... Pack.

I let them untangle me.

Slowly, my vision cleared and my brain let me process the faces looking down at me. Kai and Diego.

"There you are." Kai smiled.

"You fucked our beautiful omega for hours," Diego told me. "Luke said your tips are unreal."

I blinked, working my brain around to remember what that meant. Bit by bit, the stage and the spotlights clicked into place. "Really?"

"You made more than Kai or I did when we bonded her," Diego replied. "This is the first time we could get near you. The next audience swap is happening right now."

I buried my face against Callie's hair, huffing her sweet omega scent. It was tinged with spices and fresh air, like a carnival on a mountain top. My purr rumbled through me and I hugged her close, but not with the death grip I'd had on her before.

I felt a bit like I had been run over, but a bone-deep contentment filled me, offsetting the worst of the exhaustion. Exactly where it was coming from, I couldn't tell. It flowed from me and Callie, and delicate streams from the two alphas around me as well.

Callie was scooped out of my arms by a scent my brain didn't quite register, and I snapped my teeth.

"So vicious," Amir said with a roll of his eyes. "I'm going to take care of our omega, and Kai is going to manage you two so you don't keel over in the last stretch of the heat."

I didn't like the idea of Callie going anywhere, but now that she was no longer in my arms, I felt the sharp pang of hunger and the ache in my body. Kai drew us backstage, where I collapsed onto one of the couches and stared up at the ceiling.

Holy shit.

I bonded Callie.

Chapter 44
Amir

While Miles and Diego were occupied, I stole Callie away for a much-needed bath. I was honestly surprised Miles had held it together as long as he had, though the strength of his rut had been impressive. I'd almost worried Callie wouldn't be able to take a fucking that intense, but she'd come on repeat like a champ, her slick protecting her from Miles doing any damage. She might need to sit on an ice pack for a while once this was all finished, though.

I'd filled up the bath when it looked like things were finally calming down out there, and Callie stretched out in my arms in the massive soaker tub. She hummed happily, brushing the edge of lucidity. Her heat spikes had been longer this heat. I wasn't quite sure if that was because it was her first natural heat with alphas, or if Diego's bonding had kicked it off.

I made Callie sip from a water bottle while we soaked, lounging in the tepid bath. I didn't want it to be too hot when her skin was already burning up.

"You awake yet, princess?"

"Mostly," she replied, stretching further and rolling her ankles.

"I want to talk to you."

Callie laughed quietly. "Ominous."

"It's nothing bad," I promised.

"Okay." She sighed and tipped her face up, nuzzling my cheek with her nose.

"I've been thinking. This pack is my family, I'm closer to them than any blood, and I've realized that there's no pack without you." I breathed in her sweet scent and traced patterns over her skin. "I had no intention of bonding you when we came here, but after seeing Diego and Miles get their teeth in you, it's all I can think about."

As if on instinct, she tipped her head to the side, baring her throat to me. I dropped my mouth and slid my tongue up the column of her neck. I didn't dare use my teeth.

"What do you think about bonding?"

She relaxed a little deeper. "I think I might like an 'I love you' before we crack open our souls to each other."

I couldn't help but laugh. "I've never told any partner I loved them before."

"Have you told your pack you love them?"

"Yeah, but that's different."

"Is it? *We're* pack."

"Does getting fucked into unconsciousness turn you into a brat?"

Callie giggled. "Maybe."

"What I feel for you...I've never felt for anyone else, ever. I want to be with you, body and soul. I want to continue learning every detail of your life, your hopes and fantasies. I want to take care of you until I'm put in the ground."

Callie's sigh was deep and luxurious, her fingers snaking up to cup the back of my head. "It's okay if you can't say the words."

It wasn't, though. I hadn't heard it much growing up, and she probably hadn't heard it nearly enough in her last relationship. Withholding it from her just because I was scared wasn't fair.

"You're it for me. There's no point in denying it." I laced our fingers together and brought her hand up so I could kiss the back of it. "You've been far sweeter to me than I deserved with how I behaved when you came onto the scene. I felt it from the start but was too fucking stubborn to accept it, but I think..." I sighed. "It feels so much better not to fight it, to just let you in."

Callie wriggled around in my arms until we were face-to-face.

"I *do* love you," I promised. "I genuinely have no idea what else I'd call what I feel. I've just been a cranky chickenshit about it." I toyed with the wet ends of her hair, wrapping it around my fingertip. "I want to be your alpha."

She cupped my cheeks, drawing me in for a kiss that stole my breath. "I love you too."

"I don't have to bond you today," I said quietly. I wanted to, though. The whole pack had that connection with her and I wanted to be part of it. The thought of waiting another three months for a chance made my stomach twist.

"What if I want it to be today?" Her eyes were bright and focused on me, no sign of the heat hormones driving that decision.

"Do I have to do it on stage?" I'd take her any way she'd have me, and maybe I was feeling sentimental, but I wanted to avoid the spectacle for this.

Callie tipped her head, showing off her throat where Diego's bondbite sat alone, space for mine right alongside it. "Do it right here."

My cock hardened so quickly it smacked her, setting off a fresh bout of giggles. My teeth ached as I drew her onto my lap. I didn't slide into her, knowing that had been the trigger point for Miles to go into a rut, and I was not going to let that happen while I was in the bath with her.

Callie's smile was content and she relaxed entirely against me, purring as I kissed my way from her shoulder to the top of her throat, carefully avoiding Diego's bite. My instincts were a dull roar in my ears, demanding I claim her.

"Amir," Callie whispered, "take me."

I licked the space above Diego's bite and set my teeth against her skin, shaking with the effort not to tear into it. Her fingers curled in my hair, the soft press a silent encouragement.

I bit down until I broke the skin, and Callie convulsed in my arms with a cry of pleasure before her teeth sank into my throat in turn. Pleasure hit me like a truck, my body tensing and my cock emptying into the bathwater. The brilliant light of her exploded in my chest, and I couldn't help but feel like an idiot for having been afraid of this. All that sweet affection washed over me like waves on the shore, leaving me smooth, all the sharpest edges of my worry smoothed away in the wake of her.

All the warmth of Callie, and the delicate tendrils of the rest of my pack reaching out poured into me, the five points snapping into place, a constellation connected like it was always meant to be. I was complete, at peace in a way that made me never want to move from this spot.

Callie licked my throat, sending shivers through me. Her purr was like a buzzsaw.

Kai appeared in the doorway, an anxious Diego and Miles on his heels.

"Welcome to the pack 2.0," Kai said with a grin. "Are you gonna go into a rut too?"

"I feel in control at the moment."

"Good. We should still get back out there, though, just in case. If you're going to rock Callie's world, the audience will want to see it."

Kai helped extract her from the bath, and the five of us tumbled back out onto the stage while the audience was getting settled. Desire pounded like a drum through my body as Callie slipped into another heat spike.

"Fucking hell." I tried to breathe through the surge that came through the bond, but there was no helping it. I descended on Callie instantly. The water had washed most of her slick away, but the spike brought more, easing my way into her. She arched like a bow and the rest of the pack fell upon her.

We had little finesse in the way we crowded around her, rearranging her so we could all get somewhere. Diego propped her up on my lap to work his way into her ass, Kai going straight for her clit while she pawed at Miles to get his cock into her mouth. Once Diego was fully seated, he lay back, drawing Callie down on top of him, and I followed along, fucking her while she was sprawled over him. Her fingers curled around

Kai's cock, her body containing all four of us in some manner or another. It was a hell of a snug fit with Diego wedged up her ass and my knot threatening before I'd even come.

Her pussy squeezed me with every twitch of her muscles at the attention the pack was giving her. She looked so fucking beautiful while she was being used.

"Our perfect omega," I whispered. "All ours."

I grabbed hold on her thighs and rode her while the others did their best to make her come, unraveling Callie in an endless cascade that eroded my self-control.

I clung to the edges of reality, desperate to stay focused and present. I bucked as hard as my instincts wanted, huffing her scent, overwhelmed by the torrent of need that came from every angle in the bond. Kai spilled first, painting her skin with cum that shone under the stage lights. Miles followed next, emptying down her throat, a trail of white dripping over her cheek. Then Diego, Callie erupting as his knot filled her, the pressure setting me off a second later, my own knot locking Callie and me together.

Desperation burned through me. Kai kept teasing her clit, and I was certain my orgasm wasn't going to stop with the way Callie's cunt kept clamping down on my knot. I was breathing so hard spots danced in my vision. Callie begged for more and I wasn't sure how that was even possible.

I sank down onto Diego's legs and tapped Kai, dragging him to wedge himself in front of me. I leaned back as far as I could to accommodate while I battled for coherency, Callie's body giving way to Kai's fingers somehow wedging into her with me already filling her up.

"You really want more, little dove?" Kai asked.

"Yes!" She shuddered, rolling her hips between Diego and me.

Kai huffed out a nervous breath. "Okay. Be a good omega for me and stay still."

No one moved. I barely breathed as Kai patiently created space for himself, his fingers pushing Callie's limits while she mewled and shook, doing her best to obey his instruction. The audience was silent and watching to see if he'd actually make it inside our omega with my knot already in there. It shouldn't really have been possible, but there was something to be said for a determined omega. She whined and shivered the whole time, her scent thick as a fog around us.

All at once, Kai's cock breached the seal of my knot, the pressure setting all three of us off, Diego following after as Callie's body contracted around him.

"Fucking fuck *fuck*!" I listened to the sound of everyone's frantic breathing, the slurp of Callie getting her mouth back on Miles and triggering his knot as well, though he blessedly had the foresight to pull out before it swelled behind her teeth.

Four cocks in an omega. We'd never done that before, but considering how tenacious Callie had been, it probably wouldn't be the last time we tried this.

Time warped and faded, marked only by spikes of heat and pleasure. I lost myself in the taste and feel of our omega, drowning in the affection that flooded the bond. It cascaded in waves as we carried Callie through the final hours of her heat, giving her every ounce of pleasure she demanded and then some.

She was so perfect, and for once I didn't question it. It was impossible to question if I had made the right choice in bonding her because the reality was that I felt the truth and rightness of that decision in every ounce of my being. The pack ebbed and flowed through the bond, wrapping around one another in the ancient dance of alpha and omega.

It was just Callie and I at the tail end of the heat, and I leaned down to whisper in her ear, nipping her sensitive skin as my hips rolled lazily to drive my cock into her.

"I love you, princess."

Callie shuddered as she came again and locked all of her limbs around me, pulling my mouth to hers. "I love *you.*"

Chapter 45
Callie

I felt like I had been run over. In a good way, if there *was* a good way for that to happen. Every muscle ached deliciously and my pussy throbbed. My skin was decorated with bondbites and fingerprint bruises, some places rubbed pink by stubble that had grown in through the heat with no time for body maintenance.

Miles noticed I was awake and abandoned the lasagna he was eating. None of them had gone far, all of my alphas relaxing in the bed in the penthouse and eating while I had worked my way back toward consciousness.

"Sweetheart, I'm so sorry."

"For what?" I stretched, groaning as my muscles protested the movement.

"I didn't get to say I loved you before I bonded you, and I did that without permission. I didn't mean to."

I tugged him until he stretched out next to me so I could snuggle into his arms and rest my head on his chest. "You can't help a rut."

"I know, but I should've told you I wanted to bond you before all this happened. I got too anxious and the words wouldn't come out."

"I like having a bond with you." I tapped his chest. "You don't feel anxious to me."

Miles chuckled. "Hard to be anxious about something when I can feel all that love coming from you."

I purred happily. "You don't need to worry about not telling me the words. I feel them."

Miles hooked his fingers under my chin and tilted my face up. "I'm saying them anyway. You deserve to have my honesty, and I love you so fucking much. I used to think people were ridiculous when they talked about the instant bond they felt with their scent-matched omega, but I don't anymore. You were everything we needed, and I hope we're everything you need, too."

I brought his wrist to my lips and kissed the bite mark that was still healing there. "I wouldn't want to be anywhere else. I love you too, Miles. I'm really glad you lost control and now we're all together forever."

He gave a broken laugh and the others gathered around us.

"You need to eat," insisted Amir.

"Chewing feels like work," I lamented.

Diego chuckled. "That's probably because you spent a long-ass time trying to suck Miles's soul out his cock. Any jaw would be tired after that."

I burst into giggles and my alphas helped me sit, Amir sliding a straw between my lips.

"Drink," he ordered.

It was thick and chocolatey, with a slight aftertaste of protein powder.

"No chewing required," Kai said as he pressed a kiss to my hair.

I sucked down the entire concoction, ravenous the moment the liquid touched my tongue. I lounged like true royalty while they plied me with drinks and blended soup to help restore my energy.

Once I'd inhaled a bit of food and water, they let me sleep, which I did, like the dead, for about sixteen hours. When I woke, I felt like the raisin version of myself and gratefully accepted a bottle of fruit punch electrolytes from Amir to plump me back up.

Not a moment passed where I wasn't being touched by at least one of my alphas. Between naps and meals provided by the hotel, I barely had to move during my three days of recovery post-heat.

A knock at the door had me drowsily turning my attention toward it, and Kai pulled on a robe to answer. "Hey, Luke. What's up?"

"All the funds are cleared, and management wanted me to give you these." He passed over some manila envelopes.

"Contract dissolutions?" Kai asked.

"You bet." He glanced past Kai toward me, where I was luxuriously draped with a super soft blanket. "How are you holding up, little lady?"

I lifted a hand to give him a thumbs-up.

Luke laughed. "Are you guys going to go ahead with the new company now that you have the money?"

"We have to talk about it more," said Kai, "but that was the plan if we hit this threshold."

"Kickass." Luke beamed. "Hit me up as soon as you're ready."

"We absolutely will," Kai promised.

When Luke departed, Kai retreated back to us.

"I feel like I missed key details."

"In fairness, you've been sleeping a lot." Kai dropped a quick kiss on my mouth. "We cleared a half million between our pay and the tips."

I bolted upright. "Holy shit! Really?"

"Yep. And these—" He tapped the envelopes. "—are our freedom in print."

I swiveled my head toward Miles. "Are you still going to work for them?"

"For a while. I can double shift it while we get set up, and I can make sure we don't touch too much of our nest egg."

If I weren't so exhausted, I would have wanted to start work on everything right now, but I stayed quiet knowing my pack wouldn't let me even if I were up for it. They were very serious about rest.

As comfortable as the penthouse was, I was eager to be back in our own home. I peeked over the edge of my blankets and nudged Diego with my toes. "Nest?"

"Ready to head home, precious?"

"Yes, please."

Home with all my alphas sounded like the best thing in the world.

Two months later

"Why does three minutes feel like it's taking a million years?" Diego sighed.

"Because we're waiting for the best news ever?" Kai replied.

Diego laughed. "That was mostly rhetorical."

We were all waiting in a room at the omega clinic. I was curled up on Miles's lap, my fingers locked with Amir's while Kai and Diego paced.

The timer we had set up went off, but the doctor didn't return.

Diego slumped onto one of the empty chairs. "This is torture."

"Exterior torture for you. I'm the one waiting to see what's going on in there." I patted my stomach. My scent had just started to come in, though I could have guessed something was going on even without that. I couldn't put my finger on it, but I felt *different*.

Everyone straightened when the door opened after a quick knock. "Sorry to keep you waiting. We had some anomalous results."

"Anomalous how?" Kai asked.

"Callie's levels are exceptionally high for what we would expect this early in the pregnancy. It's a good indication she's got twins in there."

My heart cranked into gear.

Pregnant.

With *twins*.

Holy shit.

My pack erupted with excitement, four alphas hugging me tightly.

"Congratulations." The doctor grinned at our exuberance. "If you'd like to know which alpha markers showed up to indicate parentage, I have those in here."

Kai accepted the envelope. "Does that mean fraternal twins if there's more than one marker?"

"It does, yes. It's unlikely that there are more than two babies, but we'll check on that right now if you'd all like to follow me for the ultrasound."

We trailed after the doctor and she got us set up with a tech. The gel was heated and warm on my belly while the tech glided the device over my skin. "Here's baby number one." She showed the pocket on the screen with a little dot nestled on the side of it before moving the device over to show the second on the screen as well. "And baby number two."

I pawed excitedly at Kai. "Look at them!"

"I'm looking," he said with a soft chuckle.

The rest of the pack was staring at the screen as well, a mix of awe, anxiety, and elation flitting over their faces. The tech checked the babies from every angle and the doctor assured us everything seemed healthy at this phase.

"Callie, I'll get you a schedule of all your appointments, but you're absolutely free to call us with any questions or come in at any time on top of those dates."

"Thank you."

The alphas were blissfully excited on the way home from the clinic.

"We should move into a place with more bedrooms," said Amir.

"Or we could renovate," Diego offered.

"Already looking at the market," replied Miles. "Probably cheaper to move than to renovate." He turned his tablet toward me, showing a gorgeous two-story home very similar in design to our current pack house, but listed as having ten bedrooms.

"Ten?!"

Miles shrugged. "You've got four alphas and only two babies in there. Do you think we're not going to compete until everyone has put a baby in you?"

I laughed, leaning into Diego, who already had a hand protectively laid over my belly. "Let me grow the first two before we start worrying about the next ones. What's the extra bedroom for?"

"Office, probably. Or playroom."

"Ten just seems like a ridiculous number."

"There are pack houses twice that size," Amir pointed out.

"Exactly," said Kai, who was left out of the looking since he was our driver. "If we plan ahead, we can enjoy some extra space and then we won't have to move again once that gorgeous body of yours is all done having babies."

I couldn't help my grin. These kids were going to have so much love they wouldn't even know what to do with all of it. I couldn't imagine how different my life would be if I had grown up with four devoted fathers and a mother who desperately wanted me. A rational person probably would've been nervous at the prospect of twins, but I wasn't at all. I was so fucking happy.

"You're going to hurt your cheeks smiling that hard." Amir laced his fingers with mine and kissed the back of my hand.

"How am I not supposed to smile when you guys are this cute?"

"Fair point." Amir laughed and turned my face to his for a kiss. "Did you want to know who fathered the twins? Or should we see who they take after once they're born?"

"I can't decide. You guys vote."

"I bet Miles is one of them," said Diego. "That rut was wild."

Miles flushed pink.

"I can't disagree with that. Kai probably has a kid in there, too," added Amir. "He was first knot."

Diego buried his face against my skin, inhaling deeply. "Precious, how am I supposed to sniff out who put a baby in you when you smell like all of us?"

Amir tucked against me as well, the two of them sniffing around exaggeratedly like bloodhounds, making me giggle. "You guys are ridiculous."

"Don't make me pull this car over," Kai warned, humor bright in his voice.

"Drive home faster so we can all have omega time," Diego told him.

They discussed the potential parentage the entire way home, placing bets on each other. They were all pretty sure Miles was the father of one of the twins, but were split between Kai and Diego for the other. I had no preference, nor any real idea of which of them had a better chance than the others.

Once we were in the nest, Amir held the envelope aloft. "Bets are in. Let's see who's right and who's going to have an empty wallet."

I waited in a pile with my other alphas while Amir perused the document the doctor had given us.

"Well, we were definitely all right about Miles."

Kai and Diego whooped with joy, jostling Miles around and congratulating him on his virility while my shy alpha blushed red as a beet. Miles kissed me until my toes curled, his hand settling on my belly, soft affection sliding through the bond from him.

"Who's number two?" Kai asked.

"So impatient," Amir tutted. "Maybe you should just wait a while."

"Or we could toss you in the pool and read the name ourselves," Diego said with a laugh.

Amir rolled his eyes. "Don't be like that when you and I are the bet winners."

"Shut up!" Diego sat bolt upright. "Are you serious?"

"Mhmm." Amir held out the paper and Diego grabbed it, staring at the words printed there like he couldn't believe it.

"Holy shit." He turned to me, his eyes wide and full of reverence, pure delight cascading through the bond. "Precious, you're having my baby."

"You bet your ass I am." I grinned. "Now show me how happy you are about it."

Diego practically jumped on me, peppering my face with kisses while I shrieked with laughter. All the alphas curled around me. There was a hint of disappointment from Kai, but it was mostly eclipsed by genuine happiness. The twins would have all of them as fathers regardless of biological parentage, and I knew they'd all love the babies no matter what.

Kai's kiss was softer than the others, a quiet sweetness, and then he whispered against my lips, "You're going to be the most beautiful mother, little dove."

I beamed at him.

Amir caught my gaze, steady contentment thrumming down the bond from him. "Everyone quit hogging. I need to kiss our omega."

Between all of their joy and my own, I was floating on cloud nine. We had babies on the way, I had a pack that adored me, and I'd never felt this much love in my entire life.

My phone rang, startling all of us, and the LAPD flashed across my screen. I answered. "Hello?"

"Hello, this is Detective Jones. I'm looking for Miss Price?"

"That's me." I confirmed my full name and birthday for him.

"I'm calling to inform you that arrests were made on two cases pertaining to you."

I sat up sharply. "Oh?"

"Mr. Jerry McIntosh has been taken into custody for bank fraud, in addition to multiple other crimes that were reported to us by an investigator working for your pack. And Katrina Winston has been taken into custody for identity theft."

Oh, shit. "Thank you so much for telling me. Do I have to do anything?"

"Not at this time. This is a courtesy call only."

I was vibrating by the time we hung up and immediately spilled the news to my pack.

"Good riddance to both of them," Amir snapped. "Those two deserved each other."

The rest of the pack murmured agreements. I hadn't necessarily wanted either of them to be arrested, but it sounded like Jerry had been up to no good outside of fucking me over. Probably better for the world that he wasn't allowed to run free.

The mail slot squeaked, and Amir got up to fetch whatever we'd gotten. He held up an envelope when he walked back into the nest. "Callie, you have a letter from your bank."

I reached out for it and ripped it open, freezing as I read the words. "Oh my god. OH MY GOD!"

"What is it?" Kai leaned over to read it, the rest of the pack hovering around me.

"They released the account! That's another sixty thousand for the business." I opened up the app and immediately transferred over the daily limit to my personal account. It would take a while to get everything out of there, but Jerry was in no position to take anything else from me ever again. I wiggled excitedly, throwing my hands in the air. "Best day ever!"

My pack crowded around me, Amir nuzzling my cheek. "Best day ever *so far*."

Epilogue
Five Years Later
Callie

My feet ached from the all-day shoot. Amir helped me out of my shoes, insisting he would do it, even though I was perfectly capable of wiggling out of them despite my six-months-pregnant belly.

I'd been getting pretty fucking good with the camera, and our company had ballooned the last couple of years into a steady income that more than met all our needs. We were still focusing on recorded heats and livestreams, but VIP viewers were all gifted swatches of the performers' scents to enrich the experience. We even took the occasional turn on the set. Who knew people were willing to pay out the ass to watch a pregnant omega get railed? I shouldn't have been surprised, but that first paycheck had been smoking hot and almost paid off our house.

Vegas was finally home in every way possible. The pack house was immaculate and enormous. It hadn't been too difficult to convince me to move into one of the ten-bedroom places Miles had found, especially once my belly had started to show, cementing the reality that we had two little ones coming.

I heard soft voices coming from the courtyard and followed them, Amir at my side with his arm looped around my waist, to find the rest of our pack and our children sitting in the shade, lined up neatly in a row. Kai was adding rainbow baubles to Alice's light brown pigtails that stuck straight out like little arrows. She looked up at me with giant blue eyes the same shade as Miles's, grinning to show off her first missing tooth. Her twin, Daniela, was behind Kai, swiping a doll brush through his long hair, and Diego was behind her, carefully gathering her black ringlets into a ponytail directly on top of her head. She looked so much like him it was almost uncanny. Miles cradled a sleeping Yara, our sweet toddler who took after Amir in her looks but after me in temperament, always wanting to be held. All five of those awake looked up to see us enter, and the twins shot off like rockets, ruining their fathers' styling work to cling to my legs.

"Mommy!" Alice rubbed her nose on my leggings, smushing her face against my thigh. "Did you bring cookies?"

"You bet I did."

Amir scooped up both of the girls. "They're in the kitchen. We have to wash our hands first. You can share one, and the rest are for tomorrow."

Our daughter who had yet to make an appearance kicked me in the ribs like she wanted to let me know she needed attention. "Those are Mommy's bones, not a bongo set."

Kai grinned and drew me into a kiss, smoothing his hand over my belly. "Is my girl as demanding as her mother?"

I snorted. "Kailani has opinions and she needs me to know about them even before she's out and about in the world."

The twins wriggled excitedly in Amir's arms and I kissed both of their cheeks before diverting to greet the rest of my alphas and our sleeping daughter.

"Don't bend down. We'll get up," Diego said, hopping to his feet and pulling me into a kiss.

Kai took Yara from Miles so he could stand up, and a moment later I was surrounded. I relaxed instantly, all the strain of the day melting away when I breathed in their scents.

"Change into your swimsuit," Kai suggested. "Get off your feet and float for a bit while I make you some dinner."

"You're an angel."

Kai grinned and leaned close to whisper in my ear as he passed. "Only until I get you into bed later."

My body lit up with the promise.

"If they're wrangling the girls, does that mean you're all ours, sweetheart?" Miles and Diego both looked at me like they were ready to eat me for a snack.

"Pretty sure that's exactly what that means. Hope you boys fueled up because your omega needs some special attention from her alphas."

Diego's low growl had my pussy pulsing. I thanked the universe for the millionth time for helping me dodge the Jerry bullet so I could find what I had really needed all these years. Alphas who adored the shit out of me, and a family I deserved.

Finally.

Get ready for the next book in Sin City Omegas!

Also By Lexie

Vegas Baby!: A Sin City Omegas Novel

Bonding the Band (co-write with Melissa Huxley)

Acknowledgments

Thank you SO much to Melissa Huxley and Marie Mackay for helping me bring this delightful experiment to life and craft it into an actual book. Your support and encouragement have been life changing.

Double thanks to Marie for the absolutely gorgeous cover and to Melissa for the beautiful formatting!

Thank you to Alexandra for being an absolute godsend of an alpha reader. Your insight was invaluable in this book coming together <3

Thank you to my beta readers: Mickel, Alex, Renee, Chelsi, Caroline, Trinity, and Elizabeth <3